D1512060

GILDENFORD

VALERIE ANAND

CHARLES SCRIBNER'S SONS · *New York*

Library of Congress Cataloging in Publication Data
Anand, Valerie.
  Gildenford.

  1. Edward, the Confessor, King of England,
Saint, d. 1066—Fiction.   I. Title.
PZ4.A5328Gi [PS3551.N23]   813'.5'4   76-30661
ISBN 0-684-14896-X

TO THE MEMORY OF MY FATHER

John McCormick Stubington

❧ CONTENTS ❧

✍ HISTORICAL NOTE ✍

The background of this novel is authentic history. In 1036 six hundred followers of the Atheling Alfred were indeed murdered on a hillside near the town of Guildford, for which the ancient name was Gildenford. Alfred himself was kept a prisoner by King Harold Harefoot and later died of ill usage. Both Alfred's mother, Emma, and Earl Godwin of Wessex appeared to be implicated, although to what extent will always remain a mystery. I have made use of one of the more dramatic possibilities.

Most of the characters in the book were real people, although very little is known about some of them. In these cases imagination has had to fill the gaps. The chief genuinely fictional characters are Brand, Hild, and Rolf. Alys of Boulogne is also my own invention, but some historians have suggested that when Eustace of Boulogne made his momentous visit to England in 1051 his purpose was to discuss the marriage of one of his children.

V.A.

❧ ENGLISH ROYAL HOUSE ❧
979-1066 A.D.

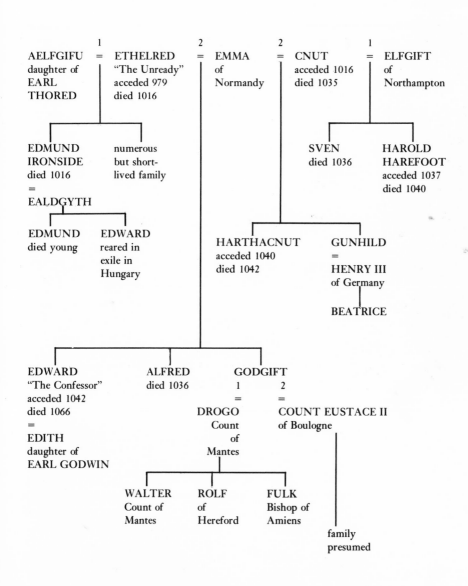

1		2	2		1
AELFGIFU	= ETHELRED	= EMMA	= CNUT	=	ELFGIFT
daughter of	"The Unready"	of	acceded 1016		of
EARL	acceded 979	Normandy	died 1035		Northampton
THORED	died 1016				

EDMUND IRONSIDE died 1016 = EALDGYTH

numerous but short-lived family

SVEN died 1036

HAROLD HAREFOOT acceded 1037 died 1040

EDMUND died young

EDWARD reared in exile in Hungary

HARTHACNUT acceded 1040 died 1042

GUNHILD = HENRY III of Germany

BEATRICE

EDWARD "The Confessor" acceded 1042 died 1066 = EDITH daughter of EARL GODWIN

ALFRED died 1036

GODGIFT
1 =
DROGO Count of Mantes

2 =
COUNT EUSTACE II of Boulogne

WALTER Count of Mantes

ROLF of Hereford

FULK Bishop of Amiens

family presumed

GILDENFORD

Prologue ✠ 1018 A.D.

King Cnut, ushered at last into his wife's bedchamber after the long day of stern, suspense-filled exclusion, at first gave only a cursory glance to his newly born son. He had fathered a son before. But he had never before seen on his queen's face anything like the expression which now transfigured it. For the moment he concentrated, marvelling, on that.

Emma of Normandy was fifteen years older than he was, a widow and a mother already when he married her. She had been a queen once already, and she had been an exile. She had never known and never displayed a single trace of tenderness, or shown any sign of regretting it. To see Emma's strong, almost masculine mouth thus relaxed in such a smile, to see Emma's sharp black eyes thus softened as she contemplated the child beside her, was a most amazing revelation.

The room was warm. A yellow patch of westering May sunshine lay across the bed, on the fine linen sheeting and the light coverlet of doeskin. A heavier coverlet of gleaming imported sables from Cnut's Danish homeland lay folded back at the foot. The curtains, crimson with gold and silver embroidery, had been tied back as well. There was luxury here, and royal state. Cnut from the beginning of his reign had set out to make it plain that he was a king of dignity and culture, and not a mere barbarian adventurer. And it was just as well. Emma, he realised very soon after she came to him, would have expected nothing less.

She looked at him as he came to the bedside and said: "He's

strong enough. He fairly deafened us all, announcing that he was born." The softness faded from her eyes. They resumed the piercing, steady gaze which was much more characteristic of them. She said: "My lord, you have a promise to redeem."

Cnut's blue eyes, narrow-socketed between high cheekbones and slanting golden brows, widened, surprised. "It will be redeemed," he said. "It was in the marriage contract and will be honoured, naturally. I will make him my heir. I shall call him Harthacnut, with my name carried on in his." Cnut shifted his gaze at last to his offspring and pushed a brown forefinger into the baby's microscopic fist. "You had no need to remind me," he said. "I keep my pledges. In any case, there was never a formal marriage contract between Elfgift and me. In the eyes of the Church, her son is not my lawful heir. But the legitimacy of this one is beyond question."

Emma said, slowly: "It was not a small thing to ask you, to disinherit your eldest son, legitimate or not. I remember wondering, when the contract was drawn up, whether you would agree to it. I realise what you have done for me, and our child. Thank you."

"Why shouldn't I do it?" asked Cnut. He jerked his head at the hovering midwife and the waiting ladies, clustered too closely round, and they retreated, giving him and his queen an illusion of privacy. "You disinherited your own children while you were about it. It was quite fair."

"There was a difference," Emma said, with an air of concession. He had promised the succession to the baby in the presence of witnesses and he would not go back on that now. She could afford to drop her guard. She said: "I detested their father. Ethelred always reminded me of a fish. Limp hands and pale round eyes." She considered Cnut's shapely young body, the sun-gilded skin and vigorous beard, and the muscular, competent hands, with unconcealed approval. "Your son will be worth ten of Ethelred's," she said. "I left his behind in Normandy when I sailed to marry you, and they can stay there forever as far as I am concerned." She looked once again at Harthacnut and that astonishing softness broke over her face once more. It was tenderness, it was wonder, it was close to worship. An artist might have tried to capture it for a nativity scene. "Children," said Emma, "I value as much, no more and no less, as I value their father."

Cnut said: "I see I did well when I accepted you as my queen."

Leaving the chamber, he received the midwife's assurance that the birth had been normal and should cause no complications, pressed a purse of silver into the woman's hands, and walked back to his hall, deep in thought.

He was thinking of Emma's children.

Their father had been a king. Well, Ethelred had been a poor king, an inefficient king, and in the end a deposed, defeated king. He had also been a perfectly legal successor to the king before him, and properly anointed. As long as his sons lived they represented danger, for they had a claim to the succession, whatever parchment contracts were drawn up to deny it.

Cnut took no pleasure in killing, least of all in the slaying of the young. But nor did he shrink from it when it seemed necessary. It might be necessary now. If you had a throne you defended it. If you ruled a people, you defended them. If you identified an enemy, you might save many lives by removing him before, and not after, he had gathered an army and come to your gates to challenge you.

He knew what his own advisors would say, Vikings to a man, tough, farseeing, unsentimental; he could hear them in his mind. "Aye, it's a pity they're so young. It'll be a bigger pity still if they grow to be much older."

Two boys and a girl. The girl he could leave alone. A good marriage, to a suitably noble husband who would have sense enough to take the dowry and not try to presume further on his wife's connections, that would provide for the girl. But the boys . . .

He reached the hall and his friends gathered round, congratulating, making jokes, and shouting for mead. He thought: I know what they'd advise.

But he was not the boy he had been and he could act without advice. No man could see the future. Death could come suddenly, in many forms, to anyone. To his own children as much as to Ethelred's. An alternative succession elsewhere could be a benefit as much as a disaster.

And in any case, the boys were Emma's sons.

Emma said that she rejected them. But there was a considerable difference between disliking your children and being prepared to acquiesce in their deaths. If Emma's boys died suddenly and she suspected that he had had a hand in it, she might well discover a love for them she had not known was there and turn against her husband.

And this he did not want. For it was a fact that this marriage between him and Emma, this political alliance made for convenience between a man of twenty and a woman of thirty-five, and entered into as coldly as an agreement to exchange corn for livestock at a fair, had burst into flame in their unexpecting faces, within a month of their wedding day.

They rarely indulged in love talk of any kind. Neither had ever uttered the words "I love you." They never would. They had no need of words. They knew.

When Emma's exiled sons showed themselves hostile, it would be time enough to act.

Part

I

GILDENFORD
1036 A.D.

1 ❈ The Unhallowed Tryst

The first to arrive at the tryst near Malvern was the man from the north, Harold of the Hare's Foot.

He was glad to get there. February was no season for journeys. The ponies were mud to the saddlegirths and the whole world seemed dissolving into the mizzle that drifted from the west. It was a mistiness full of danger both solid and ghostly—hiding bog and pit-fall from the wayfarer and subtly changing the shapes of natural things into other likenesses. The old gods were dead, his father Cnut had told him. Thunor no longer hurled his thunderbolts and old Grim, Woden's earthly self, had ceased to walk the uplands with his mantle over his one-eyed face. But Harold's mother and his old pagan nurse hadn't been so sure. Now, riding through the cloud-wreathed forests, Harold was not so sure, either. He hoped the meeting would be worth the trials of reaching it. And he hoped Godwin would not be late.

They had picked a very secret meeting place. Its reputation was so unlucky that only three of his men had been willing to go with Harefoot. He had acquired a new recruit near Worcester, however, the younger son of a freeman farmer, with some training in arms. Not much use as a fighting man, but an extra rider for the band, at least. The trouble with travelling incognito was that outlaws didn't recognise you any more than honest men did.

He gathered with some amusement, from drifts of talk behind him, that his three regular housecarles were exorcising their own fears by trying—without much success—to frighten the boy. The

lad was just now saying calmly that he knew how old hands liked to
scare newcomers and that he and his brother used to trick strangers
in their village by enticing them into the pen of the local bull. "And
then we'd let Thunderer out of his shed and sit on the gate telling
them how savage he was."

"And was he?" asked one of the housecarles, interested.

"No, that was the joke. My mother handreared him from a calf
and he only followed folk about for titbits," Brand said. A promising
youth, Harefoot considered.

The last ford appeared ahead, brown and swirling, rain-
swollen. Casual talk ended as they tussled with the task of getting
two mules laden with fuel across without letting their packs get wet.
A cold welcome they'd have if the wood and peat went under. There
was no dry tinder for miles. Halfway over, one of the mules slipped
on shifting river mud and its pack did go under. Harefoot swore.

The ghost village was only half a mile beyond the ford. They
rode in single file through what had been its main street before the
plague struck it, destroying two-thirds of its inhabitants and causing
the rest to flee. Now it was a ruin, the skeletons of old timber buildings standing naked to the weather, grass growing thick on cottage
floors, corn sprouting rank and wild in the deserted fields around.
But the stone-built church still stood, with its lead roof fairly watertight even after a quarter of a century. They rode straight to the
church door, dismounting to lead the ponies under the low lintel.

Inside, the stone-flagged floor was dry and some old furniture
stood about, stools and benches and the like. The sigh of the rain
faded outside as they put back their hoods.

"Unload the mules," said Harefoot.

A tethering line was set up along one side of the church and two
small braziers were kindled from the fuel they had brought. Enough
remained dry to fill them. The wet wood was spread to dry, along
with the soaking mantles. The fodder which each man carried in a
shoulder pack was put before the ponies and the mead-flasks were
passed round.

Of Godwin, who had sent the summons, there was no sign.

"Could be his men don't care for this place either," said one of
the housecarles, uneasily scanning the building's gloomy corners.

"Godwin's men have sense enough to know a plague more than
twenty years back won't hurt them," said his leader shortly.

"Godwin doesn't believe in anything," said the housecarle. "Or so they say. Ghosts, witches, God or devil, they say he cares nothing for any of them. Maybe his men catch it from him."

"Maybe," said Harefoot. Godwin. His father's favourite, the Earl of Wessex, everlastingly held up to him as an example and everlastingly beyond his power to imitate. The braziers burned up and wavering shadows, their own shapes in parody, ran over the sweating walls. Harefoot said: "If there is ill luck still lingering in this place, then when the careless Earl of Wessex comes, let it fasten on him."

The weather had delayed Godwin. On his journey from the south two rivers had proved impassable by their usual fords. Detours to find usable routes, through forest as tangled and wet as seaweed in its natural element, took time.

He had no housecarles with him. He had instead the company of his three eldest sons. He called to Sweyn, who was riding immediately behind him: "That was the last river—I hope!"

Sweyn pushed back his hood, regardless of the wet, and his sandy hair fell into his eyes. A grin lit up the young, virile features. In a few years Sweyn would be the handsomest male in Wessex. Even at seventeen, with his chest not yet filled out, he was impressive. The combination of his mother's high Scandinavian cheekbones with Godwin's stocky vigour was a potent blend. "At least we needn't worry about robbers!" he called. "They won't come out in this!"

"We're out in it!" shouted Harold, the eldest after Sweyn himself, and riding on his brother's heels.

"We're not robbers!"

Godwin said nothing. According to Gytha, his wife, their errand was one far worse than robbery. He looked ahead to where the mists were lifting away on a strengthening wind, and in the vista of winter woods before them one open patch was visible. They were nearly there.

They reached the church at twilight. Within it Harefoot was improvisedly enthroned on a mantle-covered bench from which he did not rise as the Godwins trooped in with their mounts. The Earl of Wessex took in the makeshift dignity, the uneasy men clustered round the braziers, and the heaps of firewood spread steaming on the floor.

"I see you had trouble with your fuel."

"The river was in flood. You are late."

"We too had fords to cross. My apologies. Let me introduce my sons."

They came forward in turn. Sweyn: very respectful because Harefoot was the son of the great King Cnut, who was one of Sweyn's heroes. Harold: fourteen years old with sun-gold hair. Tostig: snub-nosed and tow-headed, who in his own words was "nearly thirteen."

"Rather than just twelve," Godwin explained, smiling.

The boys, once presented, withdrew unasked to various tasks, to stoke braziers and set up cooking spits. The northern men roused themselves to help. Competence like a brisk wind bustled through the church, dispelling the shades. It came from Godwin. It put Harold Harefoot into an ideal mood for killing someone.

Godwin thought: He is his mother's son.

It was an indictment.

Godwin had loved his lord, King Cnut, and in return Cnut had made an earl of him and promoted his marriage to his beloved countess, Gytha. Cnut had been a mighty ruler, a great spirit housed in a fine, hard body. In his son hardly a lineament of Cnut's strong Viking face could be traced. Just a little in the bone structure, perhaps, but otherwise . . . Harefoot's hair had the look of a straw bale and his weather-reddened features were blurred already with too much food and wine. As a youth he had been fleet-footed, enough to earn him his nickname. But that was gone now. Soon he would be fat, as his mother now was. Even his pale eyes, Godwin thought, were the eyes of that mother, the ineptly named Elfgift of Northampton.

Her parents must have liked her, since they had so named her, and as a girl she had had beauty, that was true. In Elfgift the straw-coloured hair had been two ropes of twisted gold and the colourless eyes had the changeful charm of water under varying skies. But there the part the elves had in her abruptly ended. A small mind and a grasping hand, that was Elfgift. She was also—and so was Harefoot—a first-class, implacable, and enduring hater. And the person they both hated most in the world was the woman for whom Cnut had deserted Elfgift in the end: Emma of Normandy.

With, as runners-up, Emma's trio of sons.

It was generally accounted a virtue in a woman that she should be fruitful, and all the more so if the fruitfulness took the form of healthy male children. All the same, as Godwin well knew (himself the father of six sons and already accustomed to lie awake at night wondering how to secure their futures), the blessing could be a mixed one. Emma had certainly overdone it. Two boys by Ethelred. Another by Cnut. It was the latter who had hitherto incurred the worst of Harefoot's loathing, for Cnut, selecting an heir, had passed Harefoot over for him.

But at the moment Harthacnut was far away and, whatever his legal status, was imperilling no one's ambitions. This time the exiled sons of Ethelred were the menace to be dealt with. A thousand pities, Godwin thought, that Cnut hadn't seen to it years ago.

But even now, it might not be too late.

On the far side of the brazier the two of them were sharing, having drawn apart from the rest for privacy's sake, Harefoot's thought: I hate that woman Emma. She elbowed my mother out of her way and broke her heart. And this man is Emma's chief minister. For all his friendly talk, he's Emma's man and a southron. Bah!

Aloud he said: "Why have we met? It's a bad season for travelling."

"It's important," said Godwin. "Has the news from the south reached you yet?"

"What news?"

"Your elder stepbrother, Edward the Exile, landed at Southampton last month."

Darkness had fallen and the wind and rain had died away. In the quiet the rustle of the settling fire and the snort of a restless pony sounded loud. Harefoot grunted, sharply, surprised. "Edward? Southampton? What happened?" Briefly, his Viking ancestry showed itself. "He came raiding in *January*?" said the descendant of sea dogs, disbelievingly.

"There were two mild weeks, you recall. He hoped surprise would give him an advantage, I think. He was ill-equipped, however. He was quickly chased off and went back to Normandy, no doubt. No harm was done."

"Good. But in that case, why are we here?"

"Because," said Godwin, "it is a warning."

They had eaten, but the mead flasks were not yet empty. Harefoot passed his to the earl and Godwin took a long draught. He saw

that Harefoot was waiting for him to continue, having failed to see
the implications. Cnut would have been reciting them by now.

Pensively, Godwin poked the brazier with a spear butt. He
must now raise a touchy subject, which was best done with caution,
for Harefoot, despite all his stupidity, was dangerous. The earl said
quietly: "Harold Cyng, you rule today in the north of this land, but
how did it come about? At the time of your father's death, you were
not his chosen heir."

Harefoot regarded him suspiciously. "I should have been!"

"Perhaps. You were the elder. But nevertheless, your father had
named Harthacnut his successor."

"Harthacnut!" said Harefoot, as if his half brother's name tasted
foul. "That woman's brat. Emma's brat. You know the tale: why ask
me? Harthacnut wasn't here to claim his rights. He was up to his
eyeballs in a war in Denmark. So my father lost his wish. Serve him
right for sending Harthacnut to Denmark to begin with. He always
wanted Harthacnut to have everything. Denmark and England, both!"

"Yes, yes," said Godwin soothingly. He did not like Harold
Harefoot and there was no doubt that in his choice of an heir for England and a regent for Denmark, Cnut had been acting on better
reasons than mere blind favouritism. But one could not expect
Elfgift or Harefoot to agree with that. Their loathing of Emma and
all her works, including her offspring, was natural enough.

The offspring he had come to discuss, however, was not Harthacnut this time. He went on smoothly: "Because Harthacnut was in
Denmark and could not come home, other arrangements had to be
made. Finally you were given the north to rule and Lady Emma was
given the south to hold in trust against her son's return, with you as
overall protector. But the south at the moment has no real
king . . ."

"At the moment!" said Harefoot. His eyes gleamed.

"As you say. It could fall into your hands in time. If you are
quick enough to seize your chances and if you are clever enough to
outwit your foes. For you have foes. And Edward the Exile and his
brother are among them."

"That woman!" muttered Harefoot. He took back the mead
flask and swigged deep.

"They are the sons of a lawful king," said Godwin carefully.

"Ethelred was duly crowned and anointed. Your father's family took England from him by force. His children have a claim. Up to now they have been quiet in Normandy, no trouble to anyone. But last month, with your father not dead a year and the south in uncertain hands, one of them comes out of hiding and attacks. What does it look like to you?"

Harefoot had understood now. He glowered. "They think that this is their chance? Is that what you mean? Did Edward come with Norman backing?"

"Not much beyond a handful of men and one ship. But next time he might come better equipped. Next time he might come not as a raider but as a claimant. With an army. Then there would be a war. Which you might not win. The Normans are a warlike race."

Harefoot was still scowling. "What is it to you? You're Emma's man. They're Emma's sons. And Emma's Norman. Them or Harthacnut—what is it to you?"

"I was your father's man," said Godwin calmly. "My loyalty is to his house, to the house of Cnut. Do you want this menace removed from you? That is what I called you here to ask. If so, I can remove it."

"A bold and mighty claim! How? We can't invade Normandy to kill them!"

"No. But we can tempt them out of Normandy and kill them then. The way to deal with a well-supported foe is to cut him off from his support. What if the two of them came to England not as raiders or invaders but as guests? They could easily be taken then."

"Who'd do the taking? You?"

"You, I think. I would represent . . . the host."

"And your name would stay unsullied."

"If you like to say so."

The risk of a slur on her husband's name had been Gytha's final argument when she fought against this project. "I will protect our name," he had said, to quieten her.

"Very well, so I take them." Harefoot grinned. The idea did not seem to displease him. "But who in God's name is going to invite them here in the first place? They've no friends here. Even their mother hates the sight of them. She hated Ethelred. Haven't you heard the story about her when Edward was born? She looked at him when they put him in her arms, saw he was a copy of his father, and threw him bodily at Ethelred, shouting: 'He's yours, so take him! He's none of mine!' "

"I've heard it. And I don't believe it. But even if it's true, it was long ago. Everyone knows the marriage was a disaster and everyone knows Emma was a she-devil when she was young. But she's not young now and she's alone. Why should she not soften and wish to see her first children again? I think they might well believe in an invitation from her."

"You first have to get her to ask them!"

Godwin smiled. "That is already arranged for."

"You mean . . . that woman . . . but even *she* wouldn't . . . !"

"Normans are strange folk," Godwin said meditatively. "It must be a queer country to live in now, with no overlord. They say that since the old duke's boy was brought back from the French court, he has never been able to live in the ducal castles because of the unrest, and he's being secretly reared in peasants' huts on his supporters' estates. Must be an odd life for a boy bred to a court."

Harefoot waved this aside, not interested in infant dukes, whether in huts or in castles, even as an illustration of Norman eccentricity.

"You had better tell me the rest of this plan," he said.

"By all means," said Godwin equably. "I have a manor in the Surrey district, on the Pilgrims' Way. It's called Gildenford . . . and there are caves . . ."

2 ⚔ Journey Towards the Future

The boy Brand, fifteen years old and raw from the farm, became a sworn man to the Earl of Wessex the day after he first left home. No one was more surprised about it than Brand.

He had never left his home before except for a night or two at a market, and the strangeness overwhelmed him from time to time like a squall of rain blown in his face. Yet he had been well prepared.

"No one will throw you out of your home," his father had said, three years ago, between the rasping breaths of his last sickness, which seized him after he was caught in a storm while searching for a lost cow. "But our bit of land will feed . . . only so many. Orm will marry soon and then children . . . will come. You'll want to marry in time. And there's Edgiva. Finding her a husband . . . not easy . . . unless the saints she keeps praying to take pity on her face . . . or you find . . . an obliging blind man!" He tried to laugh, choked, and rested. Then he said: "I've taught you and Orm to use a sword. My advice to you is this: practise with it. Then find yourself . . . a good lord . . . and follow him, as I did."

He turned his flaccid right hand palm up on the rug of cobbled skins that covered the bed. "This won't hold . . . a sword again. I've two. Somewhere. When you go . . . if . . . take the best. Orm won't . . . grudge it. And listen. Whoever you follow, serve him well. Go where he leads you, fight his foes. In return you get food,

clothes . . . a roof . . . maybe land enough one day . . . to raise
. . . your own sons on. That's the bargain. You understand?"

He had lasted a few days after that, growing weaker hourly, it
seemed, but still able to talk sometimes in a hoarse, whispering fashion. Brand's mother brought her husband hot potions and steaming
inhalants to ease him and tried to smile at his croaked sallies. She
would not weep where he could see. Towards the end he rambled
and told his sons a tale he had told them several times already, over
the years, but could not now remember doing so. The telling was
especially aimed at Brand. ". . . A story for you, Brand boy, to
remember when you have a lord to follow. About the men of Cynewulf, King of the Southeast Saxons, three hundred years ago, they
say. Cynewulf was slain at night by a rival's men." His voice faded
but he signed for the herbal drink that stood by his bed and his wife
held it to his lips. The straining voice went on: ". . . His own men
found him dead in the morning. The rival offered them gold and
freedom if they would go away in peace, but they would not. They
fought his followers to avenge their lord, even though they were outnumbered . . . even though their lord could not . . . could not
come back to life . . . even though it meant the deaths of all of them
as well. That's the service you'll owe your leader, Brand, boy. So
choose him well."

Except for some confused murmurings and repetitions of his
wife's name, those were his last words. Brand had not forgotten
them. But obeying them was another matter. How did an inexperi-
enced lad from a farm, even if his father had been a thane's follower,
even if he had learned to use a sword, go about choosing a leader?
One could not put prospective overlords in a row and look at them.
You took what came your way. Orm married, as their father had expected. His wife conceived. And for all their assurances to Brand
that they did not wish him away, he knew that he must go. And
when, a few days since, he and Orm realised that the little party
seeking a night's lodgings at the farm were more important than they
looked, they agreed that here perhaps was Brand's chance.

"It *is* King Harefoot. I saw him close to, once, at a horse fight,"
Orm swore.

Brand felt doubtful, not of Harefoot's identity, but of his
rightness as a leader for whom he might one day have to die. He was

not much taken with Harefoot's looks. But he supposed he was no judge. The offspring of King Cnut must be of another race of beings from himself. He made his offer and showed his father's sword. Harefoot stared at him with round pale eyes and said he could use another rider. "Got a pony?" he asked.

Brand had. He and Orm had caught a couple of wild hill colts, two years before. Breaking them in was hard work but at the end both boys could fairly claim they could ride and they had steeds to prove it. Brand's was black, short-legged, hairy, and tough, with an endless capacity for eating. Brand named him Greedy. Harefoot, hearing that the mount was provided for, nodded. "Then you can come. We leave at daybreak."

He asked for no oath and made no promises. It was not at all the arrangement Brand had been taught to expect. He tagged along with the other housecarles, wondering if he were one of them or not.

And now it appeared that he was not.

He stood at Greedy's side in the church as the light of another new day spread slowly through it. The saddlegirth was in his hand. And the oldest of Harefoot's housecarles, standing in front of him, was pointing a thumb in the direction of the Earl of Wessex—that southern-speaking stranger who had swept in with his handsome sons the night before and who looked much more like a king than Harefoot did—and saying: "You go with Godwin of Wessex, not with us. He says he needs another lad." The housecarle walked away before Brand could reply. Not that a reply was needed. No one had offered him a choice.

He had heard of Godwin before, naturally. A great name, a great leader, famed from the Wash to the Welsh March, from the Scottish mountains to the Isle of Wight. His chief home lay far to the south, at a place called Winchester. In Godwin's service a man might look for a fine future. But just now Brand would gladly have traded all that unknown future, however splendid, for a glimpse of the wooden farmstead and the smell of his mother's stockpot. Winchester was so far away it might as well be Jerusalem, and besides . . .

His father had said: "Find yourself a lord. Choose."

Well, he hadn't privately considered Harefoot much of a prize, but at least he had gone to Harefoot of his own free will. Now even that was gone. Harefoot was handing him over and Godwin accepting him, as though he were a spare mule and his own opinions nothing. He dragged the girth tight, his vision hazy with anger.

When he straightened up again, Godwin was standing where the housecarle had been, waiting for him.

Never, throughout his life, was Brand good at finding words. Asked to describe someone he had met for the benefit of someone else, he would say uncertainly: "He's dark," or, "She's pretty." Pressed for more detail he might add: "He's useful with an axe," or, "She laughed a lot." Pressed still further he usually gave up and became tongue-tied. Only once in all his life did he fully break the barrier down and put a deeper knowledge into speech. Of Godwin he said: "He seems so alive, as much more alive than an ordinary man, as an ordinary man is more alive than a corpse." It was a tribute to Godwin which only Brand himself fully appreciated. When he met William of Normandy he saw the man for the taloned and talented eagle he was, but when his wife asked what William was like he only said: "He was clean-shaven and magnificently dressed."

Godwin was neither. He had a dun-hued cloak thrown back from mail of metal rings and leather, and he had a strong, springing beard, dark brown with red glints in it, like his hair. It did not hide the jutting line of his jaw. He had hazel eyes, green in this cold early light, which glittered under point-arched eyebrows. Every part of him—hair, beard, eyes, even the placing of his feet a little apart and the set of his hands on his hips—spoke of his vitality. He said, with a smile so full of charm that Brand blinked: "I must ask your pardon. My lord Harefoot let them tell you before I found a moment to ask you for myself. I want you to ride south with me. I can offer you a life worth having if you will take service with me. The best training and a chance to see the world. What do you say?"

Brand twisted a lock of Greedy's coarse mane round his forefinger. "I've heard it said that great men send their sons to you to learn, and sometimes you refuse them." He looked nervously at Godwin. "So I don't understand . . ."

"You heard aright. But why I ask you to come is my own business. Yours is to decide whether you will or not. Well?"

Since Harefoot no longer wanted him and since he could not go home, it was a smaller choice than Godwin made it seem. But at least it was a semblance of a choice. And if he had not been taken with Harefoot, he was very much taken with Godwin. Then the earl himself spoke again and clinched it.

"I saw your face when the housecarle spoke to you. You felt as if you were being passed from hand to hand, like a package or a thrall, did you not? Your name is Brand, I believe. Brand, there are no thralls in my following. You will come as a free man and freely take the oath of loyalty to me, and in return I will be all that a lord should be, and if I had any of my own men here you would see for yourself, from their horses and their arm-rings, that I keep my promises. Now, what do you say?"

This was a marvel; not only that Godwin could read his mind, but that Godwin had actually troubled to read it. And here at last was the pattern his father had led him to expect: the given oath, the received rewards, the acknowledged bond between leader and man. Brand knelt on the flagstones of the church, put his hands between Godwin's, and formally swore to be loyal to him, to fight for him and keep his counsel. As the oath was completed, Godwin pulled him up. He looked at the sword Brand carried. "I suppose you know that that blade is too big for you?"

"It was my father's."

"Keep it in memory of him, then. But I'll find you something better to work with. I will try you against my boys on the way home. If I am to teach you, I must find out how much you know. Are you ready to ride?"

The journey, on which they did not hurry, took four days. The weather had changed during the night they had spent in the church, and they set out through clear air under a high pale sky, with a southwest wind blowing. Brand was given a mule to lead and he rode behind the Godwin boys, shy of attempting any conversation at first, but finding them more natural companions than Harefoot's men, who had strongly resembled outlaws in appearance.

In the course of the first twenty-four hours on the road he learned that what he knew about swordsmanship was next to useless; even nearly-thirteen-year-old Tostig could have sliced him into mincemeat. But his eye with a bow was fair and he was handy with an axe. He admitted that he was used to chopping down trees and then regretted it when he saw that Sweyn's face was full of derision. Sweyn, alone of the Godwinsson brothers, seemed unwilling to be friendly. At the start of the journey he had, as it were, sampled Brand's possibilities, but after finding out that Brand was not yet interested in girls, he had dismissed him as unworthy of further attention. Sweyn had recently discovered that there was a separate race of humankind on earth known as the female, and all conversation with him, no matter where it started, in a very short time worked its way round to this enthralling topic and the even more entrancing subject of Sweyn's own success with the wenches. Brand did not respond and Brand was therefore nobody.

A nobody, Sweyn's expression made clear when he heard Brand's unfortunate remark about woodcutting, who actually imagined that an axe was a labourer's tool. Brand was relieved when they set off again and Tostig came to ride with him instead. Tostig was good company and did not seem conscious of any difference in status between Brand and himself. For a while, Brand forgot about it too.

The land changed as they went. They passed the nights in farmsteads or monasteries, and each day's riding brought subtle differences in the landscape. On the fourth day the track left the forestland to run along the crest of a high, short-turfed ridge. In the distance were other bare hills, grey green in colour and open to the sky. Brand, used to a forest-bounded village, felt a foreigner here on this empty plain, and he thought the vista desolate. The wind rustled in the winter grass in a fashion quite new to him, as if people he could not see were whispering together. As they came out into the open, Harold reined in and waited for him. As Brand and Tostig, who was still riding with him, drew alongside, Harold began to tell a tale of a long-dead hero called Arthur. Brand had heard the name but couldn't recall in what story. Arthur, it seemed, had lived here and fought over these hills, and was buried somewhere among them and would one day return to fight for his folk again. Tostig chipped in: "And before Arthur, before the Romans even, there were giants. They put up a great ring of huge standing stones not far away. We'll show you one day. They'll amaze you!"

Clearly they didn't amaze these Godwinssons. They belonged here, lived at ease against this background of bleak, empty hills, of immortal heroes and stone-tossing giants. Brand looked from Harold to Tostig, wondering. Homesickness, kept at bay these last few days by the comfort of his oath and by the interest of travelling and trials of arms, surged back. His sense of being different, and of a lesser breed, surged back with it. He was alone, hopelessly divided from his companions, a creature of earth looking in astonishment at the bright hair and glowing faces of beings from the sun. He wondered suddenly what kind of dwelling his new lord was taking him to.

At the same moment Godwin, riding ahead, let out a shout and pointed. "Boys! Where are your eyes today? There it is! Our hearthsmoke!"

The Godwin hall amazed him quite as much as the giants' stone ring was likely to do. He had never seen such a place in his life.

His first view of it consisted of its ditch and palisade, an enormous palisade, stretching away to left and right, encircling what seemed a vast tract of land. It was made of stout split logs with their curved sides outwards. Once through the gate, he saw that other logs were nailed crosswise on the inside. Within the wide enclosure, in the centre, stood the hall itself, high-gabled and commanding, with smaller buildings clustered about it like chicks round a hen. The nearest had its door open and he saw ponies tied inside. It was a stable. From the mouth-watering smells that issued from another, that one was a bakehouse.

But he had no chance to take in more, on account of the bemusing animal and human chaos which now enveloped them all. Geese cackled and chickens clucked, getting in the ponies' way. Dogs bounded out, barking. People of all sorts and ages seemed everywhere; leather-clad housecarles, scullions with aprons, children running, womenfolk in long, bright-coloured clothes, boys in a group round an older man who was drawing something instructively in the earth with the point of a stick.

Tostig made signals at him and he followed, into the stable, to put the ponies away. After that he found himself with the others at the door of the hall. Three smaller boys were there, younger Godwinssons, he supposed, with hair respectively copper, honey, and white-fair, as if the smallest one had been left out in the sun too long. Among them, standing peacefully still because the centre of even the most dizzily spinning world does not move much, and she was the centre of Godwin's vital planet, stood a woman who, Brand saw at once, was Godwin's countess. She was taller than her husband, who stood beside her while the little ones leapt and yelped like puppies round him. She had the Danish face: strong, slanting brows that swept low towards the nose; a strong, slightly concave profile with widesprung nostrils; high cheekbones; a short upper lip. Hare-foot had the same cheekbones, his inheritance from Danish Cnut. But where his features were coarse, Gytha's were cut cleanly. Her honey-coloured hair was braided and twisted round her head like a crown, unveiled in defiance of fashion, and her well-shaped, ringless fingers rested serenely clasped on the bulk of an unborn child. Gytha of Wessex, mother of the seventeen-year-old Sweyn and likely to be a grandmother soon if Sweyn's talk were backed with action, was herself still fruitful.

She said as Tostig led Brand forward: "Godwin, we have a young army—the royal bodyguard, no less!—eating itself to death in this house, and I add a son to the strength every second year, yet you still bring me more." Her voice was warm, a little husky, a little accented in the Danish way. She smiled at Brand and his home-sickness eased. "My husband says your name is Brand. Welcome to our hall."

"This is my wife, the Lady Gytha," Godwin said. "She looks after us all."

"More than that!" Laughing, Gytha swept them all inside. "It will be my business, Brand, to feed you, dose you if you're ill, set your bones if you break them, listen to the tale when some girl breaks your heart, and mend it for you by making you run so many errands you'll have no time to think of her. Come now, eat with us. You are our guest on this your first night with us. Afterwards, this will be your home."

Brand made suitable replies. The inside of the hall had just staggered him all over again, as much as the outside had done. It seemed huge, cavernous as a cathedral. Yet it was a home as well, he saw as he looked about. Fresh rushes, sweet with rosemary, covered the floor and glowing tapestries lined the walls, except near the door, where the household weapons hung. But even they were a decora-tion: swords arranged like the spokes of a wheel; pikes like a great open fan; axes forming a round arch over all, blades at the top and handles converging inwards. A fire burned at the central hearth and now Tostig had drawn him to a bench beside it and Gytha, beckon-ing, had summoned a thrall with ale and meat pasties. Godwin had lingered behind with the smaller boys and for the moment Gytha was in command.

"Are you from the Welsh March?" she was asking. "You look as though you could be part Welsh, with that black hair and your brown eyes."

"My mother is half Welsh on her mother's side. My grandfather met a Welsh girl at a market during a quiet time when there was trade across the border, and they ran away together. But my father was a Saxon. He followed one of King Cnut's northern thanes."

"A good heritage," Gytha approved. "Tell me . . ." She broke off at a noise behind her. "Godwin?"

Godwin shook off a swarming heap of his younger offspring. He picked rosemary out of his hair. "You have more than enough sons," he observed. "God send that the next is a girl, another quiet little Edith. By the way, where is Edith? Shouldn't she be here?"

"Why, yes." Gytha looked surprised. "The convent sent to say that the illness was still troubling it and we should keep her for another month. But . . ." Her gaze lit on her younger boys, who had drawn together at the sound of their sister's name. "Gyrth," she said to the copper-haired one, about eight years old by the look of him (a son "every second year" had been an exaggeration), "Gyrth! Where's Edith?"

It was the white-headed four-year-old with the innocent face who was pushed forward by the others, as if they were chess players and he was a pawn. "We tied her up," he explained amiably.

"You . . . where?" demanded Gytha. "And why?"

"In your bower, mother," said Gyrth, since this seemed too complicated for his junior to answer. He looked anxiously round for more substantial protection than his smaller brothers could offer and drew closer to an amused Harold. "We were playing outside," he explained hastily. "We didn't run about in there or anything . . . but we thought she might get cold if we left her on the ground. We just carried her in and put her on the bed. We haven't dirtied anything."

"Go and untie her at once! What in the name of all the saints together were you playing *at*?"

"English and Vikings," said six-year-old Leofwin, the one with Gytha's honey hair. "She was a captured heathen. We'll go and get her." They trotted happily out.

"Godwin," said his wife exasperatedly, "what are you laughing at?"

"I pay the earth to have my daughter reared in a nunnery," said

Godwin, shaking with merriment, "and when she comes home to play with her brothers, they at once decide she makes a perfect little heathen!" He cocked an ear. A frightful din had broken forth outside, compounded mainly of young humans in various states of rage and anguish. "A perfect wildcat would be more like it just now. Harold, go and separate them before they actually kill each other!"

"That Brand is a nice boy," Gytha said.

The evening meal was eaten. Edith, flaxen hair tangled and eyes bright with fury, had been soothed, brushed, and coaxed to make peace with her brothers. Now, the pallets of the household had been laid on the hall floor, Brand's among them. He had been left at last to find his level among the other boys.

Gytha and Godwin were in their own sleepinghouse. Some yards from the main hall, it was heated by braziers and lit with lamps. Gytha had sent her woman away and was combing her own hair out. Godwin, already stretched under the thick fur rugs of the bed, saddle-weary bones thankfully eased on a down-stuffed mattress, watched her, hands linked behind his head.

"Will you keep him when . . . he has done what you need?" Gytha asked.

"Why not? Harefoot was right: he *is* promising. Good nerves and an even temper. And very good reflexes. I watched him when he tried himself out against the boys."

Gytha sighed. "I've done as you asked," she said. "But I don't like it, Godwin."

"Do you want to see Ethelred's sons making war here? Seizing power? King Cnut was part of your family. You should have some feeling for him."

"He wasn't blood-close. No, I don't want to see the Ethelredsons here, not because of Cnut but because *being* Ethelred's boys, they may be like Ethelred and therefore poor leaders. But a woman shouldn't be entangled in a plot to kill her own sons."

Her voice was tired, flat. She had said it so often. The earlier times had been more violent. Godwin had laid his hand over her mouth once, saying, "For the love of God, they'll hear you in Winchester!" He gazed thoughtfully at the still-lingering teethmarks as he said: "Her family life has not been like ours. It is not so unthinkable with her. I want to save lives, Gytha. I want crops growing, not trampled flat by armies. I want cattle droppings, not blood, spread to help the corn to grow. We have contenders enough without these two pests as well. I intend to be rid of them."

"Our good name may be the worse for it."

"Harefoot's men are to snatch them out of my helplessly protesting hands," said Godwin with a faint smile. "And since Harefoot has even agreed to be away on the Welsh border when we are arranging the visit, it will look most unlikely that he and I are in partnership. I have tried to protect us."

Gytha laid down her comb and began gracefully to work on her nails. Without looking up, she said: "I think it would be a good idea if you arranged for them to be attacked by pirates on the voyage over. No one would point at either us or Harefoot then—if he cares about it!"

Half the shrewdest moves of Godwin's life had been Gytha's ideas. She usually voiced them as casual asides from some totally female activity such as baking, beautifying herself or—on one occasion—giving birth. It was this astonishing duality of the untrammelled mind in the desirably female body which had drawn his eyes across a hall in Denmark, long ago, when in the train of Cnut he had dined in the household of Cnut's sister Estrith. Estrith's husband was a nobleman called Ulf, and someone, jogging Godwin's elbow, had said: "That's Ulf's sister there . . . a handsome girl, isn't she? But stare you down as soon as look at you. She's turned down three good husbands already."

But her eyes and Godwin's had met and she was not staring him down. They regarded each other with something they would have called recognition, except that they had never met before. Their minds saluted one another in that long glance and their bodies, a hall-width apart, longed and fretted to do likewise.

That evening, later, Cnut said: "You seemed mighty taken with the Lady Gytha tonight."

"I . . . er . . ." said Godwin, who hadn't thought it so obvious.

"Time I found you a well-dowered bride," said Cnut. "You've earned the honour. If you can recommend yourself to Gytha, I will bless the marriage. I warn you she'll take some winning. There's no forcing that one." His voice was offhand but suddenly his eyes danced. "I wish you luck. Come and tell me how the sport goes!"

So Godwin went to Gytha in the morning, cutting her out from her companions as they rode out hawking, and before the time of candlelighting she had agreed to marry him. Cnut was pleased and frankly surprised. Ulf, when he heard of it, was unashamedly relieved.

Now, seven and nearly eight children later, Gytha's quality of mind was unchanged. Godwin was a Christian, nominally at least, and Gytha was decidedly pious. It would have shocked her to know what he was thinking: that if the old goddess Freya, Earth Mother and Corn Queen, had ever walked on earth in a woman's form, she must have been much like Gytha.

But she did not guess it, for she was thinking of something quite different. "I can think of no better safeguard," she said. "But . . . oh, Godwin, is there no other way? I have borne children: I know. For the sake of Mary, Mother of God, can we not do it without Queen Emma? It will bring the wrath of heaven on us! Our children are so strong, so handsome . . . I live in dread of disaster for them, of death in battle, or capture as hostages . . . to do this is almost to court such things!"

"I know. But they are likelier to happen in the war that the Ethelredsons will almost certainly bring. We are safer without them."

"God can do anything," said Gytha. "He wouldn't need the Ethelredsons."

She stopped working on her nails and came to him. He looked up into her eyes and said: "When you are happy your eyes are blue, like the sky, but when you are anxious they are as grey as the North Sea in a storm. They're grey now. Gytha, don't be afraid. Trust me. I shall bring our ship safe into harbour."

"I hope so," said the Countess of Wessex grimly.

3 ❈ *Invitation from Mother*

Robert Archbishop of Rouen was in the habit of telling guests at Rouen Castle that he was keeping it warm till Normandy produced a ruler strong enough to live there openly. The guests, surreptitiously drawing their mantles more tightly around them, would wonder if they were supposed to laugh. Neither fires piled high with logs nor the heat of midsummer could disperse the chill of that mass of gloomy masonry. It was a grey stone keep, its few private apartments mere cold poky holes hollowed from the thickness of its walls, the hall itself cavernous and inexorably cold. "You *are* supposed to laugh," Robert would tell them if they didn't. "Merriment's an antidote to frostbite."

Returning from a ride on a March afternoon, under a sky the colour of steel and through a wind full of small sleety teeth, Edward and Alfred took their mounts to the stables themselves and rubbed them down in person. It was as good a way of working up a glow as any. They could not hope for much more warmth inside the castle than out. The work done, they climbed the narrow stair to the chamber which, as well-born guests of the castellan, they had been given to sleep in, and shut the low door behind them, pulling its curtains across to keep out draughts.

The brazier had been lit for their return and fresh clothes had been laid on the wolfskin bedspreads. Edward regarded these kindly preparations with distaste.

"At times," he said, "I envy my sister."

"Why?" Alfred enquired, beginning to shed his horse-aromatic garments. A page appeared with a pitcher of hot water and a basin. "The service is excellent," he said as the page withdrew. "What has Godgift got that we haven't, except sorrow? We aren't mourning dead spouses, at least."

"Even that might be better than . . . what have we done with ourselves all day, Alfred? Recite it."

"Got out of bed," said Alfred obediently, dragging off his boots. "Went to Mass. You read books with your friend from Jumièges while I went to the mews and talked hawks. Then we ate and went out."

"Yes. Challenging, wasn't it?"

"One would not want to appear rude," said Alfred, sponging mud off himself. "But your one attempt at taking up a challenge was hardly successful, now was it?"

"I was chased ignominiously out of Southampton, you mean?" Edward was not annoyed, only thoughtful. "It was the wrong challenge. I went raiding in a fit of temper. But that's not the way to claim one's rights. The priest who confessed me afterwards said so. It did well enough for our ancestors; it still does for people like the Vikings . . . they're only half civilised. But we've gone beyond that. I wanted . . . I want . . . something real to do, but that wasn't the way to find it."

"Go on pilgrimage," his brother suggested, emptying the basin out of the window and refilling it for Edward. "Like Drogo or Duke Robert."

"Oh, *pilgrimages*!" Edward said, in tones of such bitter detestation that Alfred's eyebrows rose.

"You sound as if you don't approve of them," Alfred remarked.

In sudden anger Edward said: "Do you? Our sister has been widowed because her husband went on pilgrimage and never came back. And here in Normandy . . . do you notice nothing as you go about day by day, Alfred? Do you ride out with your eyes shut? Today, didn't we pass a burnt-out farmstead? And didn't we ride through two separate hamlets and see not a soul? You'd expect someone to be about, even in cold weather, visiting a neighbour or getting in firewood, but no. Well, where were they all? Hiding from us, peering at us through cracks in the timber! They're afraid of anyone who carries a sword and rides on a horse. The whole of Normandy is in a state of anarchy. Because her duke is a child. Because Duke

Robert abandoned his proper business here and rode off to Jerusalem to leave his bones in the sand, and his son a boy to be reared in hiding to keep him alive. While the power-mad barons squabble over the duchy's torn body. *Pilgrimages!*" Edward said again, savagely. Alfred was silent. Edward recovered his temper and said presently, towel in hand: "Our sister seems to be over the worst of her grief now. We ought to find her someone else."

"Her boys will need a father," Alfred agreed.

"You know," Edward said, reverting to the earlier discussion as he continued to dry himself, "no one would catch me wandering off on pilgrimage if I had lands to care for like Duke Robert. I took an oath to go on pilgrimage once, but I've changed my mind. I'll build a church one day to make up for it—if I can ever afford one! That's what Duke Robert should have done. He threw his life away."

"He threw his gold away, too!" Alfred laughed. "Did you hear the tale they're telling of him in Byzantium? He wanted to give largesse to the poor . . ."

"Nothing wrong with that . . ."

"Wait! He had his pack mules shod with gold, not nailed on very well. The shoes kept coming off and spinning away as the cavalcade went along, and the crowd scrambled for them. I wonder if the mules all went lame," he added as an afterthought.

"I can guess who told you all that," said Edward, somewhat coldly. He disapproved of Alfred's mistress. Her husband was another pilgrim, this time one who unlike Duke Robert had not succumbed to any eastern maladies and who occasionally corresponded with his wife.

"Mabel," Alfred agreed. "Her husband's on his way home, his last letter said."

"How disappointing for you. You're sitting on my shirt," said Edward, pointedly dismissing the subject of Mabel.

The sons of Ethelred, exiles, pensioners, gentlemen, and ne'er-do-wells, as Alfred had been heard to put it, were not very alike. Their few resemblances were subtle: a similarity in the proportions of body and limbs, and a sufficient likeness in the texture of their minds to let them understand each other's mental processes even when they did not share them. Edward was taller, with his father's mousy fair hair and grey eyes. His beard was thin and the Norman fashion of clean shaving suited him. Alfred had his mother's dark hair and eyes and her olive-tinged skin. He also had more than a trace of her waspish tongue. She had disliked him slightly less than she had disliked Edward.

Hurrying feet sounded on the stair outside. Someone tapped excitedly on the door. "Edward! Alfred! Are you there? It's Godgift—can I come in?"

Edward pulled open the door.

"A messenger!" said his sister eagerly, almost before she was through it. "From England!"

In spite of widowhood and motherhood and all the prolonged anxiety of a husband away on the dangerous pilgrimage which had culminated in his death, Godgift looked absurdly young.

"It's because she's lived a real life," Edward had once remarked. "We shall age before our time with ennui, you and I, Alfred."

"It's a letter from our mother!" Godgift was saying. "With her ring . . . the messenger's waiting for you in the hall. Come down with me now!"

They hurried after her, too surprised for much comment even if she had given them the chance. In the hall, where the familiar damp chill was staunchly resisting the efforts of the fire to dispel it, a group of English soldiers stood warming their hands at the flames, and a little apart, seated on a bench beside the archbishop, was another man, with the long hair and the gold-adorned dress of a well-to-do-Saxon thane.

He rose as they entered. The archbishop said: "This is Thane Edwin, a courier from Queen Emma."

Edward went forward and the thane, bowing, held out to him a cylinder wrapped in oiled silk, and a small leather pouch. Edward opened the pouch and a ring rolled out onto his palm. "I was told you would know it," Edwin said. "It belongs to the Lady Emma."

Alfred and Godgift came to look. The ring was of gold, fancifully wrought in the likeness of a snake swallowing its own tail. The scales were minutely marked. The serpent's eye, enormous compared to its slender body, was a round-cut garnet.

"I can't recall it," said Alfred.

"I can," Edward said. He bounced it gently in his hand. "My mother had it as a gift from her brother when first she came to England. She used to wear it to remind her of Normandy, because hardly anyone wore finger rings in England in those days. She used to show it to people—women mostly—and tell them about it. I remember hearing her. Yes, I know this ring."

"I do, too," Godgift said. She smiled at the courier. "The token has done its work. Now we must read the letter."

Edwin tactfully withdrew as Edward opened the message itself. He unrolled it and read it in silence, while his brother and sister peered over his shoulder.

It was short and explicit.

"Emma, queen in name only," it began, "sends all motherly love and good wishes to her sons Edward and Alfred . . ."

"At last!" said Edward with a snort.

". . . Since I am grieving for the death of my lord and king and since you are daily deprived more and more of your inheritance, the kingdom, I wonder what plans you are making for the future . . . ?"

Each of the three, as they separately reached that point, paused in their reading and stared momentarily at the others.

". . . You must be aware that the delay due to your hesitation is placing the advantage with the usurper Harold Harefoot. He is wasting no time. He constantly visits villages and towns, winning over the thanes by gifts and threats and prayers.

"But many would prefer that you should rule them instead. I suggest (if indeed you are interested in establishing your rights) that one or both of you should come to me and consult with me here in England. I can, I believe, help you and advise you concerning the way in which this enterprise (which I wish for) can be achieved. Send back word of your intentions with the bearer of this letter. Farewell, my dear sons."

"Harthacnut's let her down," said Alfred, breaking the bewildered silence which followed their reading of this epistle. Edward released the bottom edge and the parchment rolled itself up again.

"He must have done," he agreed blankly. "Our mother would never call to us when she had Harthacnut to summon. It's extraordinary. Well, well!"

"As you say, well, *well*! I could not be more surprised if I came on a vixen hatching chicks." Alfred let out a whistle.

"You are speaking," said the archbishop coldly, "of your mother." He twitched the letter from Edward's grasp and read it himself.

"I am sorry. But has she ever been a mother to us?"

"Could Harthacnut be dead?" Godgift asked. "That would explain it."

Her uncle shook his head. "I doubt it. If that news had reached Winchester it would have reached Rouen as well."

"But she may have given up hope of his return!" Edward said. "Magnus of Norway may be starting some new ploy against him. Or perhaps he has simply told our mother that he does not wish to claim his English throne."

The archbishop rubbed his jawline. His eyes were shrewd despite the wateriness of age. "I have never approved my sister's attitude to you, as you know, though you will not abuse her in my presence. I have hoped—I have prayed—for a change of heart. Perhaps it has come."

"Or perhaps we are all she can turn to now," said Alfred. "We are the last chance for a son of hers to rule in England, the last alternative to Elfgift's dear little boy. She hates Elfgift and Harefoot more than she does us. Given that she's despaired of Harthacnut, the letter makes sense. I fancy the news of your landing in Southampton didn't escape her, Edward."

Edward turned to his uncle. "I think we need your advice and your help," he said. "But presently. For the moment it may be best if we talk about this alone together. Will you excuse us?"

"Naturally. I will pray that in your council you have the guidance of God. This is a very heavy affair, Edward. It is not just a matter of how much your mother loves or hates you. Remember that."

By silent consent, Godgift was included in the conclave. They sat in the little sleeping chamber, and she perched on Edward's bed, elbows on knees. Edward took a stool. Alfred settled cross-legged on the floor beside the brazier. The torches had been lit in the iron wall brackets and the room was full of a mingling of faded daylight and red torch flames. Outside it had begun to snow, small sharp flakes in a gusty wind.

"So," said Alfred. "Are we going, or not? Edward?"

"If we do, it had better be with good protection," Edward said grimly. "If Harefoot heard about it . . ."

"Would even Harefoot interfere with a private visit to our mother?" said Godgift.

"He wouldn't believe it was anything so harmless," said Alfred. "And he'd be right."

Edward dangled the scroll between his knees. "There are two things," he said. "We are invited to do something that we may well wish to do on our own account. But we are being asked to do it on our mother's account. Have we any reason to please her?"

"Our uncle has just said: this is a weighty matter. It goes beyond the feelings she has for us or we have for her." Alfred looked up at his brother. "This is a kingdom we are discussing. And a kingship. If you achieved the rule of England, you would be Edward Cyng."

"King Edward. The office should come before the man. Yes. Forgive me, Alfred. You are right."

They were quiet for a little while, aware of themselves as an odd and not entirely natural gathering. They were children considering a letter from their mother, but at the same time they were a Witan Council considering an act of war. They should have met round a long Witan Council table with a bevy of clerks busily taking notes, and a dozen mead-benches full of housecarles ready to resolve difficult matters with a vote. The bedchamber was the wrong setting.

Alfred crystallised it for them. "If you think we should accept, we must ask our uncle to set up a proper council of advisors for us. But meanwhile, Edward, let me see that letter again."

Edward handed it to him. He studied it. "It's . . . more vague than it seems," he said at last. "She does not say whether we should bring a force or come privately and expect to find a force and supporters when we arrive. She talks of 'help' and 'advice.' That could mean anything. There is not a word about the resources she has at her command, nor of where the earls stand in this. Will they help or hinder? That's important."

"I take the trouble to keep myself informed," said Edward. "Leofric of Mercia would wait until we had prevailed before he supported us. He is a cautious man. Siward of Northumbria has all his territories in Harefoot's half of the country. We should be lucky to get any support from him. He's Danish-bred, too. Bound to back Cnut's house, and not Ethelred's. Godwin of Wessex is my mother's chief supporter. I would hope that we could count on him. Even though she doesn't say so."

"Tell us what you think, Godgift," Alfred said, turning to his sister. "I know something is turning over in your mind. I can tell by your face. Say it."

"I wish," Godgift burst out, "that you would go for her sake! I think she's lonely and beset! She's growing old. I wish you would go just to help her!"

Edward sighed. "Godgift, you're a girl. She quite liked you because by the nature of things you couldn't resemble father quite as much as we could—me especially. She sent you wedding gifts, I recall. But she detested us. How can we forget that? Godgift, I loved father and she despised him. She sneered at him all the time. She even called him nithing once, in front of a room full of people—churchmen, thanes, housecarles, all sorts of folk. It was in London, just before we fled from the Danes."

"I remember that," Alfred said. His eyes narrowed as he looked back into his memories. "She was pacing about the hall. She said to him: 'You paid them off and still they come. No wonder when it means such easy profit! Why don't you fight as a king should do? You're no king, you're . . .'"

"Don't," said Godgift. "It was long ago. Can't we forget?"

"You can't wipe memory out at will," said Edward. "She called him nithing, a nothing-man, of no worth. He was sitting in that big chair of his, the black oak one with the ends of the arms carved into wolf-masks. He answered her back. He said: 'You only want me to fight because you hope I'll die in battle. Maybe you'd prefer a barbarian like Forkbeard or Cnut for a husband . . . !' How extraordinary! I never thought of that before."

"Thought of what?" asked Alfred.

"He was right! She did prefer Cnut. They were well matched, or so everyone says. She was a barbarian herself towards my father and me. You don't know what happened next, either of you. You weren't there. She went to her chamber to get her belongings together, to flee. She and women were throwing things into bags. I came in. I was about eleven, I think. It was always my misfortune that I took after the English side more than either of you. You're both dark. She saw me and shouted: 'Get out, Milkface! Get out! You look like your father and I've seen enough of him for a lifetime!'"

"You never told us that," said Godgift after a pause.

"It isn't the sort of thing one willingly tells anyone." Edward paused, thoughtfully. "But I'm glad I told it today. It has cleared my mind. I shall not answer this appeal."

"But . . ." Alfred looked amazed. "You were saying when the letter came how much you wished for your own lands to administer. You could be throwing away the chance of getting them!"

"Not quite." Edward smiled a little. "I am ceding it to you. One day, perhaps, you will grant me a manor or two?"

"But . . ." Alfred was nearly speechless. Then, torn between natural ambition and fraternal affection, he became nearly angry. "I can't go without you! You're the elder. It would be wrong. And we can't stay here, either! Dear God, you've said it yourself, look at the lives we lead! A ceaseless procession from one cousin or uncle to the next. Cousin Alan in Brittany—charming hospitality and broad hints about how much all the other members of the family must long to see us. Uncle William in Eu being hearty and awkward and asking what our plans are . . . God's Teeth, *what* plans? Uncle Robert's the soul of kindness, I grant you, but this castle's freezing! Cousin Eleanor in Flanders—Baldwin of Flanders welcomes everyone and his court is nothing but a clearinghouse for fugitives. Every wastrel in Christendom ends up there like driftwood coming ashore . . . I feel like a piece of flotsam myself when I stay there. We *must* go to England! And I can't go alone!"

Edward shook his head. "I will not be beholden to my mother for anything. I bitterly regret that I owe my existence to her. You must understand that. And you must also understand something else. There's one possibility you seem to have missed. Only one of us *can* go. Only one of us dare go. And that one must travel well protected with all the knights that he can muster." The daylight had faded almost entirely by now and the wavering torchlight made their faces hard to read. He knew, however, that the thought now in his mind had begun to stir in theirs, albeit against their wills.

"If you won't go, Alfred, I shan't blame you. The choice is yours and can only be yours because of the danger. Has it not struck you that these fair words and hopeful promises may be nothing but the bait—in a trap?"

Godgift stood up. "That's a vile thing to say! She is our mother, after all! You were never fair to her, Edward, never."

She whisked out of the room. The heavy oak door banged.

Alfred said: "Godgift was always more like her mother than either of us. Natural enough, I suppose—they're both female!"

Edward commented: "We shall certainly have to find her a husband soon, and he ought to be a strong character. She is quite a lot like our mother, as you say, and our mother is hardly a weak personality. But we are not discussing Godgift now. We are discussing this . . . astonishing invitation. Well, Alfred? The decision rests with you."

4 ✖ Monk with a Gift of Prophecy

. As week followed week, Brand learned his way through the mazes of his new life, a life so absorbing, so filled with new skills and new faces that he had little time to long for home. Indeed, much that had endeared his home to him, such as companionship and the sense of belonging, were abundantly present in Godwin's household. It was a family before anything, whether one was blood-linked to the earl or not.

Days began at dawn and closed at the big sundown meal where family, followers, thralls, and guests all ate together. It was a time for singing to the lyre, talking of the day's events, squabbling a little, and passing round the mead. Squabbles were mostly muted; Gytha would have no misbehaviour in her hall. She watched over it from the ladies' table along one side where she sat with the housecarles' wives and the girls whom she was educating for various friends. A tiny frowning glance from her to Godwin at the high table was enough to make him intervene in a quarrel. If the dispute were a true one, the parties went outside to settle it.

Guests were always present. Thanes from other parts of Wessex came; Brand was told that Wessex stretched from the Kent coast into Somerset, with Godwin's manors dotted over it and along the southern seaboard. Priests and pedlars came, minstrels and merchants, and once a wild-looking sea captain with salt-matted hair and a dented helm, who stayed three days, drank the ale store nearly dry, and spent long hours deep in talk with Godwin, whom he seemed to know well.

"We'll go to sea ourselves presently," Brand's friend Peter Longshanks said. "The earl has his own fleet, did you know?"

Longshanks, too, was a recent comer, the son of a former housecarle of Godwin's. His arrival, however, had been taken for granted by the other men, whereas Brand was a curiosity. It was Longshanks who told him why.

"You've broken all the rules. How did you do it? First you get picked up by Harefoot—you don't think kings usually go about collecting stray farmers' sons, do you?—and then . . ."

"He just wanted more riders than he had," Brand said. "And it pleased my family. He's been touting for support in the north."

"All right, we'll pass that. But then he hands you on to Godwin! It's a privilege to train with Godwin! He picks and chooses even among his own thanes' sons! He only took me, despite my father's service with him, because I won a shooting match at a fair and he thought I might be worth accepting. So naturally everyone marvels at you."

"Well, I've wondered myself, at times," Brand admitted. "Sweyn Godwinsson . . . seemed to see something comic in it. But they'll get used to me one day, I hope!"

Longshanks laughed, uncurling his gangling body from his stool as he heard the horn that betokened dinner. Brand had learned his unarmed combat scrapping with a brother bigger than himself and most attempts to bully him were short-lived. "You'll do. You've won a lot of respect already. And sooner or later we'll have another newcomer who'll make a good butt and then you can have fun making his life hell, if you like. They say there's a nephew of Lady Gytha's coming soon from Denmark to be trained with the Godwin boys. That might make a diversion."

"If I have strength enough left to take advantage of it," said Brand.

For the days were close-packed. He groomed ponies and cleaned saddlery. He helped the falconer repair the broken feathers of wild passage hawks which had damaged their tails fighting their captivity. He drilled, sometimes with all the rest under Oswald Halfear, the lean, raucous sergeant who had lost part of his left ear in a

Danish war long ago, and sometimes with the Godwin boys and the other youths in a junior group. He worked with axe and sword and stave and longbow; with spear and knife and his bare hands. Sometimes Godwin himself taught them, an inspiring and pitiless trainer, on the stretch of worn grass behind the outbuildings.

That March was cold but dry. Green grass with brown patches; blue sky with cloud patches; icy fingers and rasping breath; Godwin's eyes calm and impersonal beyond his shield until the last moment when the tyro's fatal mistake was made, when they blazed in triumph as he sprang to the final attack; the whipcrack of Godwin's voice and the scuffle of feet—all these wove themselves into a pattern of sight and sound and sensation which would be part of him forever, though he did not then know it.

"My housecarles provide the king's housecarles, when there is a king!" Godwin roared at them. "And so they have to be the best in the land! . . . Hold that spear straight, boy, *straight*—a fyrd peasant could do better with a blasted pitchfork!" He took them on one at a time and wore them out successively, knocking them down with a flat-handed swipe when they were stupid. "Never mind if your head's ringing, to hell with that; you'll have to fight on through worse than that one day if you want to live! Fight it! Throw it off! Concentrate on me! I'm coming to kill you!"

And Brand, staggering to his feet, would raise shield and blade vainly against Godwin's thunderbolt onslaught and find himself once more reeling, disarmed, tripped, flat on his back, pinned under the point of a sword and a tirade nearly as murderous and much less comprehensible.

"Watch the blades, *watch* them, will you? See them shine in the sun, see their movements growing out of each other, like a dance, like words piled up to meaning in a saga! Take what your enemy does as a gift and turn it back on him . . . Oh, get up, stand back, watch!" And Godwin would signal an older housecarle over. "Now, in slow motion, see what happens . . ."

And Brand would try, shaking the hair from his bewildered eyes, unable at first to make the least sense from such exhortations, for what had swords to do with sagas? Until at last, through the days and the weeks of aching, battered struggle, muscles and eyes, rhythm and reflex, began to blend in him, to sound in the lyre of his body the first full chords. Until the day when Godwin rested on his sword-hilt, wiped the sweat off his face, and remarked: "You're learning."

That day was doubly memorable, for on that day too, Beorn Estrithson, Gytha's nephew, arrived from Denmark just as rumour had promised, and, as Longshanks had foretold, Brand's own time as a curiosity was past.

Beorn, sixteen years old and very much aware of his status as one of the family, came upriver from Southampton on a rowing barge which Godwin had sent to meet him. He brought gifts: a chest of silks, a peregrine falcon, and a pair of wolfhounds, sent from his parents to Godwin and Gytha. He had an escort of twelve Danish housecarles. He was nearly as tall as Sweyn, nearly as blond as Wulfnoth, and he was regarded unanimously by Godwin's sons, with Sweyn as ringleader, as a nuisance who needed to be sat upon, hard.

Oh his first evening he fell out with Tostig over the war records of their respective fathers. Next day he resisted contemptuously the efforts of the old chaplain, Ethelnoth, to start him in his letters. Godwin was lettered himself and so was Gytha, and they required literacy in their family. Beorn said that where he came from letters were only for clerks and women, not for warriors, and that he was astonished to find his cousins so effeminate. The three largest of the effeminate cousins instantly hurled themselves on him with a concerted howl of fury and Godwin himself had to intervene to drag the struggling heap apart. Forced to yield and attend to his alphabet, Beorn relieved his feelings two hours later by fighting so fierce a wrestling bout with Sweyn that Sweyn, as the only alternative to calling quarter, snatched up a stone and began to pound Beorn's head with it, which was strictly against the rules of the contest. Godwin, summoned once more to arbitrate, lost patience and chastised both parties, giving the major share, however, to Sweyn. Sweyn, with oaths of undying hate and imaginative vengeance, flung himself out of the hall in a rage. Longshanks, watching him storm past the weapon store where he and Brand sat scouring knife blades and sharpening them on the grindstone, remarked: "Trouble is, it's more than empty talk. Sweyn can hold a grudge. We're in for lively times if young Beorn stays." He examined a ground blade critically, testing it with his thumb. "The countess will be angry. She's short-tempered, with the baby so near."

"I wonder if it will be another son?" Brand remarked.

"My lord's praying for a girl." Peter chuckled. "Really, truly praying, I hear, and he doesn't do that often."

"He wants a daughter?"

"If you were the Earl of Wessex," said Peter, "and you already had six sons who will all want earldoms of their own one day, you'd pray for daughters too. All *they* need are fairly well-off husbands!"

The day that Gytha's child was born was memorable also. On that day Brand encountered a monk with a gift of prophecy, observed the Godwins in the throes of what, even for them, was a fairly acrimonious dispute, and sensed for the first time that there were undercurrents in this household, some hidden sources of dissension and dread, which he did not understand.

It began in the morning, when sleet was falling and weapon practice out of doors had to be abandoned in favour of theoretical discussion under cover. Sweyn had posed a question, for the purposes of the theoretical discussion.

"If your lord is outlawed," he said, "must you follow him to exile?"

Brand knew that a man's life was governed by codes of behaviour. There were procedures in time of war for the exchange and treatment of captives. There were obligations in war and out of it between lord and follower, master and thrall, man and wife. What he had not before known was that these rules were subject to rival schools of thought. But in the Godwin household where almost anything was liable to resounding argument and the merits of two different battleaxe strokes could occupy the whole of a stormy morning, the intangible laws for human relationships were matters for contention just as much as weaponry.

"No," Godwin was saying now, walking up and down before his group of attentive youths. "No, you're a freeman. It was laid down by King Alfred that a man might leave his lord and seek another as long as he told the first lord of his intent. But many men would follow their leaders to exile and be praised for it. Loyalty to your leader comes even before loyalty to your kin."

"Suppose," said Beorn, cross-legged in the front row, between Harold and Sweyn, "you had some secret knowledge about your lord—where he had a treasure hidden, or a hideout or a private anchorage—and later you took another leader, and your new lord and your old became enemies? Should you tell what you know to your new lord if it would help him?"

"Not unless it endangered him or his folk, or was knowledge concerning some deed so abominable that no oath could stand in respect of it."

"What sort of thing would be that abominable?" asked Harold.

Godwin stopped pacing and considered him. "You will know an abomination if ever you meet one," he said.

He looked towards the door, as it opened to admit Gytha in the midst of her young ladies. Gytha always kept the maidens near her. She guarded them, Sweyn was once heard to say gloomily, as if they were rare and soluble spices, and in her turn she had been heard to say that she would return her friends' daughters to them dead before she would return them damaged. If she were bringing them back into the hall now, it meant that she expected the men shortly to be out of it. And indeed, behind her head as she stepped over the threshold, one could see a segment of blue sky. The sound of rain on the thatch had died away.

"We can go back to our archery, I think," Godwin said.

As they were going out, Oswald Halfear beckoned to Brand. "I've an errand to Winchester. You'll do. I've a blade at the swordsmith's, having a new hilt put on it. I want it collected. I've no time to get it. You can be back in time for the last hour of shooting, if you hurry your pony. I ought to make you run both ways," he added with a chuckle. "All you lads get puffed too soon. And how to run down a fleeing enemy is part of the job you're learning."

Brand nodded. He went to Gytha before setting out, in case she had any commissions in the town. It was customary, if sent out on an errand, to ask if there were any others, and Gytha often did have small requirements. Not this time, however. "No, Brand, there's nothing, thank you," she said. She looked tired. This child might well be her last, for her face was beginning now to show its years and there were greying threads in her hair. But she smiled as she added: "We do have an overdue messenger from Oxfordshire but I can't ask you to scour the roads between here and there to find him! No. Get Oswald's sword for him and make haste back to your archery."

Brand liked the swordsmith's shop. Its specialty was in fitting ornamented hilts and sheaths, since Godwin's men, who were its principal customers, preferred mostly to use the superb blades of the Rhineland rather than English ones. But the swords would be finished here, and the oak-plank walls were patterned with hilts gem-studded and silver-adorned, awaiting collection, and with sheaths as decorative as the iron blades they sheltered were businesslike.

It was impossible not to linger here, however much of a hurry you were in. The smith, for one thing, never handed a sword back without drawing it half a dozen times to make sure it drew smoothly and gave no trouble to its owner's grip. When eventually Brand mounted his pony and set out for home, he knew he would have to hasten, if Greedy could only be got to hasten, which wasn't likely. He was relieved, therefore, if slightly surprised, when his urgent heels apparently produced a response and the pony broke from a slow jog into a canter. Then they rounded a clump of trees and he realised that his urging had nothing to do with it. Greedy had smelt other horses and wanted to reach them.

It was a party of three monks. One had been thrown and was sitting at the roadside examining his elbow. The other two were wheeling about on their own ponies, trying to catch their companion's. The loose pony, a stocky dun animal with a wicked rolling eye, eluded them skilfully as Brand came round the corner, and then like a sinking ship subsided onto the ground and tried to roll. The high-pommelled saddle prevented it, but two saddlebags fell from their moorings, and the unhorsed monk uttered a most unecclesiastical oath and leapt to their rescue, elbow forgotten. Brand stuck his heels once more into Greedy's hairy sides and summoning up the horsemanship which life with the Godwins was gradually instilling, came alongside the dun as it rolled the right way up again. He grabbed its bridle. The dun laid back its ears but stood still.

Brand slid out of the saddle and leading both ponies went to help the monk, who was muttering anxiously over some bright and sparkling objects which had tumbled out of the saddlebags. He flicked mud from them with hands that shook.

"Here's your horse, father," Brand said.

"My thanks, my son. My thanks. My most grateful thanks." The monk looked at the pony without much enthusiasm.

"You're not hurt, I hope?" Brand said. "Or your goods . . . ?" He leant closer to look, intrigued by the glitter, and almost gasped. The monk smiled and let him look, though the smile held a trace of nervousness. The other two now came up close to Brand, their faces watchful beneath their hoods.

Brand said: "I am on an errand from Earl Godwin's manor. I belong there. I shan't steal your goods, father, don't be afraid of me. They're . . . beautiful!"

There were several things. One was a gold box, with birds and marvellous animals carved intricately over its surface. There was also a set of jewellery, of a kind which had lately become a fashion among the women: bracelet, finger-ring, and cloak-brooch, made of gold and set with red stones. And there was what appeared to be a baby's toy, a rattle, but with beads of gold. The workmanship of all the pieces was, in its meticulousness and love, as satisfying as the swordsmith's work had been. The objects were perfect for their uses: a repository, ornaments, a plaything. And they were finished with a fineness of detail which allowed the eye to stare as minutely as it would, without finding any disappointment.

"From Godwin's house, you say?" the monk asked. "That's where we're bound ourselves."

"Are you? But . . ." Brand looked at them. ". . . Just . . . forgive me, but just three monks together, with such precious things as these?"

"A monk's habit can be as good a protection as a full set of armour," said the monk, closing up the saddlebags. "No one expects us to be carrying costly goods, or if we are, then they're holy relics and untouchable."

"Are these holy relics, then?" Brand asked. They didn't look as if they were.

"No, not this time." The monk reluctantly took the reins of the dun pony, as Brand held them out to him. "They're gifts, from Earl Godwin's cousin Abbot Sparhafoc of Abingdon, for the Lady Gytha's new child, and for Lady Gytha. Has the child come yet?"

"No, not yet. Are you the messenger Lady Gytha mentioned today, coming from Oxfordshire and overdue? She was anxious."

"Yes, that would be us. We were delayed when my pony went lame. I wouldn't set out on purpose on a spawn of Satan like this!" He nodded at the dun, which rolled its eyes again. "He was the only animal to be had in that hamlet where we left my gentle Dapple. He scraped me off under a tree this morning, and then tried to roll with me in a river."

"If you don't want to ride him again," said Brand, who had already noticed that the other two monks were not good horsemen and felt that the third was probably as bad, "you can take mine. He's lazy and you'll have to kick him along, but he won't roll or try to get you off. I'll try your dun devil! We all seem to be going to the same place, so we can ride along together."

"That's uncommonly good of you, my son." The monk looked thankful. "You have a good heart. Did you ever think of entering religion?"

"No," said Brand truthfully. Then, since this reply seemed bald to the point of discourtesy, he said: "I think I have no vocation."

The monk, pausing in the act of mounting Greedy, peered at him. "Aye, maybe you're right. If you had a vocation, you'd know. And if you haven't, then God perhaps has other work for you. If God wants you, He'll shout, that's what I say. There's many a man—and many a woman too—in the Church that was pushed there by other people and shouldn't have been." He settled in the saddle at last, and Brand helped him fasten the saddlebags to it. The other monks watched, still wary, keeping nearby.

Gathering up Greedy's reins, after a final comforting rub to his bruised elbow, Brand's new friend said: "We should introduce ourselves. I am Brother Athelstan. These are the Brothers Alfhun and Hugh, who is French and has no English. We have to talk Latin to him. And you are . . . ?"

"Brand, my name is. I am learning the skills of arms, in Earl Godwin's household."

"Brand . . . that means a sword. A good English name. But there's Welsh blood in you from your black eyebrows; am I right? And you have their love of fine works of art, I saw it when you looked at the abbot's gifts. Ah." Suddenly he leant forward and stared into Brand's eyes. "You'll fall in love with a woman for her beauty one day, my boy. And likely enough she'll break your heart."

Embarrassed, Brand said: "Abbot Sparhafoc has sent very wonderful gifts. Who made them?" As he spoke he mounted the dun pony. He was going to be very late indeed, he thought, though it might not matter now.

"Why, he did," said Brother Athelstan. "The abbot, I mean. He's one of the finest goldsmiths in the land. He's fit to turn a royal crown any time."

The monk called Alfhun said: "Should we not hurry?"

At the manor the steward took charge of the newcomers and Brand, having seen the ponies stabled, went in search of his colleagues. He saw to his surprise that the targets beyond the hall were still deserted. Then he hesitated because of a sudden uproar echoing from the hall itself. Ears pricking, he slipped through the door. It sounded as if a battle were about to start.

He stepped straight into the eye of the storm. As he shut the door, a heavy body hurtled backwards onto him. He grabbed the doorpost for support and Sweyn bounced off him, to land on the floor, where he sat angrily rubbing a reddened ear. Nearby, Beorn sat on a bench looking amazedly at his uncle. In mid-floor stood Godwin, breathing hard, furious. Gytha and the girls, by the loom, watched with great interest. Gytha was calm but the girls were frankly agog and no weaving was in progress.

Godwin caught sight of Brand. "Ah, so we're all here! You can share in this, boy. Pick yourself up, Sweyn. Sit by Brand. Now listen!" He addressed Brand directly. "The question," he said, "asked by my son Sweyn concerns the times when a man may or may not kill. An important question that we must have *clear*!" Godwin glared at his eldest son.

Sweyn glared back but did not speak.

"You may," said Godwin, adopting a public tone and standing with feet apart, "slay in battle. We all know that! You may slay from the rear if your enemy is running away and will not cast down his weapons or otherwise yield. You may by stratagem kill a known enemy to your lord or your family, to save lives among his folk or your own. But you may not kill unarmed men unless they are condemned criminals or hostages whose lives are lawfully forfeit. And . . ."—he was coming to the heart of it now, to the reason why a moment ago he had struck Sweyn, and his face hardened—". . . you may not kill for private gain, for that strikes at the roots of trust. You may not kill one who trusts you, who may even look to you for protection, such as a comrade or a follower or even a thrall . . . unless or until they in some way betray you. There must be loyalty between equals, and from lord to man also, as much as from a man to his leader."

Sweyn, still feeling his ear, said: "But if such a one, say, had knowledge that might be dangerous to you . . ."

"No!" said Godwin violently. There was an odd, last-ditch air about him, as though he were making a final defence of some private stronghold. "The killing required in war is one thing. Murder is another. God have mercy on your soul if you can't tell the difference."

Beorn said suddenly: "Uncle, you said it was permitted to kill a known foe by stratagem."

Godwin turned to him. "It is."

"What if the enemy is a man who has reason to trust you? It happened once at home. One of my father's jarls found that a friend of his was in some scheme to kill my father. He did not know what to do because his friend had once saved his life when they were on a battlefield."

"That's a good, definite example," Godwin said. "Well? What happened?"

"He warned my father without naming names. But the plot nearly succeeded because my father still didn't know which way to look for his enemy."

At the end of the hall, Gytha was studying a broken thread on the loom. She glanced round. "In such a case," she observed, with her characteristic air of having only a tenth of her mind on what she was saying, while the rest was engaged on what she was doing, "you may betray your friend, or your guest, or your follower. Or you may cause others to betray those who similarly trust them. You may not murder for your own convenience, but you may do so on your lord's behalf. One's duty to one's lord and his house is absolute. Any treachery is permitted in the cause of it."

Godwin spun round. No one could have missed the bitter edge on Gytha's voice. Her husband's expression was one of bewildered anguish, as if he had been stabbed in the back by his best friend. Anger followed the bewilderment. His face suffused. He opened his mouth.

Gytha rose. "I think," she said with masterly timing, "that our new child will be here before midnight." They saw that she was pale and she bit the last word off short. Recovering herself, she said: "Ladies! Will one of you fetch Halfear's wife Aldith and send her to my chamber?" And gathering her skirts clear of the rushes, she surged forward, past the stupefied men and out of the door. Her ladies trailed out after her. The door shut behind them.

Sweyn turned savagely on his cousin.

"Did you have to say that? You and your clever questions! Showing off how earnest you are! Making trouble!"

Beorn gazed at him blankly. "What in the name of Valhalla are you talking about? You were the one who asked if a man should follow his leader to exile, as I recall. And you were the one who suggested it might be allowable to kill someone you privately feared or disliked. If your head aches, it's your own fault and if it has started off some family quarrel in this hall, it's your own fault again. What do I know of your old disputes? I'm a stranger here, as you never tire of telling me!"

Godwin had walked up to them. He said: "Be quiet, both of you. Sweyn, Beorn asked his question in all good faith and you know that quite well. Beorn, you are as you say a stranger here but that I think must now be changed. You are a son of mine now, or as good as . . ."—he quelled Sweyn with a frown—". . . and there are —family matters—which I must soon discuss with you. You are of an age, and living here on such terms, as make it necessary. Then you will understand what Sweyn is talking about. Sweyn, go out to the archery targets with the rest and help Oswald to organise a contest. If you ever again advocate murder for private satisfaction, I will throw you out of my house. The next step after that kind of talk is the sword drawn in temper, on a man who carries none. You have much to learn."

"Bah!" said Sweyn.

"Do *you* know what all that was about?" Longshanks whispered to Brand as they went out with the rest, collecting their bows on the way. Brand, lifting his weapon from its hook on the wall, shook his head. "Some old family squabble or feud, I suppose," he said. "It's no concern of ours."

"Your daughter, sir," said Aldith, handing the bundle to its father. "Her hair," she added, "will be red."

"I should suspect the worst if it was black," said Godwin. "Gytha?"

Gytha poked a sleepy face out from the sewn fawnskins. She extended an arm and Godwin gave her the baby. "I feel I've done this before," he said.

"Eight times now," Gytha told him. She added: "Aldith says

she favours you, but they all look the same to me. Twisted up faces and nothing like anybody. Even Sweyn, and look how handsome he is now!"

They were briefly silent, remembering that first birth. Godwin had spent it in a state of dread, trying to hide his fears in busy attention to estate tasks and hearty, offhand remarks to his friends on "women's business" and Gytha's customary excellent health. He hadn't convinced either himself or the friends. When Aldith came at last to say it was a son and vigorous and the mother was safe, he had abandoned pretence and rushed headlong to Gytha, leaving his dignity behind him. And Sweyn in Gytha's arms had looked much as this girl-child did now, even to the ginger tuft of hair on top.

"Sweyn was noisier," he said. "He squalled in my face and frightened me half to death. And he's still a devil. He never profits by example."

Gytha sighed, her serenity clouded. "What is it?" he asked.

"Are the examples always perfect?" Gytha said.

Godwin sighed in turn. "Gytha, don't desert me, even in your mind. Please. I know what you think. You made it plain this afternoon. I was angry. But I know what you feel and why. Only it's too late now. Thane Edwin came in while you were birthing. Atheling Alfred has accepted. Only Alfred, not Edward, but one will be lesson enough and that lesson must be given. *Must.* I shall send Brand north very soon. Gytha . . ." He added after a moment: "Sparhafoc's messengers brought your gifts today, too, did you know?"

"The women told me, yes. Godwin, I still worry. We may be called to account for Atheling Alfred one day. Thane Edwin . . ."

"Is wholly my man and will swear he acted in good faith. Gytha, it will be all right."

"If it isn't," said Gytha, "I will be with you. If there is guilt, I share it. I have had a part in it. God have mercy on us both. What name shall we give our daughter? Didn't you once suggest Gunhild, for a girl?"

5 ✗ "He Calls Himself Alfred Atheling"

Eric Merchant of Dover was content.

By the Elbow of God he had done it. At last.

It had taken enough time and toil, years and years of putting by, of economical travel on dirty ships with pest-ridden bedding, of clever buying and cleverer selling, but now the great moment had come. He stood with a rope in his hand waiting to throw it to the first ship chartered exclusively for him, as it came into harbour with a load of merchandise all his own, back from the first voyage he had ever financed without aid.

If he could do that three times, he would merit the rank of thane. *Thane*!

What a blessing it was, he thought, weighing the rope in his hand and pushing the long flaxen hair out of his eyes, to be part of a civilised folk where one could rise through trading and intelligence, instead of only by hitting more men over the head with an axe than other people could. His own grandfather had been a Danish free-booter, but Eric was not proud of his grandfather. Most people could trace their lineage to near savages in their near ancestry, but you needn't boast of it. Reading and writing and calculation were the true skills of the future. They were the key to tomorrow's treasure chest. Not battleaxes.

The ship's oars plashed as she came smoothly to rest against the quay. There was his son Rolf on board, his second son—since

Ordgar, the elder, was on a trading trip inland. Rolf flourished an upturned thumb, token of a good expedition. A fine boy. Eric had had doubts about trusting him with the buying on this momentous trip, but Rolf must have his chance sometime and he himself had fallen sick at sailing time. He cast the rope. The sailors pulled it in and made fast, and Eric jumped aboard.

He did not doubt that this voyage was the first of a triumphant trio. Two years ago he had given hospitality to an old vagabond woman who had told the household fortunes in return for a supper of smoked pork, rye bread, beans, and ale. A mighty destiny was his, written in his hand, she said, looking up from his palm with bright black eyes that must once have been shining ornaments in a face of great beauty. They still shone from the lined and nearly toothless ruins of that face. "It's something you'll do but I can't be seeing what." He wondered where she came from, with that dark skin and those eyes. Wales, perhaps. It was a land of witchcraft. "But it'll change the course of the world," she said in her cracked singsong voice, and she smiled horribly, showing two brown fangs like those of a worn-out werewolf. "So best beware of all you do. Who knows when your hour will come?" Five minutes later she had promised his daughter Hild a visit to court and "a husband near to a great overlord." And then he thought he saw the riddle's answer. He would become a thane, of course. No one below that rank could get a powerful husband for his daughter or change the course of history either.

"Well, Rolf," he said, embracing his son, "and what have you brought?"

Rolf started an inventory as the unloading began. Unloading was a nuisance. Saving up to finance voyages was all very well, but one day they must build a better warehouse, nearer to the harbour. The stuff had to be carted much too far as things were, and hiring an oxcart was costly, too. Eric stood by his son, checking tallies against the bales and bundles as they came ashore. The Byzantine silverware would sell well in Winchester, where Queen Emma's court was, and silks were also very marketable. But he'd paid too much for the wine . . .

"No, wait till you taste it," Rolf said. "It's a find."

"Maybe, maybe, but you should have brought some cheaper stuff as well . . ."

"I did. That comes next."

Bales of cloth, dye pigments, spices . . .

"Ginger root, and a sack of peppers, and some cinnamon," Rolf said.

"Too much," said Eric disapprovingly. "Folk can grow their own herbs. There's not so much demand for these fancy eastern delicacies." But the boy had done well, he thought privately, though there was no sense in overpraising him. Eric would have done worse at the same age. He rested a hand on Rolf's shoulder as they followed the last bale to the oxcarts.

They were in the store, carrying out a fussy double-check on the tallies—Eric believed in making sure—when Hild came. She uttered a squeak of joy on seeing Rolf and ran to him. "Rolf! You're home! How brown you look! Was it a good voyage? Did you meet any pirates?"

"By God's grace, no," said Rolf. "A nice titbit we should have been for them if we had!" He pulled his sister's brown plaits. "What put pirates into your head, little Hild?"

"Oh!" Hild turned to her father. "Father, we have guests. They've just landed from Flanders. *They* met pirates. It's a young— he must be a thane at least, he's dressed so fine—and some of his men. Normans, I think. Is it all right?"

Eric sighed. As a future man of rank he felt it right to start getting used to his dignity in advance. He had built himself a bigger house during the year after the fortune-teller's advent. It had a guesthouse within its palisade and its own well and looked impressive. But it was not only prepared for guests, it also, unfortunately, attracted them. And Eric had discovered that he did not much like having strangers, sometimes rude ones, in his house. He fought an endless running battle between his wishes and his duties over hospitality. He was only thankful that as his business was now prospering there was not too much conflict over expense.

"It will have to be," he said irritably now. "Is he a well-spoken man? Is he Norman like his followers?"

"He's very polite," said Hild. "He looks like a Norman—his hair's short—but he speaks our tongue. That's why I said a thane. I think he's English, whatever his followers are."

"How many followers has he got?"

"He says six hundred . . ."

"What?"

"Only a score or so are with him at our house," said Hild hastily. "The rest are lodged round the town."

"I don't understand this." Eric signed to Rolf to finish with the tallies, and they locked up the warehouse. "I don't understand at all," he said again as they began the walk home. "A young lord with a following of that strength—and he's English while they aren't. Who is he? Why did he not go to the town reeve's house? That's the proper place."

"No room there," said Hild.

"No *room*? Are we being invaded?"

"I don't know," said Hild helplessly. "What was I to say?"

"Well, what is his name? He told you that much, surely?"

"Yes," said Hild doubtfully. At thirteen she sometimes found filling her dead mother's place a heavy task. She carried a grown-up burden, but grown-ups didn't always realise it and they gave silly teasing answers to important and necessary questions, such as those about their names and business. "He said he was called Alfred the Atheling, or Alfred the Exile. I didn't know what he meant."

"Alfred Atheling!" Eric stopped short. "But that's . . . Queen Emma's younger son, by King Ethelred! If he really is who he says he is . . . how old is he? Twenties? Thirties? Dark or fair?"

"Twenties, I think," said Hild. "He's dark."

"It could be." Eric resumed his stride. "We're in noble company if so. But what has brought . . . ? Well, that isn't our business. Rolf, if that wine is all you say it is, you had best go back and fetch some to the house. Alfred Atheling! Here! Well, well, *well!*"

"But your brother could not come? A pity. But we will give you a welcome doubly warm, to make up for it. You haven't lost your English, I notice." Earl Godwin bowed graciously and extended an ungloved right hand to his young guest. In the background, bursting with pride at this splendid meeting in his very own courtyard, stood Eric Merchant.

It was a crowded meeting as well as a splendid one. Before Eric's door stood Alfred, flanked by his friend Fulbert Fitzwarren, a fully armed Norman knight. About ten more knights were lined up behind him, a forbidding row of mailed figures who looked all alike since the nosepieces of their helmets took all individuality out of

their faces. Facing Alfred stood Godwin, respectfully bareheaded,
the sun catching the russet lights in his thick, springy hair. Behind
him stood his three eldest sons and a group of thanes, all in armour,
and inside the gate a hundred housecarles had crowded, also ar-
moured, and equipped with axes. The two principals, however,
were vivid in tunics and mantles of dyed wool. Godwin was in
turquoise and tawny, Alfred in crimson under blue. Gold and jewellery glittered expensively about their persons.

Behind the smooth, formal phrases of greeting they appraised
each other.

"I trust you had a safe journey," Godwin said as, with an arm
about the guest's shoulders, he led the way into the hall for the wine
and sweetmeats Eric was longing to serve.

"We had a short encounter with pirates," Alfred said. "At least,
we think they were pirates." His gaze travelled sideways, scanning
the earl's impassive face. "I have a few men hurt. But none seriously.
They will all be able to travel in a day or two, if the delay is permitted."

"I am glad it was no worse," said Godwin courteously. His face
told nothing beyond a correct, moderate concern, befitting news of
that commonplace hazard of the sea, a pirate attack. Alfred had
hoped at this point of the meeting to know at last whether he were a
truly welcome guest or had come as a coney into a snare. He was
disappointed.

They took their seats in the hall and Eric snapped his fingers
towards Hild, who scurried to fetch the refreshments. "Tell me,"
said Godwin calmly as the wine was poured, "more of this attack."

"That merchant was a comic little fellow," Harold Godwinsson remarked, riding at Alfred's side as the cavalcade, which with Godwin's and Alfred's men combined resembled a small army, at last set
out from Dover.

"His wine was excellent," said Alfred. "Do all merchants live so
well in England now?"

Harold laughed. "No, I think it was his own stock for sale,
brought out to honour his noble guests. Well, it should help his future trade. My father has ordered a consignment. My father sends
his apologies, by the way, for not riding with you this morning. He
has gone on ahead to see that the arrangements for our night's lodging are all they should be. He asked me to entertain you."

"Thank you," said Alfred.

In the three days they had spent at Dover, while Alfred's injured men recovered, he had seen far more of Godwin's sons than of Godwin, and now, it appeared, the pattern was to continue. Godwin had been consistently busy, occupied with a lame horse, a dispute among the men, business with the town reeve . . . it was as though he did not want too much to do with the Atheling, although when they did meet his courtesy was unfailing. Alfred shifted uneasily in his saddle and thought again of the pirate fleet. He had himself had a small hired fleet of ships—stout, fjord-built, sixty-foot vessels, with plenty of capacity but no great speed. The pirates had had a squadron of small, light ships, the kind the Northmen called skutas, which were built for speed and swift manoeuvring. They had come up fast astern. And then had come the hail of burning arrows.

Well, they'd got away, through the sheer skill and experience of the sailors. The wind was fair and they used their big square sails, aided by the power of their oars, to lengthen their lead. It couldn't be kept up long, not that kind of rowing. But the burst had won them breathing space enough to use the ebbing tide to their advantage. The hired captains knew their tides and their coastal shallows by heart and in the end they had left their pursuers enmeshed by rocks and sandbanks as the white water began to break there. But it had been a near thing. Too near. And he had voiced his doubts to Godwin, in Eric's hall, at that first meeting.

"There may be interests in the north that fear my coming."

"Perhaps," Godwin said indifferently. "But let us hope that in the north your coming isn't known. I have provided a trustworthy escort. The Wessex men are the king's traditional bodyguard, remember. You're in good hands."

Grimly, Alfred told himself he hoped so.

The route led along the old paved Roman road to Canterbury, where the first night of the journey was spent. The lodgings proved excellent. Next day they rode along the ancient way that skirted the northernmost march of Andred Forest, to pass the second night at a wayside monastery. On the third day Godwin at last gave the Atheling some of his company, telling him of the plans for the days ahead. "Lady Emma waits for you at Winchester," he said. "She travels little these days."

"Is she well?" Alfred asked. He tried to imagine his straight-backed and ferociously energetic mother as aged and frail, and couldn't. Yet she must be well into her fifties by now. Well, age came to everyone. He had not seen her for more than twenty years.

"Well, but less active than she was once," Godwin said. "We shall be there in two or three days now. We lie tonight at a town on one of my manors: they call it Gildenford, from the kingcups that turn the meads to gold where the road crosses the River Wey. I have had to make arrangements to lodge you all out among the townsfolk; my hall there is small. But there will be a feast ready."

They rode on for a while in silence, and Godwin gradually dropped back, on a narrowing stretch of road. When the track broadened again, Fulbert Fitzwarren jogged up alongside his friend. "Yours is a fair, fertile country," he remarked quietly. "If our escort were a little less overpowering, I should enjoy this ride." He glanced quickly fore and aft. "Their numbers nearly equal our own, I should say. To do us honour or to control us? Which?"

"I've been wondering," said Alfred. "And six hundred men looks like the wrong number to have brought. I should have brought six, and looked completely harmless, or six thousand and looked too strong to attack. As it is, I merely look provoking."

"We can only keep our eyes open and our swords loose in the sheath," said Fulbert philosophically. "There's a deer."

For England was indeed fair and fertile, and when Alfred could quiet his fears for a while, he found his heart going out to it. Northwards the land was more open, forest yielding place to turf and golden broom, and there were warm purple patches of clover and a silvering of daisies here and there. But southwards was the stronghold of Andred, green-shadowed under the arms of ancient oaks and gigantic beeches, with glimpses here and there of natural glades, madly, magnificently, magically green with the young spring grass. It was still early in the day and the web of a hammock spider sparkled in the wayside grasses, dazzling with dew. As a small boy Alfred had listened to his half-pagan nurse who told him that these were the beds of the Little People, who were wicked and mischievous and heartless and beautiful, beautiful beyond mortal imagining. He remembered her, his recollection suddenly grown vivid, and with the memory came others, of timber-built halls, and gold and silver tapestries, and the taste of mead. They would feast in such a hall, and on such mead, when they got to Winchester.

Winchester. Where he was going to meet the mother he had not seen all his adult life. Or was this indeed a trap? But surely it couldn't be, not set by his own mother. If the pirate fleet had been sent by anyone, it must have been by the king of the north, who had got wind of the visit. One's own mother could not be involved. Yet there was no intimacy between Emma and her elder sons. She would be a stranger to him and he, presumably, an equal stranger to her. He wondered how she would receive him.

He did not hate her as Edward did, but nor had he any warmth for her. If she had treated him less badly, she had certainly neglected him. Her attitude to him had been passive lack of interest rather than the active dislike she gave Edward. He could not remember ever running to her with any childish trouble. Always he had gone to his nurse . . . or to his father.

In the years of his manhood, away from her, Alfred had taught himself to think of her unemotionally. He had also learnt a good deal about women in general, largely from his mistress Mabel, that witty, bewitching, and faithless grass widow of a pilgrim. From Mabel's malicious but usually accurate comments about mutual acquaintances he had come to see what must have been wrong with his mother in the days when she was Ethelred's wife.

"Poor dear Mald," he could hear Mabel saying in her high, glass-edged voice at some crowded feast. "Look at that bright smile of hers. Her husband's said something stupid again and she's having to pretend she agrees with him."

Emma, as he recalled her, had been a woman strong in mind and body, married to a man who was her inferior in both, though not actually ailing. (Alfred had also learned to be dispassionate about his father.) Ethelred would never admit the truth and had demanded from Emma a conventional deference which she would not give him. Unlike Mald, Emma would not pretend to agree.

He had refused to heed her warnings against attempting to buy off the Danish raiders, and she had openly called him a nithing for it. But it had indeed been unwise. Alfred had often been sorry for his father and had loved him. But it was a love without respect. On the other hand, he had respected Emma without loving her.

In Ethelred's place, Cnut would have fought the raiders. Well, Ethelred had also fought them at times, but he generally lost. Cnut would have won. Emma had probably never needed to advise Cnut when she was married to him. Reportedly, she had been happy with him. Understandable.

In the more intimate part of their marriage, Ethelred must have been fairly adequate, Alfred supposed. He had given her three children. But you did not have to satisfy a woman to give her babies; it was enough to satisfy yourself. He recalled his mother's sudden tempers, the stormy air that went with her everywhere, the tension that gripped a room when she entered it. Mabel's voice spoke again in his mind.

"Judith's taken a lover, they say. I expect it's true. She looks so peaceful. She used to be like a thunderstorm looking for somewhere to burst. I believe poor Thorold was very inept in bed. She told me once she used to lie awake for hours afterwards, biting her nails." That Judith had had children, too.

People did tell Mabel things like that. She never kept their counsel but she was willing to advise, and her advice, if sometimes cynical, was generally sound. She was not at heart cruel but a sharp wit like a fine dagger couldn't spend all its time in the sheath. He wondered what she was doing now. Her husband was said to be on his way home. Alfred was not jealous. Long since he had concluded that it was unsafe to care too much for anyone. But he wished her image would stop haunting him. It was as though he were never going to see her again.

During the afternoon they passed through a grove of silver birch, riding up a long incline which left the thick depths of Andred behind. At the top they found themselves looking ahead to hills that rolled in a long vista, blue-tinged in the distance as if seen through clear water. A thread of river twinkled below and the road led down to it. Where the ford must be was a wide expanse of meadow, dusted gold by some field flower. Beyond the river was a cluster of thatched roofs with drifts of blue smoke slanting northeast in the light wind. On a small hill nearby, a high-roofed hall overlooked the little township.

"My manor of Gildenford," said Godwin, cantering up and drawing rein at his guest's side. "I hope that my steward is ready for us. I sent him word of the numbers."

6 ⚔ Silver Pennies

Brand's journey north was accomplished with a placid lack of incident, which was a relief. Times were more lawless since the days of Cnut.

He was surprised and pleased to be going. "I shall be away for a time," Godwin had told his household, "providing an escort for a noble visitor to England. Those remaining behind must guard Winchester in my absence. I am willing to grant leave of absence to some of you if you wish to visit your kinsfolk." Later, to Brand's stammering astonishment, Godwin had beckoned him aside and told him that he was actually required to go on leave and was to travel northwards with Ethelnoth, who was going to see friends in a monastery by Avon River, the house where he had been trained for the Church. "Given," said Godwin, "that you take in Worcester on your journey home and carry out a simple errand."

He had, he explained, promised to send King Harefoot some heirlooms of his father King Cnut. "A drinking cup and a dagger with a stoat-skull hilt. He has few relics of his father and from the way you cherish that sword that is too big for you, you know what they can mean. The relics are not of great value in themselves, but still they could be coveted for Cnut's sake. Carry them well wrapped in your saddlebag and tell no one they are there. The king is at Worcester now."

He parted from Ethelnoth the day before he reached Worcester but rode on unmolested, too insignificant with his brown homespun cloak and his plodding pony to call a robber's attention. Worcester was a hybrid of a town, with wooden, thatched houses scattered among the crumbling walls of the old Roman settlement. A few of the better-preserved walls had been patched up and used and the city walls had been repaired as well. Harefoot's hall was half stone, half wood, built on a knoll and easy to find.

To reach its gate he had to cross the open space in front of it, under the gatewards' eyes, and the lowered pike which barred his way when he got there was not lifted till he had stated his business. When he was let through it was into the care of a fierce, flaxen-maned housecarle whose cloak was made of complete wolfskins, fringed with masks and paws and tails. He said: "I will take you to the king."

"Surely," said Brand, taken aback, "the steward . . . or . . ."

The shaggy housecarle did not answer. Perforce, Brand handed his pony to the gatewards and followed his guide on foot. The court-yard was ill-kept, after Godwin's well-ordered dwelling. A midden stood by the gate, and the last object flung on top of it was—or had been—a man. Brand looked once and swallowed firmly. In his brief time with Harefoot's men he had learned to hide his feelings. This was to be expected.

"Who was he?" he asked, since the housecarle had seen him looking.

"A Welsh thrall. He tried to get away." The man's teeth flashed in his beard. "You should have come sooner, shared the fun. Or is it true they're soft down south?"

"Not so very," said Brand, thinking of Godwin's training courses.

They passed among rows of huts, where much warlike activity was going on—sharpening of blades and the forging of new arms. There were smells of charcoal smoke and hot metal, the sounds of whetstones and grinding. A campaign must be in preparation, Brand thought. The door of the main hall stood wide and a guard dog rose and growled, to be quietened by the housecarle.

Harefoot was within, eating in company with half a dozen of his chief men, whose heavy gold arm-rings and jewelled cloak-clasps proved their rank. To Brand's surprise, Harefoot rose and came him-self to greet him.

"My lord Godwin of Wessex sends you these relics of your fa-ther King Cnut," Brand said, offering his bundle. Harefoot unwrapped it. He held up the cup and dagger to the light, laughed loudly, pushed the dagger through his belt, and flung an arm round Brand's shoulders.

"So he kept his word!" He chuckled. "Welcome, Brand lad, welcome. Come and eat, you've ridden a long way. Here, fellows, this is Godwin's messenger with my father's gear!" He flourished the tokens at them. Brand was given a stool and a wooden platter and offered meat by a thrall. Rather bemused, he helped himself and took the mead-horn someone else presented. All the men were laughing as if he had brought them good news of some kind. He felt ill at ease, half fearing some hidden jest at his expense. Only a few short months ago he had been the humblest recruit among these men and would never have dared to speak to one of these gold-laden folk unless they addressed him first.

"Eat your fill, there's plenty," Harefoot said. "You came all the way alone? Meet any trouble?"

"No, sir. I came part of the way with a priest."

"With a priest, eh! Ha! Good protection, a priest!" Harefoot slapped his own knee, nudged the man next to him, and let out another peal of merriment. Brand took more meat and wished himself away.

As a king's hall, he thought Harefoot's a remarkably sorry affair. The materials in the place were fine enough: embroidered hangings, stout carved furniture of oak and pine, thick furs strewn on the seats. But nothing was cared for. The straw underfoot was dirtier than a stable, the furs were matted, the table smeared with grease. Harefoot, fingering the dagger, said suddenly: "You never knew my father, did you?"

"No, sir."

"He was a great leader. I'm glad to have these to remember him by. He was worth remembering. I'll reward you well. Going to your home, are you, where I picked you up?"

"Yes, sir."

Harefoot chuckled. "Good. Tell them not to fear the Welsh. I'm riding against them tomorrow. They've been raiding again, but we're sharpening our axes for the swart little devils. Sit there and keep packing your belly. I'll get you the silver you've earned."

Brand left Worcester with a leather pouch of silver pennies, several pounds weight of them, hanging at his saddle. He also carried a

list of good wishes to give Earl Godwin from King Harefoot and a
sense of prickling uneasiness, the same instinct, he thought, that told
Greedy when the ground beneath his hooves was turning into bog.
He went warily, leaving the straight path as soon as he was clear of
Worcester and letting the pony pick his way through a pinewood in
an unexpected direction. The reward was too much for so commonplace a service, and Harefoot had no great name for openhand-
edness. What he did have a name for was a crude sense of humour.

But no one followed him and the troubled feeling slowly died
away. It seemed that Harefoot had truly honoured his father's memory and nothing more. Brand, now committed to a roundabout route
home, cursed his own fears. It was near dusk and the shadows were
long before he came at last to the scrub-covered hillside that overlooked his home valley.

He drew rein on the slope to refresh himself with that much
missed view. Ashtree village lay in the shallow vale, its thatched
roofs a patch of brown and yellow amidst the circling fields, light
green with springing corn. Here and there were outlying farmsteads
whose masters had their own corn and vegetable patches, separate
from the communal fields. His own home was one of these, given to
his father before Brand was born, in return for services on the battlefield to the thane he followed, and only lightly burdened with dues.
The old thane's grandson collected them now. The farmstead was
one of the nearer ones, its crops lying up the slope towards him. The
white dots round the house were his mother's geese. He kicked
Greedy and the pony, sensing fodder and a rest, moved briskly
forward.

The two rough-haired dogs greeted him first, lolloping up and
trying to reach his face with eager tongues. A moment later the bent
back of his brother Orm straightened from a ditch along the edge of
the ryefield, and with a cry of recognition Orm followed the dogs.
"Brand!"

"Hullo, Orm."

"It's really you? But why so soon?" And then, sharply: "Nothing's wrong, is it?"

"No, no, only an errand that brought me this way." Brand dismounted to walk with his brother. "I've been away south, in Earl
Godwin's train, all the way to Winchester."

"Godwin?" Orm rubbed a puzzled forehead. "But you went off with Harefoot. It *was* Harefoot, surely?"

"Yes." Brand described his change of lords, distractedly. The sights and smells of home demanded his attention. As they neared the homestead he heard his name called and looked round to see his sister Edgiva waving and running towards him, shooing a herd of indignantly grunting pigs before her. "Edgiva! Well, it's good to see you again! Are you well?"

In fact, the sight of Edgiva was somewhat saddening. She hadn't changed. She was as podgy, as swarthy, as pockmarked, and as spotty as ever, and just as sullen, judging from her expression as the smile of greeting faded. But she was full of questions about him and he answered them as, accompanied by pigs, dogs, and pony, they made their way into the yard. Hens and geese added to the racket and brought his mother and sister-in-law Elfrida out to meet them. Their joy, greater even than his own, touched him.

There was food in the pot, and when the pony had been fed and installed in the byre which adjoined the house, he sat with his family at their evening meal, to their amusement marvelling because so little had altered. "As if it could," said Elfrida, "in such a short time."

The one change he did perceive, he did not mention. His mother, he thought, looked tired and in the unveiled hair that she wore pulled back from her face and knotted, there was less brown than he remembered, and more grey. Her mouth had a set to it that he knew for a sign of anger or sorrow. He wondered why. The farm seemed prosperous and Elfrida, nearly globular with Orm's child, looked blooming. Orm, questioned on the subject of Welsh raids, shook his head.

"No, we've had no trouble. Harefoot's riding against them, you say? Well, that's never a bad thing. But we haven't seen them here."

There might be a debt of some sort, perhaps. Between mouthfuls he talked of Winchester and his errand to Harefoot, and when the meal was nearly over, with the dogs contentedly chewing bones under the table, he brought out the pouch which held Harefoot's silver.

"King Harold's a strange one," he said. "I only carried a bundle for him! But I suppose he admired his father and it's true everyone says King Cnut was a great lord and a warrior. Look at this. It's the reward King Harold gave me. It's to share with you all, of course."

He undid the drawstring and shot the silver onto the table. Orm, wiping meat juice off his platter with a piece of bread and remarking "I hope he paid you well, lad," as he did so, stopped, choked, and pointed speechlessly at the shining stream. His eyes popped. Brand thumped him on the back. Elfrida said: "But . . . it's riches! I've only seen ten silver pennies together in my whole life!"

Brand retrieved a couple of overadventurous coins from the floor and looked up for his mother's approval. Her eyes were bright, but she was looking at Orm, not at him. Between her and Orm passed some unspoken speculation and reply, as if on some private matter. Brand said: "I'm fed, housed, armed, and if I wished could be horsed at my lord's expense. If you need this . . ."

"We're grateful, lad," said Orm, turning to him. His choking fit had passed. "Aye, very grateful. Not that the farm's not in good fettle, but there's no doubt we'd be glad of some silver and you've brought it at the right time."

"Are you in trouble?" Brand searched their faces. "Debt? A weregild fine? Have you killed someone, Orm?"

"No, not that." Orm pulled at his thick brown beard. "But there's one worry for all that, and this could lift it off us—eh, mother?"

"That there is," she said. The strain was already smoothing itself out of her face. It was the sudden alarm spreading over Elfrida's that warned Brand to look behind him.

Crimson with fury, her eyes ablaze like the eyes of an enraged cat, Edgiva faced him. "I hate you all," she said, not loudly but as if she were spitting out words like pieces of bone from a careless mouthful. "And Brand most of all! I'd like to kill you, Brand!" And she snatched up a handful of the silver pennies and hurled them in his face.

In Winchester, Brand had been learning fast reactions. He sprang up, shedding coins like water shaken from a dog's coat, and grabbed Edgiva, avoiding her efforts to scratch his face. He bundled her into Orm's grasp. While Orm restrained her, he swept the gleaming missiles off the table and safely back into their bag. With its drawstring tight again, he faced his family across the table.

"Now will you tell me what all this is about?" he demanded.

Orm sighed. He shook Edgiva and pushed her onto a stool. "*Sit there!*" he ordered. "And keep quiet! We were trying to get her into the religious house at Leominster," he explained in his slow voice. "But there's a dowry to find, she being no more than a plain churl's daughter, though freeborn. We hadn't got it. We were going to find another nunnery, one that didn't want so much, but we've not much time for travelling round. But now . . ."

"It would make a marriage dowry, just as well!" Edgiva shouted at him. "I want to *marry*! I won't go into a convent! I *won't*!"

"Edgiva," said her mother, and the little strain lines were back, deeper, like wheel tracks over which the cart has passed a second time. "The hens are still out and the foxes will be abroad. Bring them in."

"No! You'll talk about me when I'm outside."

"Happen you might like it better that way," said Orm bluntly. "We'll talk anyhow. With or without you. Go and get the hens."

"*Go*, Edgiva!" said her mother, and Edgiva, her anger melting into tears, sprang up from her stool and fled. Elfrida looked upset. Orm reached out a hand to her. "I'm sorry for her," Elfrida said.

"Aye, we're all that, but some things can't be mended." Orm turned to Brand. "You see now what the worry is. Don't need much explaining."

"No, but . . ." Brand was puzzled. "She's not . . . pretty," he said. "But is a convent the only thing, when she's so against it?"

He was thinking of Brother Athelstan, climbing into the saddle of Brand's pony, having found his hired steed unmanageable. "There's many a man—and many a woman too—in the Church that was pushed there." A sensible man Brand had thought him, who considered that one should stick to horses one could control and only enter the Church if led by a vocation. Edgiva had not been called of God, that was quite plain. "Wouldn't the money bring a husband?" he said. "There's quite a lot of it. How did all this start?"

"Start?" said Orm. He ruminated. "Six weeks back or thereabout. With her pestering a charcoal burner up in the woods. There was a family there with a young fellow among them. Any excuse, she'd be up there, taking them milk or ale, or going walking, or looking for a strayed pig . . ."

"And plastering her face with mud overnight, for her skin," put in his mother, "or else buying simples from the old village women . . ."

"I pitied her," said Elfrida, whose round pink face was flawless apart from a trace of windburn.

"She'd never keep her mind on her work," said Orm. "Pigs got out—or she let them out, maybe, hoping they'd make for the woods—and she forgot the hens altogether one night and a fox got some. Then the charcoal folk moved off the way they do and after that she were just impossible. Mooning all day, crying all night . . . something had to be done and how do we find a man for her as she is? She's twenty! We thought of the convent. Mother made enquiries. Leominster's a good house, with learning and a name for medicine, and a rule not too harsh . . . but as for buying her a husband instead . . ."

"That's all money can do," said their mother grimly. "Buy a husband. And a bought man's no good. A man's got to want a woman for more than her dowry. My sister was like Edgiva and my father bought her a marriage. The man took the money and he took her hand before witnesses and he took a girl from the next village into his bed. My sister kept the house and did the work and was a slave till she got the wasting fever and died, and she was glad to go, by all I heard. I want Edgiva to be safe from that. The convent is safe."

"They have enough to eat there and ladies sometimes stay there from choice," Elfrida said. "We mean well by her."

"And her face wouldn't be against her," Orm agreed. "They'd call it a blessing for being no temptation to vanity. Now, Elfrida, don't cry."

"She hates me," said Elfrida miserably. "I've got everything she wants. She's never said so, but I know she hates me." She wiped her eyes.

"And that is one reason, if you can see no others," said Orm, addressing Brand, "why Edgiva is to be out of this house as soon as may be. We'll take no more silver from you than we must, Brand, but give us her convent dowry and we'll be mighty grateful." He went to the door. "Edgiva!"

Angry-eyed, Edgiva returned. Orm pulled her in and pointed her towards the ladder that led up to the sleeping room above the

byre. "You're for Leominster in the morning. Get your things bundled together ready and get some sleep. We leave at cockcrow. I'll
take you myself. Tied up if I have to. You hear me?"

Edgiva turned at the ladder's foot and faced him. Her unlovely
complexion was uglier than ever with misery and rage. Her eyes, big
and dark, might have been beautiful in a better setting; as it was they
only made their surroundings worse by comparison. "I wish the
Welsh would come," she said. "I wish they'd come and burn the
house and slaughter us all. I'd be better dead than in that . . . that
convent graveyard with its walking, praying corpses! I'd sooner be
buried dead than alive! I wish the Welsh would come tonight!"

She dashed up the ladder and they heard her sobbing as she
rummaged about, gathering her small belongings or throwing them
round the room in despair. Orm sat down to his ale as if nothing
were wrong. Elfrida rose heavily, to gather scraps for the pigs. Her
face was kind and sad. But it was in his mother's taut, closed features that Brand suddenly saw a torment that was a reflection of his
own.

7 ✖ Guests at Gildenford

"In two days, God willing, we shall be in Winchester," Alfred said.

Fitzwarren, prowling round the upper chamber over the master weaver's shop where he, Alfred, and four other knights had been billeted, said: "I see no reason why He would be unwilling. Not now. The journey's nearly over."

"All the same, I'll be glad when it's entirely over." Alfred sat down on his pallet. The candlelight danced over the slope of the thatched ceiling, the row of bedding rolls on the floor, the table where stood the cups and the flagon of wine provided as a nightcap by their host. Food they had had already, having been heartily feasted in Godwin's hall. They were not sleeping there only because it was too small to house Godwin's and Alfred's men all at once. The feasting had spread all over the enclosure for lack of space indoors and Alfred had seen the point when Godwin said that he had arranged lodgings in the town. "If you don't mind being split up, ten here and a dozen there. The townsfolk are hospitable."

"Well, six hundred men should be protection enough," said Fitzwarren, yawning. "Your sister wedded Boulogne's son at a most convenient moment."

Alfred nodded, pouring himself wine. Edward had managed to arrange a match between Godgift, well dowered from her previous marriage, and the heir to the Count of Boulogne. The boy was younger than Godgift, but mature and vigorous, a big, dark young man to whom Godgift seemed attracted. And the alliance had proved useful already.

"Eustace has proved a staunch brother-in-law," Alfred now agreed. "He talked my escort out of his father! Unlike Baldwin of Flanders. Did I tell you he refused me any men in case Harefoot accused him of a hostile act?"

"Did he? Well, he provided some silver, I hear."

"And he isn't my brother-in-law," Alfred concurred. "One couldn't expect too much. God knows we've had enough from him already; he's housed and fed us on and off for years. He was right in a way; it would have been a hostile act. My presence here is a hostile act. If Harefoot knew I was here he would put out my life as I shall shortly put out that candle there beside you. And I shouldn't drink any more of that wine if I were you, unless your head's stronger than mine is. The mead we had at supper is making me muzzy, mixed with this."

"Let it. We'll sleep the better." Fitzwarren wandered to the window, flagon in hand. The window was covered with stretched cattle-gut, which let in light but could not be seen through. He opened the catch to look out. "Surely they've settled the horses by now, the others? Where are they? Don't worry about Harefoot, he's safe in the north, asleep or boozing. You'll be in Winchester with a palisade round you and the treasury keys in your hand before the second sunset from now."

"I wonder."

Fitzwarren, closing the window, turned sharply. "What do you mean?"

Alfred was playing with his wine now rather than drinking it, swirling it round in its cup. "I mean," he said slowly, "that we know nothing for sure of Harefoot's movements. Who were those pirates? Who sent them? It could have been Harefoot. They were out to sink us rather than take us, I believe."

"We're under Earl Godwin's protection. He's your mother's man and this is his town. And we have six hundred men of our own."

"Neatly done up into small packages, spaced apart and dotted all over Godwin's obedient town, and most of us, what's more, are drunk! That mead stuns men who aren't reared on it." He rose and began pacing. "Oh, I watched them weaving from side to side of the path as we entered the town! I was glad you hadn't had much of it. You say I have six hundred with me. I haven't, Fulbert. I've got five. The five hundred and ninety-five are out of sight and hearing and stupid with liquor!"

"I see," said Fulbert. The uneasiness had transferred itself to him. He looked round as if he expected to see enemies come sliding out of the thatch. "And so you . . . ?"

"When we came down to the ford this afternoon," said Alfred, "and we saw the grass there thick with kingcups and humming with grasshoppers and bees, it was too much, too flawless, as if all the summer afternoons there ever were had poured their essence into this one time and place."

Fitzwarren looked bewildered. "I never understand riddles. Is it the mead? What are you talking about? What is it you fear?"

"Death, of course," said Alfred.

Fulbert Fitzwarren was still sitting silent, trying to think of a wise answer, when feet thundered below and creaked on the ladder. The four knights who had been tending the horses tumbled gasping into the room. Fulbert sprang up. Alfred swung to face them. His eyes were wide open, black in the candlelight.

"Outside!" The foremost knight scrabbled among his belongings for his helmet. "Armed men! A squad of armed men! Not Godwin's, not ours! We saw them in the moonlight—drawn swords and sheepskin cloaks, coming this way!"

"Harefoot's men," said Alfred calmly, and drained his wine with an air of ceremony, as one who says farewell to all sweet pleasures and all life.

There was no defence to make. They had armour and swords and they were all comparatively sober, for Alfred had chosen his sleeping companions from those who were steadiest on their feet. But the northern housecarles, who kicked the door in five minutes later, had the weaver and his family. Alfred ordered his men to keep behind him and went down to face the raiders, stomach muscles knotted below his jewelled belt. Fitzwarren and the four knights descended after him.

"Who are you?" Alfred demanded.

The leader of the intruders smiled. He had a Viking helm and a huge axe, and there were signs of rank about him in his thick gold arm-rings and the amethysts on his sword-pommel. He replied in a falsetto mimicry of Alfred's faintly French accent. "Who am ay? Can't you guess it, shaveling?"

"Beelzebub?" hazarded Alfred coldly.

The stranger laughed. "Not so far out, to my master's enemies," he said. His eyes took in Alfred's own gems and fine wool garments. "But you are right, maybe a man should know who he's talking to. You are in the presence of Thane Thored of Alford, a chief thane of King Harold of the Hare's Foot, King of the North of England and Protector of the Realm of England. And you, my friend, are Alfred the Exile . . ."

"Atheling," said Fitzwarren.

"*Exile.* He's no crown prince. He's a foe of the realm." Thored grinned. "And King Harold waits in London, for me to deliver the person of this upstart to him." He made a sign to his followers and they shouldered forward. "Take them!" he barked.

"What about them?" one of the northerners asked, jerking his head at the frightened weaver and his household, as the last Norman sword-belt clattered to the floor and the last pair of Norman hands were jerked behind their owner's back. There was no resistance. Not with the weaver's terrified eyes upon them.

The thane glanced cursorily at the family and said: "Leave them." He spoke directly to the weaver. "You're safe if you stay indoors. Till morning. Step outside and it's the last step you take anywhere. I've men all over the town." He turned back to his captives and their waiting escort. "You know where to bring them. Move!"

"I heard a cock crow somewhere," Godwin said. In the faint starlight, Harold saw his eyes glint. "It must be near dawn."

"We should go back to the fire," muttered Sweyn. "It's cold."

"I don't want to sleep," Godwin said. "I shall stay here."

He glanced over his shoulder to where the hall door stood ajar. Through it could be seen the fire burning low in its central stone hearth, casting a dull glow over the sleeping forms of cloak-wrapped men, staining hair, skin, cloth, and leather all with scarlet. Harold said: "I can see torches. Someone is bringing us news."

They had played out the prearranged drama the previous evening, with still faces and steady speech. Even among his own men

Godwin had kept his counsel from all but one or two. To the rest, the arrival of Harefoot's forces had been a surprise.

It was done with formality, late, after Alfred and his followers had been shown to their lodgings. When the gatewards opened at the command of the stranger who spoke in the king's name, Thored marched into the hall with a squad at his heels, halting just inside the door. Godwin's men were holding a late-night sing-song, and one of them, in the act of proclaiming dolefully that mead-halls must crumble and their revellers lie bereft of bliss, stopped short with an accidental, plaintive twang on the lyre, alarmed by the intrusion. Little snorts of startled laughter sounded round the hall, and men glanced round them for their weapons. Godwin raised a hand for silence and walked to greet the newcomer.

Thored announced himself. ". . . and in the name of King Harold, I demand that you surrender to me the persons of Edward and Alfred Ethelredson and their escort, who are under your protection, in this town. They are peace-breakers." He added significantly, "I have eight hundred well-armed men out on the hillside. I would prefer that you yield your charges formally and appoint guides to take us to their lodgings. But I can order a house-to-house search without your consent if need be."

Harefoot, it seemed, had kept his counsel too. Thane Thored was taking the situation at its face value. He was not acting.

Godwin said: "You have been misinformed. Edward Ethelredson is not here. Only Alfred Ethelredson came. And he and his men are guests under my protection, in my territory."

Thored shrugged. "I repeat. I can use force."

There was a little more bandying of protest and insistence. Godwin went with Thored to the hillside and looked for himself at the strength that had come from the north. Returning, he called for silence and standing at Thored's side he declared to his thanes and housecarles that King Harold was within his rights and that his greater numbers in any case left small choice. He selected guides to take Thored and his men to the houses where the Norman guests were sleeping. "I expect every courtesy to be shown to the towns-folk," he said, looking hard at Thored. "Bring me word when it is done."

"Father?" said Harold as they stood at the gate and watched the Thane of Alford depart. Godwin's face troubled him.

"I liked him," said Godwin. "Alfred, I mean. Menace though he . . . was. If Thored had not been quite so well prepared . . . it wasn't all pretence, just now, when I argued with him. I shall keep watch here tonight. Will you watch with me, you three? I should welcome company."

The torchbearers and the first greyness of daybreak reached the hall together. The leader said: "The arrests are complete. I am to report to you that the men have been taken to the caves at the foot of the hill."

"I wish to see Thane Thored again before he leaves," Godwin replied. "I will go to the caves."

The caves were ill-lit, smoky with torches, and crowded with men. The Normans had been pushed together into one inner rocky chamber just big enough to hold them all. The caves had been made when stone was quarried to make a small stone chapel for the town and to build partially stone walls for Godwin's own hall. He had seen them made.

"Useful, these caves," Thane Thored greeted him in the entrance. "I kept men hidden here to watch for you, the best part of a week, and not a word of it reached the town. It was hard work, concealing so many. We moored the ships downstream and kept to the forest while the rest of us waited. You were late."

"Where are they?" said Godwin shortly. "Inside?"

The prisoners' eyes, reddened with smoke and lack of sleep, turned to him as he entered. They were all bound, sitting or standing uncomfortably packed together under the low roof. Some were coughing. Alfred was near the front, sitting on a heap of stones. He looked up at the sound of Godwin's voice.

"I must thank you for your hospitality last night," he said, his voice light and chilled. "And for the good service you have rendered my mother. It must comfort her to have such a trustworthy man to lean on."

"You're a fool, Exile."

"Atheling," said Fitzwarren at his lord's elbow.

"Atheling? That's the heir's title. But there are two contending heirs already and that, Exile, is trouble enough for one kingdom. The king and his earls are responsible for keeping the peace here and that is my first duty. I can be trusted with that, I promise you. To me, you are an enemy."

"Indeed? And since I landed, how many forts have I attacked?"

"When you land with six hundred men," said Godwin, "all armed and mailed, and ride with them clanking through our land, I prefer not to wait for you to start the fighting. You have lost your life for this, Exile or Atheling, but the fault is yours." He turned to Thored. "I can arrange a messenger to the Count of Boulogne, who is the overlord of most of these men, if you wish."

"A messenger to Boulogne? What for?"

"To arrange the ransom terms." Godwin frowned.

"Ransom?" Thored grinned. "But we'd have to house and feed 'em till the bullion came, and they're tough; they'd take some holding. The king's waiting in London. How would I get such a crowd transported there? Besides, it wouldn't be discouragement enough to the other Atheling."

"Then . . . ?" Behind him, Godwin sensed horror rustling through the captives like a faint cold wind through corn. He felt it himself, in his own body, the weakening of knees and bowels. His own voice sounded thin.

"We'll keep a few as thralls," Thored said with an air of concession. "But for the rest . . . sss!" He drew a thick forefinger from one ear to the other, smiling broadly.

There was a scattered outcry, quickly smothered, from the captives. They were fighting men, not serfs. But their composite, desperate gaze was like a physical dragging at Godwin's arm. He said: "Like that? Helpless? Bound? Like *sheep*?"

"You're mad. What would happen if I let them loose? They'd just go berserker!"

"You . . ." Godwin mastered himself. He was sharply aware that he and his sons were here unsupported, as encircled by Harefoot's minions as the prisoners were themselves. He said frigidly: "I had assumed that ransom terms were to be sought in the ordinary way."

"Then you assumed wrong, southron."

"You should reconsider. There is wealth to be won through ransom and the king's name would remain clean."

"Too clean." Thored spat. "He prefers his name to be feared."

"Father," said Harold quietly, "the townsfolk need you, I think. There are knots of people gathering among the houses." He pointed through the entrance. "I think they are seeking reassurance of their own safety, with such a mass of men round the town and campfires all over the hillside. Should we not talk to them?" He went on, gently, holding his father's gaze. "There is no more to do here. We could send a priest, perhaps."

Thored seemed amused. "We're not fussy. If you like to try defending my poor captives, you're welcome. There won't be much left of your men, or you, or your precious town by the time the attempt is over, but I don't mind."

Sweyn said: "If you wish, father, I will represent you here and see to . . . to any last messages. Harold is right. The townsfolk do want you."

Godwin looked once more, grimly, at the huddled prisoners, and turned away towards the daylight.

"Thank you, Sweyn. Harold, Tostig, come with me."

As he walked out of the caves he kept his face away from Harefoot's captives, and at Thane Thored he did not look, either.

Sweyn returned to the hall at noon. He walked with a curious, automatic gait, as if he were dazed or drunk. He was extremely dirty. Godwin, sitting with food untouched before him, said: "Well?"

Sweyn sat down and rested his head in his hands. "Oh, it's all over," he said. "It took all morning. You heard nothing here?"

"I was inside the hall."

Sweyn said: "We went up to the hill across the river. Thored drove them like sheep—as you said. His men . . . pretended to be herd dogs, barked at them. Told them they ought to bleat. Then when we got there they drew lots, with straws, for every tenth man and killed him. Then every tenth man of those remaining. And so on. And on."

"Dear God!" Godwin was silent a moment. Then he said: "Alfred?"

"He was stood aside. Thored is taking him to London, where the king is. I heard something about Ely, too. He's to be tried at Ely. Well away from Wessex, I imagine."

"A trial. I see. Harefoot occasionally remembers that he is a king with a law to uphold. Is Alfred the only one still living, then?"

"No. His friend Fitzwarren is still alive, and so are a handful of others they're keeping to sell as thralls. They branded them. Thored said it made a change of entertainment." Sweyn was a living battleground of incompatible emotions. His eyes spoke of sickness and horror, of fierce and violent excitement, all at once. "The dead were buried where they fell. I've never seen such a sight . . . the grass is red—crimson—over half the hillside."

Godwin looked about him, at his men in their groups, talking, eating, walking about the hall. He said: "They should have been ransomed. Perhaps—we should have tried to save them. We could have fought."

Harold said: "Our own men would have been slaughtered. It was two to one, out in the open. They came as enemies." He put his hand on his father's arm. "Alfred would have gathered others to join them, mustered an army at Winchester, for sure . . ."

"And it would have been the townsfolk and women, instead of Normans." Godwin nodded. "Babies spitted on spears. I've seen it. I sold Alfred to prevent that. Yes. How will they go to Ely?"

"By river. They have ships hidden somewhere. Thane Thored said they had one or two close by the ford, and the rest in the forest reaches. They'll carry Alfred from the ford, this afternoon."

The river was sleepy with noon, the drowsy meads seeming more kingcups than grass, and the yellow pollen brushed off on their legs as they strode through. Sweyn still talked of the killing, unable to free himself from it. He talked of messages he had taken and must send, of the priest he had run to the town to fetch. Godwin asked a sharp question or two, nodded at the answers. Under the trees the river was black, but in the middle, beyond the shadow, it rippled gold and dragonflies hovered over it. No ships were to be seen at first, but as they neared the water's edge, some overhanging alders stirred and a prow slid into sight. The leaves rustled and shook. Then with a jerk a whole bough was thrust aside and the figure of a man showed framed in green foliage. Godwin had seen too many battlefields to shy away, and Sweyn had seen it already. But Harold stopped short, his breath hissing through his teeth. The framed figure might have stepped straight out of hell.

He was not merely stained, he was drenched, head to foot, in caked, clotting, dark red arterial blood. His pelt cloak, his long hair, and his thick beard were matted with it and his arms were dipped in it above the elbow, as if he had been kneading it in the fashion of a housewife working dough. As the ship came fully into view it was seen that its boards were trodden with brownish prints and that the men who were poling her out were as monstrously stained as the first. They worked languidly, and looking to the river banks, they considered the earl and his sons with the regretful lust of cats tempted by sparrows on which they are too sated to pounce. Thane Thored was aboard, rasping at a swordblade which looked rusty but was not. He raised a hand in greeting and pointed astern. They followed his finger and discovered Alfred.

Alfred, leaning with closed eyes against the ship's side, did not see them until Fitzwarren spoke to him. Then he rose, awkwardly, because of his pinioned arms, and leaned over the side. "Godwin!" he called. "Godwin!"

Sweyn muttered: "He'll ask you to intercede for him."

But Alfred uttered no plea. He was near enough to see Godwin's face closely, to look into his eyes. Then he uttered a single word. It was the two-syllable, comprehensive insult and condemnation current among his Saxon father's folk, the word that dismissed its object as worthless, bereft of rights, no longer a member of any man's kin or any society or even of the human race.

"*Nithing!*" said Alfred, and spat.

8 ⚙ The Atheling Departs

The darkness, Alfred discovered, was not wholly black. It was shot with flame which crackled and seared although it illuminated nothing. It seemed also that memory still held, on some inner retina, scenes of the world his physical eyes would never see again, and now and then these fragmentary visions drifted through his brain.

Most persistent of all was the green amphitheatre, made from the encircling tents of Harefoot's army, on Ely Isle close to the monastery. He saw the brilliant grass, the fresh blue sky, washed clean by the rain which had fallen during the long sea and river journey through the Wey and the Thames to London, and on down the Thames to the eastern coast and the voyage to the fens. He saw the reeds of a waterway close to where he sat between his guards, and the little brown warbler bird which lived among the reeds. He saw Harefoot.

It had been an unkingly farce, that trial. He had never been allowed to speak; he had been offered no means to clear himself by ordeal or combat or sworn witnesses. Not that he had any to swear on his behalf. All his surviving men except Fitzwarren had been auctioned as soon as they reached Ely. They would be thralls henceforth, feeding the pigs and strewing the rushes for their masters till their days as soldiers were forgotten, something they had once dreamed.

But their fate was better than his. He had listened to Harefoot reciting the charges: entering the land secretly, intent to stir up rebellion, intent to seize power for himself. There was a good deal of truth in it, of course. It left out the justice of his claim, that was all.

Harefoot enjoyed the business. Alfred watched him detachedly, in fact and in memory, looking at the small red veins on nose and cheekbones and the blurring jawline under the beard. One could see how the fleet foot had gone, which had earned Harefoot his nickname. In all probability, prone as he was to overindulge in good food and drink, he would not live to be old.

But, since it was clear that Harefoot, having declared the charges, now considered them proved and was about to pass sentence without more delay, he would probably outlive Alfred.

And so the Exile, then, had withdrawn his gaze from the somewhat porcine person of the King of the North (and Protector of the Realm, as he usually added, though few acknowledged him within the Wessex borders), and given more of his attention to the sky and the grass and the reeds. His tenure of them would be short. He wondered how they would kill him.

It was with gorge-rising horror that he learned that they did not intend to—not overtly, anyway. Harefoot was mixing ungodly pleasures with practical policies. They would say in the alehouses, the fields, and the marketplaces that the King of the North had spared his enemy's life, had contented himself only with making the Exile harmless. Unluckily, the young man died anyway, but there was always a risk of that.

It was in fact possible, though everyone did not know it, to blind a man without killing him or even endangering his life much. It needed care. Harefoot's butchers, probably by order, did not take any.

Perhaps he should be grateful for it. For who wanted to drag out a life for twenty, thirty, forty years in a world without the sun? Death was now desired by Alfred quite as greatly as Harefoot could desire it for him. And it was coming. Surely it was coming. That was the only hope, the only comfort in this firestreaked blackness.

Only, dear God, merciful saints, how long would it take his strong young body to succumb?

He had been left in the care of the monks of Ely, who did their best, although his wounds were beyond their skill. He had a bed, a room—Fulbert told him it was a monk's cell—that was quiet and warm. He had attention, treatment, food, and drink as long as he could keep them down. He had Fulbert, who for some reason nei-

ther of them understood had been left with him unharmed. But Fulbert was never allowed to come to him alone, because he would certainly have heeded his lord's entreaties to kill him, and the monks
forbade it. The brother whose especial charge was Alfred guarded
the sickbed with the ferocity of a dragon out of legend, guarding
gold. Suicide was unlawful, he said. He cared for Alfred's fevered
body as best he could, but the main business of his calling was the
care of immortal souls, and he meant to save Alfred's, with or without its owner's consent.

"To take your own life is to doom yourself to hell," he said.

"I'm in hell *now!*" Alfred snarled, and beat clenched fists on his
bed in frustration and despair.

But death was coming. Now there were times when the fever
tides surged high enough to swallow all his senses up and float him
beyond the reach of pain. When it cast him back it was each time
into a body weaker than before. He became aware of his anguish as
something separate from himself, experienced as a deafening discord
or—bewilderingly in these circumstances—as something visible. "It's
dirty yellow," he said once to the unidentifiable person who was
rebandaging him. "Dirty yellow with bright red streaks."

"How does he know?" Fulbert's voice asked.

"He's delirious," the attendant monk's voice said.

Pain, flame, memory . . . and one obsessive thought of which
at first he did not speak. It did not break through to speech until the
end was very close, and then he had to croak it, for the infection had
attacked his larynx and to talk at all was hard.

"My mother," he whispered, clutching at Fulbert's wrist. "My
mother . . . sold me . . . into this."

He felt the bed give under Fulbert's weight as his friend sat
down on it. A hand was laid over his. "No, my lord," said Fulbert.
"That cannot be true. She was tricked too, be sure of it, even as you
were."

"She sent her . . . ring. Saw it. Don't suppose she meant . . .
this to happen. Just wanted . . . me dead. Bad enough. She always
hated . . . us . . . Edward and me."

"My lord . . ."

"She wants it all . . . all . . . for Harthacnut. Just using . . .
Harefoot . . . hates him too. All for . . . Harthacnut. Always,
always . . . Harthacnut."

He heard Fulbert murmuring reassurances. He tried to draw

away within himself, away from the horror he had just spoken aloud, confessing it for the first time, that he had come with a hand stretched out to Emma after the long cold years, and this had been her greeting. He tried too to withdraw from the burden of his body. But then without warning the agony leapt on him. He fought, plunging against his sickness as if it were a fetter he might break. Hands pressed him down. Voices sounded. Feet. An aromatic, drugged liquid was being poured down his throat. There came a patter of sandals and a swish of robes and what he hazily recognised as the last rites. He tried to respond to questions but could no longer understand them.

After an hour as long as eternity, the rising fever swept him away for the last time and he lost consciousness. In the night, he died.

Harefoot came in the morning while the monks were making ready a tomb in one of their chapels. He had been waiting for the news.

"Bring me the Norman, Fulbert Fitzwarren," he said without preamble to the abbot.

Fulbert had aged since Gildenford, fresh grey speckling his short dark hair and lines deepening in his face. Fitzwarren, knight of Rouen Castle, had seen his young wife die, ten years before, of plague, had seen many battlefields. He thought himself inured. But treachery, and the slaughter of helpless men, and this bitter death of Alfred to whom he had given all he still had of human affection, had now pierced his armour three times over. He was afraid for himself, but who was he to live and be free when his companions and his lord were not? He stood, not speaking, before Harefoot and waited.

"No need to quake," said Harefoot, who had his perceptive moments. "I need you, Fitzwarren, alive and all there. If the Exile had lived he might have told his own tale and made the warning plain, but as he's dead you'll have to do it for him. You are to go to Winchester and put his mother out of her misery. She'll be waiting eagerly for news. Hah!" The king let out a snort of laughter. "Then you can go to Rouen and tell Edward. You can give him a touching eyewitness account of his brother's last hours. Make sure he knows what to expect if he ever tries the same trick. Cheer up, Fitzwarren, you're a free man! The one free survivor of Gildenford! Don't you know your luck? Are you ready to leave?"

"I will leave," said Fulbert coldly, "one hour after the burial."

"He was her son," said Edward. He stood on the walls of Rouen Castle with his friend, Abbot Robert Champart of Jumièges. "Fitz-warren says she shed no tear, uttered not one word of grief. You heard him."

Fitzwarren, standing at a little distance from the man to whom he had brought this terrible news, said: "It is true. She just looked at me out of those black falcon's eyes of hers and said: 'What kind of tomb did they give him?' But she denies she sent you any letter, my lord. She said it was forged."

"Naturally she would say that," Edward answered.

Champart, a sparely built and unemotional man, interposed. "Could her tale not be true, my lord? Or the letter sent in good faith, even, and intercepted in some way by Harefoot? Her denials now may be only meant to reinforce a genuine innocence."

"She sent her ring," said Edward dully, not heeding him.

"That is what Alfred said," Fitzwarren agreed.

Edward said hesitantly: "He . . . realised what her part must have been?"

"Yes."

"She always detested us. What did she say about Godwin?"

"She sent for him and rated him in front of me," Fitzwarren told him. "She said he had let himself be fooled by Elfgift's whelp. There was talk of some messenger he said had brought her instructions to him, that she denied having sent. It sounded like just talk to me, arranged for my benefit. She told him he'd been 'tricked, bewildered, surprised, and befooled by a descendant of a drab.' Those were her words." He added viciously: "She did it very well. And Godwin is a fine dissembler, too. He said Harefoot had taken him by surprise and that he was outnumbered. He was all horror at the news from Ely. I didn't know where I was with either of them."

" 'Tricked, bewildered, surprised, and befooled by a descendant of a drab!' " Edward repeated softly. "Yes, that sounds like her. Alfred used to say . . ." He stopped. He raised his hands to his face. They watched the truth of Alfred's death strike home. In a muffled voice he said: "It was . . . is . . . a way she has of talking. A stream of angry words in French—it flows, it's liquid compared to English—and then a single rough earthy word from the English she learned with my father. Alfred used to say it made him think of a seagull."

"A seagull?" Champart asked, puzzled.

"Yes. Like a seagull gliding down on graceful wings and landing with a thump of flat wet feet. That was how Alfred put it. He had a turn for words. Inherited from her, perhaps. *Alfred!*"

"She sent you a message, my lord," said Fitzwarren. He passed a tired hand over his face, feeling the deep lines in it where the skin had folded over them. Godwin, seeing him for the first time since Gildenford, had said: "I would not have known you."

"You might have found the Atheling hard to recognise at the end, too," Fitzwarren had retorted.

"What did she say?" asked Edward.

"She hoped you were in good health and bade you stay away from England."

Champart said: "Her reputation will suffer for this."

"Yes, she said that too. She said that the truth would never catch up with rumour now. Then she drew her cloak round her and sent me and Godwin away."

"I am certain," said Champart firmly, "that she never wrote a letter meant to bring you and your brother to your deaths, Edward. Many people, when they hear dreadful news, show no sign at the time because their feelings are beyond expression. That she did not weep at once means nothing. It would come later, secretly. I am in the Church. I attend the dying and tell the bereaved. I know."

"My dear Robert," Edward looked at his friend kindly. "You are a good and trustworthy friend . . ."

"I hope so, my lord."

". . . and you know about men, or you wouldn't have made such a successful career. But you know nothing, nothing at all, about my mother!"

"So you haven't heard? You haven't heard what happened? To Alfred Atheling Ethelredson?"

"No, I haven't heard," said Brand, exasperated. "I've heard nothing but rumours about the Atheling and his men and Gilden-ford, ever since I got back. All I know is that the last few days it's been worse than ever. People huddling in corners, whispering. My lord stalks about like a spectre. It's as if he doesn't see the people all round him in his own house. My lady watches him with a sad face as if he were sick of some deadly disease. The Godwin boys keep together and speak to no one. Sweyn doesn't even quarrel with

Beorn any more. Well, what *has* happened to the Atheling? I thought he was arrested."

Quietly, gravely, Peter Longshanks enlightened him. Brand listened in silence, picking out Greedy's hooves as Peter's voice went steadily on. At the end he said: "Do you think it was true that Godwin knew Harefoot was lying in wait? A lot of people say it is."

"It's possible. The Atheling came with what amounted to the seedcorn of an army. My lord and King Harefoot may well have worked together to remove a danger such as that. No one criticises Earl Godwin for it."

"No . . . no, I see." Brand thought of the day he had himself met Godwin for the first time. That had been a tryst between the earl and Harefoot. Perhaps they had discussed their plans then. But . . .

"But if it was right for Godwin to lay such a plan, why is everyone now so shocked and silent?"

"It's my belief that Harefoot did trick him," Longshanks said, "not over lying in wait, but over the way he dealt with the captives. He slaughtered most of the Normans instead of keeping them for ransom. And . . . Godwin would not have consented to Alfred's death by such a means. I saw his face the day the news came. He looked stricken."

Brand rubbed his forehead, confused. Indeed, the matter hardly seemed of great importance to himself. He had other things, troubles of his own, to think about. Despite reassuring messages, since his return, of his sister's welfare in Leominster Abbey, he would not quickly forget the wounded anger in her face, and her agonising despair, when he and Orm had left her at the convent. He had given much of his remaining silver to Ethelnoth for charitable purposes, feeling vaguely that this might absolve him if he had done wrong. Gildenford was a tragedy but it was not his tragedy.

Longshanks was still talking, fingering a halter.

"The thing that has sickened us all is Queen Emma's part in it," he said. He spoke very low now, almost in a whisper. "The Atheling came in answer to a letter from her, after all. Every one is saying she was in it too. Their own mother."

"Oh, surely not." Brand let down the hoof he had just cleaned and ran a hand over Greedy's quarters and down the other hind leg to pick up the next.

"It's quite likely. She never cared about Ethelred's children and she adores Harthacnut. And she's regent here for him."

"That's horrible if it's true. Get up, you brute!" Greedy was trying to lean on him. Brand gave his pony a shove. "But," said Brand, plying the hoofpick, "it's all a bit beyond us, isn't it? What can we do about it, after all?"

Part

LIONS GOLDEN
1043–1045

1 ※ The Road to a Coronation

Brand turned in his saddle and cast a practised glance along the line. It was orderly. Twenty pack mules and four shaggy ponies, two fore and two aft, carrying Eric Merchant, his son Rolf, and two hired mule-boys. A dozen mounted housecarles were strung out on either side of the cavalcade and a further score brought up the rear, the bright, pale March sun catching their spears. Others were riding ahead to intimidate would-be robbers. Their ponies' feet had churned up the soft track and the muleteers' remarks were far from grateful.

But an escort was necessary. Godwin, putting in at Dover during a training voyage from Sandwich, had found Eric in his newly built quayside warehouse checking a consignment of spices and silks and promptly bought up half of it for the coronation festivities. It was worth a young fortune. Hence the fifty men under Harold Godwinsson who were now in charge of it. Harold was in front with the leaders, keeping their speed down. You couldn't hurry a mule train. And mules it had had to be. The waterways were too roundabout and Eric had other customers to visit in Kent, which made the coastal route unsuitable.

At twenty-two, Brand was acquiring the outlines of maturity. His Celtic blood showed in his stockiness, in his brown skin, and in the blackness of his hair. He had seen action in a border war with the Welsh, however, for he had no sense of kinship with them. He had a scar from a glancing axe-blow, gained while guarding Harold Godwinsson's back. Because of it, a friendship had risen between himself and Harold.

"I'll have Brand for my right hand," Harold had told his father when choosing a second-in-command to help him guard the mule train on its way to Winchester.

Brand, in fact, had without ever thinking much about it become a fighter of experience. The border fighting had taught him the meaning of a battle, all the way from the nerve-taut eve, spent singing bawdy songs round a campfire to keep one's heart up, to the cloak-wrapped, uneasy sleep that was vital and so hard to win, to the bestialities and extraordinary joys of the shield wall, to the night that followed. After a battle they had camped, many times, on the edge of the field to feast off stolen sheep and pass the mead round and make songs of their exploits, grateful to be there and not among the sad heaps of human refuse that lay beyond the firelight, given over to the wolf and the raven and, as night deepened, to the ghosts who in the morning had been men.

He had also learned of ships and the sea and had discovered within half an hour of going aboard for the first time that he had a sounder stomach than many more hardened sailors. He liked the sea immensely, liked its changing temper and its power. He liked the feeling of his own strength as he plied his oar, while the steersman beat out the stroke or maybe chanted rhythmic verses to which the oars could fit. Brand, on the whole, liked living and above all he liked living in Godwin's household.

He was, it seemed, a natural follower, and in the Godwin family he had found leaders he could admire. He was himself quite good-looking now and his friendly brown eyes, surveying the world from his square, vigorously bearded face, often encountered inviting glances from the girls, which he found pleasant. But in the company of the Godwinssons, with their height and their sunny hair and their fine skins which the weather only burnished to the lightest Scandinavian gold, he knew himself a mere rustic. The Godwin boys had something more than looks. They had magic. And their father, though he did not look as spectacular as his offspring, had a double share of the magic to make up for it. Because of this, Brand worshipped without resentment even when the exalted persons he served drew attention to the differences between himself and them. He had even let Sweyn give him a nickname. Sweyn had never forgotten Brand's admission on his very first day that he was used to chopping wood. After watching Brand's stolid and workmanlike performance at sword practice one day, Sweyn commented: "You're still a woodsman felling timber, at heart, aren't you, Brand? Rather than a warrior fighting a foe. Brand Woodcutter, you should be called." And Brand Woodcutter he had been called ever since. He answered to it.

There was a shout from the front and the leading riders were seen to have halted. Brand signalled the string to stop and spurred forward.

"It's a tree down," one of the housecarles called. "But we can shift it!" Some of the men had dismounted and were attacking the obstacle with axes. It was a silver birch, not large in the trunk. Brand rode back to the mules.

The mule at the very end of the line had a passenger as well as its bales of silk. Eric had wanted his daughter to come. "She's never left Dover, and this is the time for her to travel, if ever," he said. "With a coronation to see!"

Now, having paused to tell Eric about the tree, Brand out of courtesy rode on to tell Hild. She was not in his opinion an interesting girl, but she looked lonely, perched awkwardly between sacking-covered bales and isolated from her father and brother, who spent more time nagging the muleteers to go faster than they did in talking to her.

"If those bales are a nuisance I can fasten them better," he said.

"No, I'm quite happy," Hild said, smiling. "It's warmer now, isn't it? That wind has gone."

"I think it was the wind that brought the tree down," Brand agreed. "Yes, it's warmer. Spring is coming. The chestnut will be first into leaf." He pointed to a tree near the roadside, whose twigs were bulbous and sticky with new buds.

"Will it?" Hild was interested. "I've never noticed. The forest is strange to me." She looked gravely into the colonnades of Andred. "It seems so big. It must go—how far? A hundred miles? A hundred leagues? Do you know?"

"More than fifty miles southwards, so my lord Godwin says," Brand told her. "Most of the way to the sea. And more than a hundred miles east to west. It gets thicker further in and there are wolves. But surely . . ."

"I've spent most of my life at home or running to the harbour to see the ships come and go. I know more of ships and tides than you, perhaps."

Brand laughed. "I doubt it. I'm a seaman too. We fight on the water as well as on land.

"Are you ever seasick?"

"No," said Brand, wondering how, politely, to end this dull conversation. He liked girls to be lively in mind and appearance, flaxen or redheaded, with spirited tongues. This little brown sparrow was a long way from his ideal. There was movement ahead. Perhaps the tree was cleared. He gathered up his reins.

But Hild, who had been riding alone for three hours, went on talking. "This is an adventure," she said as the string moved forward again. The tree *was* removed. "My father thought I should see the king crowned. He thought I should see more people, too." She was stating a fact, without archness, although in the next phrase she made her father's reasons plain. "There's a wool merchant in Dover who wants to marry me but my father won't promise him anything till we've been to Winchester." Suddenly there was a gurgle in her voice. "He hopes I'll catch a thane."

Brand grinned. "And what do you say? Do you like the wool merchant?"

"Yes, very much," said Hild, without a trace of ardour. "He's cheerful and has a good business. But my father hopes to be a thane himself one day, so he keeps his eyes open for a good match for me. A wise woman told his fortune once and she said he would become important. He has already put up money for two voyages. All these things on the mules are from the second. The first was years ago, but we had a disaster in between. We sent out a ship that was taken by pirates on the way home. I lost my other brother then." Her face saddened. "But now we are getting to rights again," she went on, brightening. "We've a new warehouse nearer to the unloading quay, and my brother Rolf has started a new trade in sword-blades and ship-masts with the northern lands. He's been to Denmark, all among the wild Danes, to trade with them! My father says that's how people ought to live, travelling and trading instead of fighting. Do you travel far, when you go to sea?"

"No, we sail along the coast most of the time and practise sea warfare on each other—how to chase and board and sink an enemy. Your father wouldn't approve! You would like to travel too?" He smiled at her, thinking that she was quite an engaging lass, after all. "It must be exciting to see goods arrive from distant places. The

spices and silks come thousands of miles, I've heard, on great beasts
with humps and big soft feet."

"Camels," said Hild. "Yes, they do." She looked down at the
bales. A gleam of some brilliantly dyed material showed through a
tear in the sacking. "That's why they're so valuable—they've come
so far and through such dangers. I always worry about Rolf when
he's away now, after what happened to Ordgar. There are always
dangers. Have you any brothers or sisters?"

Brand said: "I've a brother on a farm and a sister in a convent."
He didn't like being reminded of Edgiva. He had never seen her
since the day he and Orm took her to Leominster, although oc-
casional news had reached him from his family, and Ethelnoth had
visited the place once, bringing back a report that she was settled
down, in good health, and quickly mastering the skills of medicine
and literacy which the nuns learned there. Brand had been thankful
to hear it. But he could not yet get up the courage to visit her himself. And he didn't want to talk about her. He gathered up his reins
for the second time, more decisively. "If you will forgive me," he
said, "I must see what is happening in front."

"I get greyer every day," Godwin said frequently, examining his
hair in one of Gytha's silver mirrors. "I feel as if I were living
through an endless game of dice, with every throw reversing someone's fortunes. I hope that in the finish all my hoard isn't in someone
else's treasure chest."

"I sometimes wish we could divine the future," Gytha agreed.
"Once I even thought of consulting a witch-wife. But the Church
forbids it."

"And her forecasts might be discouraging! You used to be able
to see the future yourself, at times, did you not?"

"I know." Gytha smiled. "I knew the day before I saw you that
you would come. I was fey, waiting for you. But now—no, I can see
nothing. I can only pray."

Godwin, after Gildenford, had taken Harefoot openly for his
overlord. He had stayed in his hall, diplomatically unwell, when
Harefoot swooped on Winchester—at a pace which for once justified
his name—and snatched the treasury keys from Emma, at one and
the same moment depriving her of the power to buy support while
transferring that power to himself. He'd done the snatching per-

sonally, report said, tearing the keys by force from the girdle of the woman who had supplanted his mother. The mother in question, Elfgift of Northampton, now failing in health but still his chief advisor from her hall in York, had laughed to hear of it. She laughed again when he told her how he had gone straightaway to the underground strong-room where the hoard was kept, unlocked the door, and entered the dank, stone-lined chamber, to fling open the chests. He had paraded round the place with three gold circlets at once on his head, and great gold arm-rings spinning in his hands, flashing in the light of the torches his whooping followers carried.

Her only regret, said Elfgift, was that he had let Emma go. But even Harefoot stopped at drawing steel on a queen, and a grey-haired queen at that.

Emma went, silent and proud as ever, to Count Baldwin's amiable court at Bruges, where all the fugitives went and where her niece Eleanor could be trusted for a welcome. Godwin put his hands between those of Harefoot and was at his new lord's side two years later to see Harefoot do what everyone had been prophesying he eventually must do: complain of pains in his chronically overfilled stomach, take to his bed in anguish, and die.

He had been the last representative of Cnut's house still in England, and so Godwin had borne with him. But he was not and never had been Cnut's named heir. In Denmark, when the news came, Harthacnut at last made a hasty truce with his foe, Magnus of Norway, and promised him the reversion of Denmark should he, Harthacnut, die without issue.

It was a somewhat empty treaty since a lawful heir, in the shape of Magnus's Danish kinsman Sven, already existed and wasn't likely to surrender his rights without protest. But it was mouth-watering enough to make Harthacnut lose no time in removing himself from Magnus's acquisitive reach, to claim his English throne at last.

Harthacnut resembled his half brother Harefoot a good deal in physique but proved a better ruler. He came to London for his crowning. He received Godwin's new oath of loyalty while Emma, restored, sat by her best-beloved son's side and smiled dourly. Soon, the house of Godwin learned why. Harthacnut had heard the tale of Alfred's death and had condemned it. He condemned all parties to it, dead or alive. Thane Thored he banished. He ordered the body of Harefoot to be torn from its tomb and cast into a marsh. Godwin at this point judged it wise to reinforce his oath with something more practical. The magnificent, gold-ornamented ship he chose to present to Harthacnut as a demonstration of his loyalty was embarrassingly costly.

Harthacnut's final act in the matter was to send for Alfred's exiled brother to be his right hand and his heir in England. He did not expect to have heirs of his own, he said bluntly. The girls he had known in Denmark had none of them got children by him, though two were now married and had babies by their husbands.

In Godwin's hall, the news of Edward's coming was greeted with an alarm which even outweighed the public condemnation of Alfred's betrayal.

"How *can* I take an oath of loyalty to Edward?" Godwin demanded. He strode about, grinding rushes under his heel when he spun round at the wall. "I yielded Alfred because then he was an enemy, yes. But he was still Edward's brother. To Edward, I'm the man who sold his brother, that and nothing else!" His beard jutted over jaw muscles knotted in exasperation.

"The question should rather be: How can Edward accept an oath from you?" said Gytha calmly. For once her hands were empty and her whole mind on the crisis.

"Oh, he'll accept it! I hold Wessex. I've held it more than twenty years and its men follow me. I've an army, a sea force, and I hold the most valuable seaports of the land. A king is most unsafe without my support, even with Leofric of Mercia and Siward of Northumbria both to back him. Harthacnut has accepted my oath and he will advise Edward to do likewise. It isn't Edward's problem. It's mine."

"What else can you do but offer the oath?" asked Beorn. He was sitting near Gytha, a well-grown young man now with a niche in the household except with Sweyn, who did not like him and never would, though nowadays he tolerated him. Out of Beorn's hearing he referred to his cousin as the Cuckoo.

Sweyn cut across Beorn's voice now. "If father won't take the oath, or if Edward won't accept it, there will be fighting. Either to subdue us or to throw us out. And for all our strength . . ."

"We might not win," Harold agreed. "If we did we could throw Edward out. But if we didn't . . ."

"We should be banished, if we were still alive," Tostig said. He sat with a hound between his knees, rubbing the animal's ears. His voice was serious. "We should have to go to Baldwin in Bruges, like all the other exiles. Or on to Byzantium to seek our fortunes like that mad Norwegian."

"What mad Norwegian?" asked Godwin, momentarily nonplussed.

"The one Harthacnut talked about at his coronation feast, when he was telling news from Denmark. Magnus's uncle—Harald the Ruthless. You remember."

Godwin smiled for the first time that day. "Yes. Now I do. A gambler and showman as well as a soldier, and I'm neither. I wouldn't get a fortune in Byzantium. I would be no use at seducing empresses!"

"Oh, I'm sure you would be," said Gytha serenely, raising a laugh from the uneasy men clustered about the hall. "But I'd probably poison her . . . I think Beorn is right. There is little alternative to offering the oath, that is, if we want to keep our home and our lands without fighting for them. Godwin?"

He recognised that it was an appeal. He had gone against her counsel when he laid the trap at Gildenford and now, because of that, they were in danger. She was asking him to avert that danger. He looked at her. *This time, listen to me*, said her eyes, fixed on his face.

"Harthacnut is ill at times," he said uncertainly. "Edward may be king one day."

"Make peace with him," said Gytha. "You were *not* party to the blinding. And you were obeying the orders of a lawful overlord. Make your stand on those things."

"We all agree, father," Sweyn said. "You have a large family to look after, remember."

"You want an earldom!" said his harassed parent.

"We must find futures somewhere," Harold said quietly.

Godwin sighed, and nodded in acquiescence. Gytha, relieved, reached behind her and picked up the linen she had been stitching before the council of war. "I wonder," she said thoughtfully, "how our Edward and his mother will get on?"

The land at large was wondering the same thing. It continued to wonder when travellers to and from the court reported the astounding spectacle of Emma and her despised eldest son side by side in talk at the same feasts. Whatever they said to each other in private, if anything, their public manners were patterns of civilisation. It was said as time went by that Harthacnut had refused to believe that his mother had any hand in Alfred's capture and had threatened dire penalties for anyone who repeated the slander, that he had virtually ordered his half brother and Emma to be reconciled. At any rate, they were side by side when Godwin came and promised his faith to a cold, silent Edward as Harthacnut's deputy, and they were side by side again when Harthacnut, whose physical makeup was even more like Harefoot's than anyone had guessed, collapsed in the midst of a friend's marriage feast and died beneath the table, his drinking horn fast in his death clutch.

Leaving the kingdom, subject to the approval of the Witan Council, to Edward.

He would be crowned in less than a month, at Winchester. Queen Emma would be there. And Godwin, Earl of Wessex, would renew his oath to Edward, this time as king, and he would entertain the king and the king's remarkable mother, that centre of appalling rumour, together in his own great Winchester hall.

As a social occasion it had already, before it even began, the hallmarks of an event to remember.

Edward himself chose the city of his coronation. He liked Winchester, he said, and meant to make it his central court. The word went out by fast-horsed messengers that galloped from shire to shire, from town to hamlet, from Andredsweald to the northern Danelaw, from the Devon moorlands to the East Anglian fens. It was proclaimed in marketplaces and at Hundred Courts. The king would be crowned on April the third, 1043, in his cathedral city of Winchester. Almost instantly, the city felt the bow wave of the invasion as thane and earl and abbot set out from every district to gather for the ceremony; and with them, converging on Winchester by mule-train, river barge, and sturdy leather-sandalled feet, came the merchants and the ped-lars, their finest wares in their packs and the light of profit in their eyes.

When Eric Merchant's string arrived, the city was already half-swamped. A fair was in progress as they left the town reeve's office, where they had declared their goods and Eric had taken an oath of good behaviour on behalf of himself and his companions. They rode

on through chaos. Ponies were being trotted out for buyers to inspect, shying at the skins and fabrics hung up for display upon the
booths. Cattle bellowed and pigs squealed and an oxcart with a load
of flour sacks, cheeses, and some angrily squawking poultry in coops
blocked half the road, having stuck while trying to get between two
booths. While they waited for the cart to shift, Harold rode back to
talk to Eric.

"We should divide the string here," he said. "I heard that the
steward at the royal hall is seeing merchants now. I'll take my father's purchases straight to his hall and you can follow. You can take
the unsold goods to the royal hall straightaway."

Eric had been thinking along the same lines. He said: "Rolf will
go with you. Hild can keep me company—she's sitting on top of an
unsold mule-pack anyway. You'd like to see a real king's hall,
wouldn't you, Hild? Of course you would!"

The courtyard of the royal hall was remarkably like the market, only
more so, because its occupants were crowded into a smaller space.
Animals from several mule and pony trains stamped and snorted,
switched tails, and laid back their ears at one another. Pens of assorted livestock bleated and clucked. Bundles were heaped on the
ground and in one corner a queue of those with goods to sell had
formed in front of a tall, bland-faced man wearing enough costly
jewellery to dignify an earl, but who was apparently a chief steward.

When it came to Eric's turn, his welcome was short.

"What do you bring?"

"Rare spices, finest quality . . . cinnamon, pepper, ginger,
cloves . . ."

"My dear man, we've spices enough to last for a score of coronation feasts and five years of ordinary eating besides! What else?"

"Silver dishes from the Mediterranean, the best white ivory in
the tusk . . ."

The steward waved these precious commodities away, implying
that Edward's treasury was overfilled with their like already and that
the surplus was being given away to beggars as charity. "Silks," said
Eric desperately, "woven silks and thread for needlework . . ."

The steward looked for the first time as if he were really listening. "Silks, eh? Well, Lady Emma's buying those, yes. You can take
your samples up. Which are they?"

"The bales on that mule. My daughter's sitting on them."

"Your daughter? What's she doing here? You'll have to take her up with you; she can't sit here in the yard with all these mule drivers. I can't look after stray daughters as well as all these!" He waved an arm at the milling crowd. Then he snapped his fingers at a passing thrall, who came to him.

"Take this merchant and his daughter to the Lady Emma's bower. You address her as madam," he added to Eric.

Eric thankfully called to Hild to dismount and take some sample materials from the bales. They followed the thrall to the queen's apartment.

Emma, who had lived at the royal hall itself since Cnut's death rather than in her own house in Winchester High Street, had had an apartment built there for her, Norman fashion. It had a sleeping chamber on the lower floor, with an upper room where she might sit and receive visitors. The room had south-facing windows, open in good weather to let in the sun. Like everywhere else just now, it was crowded. Purveyors of this and that jostled for attention. For Emma, who was instantly identifiable, because in a queen's chamber no one would dare to look so regal other than the queen, was doing her own choosing.

Emma of Normandy was a study in black and white: white veil over her hair; black overtunic and white, silken underskirt; dark eyes and pale skin; a necklace of mussel pearls and jet round her throat. She sat straightbacked behind a table where lengths of fabric and cases of gems and pots of unguent were strewn. One vendor, the jewel merchant, was importantly displaying his wares. Two others were disappointedly tying their samples up. Three of the queen's ladies were exclaiming over a length of sendal and Emma herself was passing a piece of white linen through her hands, talking to a tonsured cleric at her side. She turned at the sound of more arrivals.

"More merchants? Tch! Boy!" She pointed at the thrall. "Go to the steward and say I've seen enough. Oh no, *you* can stay." Her sharp voice arrested Eric as he was about to withdraw, pulling at Hild's sleeve. "If you've been brought up here, you may as well show what you have. Come here."

"Undo the bundle, Hild," said Eric hastily, before this snapping-eyed lady could change her mind. He thrust Hild forward. "My daughter will show you the silks. She is very knowledgeable."

Emma's strongly marked eyebrows rose. "Indeed? She is very young. Are you training her to be a merchant too?"

"Oh no!" Eric was embarrassed. "I brought her to see the coronation. But she does know about silk."

"Here, child." Emma had somehow brushed aside the jewel merchant and had cleared a space on the table, apparently by giving it one commanding look. She tapped its surface where Hild was to spread her samples out.

Hild, less nervous than her father because she had barely understood in whose presence they were, unrolled her burden. "Here are plain weaves," she explained, shaking the silk free. "But I have embroidered lengths too, and some weaves heavier than this . . ."

"So you're here for the crowning," said Emma, finger and thumb investigating the texture of a glistening fold. "And where have you travelled from? I will see the heavy weave as well."

"Dover, madam. I've never left Dover before."

Emma smiled. "A first journey from your home and you are in the bower of a queen! You'll have some tales to tell your friends. Hm. I suppose you would call this heavy compared to the other. Yes, I like this better. And these are the embroidered pieces? Not so good, I think. I can do as well myself." She considered the thick plain silks again. "Ladies! Gertrud! Adele!" She crooked a finger at them without looking at them and they came to her. "What do you say to this for your overtunics on the great day? If there's enough of it."

The girls leant over the table, a little doubtful, as if not sure whether their mistress wished them to approve or not. Amused, Emma said: "You may have it if you like it. What about the colour? This is green. Gertrud looks muddy in green."

"There is tawny as well," said Hild. "How many girls are there, madam?"

"Twenty."

Hild did a quick calculation on her fingers, lost herself, bit her lip, and was rescued by her father, who said: "We have enough for twenty in either colour, madam."

"What else have you?" asked Emma. "Apart from silk. Anything?"

Eric began on his inventory again. "Spices. Silver. Ivory . . ."

"Pooh! The kitchens reek of weird condiments, and as for silver . . ."

"Guarding it keeps the men occupied," remarked the cleric at her side, with a chuckle. He was an odd-looking man, quite young, but his tonsured ring of hair was prematurely white.

"Perfumes?" Emma said.

"Not this time, madam, I regret."

"My brother is starting to bring in sword-blades," said Hild. Her father frowned at her but Emma, surprisingly, showed interest.

"From where?"

"Sweden and Denmark, madam," said Eric respectfully. "He has just opened trade with them. He is with me in Winchester now, but he will sail for the northlands very soon."

"Ladies!" The queen reverted suddenly to the matter of their dress. "Settle among yourselves who wants green and who wants tawny. I require half of you in each." She watched them withdraw into a chattering huddle at the other end of the bower and added: "Stigand, leave us. I will talk about the altar cloth another time." The other vendors had already gone, and the various servants who stood about the chamber were expertly trained, out of earshot until beckoned into it. Emma was virtually alone with the silk sellers from Dover. She was still examining their wares. She spoke to Eric in a matter-of-fact voice.

"No doubt you had some idea in your mind of showing off your intelligent young daughter while you were in Winchester? Am I right?" She scanned his face and correctly interpreted his pink-flushed puffings. "Very natural," she said dryly. "Why not? It's a father's duty. She's prompt-spoken and neat when she moves. I take it she is neither married nor betrothed? Tell me, would you like her to have a place among my ladies?

2 ✵ Eadgyth

Godwin's hall was as near to upside down as a building well can be that is not actually balanced on its rooftree. He had said openly that his chief reason for going to sea in the unsuitable month of March was to escape the frantic domestic preparations for the coronation and the feast: the buying and baking, the slaughtering and salting, the flying shuttles and darting needles, the spattering paintbrushes and the bubbling stockpots, and above all the reeking dyebaths which always attended the making of fine new clothes.

But the maelstrom was still whirling when they all returned, complicated even further now by the arrival of the first guests. Only a few hours before Brand and Harold rode in with the mule-train, an old friend of Godwin's, a Norfolk thane, had arrived with his wife, daughter, and servants and had cast the household into a renewed fever of effort to get the hall into a fit state to house the evening meal. The thane had fought at Godwin's side in Denmark long ago, and although he had no importance in himself, for friendship's sake he commanded a respectful welcome.

At midday, when the mule-train came, the hall was still in confusion. Most of the hangings were down, draped across trestles as the womenfolk toiled at them antlike, with needles for antennae. A master craftsman and his apprentice, visibly keeping themselves to themselves as far as housecarles and other workmen were concerned, were tenderly laying gold leaf on a new design round the main door. Hired hands, aided by thralls seconded for the purpose, were touching up the paintwork. Buckets, tubs, and baskets of curious substances were everywhere. By the kitchen door stood a row of containers full of dyeing materials: oakapples and waterlily roots, saffron flowers and kingcups, madder roots and cockles. The hall had smelt terrible when Godwin left it. It still did.

The earl himself was nowhere to be seen. Brand and Harold, invading the kitchens to see what they could find for themselves and Rolf and the muleteers to eat, were driven out again almost immediately. Gytha had three big fires going in the outdoor enclosure, and from cauldrons above them came fantastically hued vapours and evil stinks. Treated cloths, hung up to dry, dripped everywhere. Over one of the pots a witchlike kitchen crone, the oldest of the thralls, crooned incantations with obvious enjoyment as she stirred the disintegrating vegetable matter it contained. Gytha, bright green to the elbows, perspiring and preoccupied, made shooing gestures at the new arrivals.

"Bread's in the bakehouse, cheese is in the dairy, and I don't have to tell you where the ale stores are! There'll be no cooking done until tonight. Be off and look after yourselves. I've no time for you now."

"Women!" said Harold as they retreated in the direction of the bakehouse. "God's Teeth, why don't they tear the hall right down and be done with it? I shall take my hawk out this afternoon and get away from it. They go out of their minds whenever there's a festival, the womenfolk! Find the mule-lads somewhere to eat in peace, will you?"

Brand obeyed. He ate and drank with the muleteers and Rolf, sitting on benches in the angle of stable and byre, watching the excitement but keeping out of its way. He was glad to be off-duty at last after the long, watchful road from the east. Having eaten, he excused himself and wandered off. Rolf could find his own way about the household and look after the mule-boys now. As for himself, he could laze, or rub down his pony, or clean his sword, or gossip with Longshanks, just as he liked.

He walked across the courtyard, looking about him for Longshanks. He felt happy. The mule-train had been brought in safely; a task had been completed. He had a full stomach and the lingering taste of fresh-baked bread in his mouth. He was young and in good health and the sun on his back was warm, like a friendly hand. He skirted the kitchen enclosure, where the dyestained sorceresses were still at their cauldrons, and went on towards the little cluster of guesthouses, his attention now caught by upraised voices. Someone, by the sound of it, was having the great-grandfather of a quarrel. He moved easily, drawn by curiosity, thinking of nothing in particular, cheerful and content. He had not the least premonition that this young freedom was about to end, would be gone forever in another six strides, that never in all his life again would he recapture that unthinking peace.

For it was the peace of the unawakened, and as he came in sight of the guesthouses and saw the trio who were arguing there, like a dragonfly bursting from its chrysalis to exchange the world of water for the world of air, like a sane man stricken with madness or a madman becoming sane, Brand in body and soul woke up.

Two of the trio were Godwinssons, Harold and Sweyn. They were glaring at each other, angrily planted face to face in front of the largest guesthouse. But the third was a young woman, about Brand's own age, with flame-coloured hair half-braided and half-loose as though she had been interrupted while plaiting it, a small neat head on a slender neck, a green tunic above a long, well-worn orange underskirt which did not go with her hair, and wide-set, almond-shaped, baleful grey-green eyes. With one hand she held back the loose hair from her face, while behind her in the doorway of the guesthouse hovered a resigned-looking maid. The maid was being purposely unobtrusive, however. For the young lady was in a temper more fiery than her tresses.

The voices he had heard in the distance had been male: Harold and Sweyn, presumably. They had stopped shouting now, to listen to the girl. She had not raised her own voice. But her words, though soft, were coming out with enormous force, like jets of steam from under a clamped-down pot lid.

"Must you . . . *must* you come and squabble *here*?" A long forefinger jabbed in the direction of the guesthouse. "My parents are trying to rest—in *there*! They're both tired, they're both ailing! We've been days on the road!" Her finger swivelled to accuse Sweyn. "You were here when we came! You welcomed them with your father. You *know* this is their apartment! Yet you come and stand out here and screech at each other like . . . like . . ."

"Corncrakes?" suggested Sweyn helpfully. His eyes were dancing. He seemed dissatisfied with his simile. "No, they croak. Barn owls? Tomcats?"

One of the workmen had dumped a bucket of whitewash carelessly down outside the guesthouse. The young lady's malevolent gaze alighted on it. She picked it up and swung it threateningly. "I don't care what you think you sound like," she said to Sweyn, still in that passionate undertone. "But don't come and sound like it *here!* Think of other people for once! Go and fight elsewhere!"

"I'd empty that whitewash over him if I were you," Harold advised her, as virtuously as though he were her ally instead of the second object of her indignation. "Don't hesitate. I wouldn't."

Sweyn turned on him. "Who began this? Let me remind you . . . !"

"Oh, Sweyn, be quiet!" Harold seemed to be struggling with internal merriment. He turned to the girl. "Eadgyth—it is Eadgyth, isn't it?—I am sorry. I didn't know anyone was in there and I think Sweyn didn't notice just where he was. Please apologise to your parents for us and . . ."

"What by the Elbow of God is going on here?" Gytha arrived in their midst. The sounds of strife had carried to the kitchen. She looked at Eadgyth and her simmering eldest son. There was a pause, during which a workman with an expressionless face walked up, took the pail from Eadgyth's grasp with a murmured "I want thát, lass," and strolled away with it. Faint grins flickered over everyone's faces. Even Eadgyth fleetingly smiled.

"Well, Sweyn?" said Gytha, demanding an explanation.

"I was quarrelling with Harold," Sweyn said blithely. "And Eadgyth thought we might disturb her parents."

"A quarrel over some girl by the sound of it," said Eadgyth disdainfully. She waved a hand at Harold. "I heard him say she was his. Then Sweyn said . . ."

"You heard *Harold* say some girl was his?" asked Gytha in amazement. Harold's indifference to girls was a byword. It had infuriated scores of them.

"It isn't a girl, it's a goshawk," said Harold, his mirth beginning to bubble. "Sweyn took her from the nest but I trained her and then I went off with father and when I came back I found he'd claimed her! So we fell out."

"I bloody near broke my neck getting her out of that tree!" Sweyn thundered. Eadgyth glared and his mother interposed.

"If it's so important, you can fight it out fair. We'll have the pair of you as part of the king's entertainment at the banquet. I'll tell your father. Meanwhile, go and find something useful to do where you won't make any more trouble. Eadgyth is right. Her parents *are* trying to sleep, and they need sleep. Go along!" Gytha stood triumphant, mistress of the battlefield, as her sons reluctantly took their departure.

"I'm sorry." Eadgyth rubbed her sleeve across her forehead. "I was angry. I wouldn't have thrown paint at Sweyn, not really, but . . ."

Gytha laughed. "Why wouldn't you? The girl who throws a bucket of paint at Sweyn instead of falling into his arms, that girl I shall marry him to!" Her eye discovered Brand, rooted and silent, standing a few feet away. "Brand—have you eaten?"

"Yes, I . . ."

"Then you can amuse Eadgyth." The world burst into songs of enchantment and there were stars in the heavens at noon. "Take her to see the goshawk my two boys were fighting over. Eadgyth, tidy your hair and Brand will show you the mews. Wait here, Brand, she won't be long." She led Eadgyth back to her maid and the guesthouse. Brand waited willingly. He was quite prepared to wait if necessary till Doomsday, if he could be alone with Eadgyth when it dawned.

The astonishing thing was that no one realised what had happened. He was just Brand, Godwin's housecarle, Harold's friend, young Brand at a loose end, told to show a guest round the mews. And here he was in the shadowy wooden building, where the birds— falcon, goshawk, and merlin—sat on their carefully spaced perches, too far apart to savage each other; and here with him was Eadgyth, whose every movement of her long fingers and her graceful neck turned his vitals to molten gold.

"This is the goshawk they meant," he said.

The bird roused her feathers a little as he lifted her. The huge talons, monstrously powerful for her size, curved strongly round his arm. Her beak clacked.

"I can see why they quarrelled!" said Eadgyth admiringly.

"You have a hawk of your own?"

"A merlin, yes. At home. My father keeps a goshawk but not as fine a bird as this."

She smiled at him and he wondered if his own heart-stopping sensations had any counterpart in her, and if so how he could find out. He put the goshawk back on her perch. "There's a peregrine falcon here." How could he keep her with him long enough to build a bridge of talk between them, strong enough to carry so heavy a meaning?

He knew that he was being a dull companion with nothing to say except commonplaces. Yet Eadgyth seemed happy and interested. "Your mews is much better stocked than ours," she said after duly appreciating the falcon. "But I have a very fine horse!" Her eyes were bright. "My father went to the Holy Land when he was young and he brought back two Barbary colts. My mare has them both as grandsires. The rest of her blood is local pony but it's a good mix. She's fast like the Barbary horses, but she can go all day and never tire."

"Can I see her? You brought her?" Anything to stay in Eadgyth's company. They would go through the stable one horse at a time and scan every animal from nostrils to tail. He wondered what she would like to see after that.

The mare turned and whickered at her mistress's step. She was sorrel-coloured, sturdy in the barrel but with a sculptured concave profile and a tracing of veins under a fine skin, which proved her Eastern blood. Her mane and tail might have been made of silk thread. Brand had seen Barbs before. Godwin had a black pure-bred stallion and the queen's confessor, Stigand, had been seen about Winchester on a strawberry half-bred mare. He judged Eadgyth's steed to be valuable and worth her owner's pride in her. They suited each other. Creatures of air and fire, the two of them. Whereas he, Brand, was solid, earthy clay and he had a mount to match. Godwin had offered to remount him, but he was fond of his old Greedy. Was. Had been. Now he felt ashamed. "Which is yours?" asked Eadgyth at that moment, tactlessly.

He had to show her. Red plaits swinging, she walked ahead of him to the pony's stall. She held her skirts just clear of the floor, gracefully and without trouble; she was used to stables. She knew about horses. Greedy looked more hairy-heeled, serviceable, and lumpish even than usual, to his master's jaundiced eye. But Eadgyth, to his surprise, stroked the rough black mane that always wanted to stand up on end like a donkey's and said: "He has a good wide forehead. He's no fool, is he? I learned to ride on a pony very like this. He never lost his way and never fell into a bog by mistake. My Thundergift might, for all her fine foreign blood."

"Thundergift?" said Brand. "Is that her name?"

Eadgyth chuckled. "Yes! Our chaplain said it was a pagan kind of name and was cross with me. But she was born in a thunderstorm; we had to go out in it to fetch her in, her and her dam. We thought they might not be strong enough to weather it, being part Barb. The name was really my father's idea. My parents are old-fashioned in some ways. We keep some of the old customs still— evergreens in the hall at Yuletide, and the Midsummer Feast. The priest puts up with it. He always gives us an improving sermon at the same time."

"What other old customs do you keep?" Brand asked, daring as much by not giving himself time to think.

Eadgyth gave him a sidelong glance full of mischief. "May Eve and the sultry August Yule? Ah—not quite." She sounded regretful.

"I've never kept them either," said Brand. "But they must have been merry festivals in the old days. If one had the right company."

The bright rectangle of the stable door was blocked. In the midst of exchanging glances of laughter and comprehension, they turned. Silently, Brand cursed. It was not Sweyn, at least. It was Harold. But even Harold, just now, was unwelcome.

"Eadgyth? Your mother is looking for you. Have you been showing Brand your mare? I should like a horse like that, myself."

"You must talk to my father." Eadgyth went towards him. "I saw the goshawk. She's beautiful." She smiled back at Brand, an enchanting smile except that it was one of farewell. "Thank you for showing me the mews," she said.

Left alone in the stable, Brand sighed, gathered up a handful of straw, and began to rub his pony down. He was not a great one for show. Most of his fellows vied with each other in the number of gold arm-rings they had and desired jewelled sword-hilts and saddlery above anything. Hitherto, these desires had hardly touched him. He had not been bred to them. But now he wished for a garnet-set cloak-clasp or gold and silver studs on his pony's tackle, because such things might impress Eadgyth. He understood the yearning for the first time. It was the man's equivalent of the cock dove's outspread tail or the plover's aerobatics.

"Brand, bach," he said to himself, with the old Welsh endearment his mother had used when he was small, "Brand, bach, what a fool you are."

3 ✠ Young Lions Embattled

The eve of coronation feast in Godwin's hall on the second day of April, 1043, would have been quite unimaginable on the second day of April, 1042. A year had brought astonishing things.

The hastily convened Witan Council in the July of 1042, summoned to settle according to custom who the dead Harthacnut's successor should be, hardly knew what to do with the problem in front of it. Edward Ethelredson was the obvious choice, Harthacnut's own nomination. But Godwin, the most powerful earl in the land, commander of the royal bodyguard and master of all the chief southeastern ports, had every reason to object. Godwin had after all betrayed Edward's brother. Godwin might well have some other candidate in mind. If so, the future did not merely look uncertain. It looked hideous. The council members gathered with grim faces.

They met in London, at the hall of the city's Bishop Elfward. Edward himself had convened them, which amounted to a demand for his own election. But London was in Godwin's territory. Most of them came fully armed, with large and well-armed escorts.

They gathered out of doors, for it was fine weather. There was a wide stretch of greensward outside the bishop's palisade, with the river at the foot of the slope, an oak tree for shade over the principal personalities, and Elfward's barley fields ripening on either side. The wide view also provided ample notice of any new arrivals.

Godwin came early, with his two eldest sons but a smaller escort than anyone else. Tacitly he seemed to be saying that he neither expected trouble nor intended it. Leofric Earl of Mercia, short and red-faced, with dull yellow curly hair and round, wary blue eyes, came next, accompanied by his son Alfgar and riding at the head of four hundred men. Siward of Northumbria followed him. Siward had left his family at home in the north. He was the oldest of the three earls; his sandy hair was now grey-streaked and receding at the temples, although his huge Danish frame was as mighty as ever and his skin was weatherbeaten to the hue of the oak tree's bark by his hard way of living. He was almost pure Viking, with a battleaxe so heavy that few but he could wield it. It was much in evidence, and so were the axes of the three hundred northerners riding at his heels.

Bishop Elfward, aged and frail but sharp enough of eye, presided from the bench he had to himself immediately under the oak. On his right sat Alfric Kitehawk, Archbishop of York, well-fleshed, tall and round like a pillar in a stone church, magnificently robed. On his left was the other archbishop, Eadsige of Canterbury, thin, yellow-faced, with skeletal hands. Their combined escorts made a semicircle facing another formed from the earls' followers. Together they ringed the Witan round. Brand had been there among Godwin's men. Edward Ethelredson himself, he noticed, was absent.

"He has to be," Harold explained to him while they waited for the proceedings to start. "He can call the Witan. But he has to keep away while they talk about him."

Elfward called on the earls to speak in turn, Siward first and Leofric second. They spoke for Edward. Neither let his eyes turn in Godwin's direction.

"Godwin?" said the bishop in a carefully neutral voice.

Godwin rose, came forward. If he had limited his escort, he was still flaunting his rank. No one else present had so much gold about him, such a crusting of amethysts on his shield, or so much gilding on his helmet.

"For whom do you speak?" asked Elfward.

"Edward Ethelredson," said Godwin briskly.

He took them all by surprise. There were gasps, a dropped jaw or two. Godwin's eyes showed amusement.

"Your reasons?" said the bishop after a pause.

"Because," said Godwin, "in the first place he clearly has the support of almost everyone here and above all that of the Church." He bowed towards the prelates. They had not yet spoken, but their nodding heads while Leofric and Siward talked had shown their views beyond doubt. "And in the second place," Godwin continued, "for the good and simple reason that he is *here*. All the other claimants are somewhere else. The other branch of King Ethelred's family, the descendants of his first marriage, are in Hungary, a long, dangerous journey away, and perhaps they are not interested. In all these years of change they have sent no word. King Magnus is in Denmark . . ."

"Magnus has no claim!" said Eadsige irritably. Siward had already raised the subject of Magnus and knocked it down in the same sentence. "Harthacnut made him heir to Denmark only, *not* to England. Harthacnut summoned Edward Ethelredson here to be his heir in England. My lord Siward has already said all this."

Godwin nodded. "I agree. Though I have heard that Magnus himself thinks he has a claim. But if he had, I would not support it. Edward Atheling is English-bred and was the last king's right hand for more than a year. Of all men he is the one best placed to take power here and find his rule accepted, without bloodshed. There would be opposition to Magnus and probably to the Hungarian branch if they sent anyone." He caught Leofric's eye. Leofric, of all those present, had the most disbelieving expression. "Let me say something else. I have said it before." He did not specify where. "I like to see the crops growing, not trampled flat by armies. I would have the corn harvested in season, not left to rot where it stands while the men swing swords instead of scythes, harvesting in fields of war. I am a warrior but I fight to defend the corn, my own and my overlord's, not to harm it. I was King Cnut's man first and I upheld his sons when he was gone, but now the sons are gone as well and I must choose a new lord. I choose one who will defend the land as Cnut did, not a trouble-bringer. I see no choice but Edward. I speak for him."

"Edward," said Leofric thoughtfully, "has promised great rewards to those who follow him."

"And we all have sons to provide for," Siward added in the broad accents of the Danelaw.

"Ah, so we have," said Leofric, as one who has got to the bottom of a mystery. Eadsige clicked a disapproving tongue but Godwin smiled.

"I have sons," he agreed. "But if that is true, so are the things I have said about the crops. I'm a man, not an angel. All my reasons

for upholding Edward aren't pure. Neither are yours. As you say,
Leofric, Edward will reward us. As you have remarked, Siward, we
all have sons. Here on earth, reasons rarely are pure. But they can
be, and mine are, *sound*."

He waited to see if his fellow earls had any more hints to drop,
but they were silent. He added: "I respect Edward as a man. He
came alone to England when Harthacnut sent for him. The king was
Queen Emma's beloved son, and he must have remembered what
happened when *she* sent the Athelings an invitation!"

The Witan goggled. The last thing they had expected from
Godwin was this ruthless exhumation of Alfred's body. They had
meant to leave it buried, out of tact.

"He took the chance, " said Godwin, "that the summons was
honest. That it meant a share of the rulership, not death or the
blinding iron. He gambled his body in cold blood. Once more I say:
I will trust England to him, I will follow him."

"If, of course," he added after a pause, dragging into the open
the final horrid possibility, which no one yet had braced himself to
mention, "Edward Ethelredson himself accepts me."

Alfric Kitehawk said: "We shall recommend that he does so."

Siward drew his sword, another huge weapon which like his axe
was too great for most other men. He pointed it to the sky. "*Edward!*"

And with a unanimous hissing of steel, the blades of the Witan
Council and the watching escorts were drawn and raised, a thicket of
sharp-honed, sunlit edges. "*Edward Cyng!*"

Hence, on a day of swiftly alternating sun and showers, with a stiff
wind shaking the horse chestnut blossoms, this feast in Godwin's
hall, to entertain King Edward and his mother Lady Emma.

The first event of the day took place in the morning, by the
river that ran behind Godwin's palisade. Here an existing landing
place had been widened and the folk of Winchester had come complete with stools and benches and cloaks to sit on, with packets of
food and leather bottles of ale or mead, to watch Earl Godwin
present the king with the coronation gift of Wessex.

Everyone was there who had been at the Witan, including Siward, with his family this time, and Leofric with his wife,
Godgitha. Gytha stood with the womenfolk of her own household,

her younger children grouped before her. Edith, home for good from the convent now, looked unassuming and somewhat lost among her brothers. She held redheaded little Gunhild by the hand and Gunhild in turn held the last of the family, the toddler Elfgiva. There had been one more child after Gunhild, but there would be no more. Gytha had nearly died of this one.

Close by, Eadgyth stood with her parents, her father aged before his time by some disease that had knotted his joints and bent his back, her mother thin and fragile. It was as though they had given her all their vitality and kept none for their own use. Brand, standing among the other housecarles, found it hard not to stare at her and almost missed the arrival of the king.

Edward walked to the landing stage with the Archbishops Eadsige and Kitehawk beside him. He was mantled in blue, bright with gold and silver thread. His mother followed, small and upright in red and white. A bevy of green- and tawny-clad ladies followed her. Among them, breathless with excitement, the wool merchant quite forgotten, was Hild Ericsdaughter.

Harold and Sweyn Godwinsson were the Masters of Ceremony. They greeted the king and Lady Emma, set chairs for them, and served wine. In the crowd, Eric Merchant grew fatter and redder with pride. He had supplied it.

Godwin waited, bareheaded, on the riverbank. When Edward and Emma were seated, he signed to Oswald Halfear, waiting a little way downstream, and Oswald sounded his horn. Half a minute later, round the downstream curve of the river, a barge was rowed into sight. The gift of a ship to Harthacnut had proved a success; Godwin was repeating the effect. With improvements, for this was a sight which drew gasps.

The crowd pushed forward, parents lifting children up for a better view. The barge's dragon prow was sheathed in gold and in the stern a great lunging lion of solid gold was poised, the sign of royalty, flashing in the opportune sunlight. The clouds had chosen that moment to break. Oars in flawless unison rose and dipped, their spray feathering silver round the blades. The rowers were dressed in green cloth against the sharp spring air, but their arms were bare to the elbow and they wore gold arm-rings to prove their free birth. Gently they brought her to the bank. The burnished lion looked hot to the touch. Harold cupped his hands round his mouth and shouted to get a hearing for his father's presentation speech, above the chatter of admiration.

Silence fell, rather unwillingly, as Godwin stepped forward to face the king. But the address was for them all, as the pitch of his voice told them in his opening sentence.

"This is a day of the greatest joy for me," he declared. He held the king's eyes but even the back row of the assembly could hear him. Godwin's voice production was skilled. "It is also," he continued, "a day of pride and of hope in a new beginning for us all." Some just perceptible change of timbre entered the last few words. Edward stiffened and those in the crowd who had been fidgeting with food packets or tidying their children became still. The silence was no longer unwilling.

"This day," said Godwin steadily, "is the coronation eve of my lord Edward of England, and I, as Earl of Wessex, in whose earldom he has his chief city and from whose followers, by long custom, the main part of his personal guard is picked, will tomorrow make my oath of loyalty to him. These are the causes for joy and pride.

"They are also the foundation of our hope. All of us—my brother earls and the prelates of the Church—who chose Lord Edward as king pray that he may have a long, peaceful, and prosperous rule. And I trust that my followers will throughout that rule continue to be the backbone of his bodyguard. I pledge that my own loyalty will thus endure.

"But men who are shaping the future can never be quite indifferent to the past. It is to the past that we look for example and for warning. Many of you here today must have recalled the past even as you gathered for this ceremony . . ."

Edward had not stirred. His rather thin-lipped mouth was a straight line. The earl did not look towards his own family. They, however, were looking at each other. *Did you know?* Gytha's eyes were silently demanding of Harold and Sweyn. *No, did you?* their startled faces were asking in reply. There had been days of rehearsal for this presentation. Godwin had even practised parts of his speech out loud. But it hadn't been this speech.

"In the recent past," Godwin was continuing, strongly, steadily, into the attentive silence, "we have had times of disturbance, of many contenders for the throne, and blood has been shed. There are those here today, my lord Edward, some of them among the people closest to you in rank and in blood, whose loyalty you may question in your heart. I wish to say this: that you need not doubt the loyalty of any person here present on this day. Those who owe you love have never failed of it. And those whose task it is to support the royal office with their swords have never failed in that duty either."

He took a long breath and the people nearest to him saw sweat beads on his temples. But his voice as he resumed was still resonant and level.

"In days gone by, I myself gave loyal—and honourable, only honourable—service to the house of King Cnut, for he and his heirs were my lawful overlords. If I did not condone or take part in all their enterprises, nor did I ever lift a blade against them, not even when I might have justified it. Nor, by the same token, will I raise a blade against you, my lord Edward, whom I also take now as my king.

"It is my pleasure now to ask if you will accept this token of my faith, this rowing vessel, named *Lion*, a gift from the earldom of Wessex. She was built in my own shipyards and is manned by my own men. It will be my care to provide rowers for her whenever they are needed. I should also like to present to you the master shipwright who saw to her construction, if he will come forward . . ."

The shipwright came and knelt before the king. The bemused gathering saw the apparently equally bemused king raise him and then accompany him and Godwin aboard. Emma, stony-faced throughout Godwin's address, was approached by Gytha, and she too rose and walked to the barge. In the stern, a harper struck up a tune and serving boys ran to plump up the red and blue silk cushions and offer more wine. Ceremony, itself like a great ornamental barge with an irresistible way on it, bore them all inexorably forward—king, queen, earls, and audience. No wandering from the set course was possible.

"I take it he was talking about himself and Lady Emma," Longshanks muttered in Brand's ear. "I've never seen her close before. Do you think he really knows the truth where she's concerned, or not? She looks capable of anything to me."

Brand nodded absently, his eyes still on Eadgyth. He thought he had understood Godwin's speech, and that it was a declaration that Godwin and Emma alike were innocent of the plot to murder

Alfred. He was glad. But today he could not think about either of them for long. He was in love and this evening she had half promised to see him after the feast, alone.

The feast started in mid-afternoon.

As far as weather went, it was well-timed. Brand sat at a lower table, near the door, and listened to the drumming of a rainstorm on the roof. The hall, though nightfall was far away, was dim. Or would have been had Eadgyth not been there. She was some way from him, sitting with her mother and the other women grouped round Lady Emma. But she smiled at him once, and he could look at her and faintly catch her voice. She was talking to Edith. They were a contrast. Ten years in a convent had smoothed all the wildness out of Edith. She walked with a nun's small, soft steps, spoke with a nun's low, soft voice, and scarcely moved her hands to help out her speech; Eadgyth never stopped moving hers, and her gold and amethyst bracelets sparkled whenever she spoke.

At the top table the king had the place of honour, flanked by the Godwin menfolk. The archbishops were there as well, and one or two guests of importance, including relatives of the Godwin house. The goldsmith abbot, Sparhafoc of Abingdon, had been pointed out to Brand, as had the group of monkish clerks who were friends of the king from his Norman days. The talk among them was brisk and bilingual, French crisscrossing with English, question in one and answer in the other, even both in the same sentence. Brand could follow quite a lot of French now, but he would never be a linguist, he knew. Sweyn had said as much, mock-sorrowful.

Edith had risen and was presenting a beaker of wine to Edward, who was smiling at her and complimenting Godwin on both the wine and its donor. The courteous formalities of the morning still held. This, it seemed, would be the pattern of commerce between Godwin and the king. It remained to be seen whether there would be any of the usual favours for Godwin's house. Sparhafoc was hoping for some, no doubt.

"Not," Edward was saying, "that I dislike English mead. I was bred to it. I missed it in Normandy."

"Normandy and England are surprisingly different, though the sea between them is so narrow," Eadsige, a travelled man, commented. "The stone castles of Normandy always amaze me. We have only a few stone buildings here."

"I have it in mind to build a stone abbey near London," Edward agreed. "We should have more such. Stone endures when wood has crumbled. But it pleased me when I came to England to see how open and fearless the buildings were. Only the greater halls have palisades, and only towns have walls. The small houses lie open to all comers."

"Ours is a more peaceful land, perhaps?" Kitehawk suggested. "King Cnut did that for us. We used to defend the houses near the shores, of course, in the days of the raiders."

"Normandy is turbulent by comparison," Edward said, nodding. "But it may improve as the young duke grows up."

"If he grows up," Godwin commented sombrely.

"As you say, if he grows up. He's thirteen now and out of hiding, in the company of trusted men, and I hear he is already showing strength of character. If he lives through five more years, we can look for new times in Normandy. But . . ."—he smiled on the company and gracefully pledged his host and hostess in the wine Edith had given him—"the new times for England are already here, I trust."

Siward of Northumbria, pushing back his bench, declared a toast to the new times, and it was noisily drunk. Gytha pushed Edith forward again to refill the royal cup. Edward held it out for her, gravely thanking her.

Lifting the cup, he caught the eyes of Godwin and then, across the hall, of Gytha. Raising his voice so that the ladies could hear him easily, he said: "My meeting with your family, my lord Godwin and Lady Gytha, has been a very happy thing for me. It is a heartwarming wonder to me to see so great a brood of brothers and sisters—and a cousin too!—living so kindly together under one roof. Your hall impresses me! Family unity and loving trust between parent and child are very precious things."

The king looked round him, smiling with mouth closed in a thin, sharp curve like a crescent moon. Beorn and Sweyn, who had both choked faintly at the reference to cousins, were still. And from Emma at the ladies' table came a palpable sense of anger, like a cold airstream through the hall. Gytha opened her mouth to speak, quickly. But Edward had not yet finished.

"Of course it seems especially so to me," he said, "because I have so little family. My sisters are far away and my brothers are all dead." On Godwin's right forearm, resting on the table, a muscle ridged out. "I hope," said Edward smoothly, "to profit by this admirable example today. Lady Gytha, you are, I am sure, the one most responsible for the happy state of affairs in your husband's hall. Your health!" He rose and pledged her. Obediently, wordlessly, the rest of the guests rose with him.

"I can only hope," said Godwin, moving strategically into the hush as the toast ended, "that my family is not about to disappoint you, my lord! We have as entertainment this afternoon arranged for two of my sons to fight each other for a goshawk!"

It was still raining, so they made an arena inside the hall, sweeping part of it clear of rushes and snoozing dogs, shifting the long trestle tables and the benches in order to make a wide open space and a barrier between the contestants and the fire. Brand was sent to bring the goshawk and a movable perch, and he arranged them where the bird could be admired but was out of harm's way. By then the fight was nearly ready to start.

Harold and Sweyn were half-stripped, limbering up and making challenging faces at each other. Their weapons were piled on a bench. This was to be barehanded fighting.

The company jostled good-naturedly for a view, commenting on the beauties of the hawk and the muscular development of the young men. But the announcement that Edith would present the prize to the winner caused discontent.

"She's their sister, that's spoiling sport," someone said.

"Eadgyth was there when the fight was . . . er . . . suggested," Gytha said. She looked at Eadgyth's father, whom Tostig and Gyrth were kindly helping to a good position on top of a table. At close quarters he was more like Eadgyth than one at first realised. His colourless hair had once been red and the fingers knotted round his ash staff had once been long and elegant. "Will you let your daughter give the prize?" Gytha asked.

"Yes, yes, why not? Here, girl!" the old thane said, and Eadgyth too was helped to a seat of honour on the table. She was near Brand now. She smiled at him again, tidying her skirts and clasping her hands before her. The crowd sorted itself out, those in front squatting down to give those behind a view. The floor was prepared.

Godwin placed his gladiators one on each side of him, facing each other beyond the reach of his outstretched arms. Then he stepped back quickly and shouted: "Go!"

Eyes wary, hands spread, and bodies arched forward, Sweyn and Harold circled each other, watching for a hold. "Hawk thief!" Sweyn said, his fingers crooked like talons. "Who took her from the nest?"

"Any treecat can climb. Save your breath, mog," Harold advised.

They closed in, and the front row of the audience found itself shoving backwards into the others as the pair swayed round their improvised ring. Feet scuffled on the beaten earth floor. Sweyn was playing to the audience—breaking away, dancing, leaping, making rabbit faces at Harold, issuing taunts. Harold kept his feet on the floor, his mouth shut and his gaze unwaveringly on Sweyn. He came in swinging a hammer of a fist straight for his brother's face. Sweyn dodged and dived under it. They clinched, tangled. Harold's knees bent. He had Sweyn half-lifted. Sweyn hooked an ankle round one of Harold's and both lost their balance together. They crashed to the floor. In the crowd somebody—it sounded like Leofric of Mercia—banged a table and started laying odds. He was betting on Harold.

They rolled over in a flurry of groping hands and scrabbling toes. Blood had appeared from somewhere; both the straining backs were smeared. They broke apart and sprang up, and it was seen to be coming from Sweyn's left nostril. Harold had a half-shut eye and a graze on his jaw, just beginning to bead red. There was no more playacting. They had forgotten their audience. They could not hear the flying bets. They rushed in again, roaring like stags. Sweyn's hand clamped over his brother's face, blocking his breath. Harold gave ground, collided with a table, and went backwards across it with Sweyn on top. Harold's feet, off the ground, began to swing, one crossing the line of the other above and below Sweyn's thighs until, with a pelvic earthquake and a sweeping scissors, Harold rolled on top of his foe. In doing so, he slithered both of them along the table. As they reached the end of it, still locked and grunting, the table tilted, throwing them off. It fell on them. The nearest members of the audience rushed to lift it clear. Sweyn got up, shaking hair out of his eyes. Harold, eyes closed and face ashen, lay still. Godwin knelt beside him. "Knocked out," he said a moment later.

There was a pause while Sweyn stood panting, absurdly worried, above the supine brother he had earnestly tried to smother not sixty seconds before. Godwin seized a bowl from the nearest table and began to lave the visibly growing lump on the patient's head. Harold's good eye opened, and then screwed up as if the light were painful.

"You were hit by a table. Can you remember how?" Godwin asked quietly.

Harold grinned. "I was fighting Sweyn about a hawk, and my name is Harold." He pushed himself up on an elbow. "My memory is all right! And I didn't finish the fight." He started to get to his feet but failed. He felt his head and discovered the bump. "Sure it was a table? Not an axe?" he enquired.

Godwin propped him up against a bench and stepped into the middle of the ring. "The contest seems to be over but I can't declare a winner. Harold was defeated by a table, not by his opponent, and we can hardly present a goshawk to a table! What shall we do?"

"Let Sweyn fight someone else!" shouted Leofric. "Who'll volunteer?"

"Ay, let's have another challenger!" Siward of Northumbria took up the cry. Beorn suddenly pushed his way out of the crowd. "I'll take him on! I fancy that hawk!"

Cheers and table thumping made him welcome. Leofric shouted: "Sweyn's bigger but he's tired! Beorn's lighter but he's fresh! I back Beorn to win!"

"Ye'll lose your stake," Siward warned him. "I'll back Sweyn. What'll it be?" They started pulling arm-rings off. Alfgar, Leofric's son, politely held a trencher for the bets to be deposited. Brand edged back to Eadgyth, waiting, her prize still ungiven.

"Is Harold hurt much?" she asked. "I can't see from here."

"He's sitting up and he knows what happened. I don't think he's much harmed. His cousin is taking on where he left off. This should be exciting."

"More exciting than Harold against Sweyn?"

"I think so. Harold and Sweyn are fond of each other at heart. Beorn and Sweyn . . . aren't."

Some inkling of the difference between this fight and the last had got round. After the noisy encouragement while Godwin stripped off his nephew's tunic and shirt and weaponry, silence fell. Once more Godwin arranged the opponents and signalled the start.

They were a less even match than the first had been. Beorn was a good three inches shorter than his foe, and although wiry he weighed much less. The plucked-chicken whiteness of his chest looked puny against Sweyn's gold-thatched torso.

But Beorn, it quickly transpired, had not spent seven years battling for recognition among the spirited Godwinssons for nothing. He had learned, out of need, that skill can upset strength, and he had developed the skill, perforce. He was a natural stayer, and he had taken advantage of his light weight to train his speed. He was fast and he was wicked. Two minutes, and Leofric was standing on a table bawling encouragement to Beorn and stamping his feet. The other Godwinssons were loudly supporting their brother, but in despairing voices. And Sweyn had lost his temper.

The fight, conducted in a savage silence except for involuntary gasps and grunts, lasted a long time. Sweyn's face, streaked with clotting blood from his nose, was stretched in a snarl. Beorn fought with concentration, nostrils flaring, teeth-tips a glitter of white between his lips. Sweat poured down their bodies. The ring shrank as the audience pressed excitedly in. Eadgyth leant forward, white-knuckled, eager.

The end came when no one expected it. They were down, struggling near a table which they had knocked over, strewing its contents over the floor. Sweyn, as he rolled, was seen to have a piece of bread stuck between his shoulder blades. The bench that held their weapons had been upset too by a sweeping foot, and some spilt wine had splashed them both a lurid, gruesome red, which made the audience laugh. Beorn, twined serpentlike about his enemy, was slowly and efficiently working his legs round Sweyn's right knee to achieve a bonelock. His left foot slid into place with a last smooth thrust, and there were indrawn breaths from the watchers as Sweyn's leg began to turn dangerously against the joint. They waited for the cry of surrender or the crunch of a cracking cartilage.

Sweyn, his face half-flattened by Beorn's body and only his furious eyes visible, fought vainly back. His right hand, groping for a grip that would help him, closed not on part of Beorn but on the handle of a fallen knife. There was a metallic glinting, a spouting of red, true blood red now, and a roar from the crowd. Beorn rolled clear. Godwin, bellowing, hurled himself between them. His nephew sat up, gripping his shoulder, the blood running between his fingers. He had moved barely in time to avoid a stab in the armpit. Godwin snatched the knife from his son's hand and flung it away. "Steel was forbidden!"

"It was that or breaking my knee!"

"Breaking your knee, you stupid oaf!" thundered Godwin. "You should have yielded!"

"He was lying on my face! How could I?"

"I'd have moved if I'd heard you try to speak," said Beorn.

Godwin came and peered at his shoulder. "It's a surface cut, saints be thanked. You moved fast. Just as well! Someone get me water, and a cloth."

"Great Cnut's admirer!" Beorn sneered at his cousin. "A follower of the great lawgiver! Can't even keep the laws of a simple contest!"

The audience was now taking sides. Edward, since Godwin was engrossed in binding his nephew's hurt, took them in hand. "The judgment is clear enough this time!" he announced loudly. "Sweyn Godwinsson was already conquered when he used the knife. The winner is Beorn Estrithson! Lady Eadgyth . . ."

"I won't forget this!" Sweyn shouted at Beorn.

"Nor will I," his cousin assured him, as Godwin tightened the bindings and led him forward to be made formal master of the goshawk.

Afterwards, Beorn murmured to Brand: "Will you take her back to the mews for me? I can't manage the jesses with only one hand." Brand took the hawk on his own fist. Everyone was crowded round the combatants, or paying up bets. Eadgyth was momentarily alone. "Come to the mews with me," he said to her softly. "You said you would see me this evening. And it's stopped raining."

The mews was peaceful after the din in the hall, and beyond its open door they could see the gold reflection of the evening sun on the puddles in the yard. The air was damp and mild, sweet-smelling. "I should love to fly her," Eadgyth said, as Brand secured the hawk on her perch. Her voice was tight, as though she spoke for the sake of it and did not quite know what she should say. Brand took a deep breath. He did not give himself time to hesitate.

"Eadgyth."

"Yes?"

"Are you betrothed to anyone?"

"No, not yet. My mother isn't strong and I keep our hall in order. My father says there's plenty of time . . . and I haven't much dowry."

"Is there anyone you want to marry?"

"Why do you ask?" She did not move, either towards him or away.

"I have no land," he said. "But if I wished to marry, I could ask Earl Godwin for a hide of my own, and he might grant it or get one of his thanes to grant it. And in time I might add to it. I am a freeman and so were my forebears. My mother has Welsh ancestors, they say of good family with land, and my father was a thane's follower, a housecarle."

"You need not worry about that," Eadgyth said with amusement. "Ours is a thane's hall but half of it is falling down. The land's badly drained and we get a living from it but not much else. We sell a few good colts each year; the Barbary horses were the best asset we ever had. My father is Earl Godwin's guest for old times' sake, not for his nobility or wealth! So don't be too humble!" Her wide eyes danced. "But as to marrying—I don't know. I can't say, Brand. I think not yet. I only saw you for the first time less than a month ago."

"It doesn't take a month to know," said Brand. "I knew—in the blink of an eyelid."

But it was not a time for talk. He put his arms round her. She held back at first, but after a moment gave way to him, hip to hip and tongue to tongue, awakening his manhood. He said her name, over and over, as if it were a spell to bind her to him. But she pushed him away, freeing herself. "Too fast!" she said, though she smiled as she spoke. "One day . . . perhaps . . . dear Brand!" Then she vanished, darting out of the door, gone in an instant like one of the fairy folk in the pagan tales. He followed her marvelling, thinking that he knew now what was meant by witchcraft, and being under an enchantment.

He slept with difficulty that night, images of Eadgyth drifting through his dreams, and his body burning where she had pressed hers against it, as if she were made of flame.

4 ✻ *Messenger to Denmark*

"Certainly I lied. What else could I do? Now can we go to sleep?" Godwin sat angrily amid the wolfskins on the bed, lamplight glittering on the coppery fuzz of his chest. His thick hair was flattened where he had lain on it. Gytha's voice had dragged him up when he was already halfway to slumber. He felt at a disadvantage.

Gytha, propped on an elbow, said: "You could have kept silent."

"I could not. It had to be exposed to the sun to be got rid of, like fog. It was between us. I felt it the first time I met him—and I told a lie or two then, I recall. He asked where my instructions came from, to meet Alfred. But he wasn't convinced; I felt that too. I have to work with him, Gytha. No one can serve a lord who distrusts him. I had to tell him plainly that I am not his enemy, that Edward Cyng can put his faith in me as Harold Cyng once did."

Gytha said: "When he asked you outright, you had to reply, yes. But this time no one asked you anything. Unasked, you implied, in public, that you were not in the conspiracy. You said: only honourable service. Godwin . . . it was perjury, without need."

"There *was* need! Alfred was Edward's own brother. He couldn't forgive anyone who had conspired to trap Alfred, for whatever reason. As far as Edward is concerned, I had to be taken by surprise at Gildenford. In his place, I would be the same. Brothers stick together. And it could have been Edward himself, remember! The invitation included him." He added sourly: "Judging by Edward's remarks at the banquet, he still has his doubts! And I would point out that I didn't take part in the killings. As you know."

Gytha lay back slowly. "Whether Edward is deceived or not hardly matters. God will know the truth."

"If God really cares about our little affairs—which I doubt—He'll know my reasons. I trust Him to understand them. I wish you understood too." Suddenly he sat up and banged a knotted fist down on the wolf-pelt. "Religion lays down rules, Gytha, but the rules are too simple! This isn't simple; from the beginning it *wasn't simple!* The rules never tell you what to do when *whatever* you do leads to slaughter and bloodshed and hell for someone! All I could do was put my own lord and own folk first! Suppose I'd let Alfred alone? He and Edward could have been here within a year with a Norman army. I'm certain of it and so was Harefoot!"

"Harefoot was a . . . !"

"Gluttonous degenerate and as cruel as Lucifer, but how many people did he actually harm? Not many. It isn't usual for a king to harm his own. And how many people would a Norman invasion have harmed? Hundreds on hundreds! And what about you and our children? Did you want me to tell Edward all the truth and ruin not only my future but yours and theirs?"

"No, I would have had you say nothing and win Edward through the years ahead."

"Dear God! *Women!* Very well, Gytha, my darling, my love. I was wrong. I should have held my tongue and imperilled the future, or said all and assuredly wrecked it. But since I can't roll time back and unsay my words, or resurrect Alfred either, come to that—will you accept my apology and let me go to sleep?"

Gytha sighed. Presently, since although Godwin had lain down again, his eyes were still open and the lamp at his side was still alight, she said: "I have asked the girl Eadgyth to stay on after the coronation as one of my women."

It was a peace offering.

Godwin accepted it. "Why did you do that?"

"I took to her."

"Look . . ." Godwin, seeing a new cause for dissension loom up, almost groaned. "I know you were pleased with her for brandishing a bucket at Sweyn, and I agree that Sweyn might profit by some rough treatment at female hands. But I don't want him to marry an Eadgyth. Her father is my friend, but that's another matter. Our sons will be able to marry any wealth and any rank, and I'd have them aim high. A good marriage can make a career . . ."

"Indeed?" said Gytha dangerously.

"Yes, indeed! They'll have brides enough to choose from before
I've done. I'll have great men throwing their daughters at us. Somewhere among them will be girls my sons can love. I wish Eadgyth a
good husband, but not Sweyn."

"There's nothing to worry about, in any case." Gytha's voice
was growing sleepy. "She decided not to stay. She looked at her parents and then she looked for advice to her own generation—Edith,
Harold, and, yes, Sweyn himself. It was after the king had left last
night and we were all together tending Harold's bump. She said to
them: 'Shall I stay or go? You know I am depended on at home. Yet
this is such a chance.' Her father muttered something about not
spoiling her opportunities and that she should stay if she wanted to.
Sweyn said: 'Stay!' . . ."

"Oh, did he?"

"But Harold said: 'You would be very welcome but for your
parents' sake I think you should go home with them.' Then she nodded as if he had only said what she was thinking, and politely said to
me that she thanked me for the invitation but could not accept it."

"Good!" said Godwin candidly.

The coronation was over. The king had been led by the hand, by
Alfric Kitehawk of York and Eadsige of Canterbury, to the cathedral, round which Winchester clustered. He had been anointed with
consecrated oil and crowned with a circlet of red gold and exhorted
by the two archbishops in antiphony to uphold the Christian virtues
of charity, humility, and justice. Eadsige laid extra stress on the forgiveness of enemies and on doing good to those who attempted to
harm him. If any eyes turned at that moment towards Earl Godwin
or Queen Emma, neither they nor Edward acknowledged it. After
the ceremony there was banqueting in the royal hall, where Edward
sat enthroned between his archbishops and all the company drank
deep.

The day after that, Edward seized on the business of govern-
ment as a hungry man seizes on a platter of food. He had, it seemed,
come into the estate he had longed for all his life. His counsellors
and administrators, before the first week was out, started to feel
dizzy.

Edward, it appeared, wished to study his realm in detail. He wished to inspect things: mints, ships, manors, shire courts, potteries, tanneries, vineyards, and abbeys. He wished to meet people: thanes, bishops, merchants, town reeves, and master craftsmen. His earls and prelates trekked round the land in his wake, breathless with astonishment. And, very soon, with exhaustion.

Edward also wished to mark his official accession by handing out gifts and honours. Sweyn, Godwin's firstborn, was unexpectedly presented with an earldom of his own. Edward, hardly impressed with his first close view of Sweyn, resisted the idea at first, but Godwin's repeated pleas that "the boy is ripe for responsibility and needs it," coupled with tactful hints about the size of the territory Godwin himself had brought into painless acceptance of Edward's sway and the fact that the earl was willing to share some of it to accommodate his son, at last induced a sympathetic hearing. Sweyn was promoted to charge of a length of Welsh March and departed from Winchester with a dozen men, a mule-train of belongings, a couple of girls picked up from somewhere, and a half-Barbary horse sent as a congratulation gift by Eadgyth's father.

The horse was magnificent enough to cause a public stir, and Harold, at the first opportunity, escaped from the governmental whirl and rode to Norfolk to return with a half-Barb of his own. It was a sorrel like Eadgyth's mare—beautiful, swift, and so spirited that it was almost unmanageable. It was well-nigh impossible to ride the fractious Stormcock in the presence of other horses, and Harold was forced to exercise him in his spare time, alone, which slowed down the horse's education, as Harold did not have much spare time to give him. Occasionally Gyrth, who had a well-mannered pony, and Brand, whose mount was famed for stolidity, did go with him to help him accustom Stormcock to company, but their free time was equally limited.

"There seems no end to it. Edward's a fiend!" Gyrth complained one day when only two hours after they had rowed upriver to Winchester, after going with Godwin on a royal errand to the east coast, they learned that a Witan Council meeting was set for the next day, at which both Gyrth and Brand would be required as part of Godwin's escort.

"I'll have to ride Stormcock on my own," Harold agreed. "Well, I shall have a day off duty, at least!"

Brand, shaking his pallet out on the hall floor, felt envious. Of all duties, escort duty at council meetings was the most tiresome. It meant a weary day standing at a door with nothing to do but think of Eadgyth, and that was no pleasure when she was so far away.

"Will Emma be there?" Gytha asked her husband as he prepared to leave. She drew her cloak round her as they stood talking in the hall porch. The weather, hitherto fine, had broken with a thunderstorm in the night.

"I doubt it. She keeps a court of her own in her own quarters now. Edward's offended with her."

"About Stigand? I heard she'd made him a bishop and the king didn't approve. Was that it?"

"It was. Bishop of East Anglia. Edward doesn't have anything against Stigand for the post—but Edward thinks that promoting bishops is his prerogative and he hasn't spoken to his mother for three weeks. She does it to make sure some power is still in her hands, I think."

"I will never understand how it is between them," Gytha said. "Did the king believe you when you swore her innocence, or not? Do you know for sure? Does anyone?"

The pony was brought and Godwin turned to check the girth, stepping out into the rain. "He never says. But he has other things against her, besides that."

"Yet she stays at court. It's a mystery to me." Gytha smiled. "I don't hear as much gossip as I used to do. I avoid Emma. Why does she stay? Why does Edward allow it? He would be happier if she were elsewhere, surely?"

Gathering his reins to mount, Godwin turned and stared at her. "I thought you knew."

"Knew what?"

"Edward can't banish her from the court. She holds the treasurehouse keys. Harthacnut gave them to her." He set foot in the stirrup and swung himself up. "It was his way of recompensing her for what she suffered at Harefoot's hands, and protecting her if anything should happen to him. He knew—although to you it's outrageous—that Emma does not love Edward her son and never has, and that Edward, to put it mildly, does not love her!"

The Witan Council sat round a long trestle table set across the hall midway between door and hearth. A small fire burned there, for although it was July, it was cold. A chill downpour slanted from a ragged sky to flatten the half-cut hay, and the moaning wind was the kind that made the old folk huddle round their fires and whisper that they heard hounds' voices in the sky, and that Woden's Wild Hunt was abroad. The businesslike air of the council itself was a striking contrast to the elements.

Brand had been posted inside the hall and could watch the proceedings. Edward sat at the table's head, on a thronelike chair with furs flung over it. He was a figure of dignity, his chiselled profile pale against a background of dark red hangings. Edward was a lover of the chase, but the weather never much changed the tone of his white skin.

The earls sat together: Siward, Leofric, Godwin. Sweyn was absent, being already at loggerheads with the Welsh on his borders. Opposite were the two archbishops: Kitehawk as majestic as ever, Eadsige yellow and lean to emaciation with dark hollows about his eyes, a man visibly ill. Next to them was the prelate Sparhafoc, whom Brand recalled from the eve of coronation feast, a small aggressive-jawed man with very bright eyes. Beyond him at the table's foot sat three Norman clerks with vellums and quills before them. Other guards were posted round the hall, and on benches set a little back from the council table were the thanes who were in attendance on the king and his earls. Thane Thored of Alford was one of them, reinstated, it was said, by an Edward who had said with a shrug: "If I have Godwin at my council table I can hardly refuse to have Thored in my country. He at least offered Alfred no lying friendship. Request granted!" On his first appearance at court, it was reported, Thored had done Godwin some unexpected service by commenting thus on his encounter with the earl at Gildenford: "I don't think he was expecting me." This remark had done something to ease the tension between Godwin and his king.

Godwin had been pleased, and coldly amused. "I suppose his testimony carries weight because he dislikes me," he remarked. "He's honest in his crude way, I think. I wouldn't do any favours for him, not after that slaughter! He could moulder away in banishment for the rest of his life, for me."

Besides the Witan members and the thanes, the hall also held
numerous minions—pages and servants who were ready to answer
questions, usher late arrivals, carry messages, fetch wine or cloaks or
documents, sharpen quills, build up the fire, or refill the inkpots.
The floor was sweet with fresh rushes mixed with herbs, and the
king's dogs were asleep in a furry heap on the far side of the fire.
There would be no hunting on this foul day, even if business allowed it.

"The first item," said the principal clerk when greetings had
been exchanged and Kitehawk had formally requested God's blessing on the Witan's work, "is the design for the proposed new issue
of silver pence." He looked at the clerk beside him, who rose and
passed a set of parchments along the table.

"Ah!" Edward leant forward. "Your work, Sparhafoc? My
lords, I should present to you Abbot Sparhafoc of Abingdon, whom
I have lately appointed my royal goldsmith." Sparhafoc stood up
and everyone murmured appropriate congratulations.

The parchments were distributed round the table and passed
from hand to hand. The archbishops paid them more attention than
the earls.

"Hardly see it matters what picture's on the coins as long as the
silver weighs right," Leofric said frankly. "I like this one, though."
He paused over the last drawing to reach him. "Good, warlike air to
it."

"My choice also, sir," Abbot Sparhafoc told him.

"Aye, it would be." Siward chuckled, moving on the bench,
which creaked under him. The muted, formal air of the council did
not suit him. He was too large for it, too untrammelled, too powerful. "Remember you before you joined the Church, Sparhafoc. An
able axeman and a bonny berserker, you were."

Sparhafoc raised a pleading hand. "You remind me of things I
would forget. I did great harm to my fellow men and made many
tears fall before I saw the light and became a thane of the Lord and
poured the violence of my spirit into the creations of my hands. But
a king must look able to lead an army. His folk look to him for protection."

"My own choice," said Edward, overriding all of them, "is
this." He picked a sheet off the table. "Dignified—you have flattered
my face, Sparhafoc—but with more the air of a shepherd king, a

peaceful prince. I would be thought a bringer of peace rather than war. Does anyone object?"

No one did. The drawings were returned to the clerks, with a cross on the one chosen, and the chief clerk announced a fresh item. "Earl Godwin to report on the ports willing to provide ships for the new navy."

Godwin put his fingertips together on the table and said: "I returned only yesterday from the coast, where I met the local thanes of Sandwich and Romney and also port reeves and harbourmasters and the captains of ships plying round the southeast coasts. Both those ports are willing to maintain ships ready for any call. I found them, in fact, well aware of the necessity. Sandwich offers ten and Romney fifteen. Sandwich has her vessels already; Romney must provide five new ones. Recruitment for the crews has begun and timber been marked down."

"What size ships?" Siward asked.

"Mostly eighty-foot, thirty-six-oar warships. Romney offers two larger, sixty-oar vessels among the new ships and proposes that the other three should be small, fast skutas. Of the Sandwich fleet three are skutas."

"And who'll be responsible for seeing that recruitment, building, and training are carried out?" Leofric enquired.

"The port authorities, with my eye upon them. I shall carry out a certain number of training exercises myself."

"And what," said Edward, "will be the total cost?"

This proved to be a knotty question, involving the conversion of royal dues to be balanced with a charge on the treasury. Edward seemed concerned to avoid payments from the treasury. The financial problems of the Kent coast fleet were finally shelved for the time being as beyond immediate solution and Edward raised the question of hired ships. He had to raise his voice at the same time, for the weather outside was worsening. Gusts of wind had begun to drive through the walls and hangings like attacking swords, and the tapestries were billowing.

"It's to be hoped that our ships will be more weatherworthy than this hall! Godwin?"

"I have recruited ten mercenary warships so far and I have a promise of a further four. I am waiting for news to reach me from Flanders concerning those. The ten so far include . . ."

He broke off. The wind, at a new crescendo, was doing damage somewhere. Something struck the outside wall with a crash, and from the courtyard came voices and running feet. Another crash overhead made them look up startled to the roofbeams. Godwin glanced round the hall and found Brand. "Go out, Woodcutter, and see what it is," he said.

Brand went, hurrying across the small antechamber to the outer door and down the steps into an onslaught of weather. Wind and rain driving into his face stopped him on the lowest step. He had to wipe his eyes in order to see.

On the other side of the courtyard was an outhouse meant to hold pitchforks and spades for the stable and the kitchen garden. It had been run up quickly and no one had bothered to thatch it. A few split pine logs laid close and roughly nailed had been enough. Now the nails were rusting and the wind had got at the logs. It was spiritedly tearing them off while a crowd of thralls stood in the porch of another building and pointed excitedly.

There was nothing here that concerned the council. Brand, however, paused on the point of going in again. Out of the kitchen-house a few yards away a girl had come, carrying a tray with a leather wine bottle on it and some wine cups. She plunged into the weather, head bent against the wind, and set off across the court-yard. A gust blew her loose-fitting hood back and Brand recognised her. It was Hild Ericsdaughter, that hedgesparrow of a girl who had somehow got a place now in Lady Emma's service. Gytha, who had heard all about it from Eric Merchant, to whom it was a matter of enormous pride, had remarked afterwards that she was sorry for the girl. "She sounds like just a simple child and those mannerly cats Lady Emma keeps will put upon her. She ought to go home and marry her wool merchant. When a girl has a good man waiting for her, she shouldn't waste him."

And here she was, no doubt being put upon as Gytha had foretold, since she was the one sent out in the rain to fetch refreshments. And there, spinning into the air above her bent and heedless head, was a great, black, nail-studded pine log. Brand bounded forward and yanked her out of the way. He was barely in time. It fell at her feet, splashing both of them with puddle water. The goblets jarred on the tray and slid, and the wine bottle went after them.

"Oh, *dear!*" Hild knelt in the mud to rescue them. On the roof of the outhouse another log shifted ominously.

"Come away for the love of God!" Brand said urgently. "The rest of that roof's about to . . ."

He meant to say "go" but the event got ahead of him. The wind, pouncing out of the sky like a huge, invisible falcon, seized the last few logs in its talons and snatched them upwards. Brand grabbed Hild's arm and dragged her forcibly to the shelter of the main hall porch. The logs descending smashed against a stable wall and the horses inside whinnied anxiously.

"The *tray*!" Hild wailed.

"Thunor take the tray! He's already taken that roof!"

Hild giggled, but the tray and its contents still lay in the mud and her merriment stopped short.

"Lady Emma's waiting for the wine. She'll be angry."

So she feared her mistress. He was not surprised. Brand had now seen Emma several times. He had never spoken to her but he had heard her address others. Report said she never struck her women, but when you had such piercing eyes and such a stabbing tongue, you didn't need to lift your hand. Emma looked, and her household quaked. Emma spoke, and her household wept.

"Wait," said Brand.

He went forward warily, one eye on what was left of the shattered roof, picked up wine cups and bottle—fortunately still stoppered—and came back. "The goblets need a wash," he said. "But no one can blame you."

"She expects things at once," said Hild miserably. "I must hurry. Thank you."

Brand eyed her thoughtfully and beckoned to a thrall. "Go into the hall, find someone who can give a message to Earl Godwin, and say I am helping clear the wreckage of the roof that the wind tore apart. My name is Brand Woodcutter." He turned back to Hild. "I'll come with you and say what happened. I must go back soon too, so I must also hurry."

Hild led the way towards the kitchen in search of fresh wine cups. "Are you unhappy here?" he asked as they hastened through the rain. "Couldn't you go home if you liked?"

"Yes, but my father would be displeased. He's so proud that I'm here, serving the queen. Only it's still all so new. I make mistakes. I'll learn to fit in, in time."

She didn't look the part either, Brand thought. Not now, anyway, with her green wool underskirt dabbled in mud and her hair in two dripping tails, coming out of plait. "Put up your hood," he said. "It falls off. It's too big. One of the girls let me borrow it because mine is old, but it doesn't fit."

"How in the world," Brand asked with some annoyance as they reached the steamy kitchen and stood drying themselves off beside the fire, over which the day's supply of chickens was sizzling on the spit, "did your father get you the post?" He shoved the wine cups into the hands of a scullion who appeared through the vapours. "Get clean ones. It's for Lady Emma and she's waiting." Eadgyth, he thought, would have filled the post much better. If only she were where Hild now was. In Winchester. In the royal hall. Saved by him from the storm. Beside him in this kitchen.

"He did some service for her," Hild said, "I don't quite know what. A letter or a message. My brother Rolf carried it to Denmark. He trades there—I told you, didn't I? Sword-blades and now ship-masts. Thank you." She took a fresh set of silver cups from the scullion. "I must hurry back."

He went beside her across the courtyard. Their first dash through the downpour brought them to the hall porch where they drew breath for a second plunge. As they paused, Brand said awkwardly: "I shouldn't have questioned you. You shouldn't talk about your mistress's business—her letters and messages and who she corresponds with. Not to anyone."

"Shouldn't I? Was there something wrong about it—about her writing to Denmark?"

To Hild, bred in a house where only sins were secrets and sins of any magnitude as rare as cuckoos in February, the idea of secrecy as a duty was quite foreign. Her wide, innocent eyes irritated Brand. Her father was a fool, he thought. He should have kept her in Dover and married her to some worthy man, as Gytha had said. Her brother had taken a message to Denmark, had he? She had chosen a private man with other business there already, instead of an official courier, had she? And neither Rolf nor Eric had thought it odd. The whole family were wantwits and simpletons who shouldn't be allowed within five hundred forest and fenland leagues of a she-spider like Emma. With a huge effort he throttled his fury.

"Not wrong," he said slowly. "But for royal folk . . . all folk of rank . . . life is . . . is complicated. They have enemies. They have people in their care. They must choose sometimes between this man's good and that of someone else. Don't tell your mistress you have talked about her. And don't talk about her to anyone else. You understand?" He could have shaken her. "Well, this rain isn't stopping. Come on or we'll never get there!"

He went up to Emma's bower with her and told the formidable lady who reigned there that her newest waiting maid had come near being killed while fetching a tray at her behest. He did it neatly, not as one defending a timid girl from a harsh mistress but as a courteous passerby telling an anxious employer news which she would be grateful to hear. It worked: Emma, who had already taken a breath for a set-down, let it out again, thanked him, and told Hild quite amiably to go and dry and tidy herself. Brand bowed, withdrew, and made haste back to his post. To the rest of the Witan proceedings he paid no attention at all.

Hild had escaped being stunned by the pine logs. Instead, she had almost stunned the man who rescued her.

Denmark. *Denmark!*

5 ✠ Summer Thunder

August came in gold and glowing, the July storms forgotten. The corn harvesters were in the fields, working with rhythmic scythes, muscular brown backs deepening to seasoned oak in the sun. Farmers watched cattle fatten in the rich grass and the milk gushed merrily into the pails. Fruit bulged on the twig; forest paths once broad grew dim and narrow between growths of heavy foliage. It was a good year, a golden year, an omen of promise for King Edward's new-come reign.

Through the effulgent weather the life of house and court went on. Godwin journeyed off with the king once more, this time taking Gyrth and Tostig and leaving Harold behind. He also left Brand, who found himself once more bidden to accompany Harold about the countryside to assist the volatile Stormcock's education. It was sometimes a doubtful privilege; he met jealousy among his peers, although not from Longshanks, who thought that foolish and once clouted the head of a colleague who made a remark about belly-crawlers.

Brand himself was faintly embarrassed by this singling-out. In a complex way the Godwins were embarrassing. They had a knack of making him feel, in the presence of any of them, physically under-sized, slow-witted, and clumsy. Only Beorn, who was after all only Godwin's nephew, seemed of normal human stature and attributes.

Though Brand did not resent this state of affairs, it still worried him. He knew others shared it. He had heard one of the thrall women say admiringly of Harold: "He's like a lion, a golden lion—

there's something that wonderful about him." And the woman she was talking to, the old kitchen crone whom everyone knew as a pagan still, said: "Aye, he's like the Corn King come among us again, with that hair and those blue eyes."

He had also seen the men in the fields look up and grin as he and Harold rode by, himself short and dark on a stumpy black pony whose legs twinkled in the effort to keep up with its companion, and big blond Harold on his fiery, elegant sorrel. He did not blame them, for no doubt the contrast was funny. Yet at times he saw an image of himself that he disliked. "I'm for the Standing Stones today. There's a man that way I want to see. Coming, Brand?" Harold would say, striding through the hall and picking his bow off the wall as he went, his voice offhand but his grin friendly, melting annoyance. And Brand would fall in behind, to follow Harold to the stable. And in his mind's eye he would see a picture, of a small black dog running at its master's heels, summoned by a whistle.

The extraordinary Godwin air of belonging to an altogether more exalted and wiser race of beings had some uses, however. It was natural to turn to them for advice when in uncertainty. In that August, one month after the stormstruck Witan Council meeting at Winchester, after long hesitation, Brand did so.

They had ridden through the home farm and Harold had commented rudely on a poor piece of thatching. They had visited a thane, Ethelwulf by name, whose lands lay to the northwest of Winchester and who was involved in a dispute with a neighbour about field boundaries. They had come at midday to the circle of immense, grey, upright stones that stood out on the open plain far from human dwellings, the stones that Tostig had said had been raised by giants before history began. Here Harold and Brand rested; the horses hobbled nearby. They had rye bread and white cheese, wine flasks and a piece of cold roast fowl each. They sat with their backs propped against sun-warmed stone, looking out on a vista of rolling plain under a wide, clear sky.

Brand swallowed a mouthful and said: "My lord, I need counsel."

"What about? You sound very solemn." Harold flicked meat juice off his fingers and considered the blue distance with screwed-up eyes. "There's a peregrine falcon over there. We should watch where it goes. Two died in the mews last month. Is it about a girl?"

"No . . ."

"Because if it is, I'm the wrong man to ask. They confuse me too. My mother is at me to marry, and half of me wants to. But the other half wants to be free, to go adventuring at will without leaving a wife at home to grieve. But I have heard that you lately asked my father if he would give you a holding if you married so I thought . . ."

"I did and he agreed, but that isn't it. It may never happen; the girl has plenty of choice and perhaps she won't choose me. I . . ."

"What's her name? Can I help?"

"No. No, I don't think so." Harold would only laugh if he heard that the Woodcutter had raised his eyes to Eadgyth Thanesdaughter. "No, I want to ask you about something quite different."

He heard a trace of desperation in his own voice. Harold also heard it. In a different tone he said: "Tell me."

"I want to know," said Brand carefully, "whether it is right to pass on news learned by chance—from someone who shouldn't have told it."

"What kind of news?"

"I'm . . . not sure. It could mean much or nothing. The . . . the man who told . . ." He stopped.

"Told you. If you pretend it all happened to a friend of yours I will pick you up bodily and dash out your brains against this stone." Harold patted the bluestone upright behind him. "The man who told you. Yes. Go on."

"He's harmless and ignorant." Brand took the plunge. "He knows nothing of courts and affairs. He didn't in the least understand what his bit of talk could mean. But it was gossip about his . . . lord and he would get into trouble if it were known he had talked. What shall I do?"

"Can't you find out more? If this mysterious titbit, whatever it is, has no importance, then you can forget it. But if it has . . . look, what do you mean by importance? Important to whom? You had better tell me the rest."

Brand wished he had held his tongue. Harold watched him. The blue eyes had narrowed and hardened, were probing into Brand's mind as a surgeon probes a wound. "Brand," said Harold Godwinsson quietly, "why are you silent?"

One of the difficulties, Brand discovered, was to say openly that any knowledge in his, Brand's, insignificant possession could possibly matter to anyone like King Edward. But he got it out in the end. "It could concern the king."

"As a man or as a king?"

"I don't understand."

"If it only matters to the king in private, to the man called Edward, that's one thing. If it matters to Edward the king then it probably matters to half the inhabitants of the land. That's the difference. Which?"

"Both, I suppose." Brand spoke doubtfully.

Harold straightened his back with a jerk. Stormcock flung up a nervous head and laid back his ears.

"Brand, are you telling me that you've heard some rumour that quite possibly concerns this whole land and the folk in it and that you're wondering whether to *keep it to yourself*? This isn't your farm now, where nothing ever happens that ripples beyond your own fishpond! Tell me what it is at once!"

Brand flinched. Like Hild herself, he thought bitterly, he had talked too much. And Hild might pay for it. Obstinately, he said: "I must protect the man who told me."

"Brand, are you out of your senses? I'll protect your fool of a chatterer if I can, rest easy on that. But *what did he tell you*?" The blue eyes were the colour of summer skies. With thunder about.

"At or just after the crowning of King Edward," said Brand unwillingly, "the Lady Emma sent a private messenger to Denmark. He was a man who was going there anyway on other business, not a court courier. And she rewarded his family well."

"A private messenger to Denmark," said Harold thoughtfully. "To whom in Denmark?"

"I don't know."

"Who was the messenger? Brand, I have a right to command you!"

Into Brand's memory flickered the image of Godwin by a sun-flecked river with an ornate barge on it, claiming that he had given honourable service to the house of Cnut. But because of that honourable service a young man had lost his eyes and died of gangrene, and six hundred men had been massacred. What would Emma do to Hild? Or Edward to Hild's brother?"

"You had better tell me." Thunder could also be soft.

"He was a Dover merchant with business among the Danes. Rolf Ericsson. We brought his father's mule-train up from Dover last March. You met Rolf then."

"Ericsson? Yes, of course I know him. He's in Denmark now, that's right. We're going to look at the blades he brings back, and there was talk of masts for the Romney fleet. He's due back in October. What in the name of Christendom did he want to turn errand boy for Emma for? And what was the reward?"

"A place in Emma's court for his sister," said Brand wearily.

"Ah! It wouldn't be the sister and not a man at all who let it out to you, would it? Is she the girl you want to marry?"

"Yes. No." said Brand shortly.

"Then how did you come to be talking together in such a trustful way?"

"It was chance. She's a simpleton in many ways but perfectly innocent. I wouldn't like . . . Emma isn't kind to her."

"Emma's never been kind to anyone in her life except her beloved Harthacnut!" Harold's face darkened. "They say she hated Edward. Her own son!" He shook himself, as if throwing off a nightmare. "Listen. I will safeguard this pair of idiots, Rolf and his daft sister, if I can. Thank the saints you had sense enough to talk before it was too late. Don't look like that! Do you realise what Emma must be after? If the message had been important but honest she'd have sent a proper courier with an escort. If it were trivial but honest she wouldn't have rewarded it past a handful of silver. You don't elevate a Hild Ericsdaughter in the cause of ordering a cargo of pine logs! That message wasn't honest and it wasn't trivial. And I'd remind you that Emma holds the treasury keys. The treasure's Edward's by right, but he has to go to her for access. Maybe she's found another use for it."

"But we can't be sure . . . ." Brand began feebly. Harold's ideas matched his own, worked out miserably through restless nights.

Harold was up and tightening Stormcock's girths. "No, we can't be sure. So we'll make sure. We must go to my father. Back to Thane Ethelwulf first—his is the nearest house—for a pack of food and a better mount for you. That slug won't keep up with the pace I'm going to make, and it's time Stormcock here learned to be useful. And then we ride east. Get into the saddle! Hurry!"

As they thundered at full gallop along the track to Thane Ethelwulf's domains, the men in the cornfields straightened and stared after them, scythes arrested in the air.

"Anyone 'ud think," said one gnarled gaffer watching the dust cloud dwindle, "they'd seen the Northmen coming!"

6 ⚔ Messenger from Denmark

To belong to the entourage of Queen Emma, Hild knew, was an honour. But within a very short time she had learnt that the post of honour is not a guarantee of content.

The first warning came at nightfall, the day her father left her there. In the chamber the girls all shared, her belongings looked plain among the fashionable clothes and jewellery of the others. One girl asked in a bored, amused voice whether glass beads were all Hild had. "No amber, even? Where is your home?"

She told them her father was a Dover merchant. A merchant, in Hild's understanding, was a person who travelled, whose knowledge and dignity were worthy of respect. But the girl, who was Norman and had a thick accent, said: "Oh, a merchant? *Mon père*—my father—he is a knight," and spoke to her no more.

But she pushed the first unease away. It was a splendid thing to be here. She would get to know the other girls and make friends with them. They were a mixed group: Normans from Emma's homeland, Danish and English daughters of Cnut's one-time followers. Dover was a cosmopolitan place, and Hild found this natural. She had a smattering herself of several tongues and a fair command of Norman French. She would soon fit in.

She had been there over a month, and her father and brother had departed coastwards out of reach, when she at last saw that she would never fit in, and saw why. All the others, whatever their homeland, were daughters of warriors. To them, a man who wore no helmet and bore neither axe nor shield was not worth a second glance. Hild, who like her father considered that it was the men of learning and commerce who were the apex of civilisation, found this both odd and absurd. Most of the girls could read and write, she found, but not as well as she could, and they set no store by it. Some of them considered such things actually unfit for their menfolk. Their minds and hers could not meet. The fact that Emma sometimes asked her to read aloud to them all, and approved her fluency, did not increase her popularity.

Hild, without thinking about it as strange, had spent much of her life among men. She had no sisters and her mother was long dead. She had kept her father's house and welcomed his guests: merchants, sailors, travellers of all kinds. The few female thralls he kept obeyed her, and she did not share their living quarters. The bitch potential of concentrated femininity when one had no means of retaliation was a new and monstrous discovery.

So too was the power of fear. For Emma's ladies went in dread of Emma's tongue and Emma's summary dismissals and would divert her anger onto anyone else rather than support it themselves. Hild, the odd one out, from a lower social class, became a scapegoat. She thought Emma was probably aware of this but found it only amusing. Emma largely despised her own sex.

She also enjoyed wearing other women out. Never, Hild thought, as one marathon of a day succeeded another, had she been so weary. Emma rose at dawn to attend Mass and her women rose with her, forbidden to yawn. The breakfast that followed was scanty and was succeeded by a prolonged business session in Emma's solar, where her women stitched or wove while she received callers. Emma liked to hear news of the outside world and paid well for it. Thanes came, returning from their annual service at the king's court, and told her of its doings. Bards came and merchants. Travelling priests came to offer additions to Emma's well-known collection of saintly relics. Pedlars came and itinerant workmen. Emma talked to them all.

The gossip ranged widely. A wizened merchant who had been to the eastern verge of Christendom brought news of the intrigues and triumphs of Harald Hardraada, the exiled uncle of Harthacnut's old enemy, Magnus of Norway. A Norman knight riding to offer King Edward his sword told of the young Duke William's strengthening grip on his surprised duchy. There was news of a family feud here, an outbreak of plague there. Hild pushed a needle back and forth through an altar cloth and listened. It was interesting, no doubt. But why Emma so wished for information now that she was retired from power and growing old, she could not understand.

Not that it concerned her. Her job was to stitch evenly, fetch Emma's gloves or wine promptly on request, and pray that if anything got mislaid today, the culprit would not think of saying: "Hild had it last." Later she might have to read and suffer Emma's two-edged compliments, which would always include a slighting reference to someone else's shortcomings and so would breed spite in the someone else. They were the only compliments Emma ever paid her and she could have done without them. If they didn't read, there would be singing, and she would suffer in the opposite way. Either the lyre would pass her by or she would have to sing and have her performance greeted with pointed silence or silvery titters. Whether she did things well or ill, it brought trouble. She had seen hares cowering in the grass, hoping by their stillness to escape the eyes of the hawk. She knew how they felt.

She supposed she should be glad there was no physical abuse. But if the girls had ever hit her, at least she could have hit back. Against these subtle cruelties there was no defence.

In the August after the crowning, Emma moved her court from the royal hall into her own house, whose gateway opened on Winchester's main street. It was rumoured that Edward had recommended her withdrawal there. Winchester gossip had it that the king and his mother were on bad terms. Hild did not know if this were true.

But she preferred the new surroundings. Emma's private hall had been part of her morning gift when she had married Ethelred long ago and, following the English custom, had asked her husband for a present on the morning after their first night together. This house too had a Norman-style hall and bower and was furnished with fine tapestries and carven stools and settles. The life of the main street went on beyond the fence, but one did not constantly encounter intimidating nobles and swaggering housecarles, as one did at the king's court when Edward was in residence.

The mellow summer faded slowly. October came, and November. It turned grey and chilly, with dark mornings when they all rose shivering by candlelight. There were fogs.

Hild was used to sea mists but had somehow thought that inland fog would be rare. The clammy pall that now descended on
Winchester surprised her. The skylines vanished. Droplets of water
beaded the fence and plopped from the thatch. Candles were lit at
noonday to make needlework possible. By the third day of it Hild
had come to hate it, for it made her feel more shut in than ever
amongst her uncongenial companions. She sat by a window glazed at
vast expense to let in light without weather, toiling at the altar cloth,
which had been their principal opus now for months. Emma was
stitching too, since no callers had arrived today, while Rohese, the
Norman girl who had been rude on Hild's first evening, had the task
of reading. Hild was glad it was Rohese and not herself, but she
winced inwardly at the Norman girl's halting efforts. The book was
a life of King Alfred and should have been interesting, but Rohese's
dreadful accent and arbitrary pauses for breath made it nearly impossible to follow. The Bishop Stigand had made them this English
translation at Emma's behest. Rohese was wasting his work.

" 'At that time Alfred with his lords. And some of his followers
lived in the woods . . .' "

" '. . . with his lords and some of his followers lived in the
woods,' " said Emma irritably.

" '. . . lived in the woods and marshes of Somerset . . . a
wretched life of trouble. He had nothing to live on. Save what he
could carry off . . .' "

" 'Nothing to live on save what he could carry off.' You breathe
when the sense tells you, not when you feel like it. Read that passage
again."

Rohese flushed. " 'At that time Alfred with his lords and . . .' "

"Stop!" barked Emma.

A sound outside had caught her attention. At the gate beyond
the blanketing fog there was a clatter. Hild pushed the window a
little open. Horses snorted, voices challenged and were answered.
Riders loomed below, their mounts' breath rising to mix with the
November vapours. Rohese, glancing at Emma for permission and
receiving a nod, put the book down and came to look.

"It is the king, madam," she said.

Below, Edward was dismounting at the steps of the hall. His
companions did likewise. Among them Hild recognised the Earl of
Wessex, whom she knew by sight, and others that she thought were

his sons. There were some nobles she could not name, and a woman, tall, wrapped in a green cloak and without attendants. Then there were some soldiers, gathered round a man without helmet or arms, who seemed to be a prisoner.

Her heartbeat checked, jumped to catch up with itself, and began to gallop frantically. The captive was Rolf.

Her brother Rolf. His hands were bound to his saddle pommel and mist silvered his bared head. They were freeing his hands now and pulling him off the pony.

"Ladies, take up your work again," said Emma. "Hild, shut the window. The fog is getting in."

Hild obeyed and sat looking at her work. Her hands trembled. Footsteps below announced that the newcomers were passing through the hall. Then Edward, his companions close behind him, appeared at the top of the bower stairs, and like the rest she dropped what she was holding and rose to curtsey. Edward ignored them, and confusedly they sat down again. He strode towards his mother. The chamber, suddenly full of men, apparently dwindled in size, and the ladylike atmosphere was shattered as though it were a glass vessel struck by a stone.

"Good morning, Edward," Emma said. She did not rise. "What a distinguished company! Earl Siward . . . Leofric . . . my lord Godwin too. Harold Godwinsson . . . Sweyn . . . no, Earl Sweyn now, of course. My felicitations, Earl Sweyn. My lady Gytha . . ."

That was the woman in green. Hild recognised her now.

"We can dispense with the social formalities," Edward was saying coldly. He spoke in French, as Emma had done. But in the next sentence he abruptly switched to English. "Our business today is business *only*." He pulled a rolled parchment from under his mantle and thrust it at her. "Your answer from Magnus in Denmark, madam. I brought it myself. I felt sure you were waiting for it."

Emma's carven face did not alter. She unrolled the document calmly, as one who enquires the nature of an unsought gift. She read the strong black lettering with attention and without haste. "So he is occupied elsewhere just now. A pity. How did you come by this, Edward?"

"We caught your messenger boy," said Leofric. His tone was unmistakable. The king's man spoke to the king's enemy. Emma's eyes narrowed. The housecarles had brought their prisoner up in the wake of the earls, and now they thrust him forward. He fell kneeling before Emma's chair. Edward stepped away from him. Rolf's glance, darting about the chamber, found Hild and sent her a message of terror and appeal. At close quarters she saw that he was not only frightened; he was also exhausted and hurt. Blood was crusted round his nostrils and a fresh thread of it ran from the corner of his mouth. His face was bruised. She clasped her cold hands tightly, afraid too, and bewildered.

"He was brought to me at Gloucester," said Edward. "Caught with the letter on him."

Among the housecarles Hild suddenly discovered Brand. She saw the red starting under his tanned skin when he found her eyes on him. She wondered why.

"I have never seen this man before," said Emma truthfully.

"We know that. Don't play at innocence! His father made the arrangement with you. Why did you do it?"

"You'd never understand," said Emma after a pause.

"I wish to hear." Edward's face too might have been a carving, out of ivory or pale stone. They looked alike.

"Very well," said Emma grimly. She sat with hands folded uncompromisingly, left above right. "Because you are the son of your father, Edward. And this land needs a stronger leader than either of you. I sent for one."

"A strong leader!" Edward sounded as if his breath had been punched out of him. "A strong . . . ! Do you *know* what you've tried to do?" He leant over her, his palms on the acorn-carved arms of her chair. "I can remember," he said savagely, "when I was a child, you were afraid of the Northmen too. Think of the days when we went in dread of the Vikings, when guards watched day and night round the shores, looking for the serpent-prowed longships to slink in out of the haar, listening for oars in the dark. When folk prayed in their churches week in, week out, 'From the fury of the Northmen, good Lord deliver us!' You prayed too. I heard you. Don't you remember how we once came on a settlement they'd attacked on the east coast? The burnt-out homesteads? The bodies? The little girl, no more than eleven, they'd raped and killed doing it? You were afraid then, too. Before Cnut came. Before you found that . . ."

"There are maidens in this room," said Emma stonily.

Edward looked taken aback.

"You were about to make a coarse remark. Never mind how I know. I do know. Behave yourself, Edward. As for fear of the Northmen, a raider is one thing and a ruler another. Magnus would have come as a ruler . . ."

"Would anyone in his path have thought so?"

"I wanted him here," said Emma, her voice roughening with anger, "to keep raiders off! There were raiders long ago, in your father's day, the father you resemble so closely! I wanted no repetition of those times, no more ineffectual resistance, no more weakness and foolishness and defeats!"

"My father was not weak! He was betrayed."

"He couldn't judge men. That's a weakness. He trusted where he should have killed. And he never fought hard enough. He tried promises and inducements where he should have stuck to the sword. He even tried marriage. He married me!" Emma snorted. "All in the hope that my brother would forget our northern forebears and close the Norman harbours to the longships. Well, Richard didn't, because their trade was good. I could have told Ethelred that! So then your fool of a father taxed the folk to the edge of starvation to buy the raiders off. Twenty-four thousand pounds of good English silver in one year went away in the longships to swell the Keep Scandinavia Solvent Fund . . ."

Black eyes glittering, Emma took stock of her audience. They were speechless and immobile, as if mention of that colossal sum had been a Medusa spell turning them to stone.

"And when the Danegeld failed," Emma went on ruthlessly, "he tried hostages. And when the truce he struck for their lives was broken, he slaughtered them. And one of them was Sweyn of Denmark's sister!"

"She *was* a hostage, and her husband was one of the truce-breakers."

"She should never have been accepted as a hostage in the first place! Your father was a wantwit! For that piece of madness we had Sweyn Forkbeard and his son Cnut here to take her weregild out in blood. Whose fault was that? When we were driven to Normandy, I heard that folk turned out of their homes to *welcome* Forkbeard, because he'd sworn that if they took him for king in Ethelred's stead, he would be a faithful lord to them. And he was, and Cnut after him. Northmen make fierce foes but honest kings and strong ones, who keep the other foes off. Cnut guarded England as though it were his treasurehouse . . ."

"Ah," interrupted Edward. "The treasurehouse . . ."

"I didn't want England at the mercy of another Ethelred. You, Edward, even look like your father . . ."

"I am amazed," said Edward furiously, "that you forbore to poison me while you were at your scheming. Why didn't you?"

"Because contrary to rumour," snapped Emma, "I do not murder my own children! You have a hundred friends in Normandy. You could live there in peace. I wish you would. Then I would not have to live in the company of a son who thinks I once plotted his death!"

"I see," said Edward. "Now we come to it!"

"I shan't waste time trying to convince you, Edward. I don't believe in waste. Godwin has said I am innocent. Unfortunately, Godwin has also told a tale of a courier, purporting to be mine, who brought him instructions to arrange my son's escort from Dover—a courier he could not afterwards name or trace. A clever story, Godwin, which no one now can prove or disprove. And Thane Edwin told the same story, except that in his case it was a clerk who approached him at court, asking him to bear a missive to Normandy on my behalf . . ."

Godwin shrugged. "That is what happened. Perhaps they were Harefoot's creatures and we were deceived. I have often said as much."

"And much good it has done me!" Emma turned once more to Edward. "The archbishops have also declared that I would never do such a thing. But you think you know better. Magnus was a fool to address his letter to me so openly. I sent his to one of his followers, a man called Olaf Goatbeard, who would pass the enclosure on . . ."

She stopped, sensing a change in the air. Godwin, Harold, and Edward were exchanging looks and glancing at the still-kneeling Rolf. Rolf raised his head. He said sullenly: "I told you, I *did not know* the letter was for the lord Magnus. I was told to give it to a private man, this Olaf Goatbeard. And I did. What was so wrong in it? It was an errand for the Lady Emma." He stopped, breathing short, near crying. The blood from his mouth was running freely now, and Hild saw that two teeth were gone. He scanned the faces round him, the king's, Emma's, searching for hope. "They're going to hang me!" he said hoarsely to Emma. "For the love of God, for taking a letter to this nobody, this Olaf Goatbeard, for you!"

Hild, in whom a terrible confusion of horror, guilt, fury, grief, and pity had been mounting one upon another, broke into a wail.

She threw down her section of altar cloth and overturned her stool, flinging herself down by Rolf. She said frenziedly to Emma: "They can't! He's done nothing! Save him! Please, please, save him!"

"I would," said Emma, "if my son would listen to me. But I am afraid my appeals would find him deaf. You had best ask him yourself."

Edward was too tall to be easily addressed from the floor. Hild stood up, and standing, regained dignity. She looked into his face. She had forgotten he was a king. She said: "Taking that letter was a service done in return for my place here. Rolf is my brother. I heard the agreement made. I am as guilty as he is. But it was only a letter to someone called Olaf, in Denmark. So is the guilt so great? That is the truth."

Edward did not reply, or even look at her. Her gaze slid off him like clawing fingers off a granite cliff. She found herself looking at Brand instead. He too turned away, and this time she understood.

"I told you by accident!" She pointed at him. "I told you by mistake, and you told *them*. You *told* them!"

"I see," observed Emma from behind her. "You let it out, did you? Then this sorry scene is of your making. I see."

Uproar suddenly broke out while Hild, sobbing, sank down beside Rolf and wiped his mouth. The earls were all talking, shouting, and gesticulating at once. Brand pushed his way through them and came to her. She looked ready to spit at him. He said: "Hild, I'm sorry, I had to. You don't understand. There might have been an invasion. War with the Danes. Hild. I'm sorry."

"I wish they'd hang *you!*" she shouted into his face.

Harold heard her. He too detached himself from the crowd and came to her. He put his hands over her wrists and pulled her to her feet. His grip was steadying; no one else could ride Stormcock at all. "Hild. Listen, Hild. He is telling the truth. No, *listen* to me. That's right. He had to tell us. Do you know the tales of the Viking raids? The first raid on Dorchester long ago, and how the king's reeve rode down in friendship to greet the three strange ships he took for merchantmen and tell them where to bring their goods, and how the berserkers slaughtered all his men and made a bloody eagle of him there upon the sand. Do you know what a bloody eagle is? Yes, I see that you do. That is what that letter to Denmark could have loosed on us, Hild. Brand did not tell lightly, believe me. It was I he told in the end, hesitant, fearful for you and your brother. I did the rest. Blame me if you will. But if I had not, it could have been your home in flames, your menfolk slain, yourself forced on the threshold of your own house . . ."

"But *Rolf*! They're going . . ."

"You remind me," said Harold, smiling, "of a promise."

The clamour had died down. Harold said into the new quietness: "I plead for the life of this man Rolf Ericsson. I will represent him in combat if the king desires, or find oathswearers for him. I declare him innocent of wrong."

The noise at once began again. Through it Leofric's voice could be heard advocating Rolf's instant death and Siward's booming tones enquiring if Leofric would fight Harold to settle it. Harold was a much better warrior, they all knew that. And then Gytha came forward, whom they had all forgotten. She borrowed Harold's sword and got a hearing by pounding the hilt on the floor. Once again the din subsided.

"I came," said Gytha, collecting the eyes of her audience, "because Harold's man Brand begged me to. Because of this girl Hild and her foolish family, for whom he feels responsible." She addressed herself to Edward. "There is only one traitor in this room, and it is not this frightened boy. Send these children home, my lord, and deal with your real foe."

"The girl will go home anyway," said the real foe icily. "I won't have her about me." Emma reverted to her habit of mixing French with English. "A timorous, loquacious nitwit!"

"That's enough," said Edward. He had been far away in thought. Now he came to life again. "Now we shall speak. Let us deal with . . . shall I call them the pawns? . . . first. Some would advise that we hang both before your eyes, madam, hoping to sicken you by the outcome of your own evildoing . . ."

"I would, for one," muttered Leofric.

"But we shall not do so," Edward continued, "because frankly we fear you are beyond the reach of pity, madam, beyond even the saving grace of remorse. Therefore they are set free." He nodded at Rolf and Hild, who stared, unbelieving. "Out!" he said. Gytha hustled them to the door. "You too," she whispered to Brand. "Someone must escort them home. You go, and make your peace on the way. Get provisions at our house." She chivvied the bewildered trio down the steps and came back.

"So much for the pawns. Now for the queen." Edward surveyed his mother. "You, madam, will go into retirement. You may choose a convent and one woman to go with you. As long as you choose and leave Winchester today. Before you go you will hand the keys of the treasury to me. You are not to be trusted with them. Who would you offer them to next, I wonder? Have you anything to say?"

"I repeat," said Emma, "I never waste my time." She added softly, as if speaking to herself: "I'm glad I have outlived that woman Elfgift, at least. I was pleased when I heard she was dead. I wish Harthacnut were still alive. That is all."

"That is my family life," Edward observed as Emma, upright and haughty, rode into the fog with Rohese as her sole companion, apart from the armed escort. The other ladies were making ready to go to their homes and Edward was preparing to make himself comfortable in Emma's hall, since his own was not expecting him.

Godwin said carefully: "You should found your own family, my lord, and change your luck."

"Marry?"

"Most men do. And kings need heirs."

Edward nodded. His rage against Emma seemed to have exorcised all other angers. His usual prickly air in Godwin's company was gone. He said: "I'm afraid of it. Afraid of taking the wrong wife, as my father did."

"Your father wed a stranger from over the sea. You could have an English wife, someone you already know. Does no one attract you among the nobles' daughters?"

"It isn't so simple. She must not only attract me; she must be a queen. What sort of woman should she be? I don't know."

"A gentle girl, with an interest in religious matters as you have, someone reared in a happy household. She would be your friend and make peace in your hall."

"Eadsige has been saying the same things." Edward sighed. "He won't like this morning's work. He'll preach forgiveness at me and tell me to reinstate my mother. Come inside. It's cold." He added as they went in: "The Norman style of this house pleases me. I feel at home. I am well aware, Godwin, that the wife you picture for me is the image of your daughter Edith. But I shall please myself."

"Edith?" said Siward of Northumbria, before whom Edward placed his problem, because the hulking northerner was so unlike himself and perhaps might see things Edward could not. "Edith Godwins-daughter? A man might do worse. Ye've no love for her father but ye'll maybe have to live for years in that crafty southron's pocket. Marry her and it'll keep him sweet. It might be wise. It might."

"I am much dependent on the support of Wessex," Edward agreed. "And the past—perhaps—should now be buried?"

Siward shot him a shrewd look. "Would that include the quarrel with your lady mother?"

"That quarrel concerns the present, not the past. And it does *not* concern you. But the matter of Alfred is . . . over."

His voice still held uncertainty. "What of the lassie herself?" Siward asked. He added bluntly: "Ye hate her father's guts, so there'd best be something to put the balance right. Does she stir your blood?"

"I like Edith," said Edward slowly. "She's gentle and modest and convent-reared. I dislike commanding women."

"Well, if she suits you, court her. It's as good a way to end a feud as any. The land wants heirs. Tell us when the marriage day is!"

"So marriage is in the wind." Leofric of Mercia, who had been hovering within earshot, drifted to Siward's side as the king walked away. "And with the Wessex girl. A good move. But it surprises me."

"She's an old foe's daughter," said Siward with a chuckle. "There's a conquest with a good spicy taste to it. Excites him, maybe."

"Our pious Edward? Could any woman excite him, I wonder?

And for all his talk of ending feuds, he has a long, long memory. We shall see," said Leofric.

"I've brought your daughter home, sir," said Brand. He helped Hild descend from the mule which had carried her to Dover. Rolf also slid out of his saddle. The three of them looked at Eric instead of each other, waiting for him to speak.

"Home?" said Eric. "Why?"

"The errand which was the price of my sister's post at court failed," said Rolf shortly. "I nearly died for it." His young face still had the blank look of one who has passed through terror and hardly dares even yet to believe in his own safety.

Brand said: "The message to Denmark was an invitation to Magnus to invade England and an offer to pay his men while they did so. I learnt of it and warned my overlord Harold Godwinsson. I make no apology. Unless you feel you would welcome a horde of wild Norsemen rampaging through your hall, you will not ask for one. Both your son and your daughter have been pardoned their part, and your daughter was not happy at court. I hope they may forgive me one day for endangering them."

Another man came out of Eric's hall. He was a broad-built man with a thick brown beard and a round, sun-reddened face. He slapped a large hand down on Eric's shoulder and let out a bellow of laughter. "So there *was* some wicked scheme behind the old lady's errand! What did I tell you? No wonder she rewarded it so well. Oh, Hild's place meant more to Eric here than a sack of silver—and he didn't go without the silver, either, did you, Eric? Well, I wouldn't want Magnus's horde on my doorstep, and I'm glad to see Hild home, if you aren't. Hey, Hild?"

A faint smile passed over Hild's face. Eric humphed. The big man swept on. "I'll have no more delay now, Eric. You get the priest and I'll arrange the feasting. Hild, my little love, come here." She went to him and when he hugged her, hugged him back. Over her head her self-appointed betrothed said: "Stop pulling that po-face, Rolf. If you get tangled with princes' affairs, you're bound to find trouble. What would you do if you found a Viking with an axe at your gate? Ask him in to dine? I take it you were arrested for your part in it all?"

"I was nearly hanged!" Rolf snapped.

"Well, but you weren't quite hanged, were you? If the North-men had come, you'd have wound up skewered, as likely as not." He grinned at the silent Brand. "I'm Ragnar Wulfson, wool merchant of Dover, and I have to thank you for bringing home my bride. We're having a feast here tonight. The town reeve, Alfwold, has become one of my prospective father-in-law's customers and is to share his meat tonight. If I don't tell you, Eric soon will. You'll stay to feast with us? What is your name?"

"He's called Brand Woodcutter," said Hild. Throughout the days of their journeying he had had nothing from her or Rolf but recriminations and silences alternately. But in the overwhelming warmth of Ragnar's greeting, her anger had begun to melt. Her voice was not unfriendly.

Eric pulled his lip and huffed. "Ragnar, I know I have made you wait. But when one has only one daughter, one jewel . . ."

"One wants the best setting for her. But maybe that setting should be my hall and not the court of that she-devil Emma. She's a monster, my friend. Threw her eldest son across the room the day he was born and had her younger one murdered when he grew up. Give Hild to me, I'm a safer guardian. Now, Brand . . . Woodcutter, was it? Is there a tale behind that name? Do you join us tonight?"

"If Eric here, and Rolf and Hild invite me too," Brand said.

"Oh . . . ah . . ." Eric caught his future son-in-law's eyes. "Yes. Of course. You will be welcome."

"Rolf?" said Brand.

"Rolf!" Ragnar barked.

Reluctantly Rolf met Brand's eyes. He did not smile but some nascent amity showed in his face. "Very well. Yes, Woodcutter. Come—you need it after the journey."

"Hild?" said Brand.

"I hated Winchester," said Hild from the curve of Ragnar's arm. "I hated *her*. And Rolf is safe. Yes, Brand. Feast with us."

"Then I will," said Brand.

7 ✖ The Stricken Hall

Five months later, a year after Eadgyth had gone away, with the thought of her still a fire in his bone marrow, Brand asked Godwin for leave of absence. If she did not want him, she must tell him so herself.

Marriage had been inescapably in the air all these months, for rumours were flying now that the king was seeking a wife, and Edward had visited Godwin twice for no real reason, but on both occasions had held long conversations with Edith. Edward had left Gildenford behind at last, it seemed, and nowadays went hunting with Godwin. It would be Edith, Edith, the gossip said, and the air of the earl's hall grew thick with hope. Gytha began to instruct Edith on the care of her complexion and taught her a more sophisticated style of hairdressing—ringlets instead of braids, with herbal washes to improve the colour. "Let's see if we can find some buttercups in the middle of all this hay," was Gytha's comment. In this atmosphere Brand's longings grew deeper.

"You wish to go home?" Godwin asked.

"I . . . yes." He could not speak of Eadgyth to Godwin any more than to Harold. Save for his one cautious request for a holding if he married, he kept his own counsel.

"I need you for training exercises in a few days' time. You can leave eleven days from now. Or is someone sick and asking for you?"

"No, it isn't that. No, eleven days will do very well. Thank you."

They went faster than he had expected, for they were exhausting. Godwin had been seized by a warrior equivalent of the feminine urge to spring-clean, and day after day, with the other men, the Godwinssons, and Beorn, Brand went on survival treks through plain and forest, foraging for food and sleeping rough, charging up slopes against walls of locked shields, and fighting endless duels under handicaps of increasing severity ("Now fight without your shield . . . now without your left arm; it's broken . . . Now I'll cover your right eye"). As a result he was still in Winchester when the astounding news broke that Lady Emma had been reinstated as queen mother and was on her triumphant way home, in jewelled, cloth-of-silver state, riding in a litter, with an escort of two hundred.

It was the outcome of strenuous efforts by the archbishops and also by Bishop Stigand. Stigand had made his peace with Edward, who had recognised that he was capable in his appointment, even if Emma had made it. He now joined Kitehawk and Eadsige in the effort to coax Edward into setting an example of true Christian forgiveness.

It was an uphill toil to begin with. Edward's first reaction was to rout out one or two of Cnut's less important relatives who were living peacefully in quiet corners of the realm and send them unceremoniously into exile. Most went to Flanders and Count Baldwin and the most hospitable court in Christendom, and Edward turned a stony face to his disapproving prelates.

"Forgive her?" he said. "Or any of Cnut's kin? My father forgave treacherous friends more than once. They sold their swords to the Danes in the first place and sold them again after they were pardoned. I know. Do you expect me to be like him?"

Emma's remarks had gone home, that much was plain.

"We said *forgive* and *reinstate*, but not necessarily *trust*," said Eadsige patiently. The archbishop was thinner than ever and often in pain, but he would not leave his work. "You must guard yourself from treachery, but there are ways to keep watch over Magnus's movements and ways to track the queen's messengers if need be. There may not be need. Grief is a strange thing, my son. It matures like wine. At the time when you think the bereaved are forgetting, their sorrow is at its keenest. Hers was, I do believe, only the passing madness of a woman who mourns a beloved son and is tormented by the accusations of a surviving one."

"I never accused her openly."

"But your suspicions were plain. And when all these things came to a zenith, she acted under their influence as a madman is driven by the moon. Forgive her, my lord. You need run no risk, and it will be a shining light for your people to follow."

"Your mother is your mother," Kitehawk added gravely, "and growing old. Remember Our Lord's words. Do good to them that despitefully use you. Love your enemies . . ."

"If Magnus arrives with an army, am I to embrace him on the beach?"

"We speak of personal wrongs, my lord. If a man shall compel thee to go with him a mile, go with him twain. Extend to her a royal, open hand of clemency. You need not disarm yourself as well!"

This exchange, which took place in the Witan Council in the presence of bystanders, became common knowledge. And so did the subsequent words in which a worn-down Edward, in formal Norman French, welcomed his mother back to public life. His interpretation of second-mile Christianity was decidedly double-edged.

"Be pleased, madam, to resume your former honours and dignities and the possession of all your lands and houses. You need fear no persecution, even if you intrigue against us again. Do so if it amuses you. You will find your efforts ineffectual."

Whereat Emma coolly repossessed her Winchester hall, and although she had in the past publicly called Godwin the murderer of her son, and had excellent reason to be chilly towards Gytha, she extended to them every sign of friendship. "Emma would make a compact with the devil himself to keep near the source of power," the cynics said. "And the power's with Godwin now—or will be when he makes that marriage."

On the tenth day Godwin called Brand and said: "Tomorrow you can leave."

Norfolk! His pulses thudded.

"But I have an errand for you. My son Sweyn is with Earl Leofric near Worcester. He is wanted at court to take his place at the council table. Take word to him to come and save me a messenger. You'll have plenty of time to see your family. You're to be back before we leave with the king in early May. You have thirteen days."

Thirteen days. Not time to get to Worcester and then across England to Norfolk and Eadgyth and back to Winchester. He must tell Godwin the truth or give up his plan. He opened his mouth.

"We shall travel to Norfolk with the king," Godwin said casually, gathering up cloak and gloves, about to go out. "You've never seen it, I think? A queer, wild land with queer, wild people. They live in the midst of marshes, and the sea journey to Flanders is easier than the road to the rest of England. Rumour has it that half the babies are born with webbed feet. And that's where Harold's Stormcock was foaled! You'll find it interesting."

Brand blinked, and smiled. He would go to Norfolk after all, then. And meanwhile he could go home.

When he got there he found that his mother looked older but seemed well, and that Orm and Elfrida were in full bloom, parents now of two hearty sons and a daughter, while Elfrida was growing big again. The farm was in good order. He enjoyed their welcome, though the talk went haltingly at first, so far was his life now from theirs. Orm left the farm only to go to market and Elfrida only to visit village neighbours, while Brand's world was the width of England. He asked after Edgiva.

They had seen her very little, they said. Elfrida had the children to see to and his mother could not travel so far now. Orm had been to visit her two years ago. Brand nerved himself and at long last rode to Leominster.

The abbey was a little bunch of buildings of local stone, just outside the town palisade. It was walled round but the gate was open, and the porteress was there to greet travellers between dawn and sunset. Inside stood a guesthouse and a hospital building. Beyond these was another wall and a further gate, and within that stood the nuns' house and their chapel. He heard from the porteress that Edgiva was now a woman of consequence among the nuns, skilled in calligraphy and Latin . . . *Latin? Edgiva?* . . . and gifted in manuscript illustration with tinctures and gold and silver leaf. He waited, astonished, in a visitors' cell of bare stone. When she came he didn't recognise her and asked where his sister was.

"I am your sister, stupid!" said the young nun with the great dark eyes and the clear olive skin in which the marks of the childhood smallpox were hardly noticeable. Brand's eyes widened. Plain food, clean intellectual pursuits instead of the toil of byre and pigsty, and perhaps some help from natural maturity had worked a miracle. Or perhaps it was a blessing conferred by prayer. The puppy fat was gone too. She was strong and sturdy, that was all. Her mind had changed as well, grown. Her expression told him that. Her voice had lost much of its accent. She was a senior nun. The abbess was old now and often sick. The novice mistress did most of the administration and Edgiva helped her.

"You're happy then?" he asked warily. She was twenty-six, he thought. But she looked less.

"Why, yes. This is a happy community. Where else would I have learned so much? I'm truly glad to be here."

She asked about his life, eager to hear of the world outside. He found himself telling her about Eadgyth. She listened seriously. "Poor Brand. But *your* hopes may bloom yet." Had he imagined the emphasis on "your"? But he had not imagined that sudden hunger in her eyes. She said she was happy but . . . oh, God, poor Edgiva, immured in this place amid walls and vows for the rest of her life, spending her passions on illuminated manuscripts! All very well for those who had been called of God, but He hadn't called Edgiva. She was the bride of Christ by a forced marriage. She read his face.

"Brand, I *am* happy. They feed my mind. A hungry mind. A hungry mind could be worse than a hungry body. I don't mean food. You know what I mean. Tell mother I am all right."

"I will," he said.

For his mother's peace of mind he would have done that anyway. For the vows were taken. Whatever they had done was irreversible now.

Later they were to inspect the newly assembled fleet at Sandwich, but meanwhile Edward wished to tour East Anglia. It was a packed itinerary. A visit to a new mint at Bury St. Edmunds, to a monastery where Edward meant to endow an orphanage, to a shire court. Brand wondered anxiously if he would be able after all to reach Eadgyth. But Godwin apparently wished to see her father, and Harold wished to accompany him; so quite naturally Brand found himself among Harold's companions on that visit. It was surprisingly simple.

He rode in a daze of happiness through the strange, waterwoven country that was Eadgyth's home. Waterways threaded everywhere, strands of silver through green cloth. They had a local guide and needed him, for on either side of the narrow paths were clumps of rushes and patches of virulent emerald. It was a cloudy day but soft; the pools shone under the pale sky and the reed warblers called. Eadgyth's land.

But his first sight of her actual dwelling was a shock. An instant later he knew that he was not alone. Evidently this was not normal. Harold had reined in and was staring blankly about him. He raised a hand and pointed. "What in God's name has happened? That barley field—it's scarcely half-sown! And *there!*" He pointed again, at an enclosure made of hurdles, with mares and foals within. "Those hurdles are falling down; the horses will be out and in the marshes if something isn't done at once! And where on earth are all the men? I can't see a soul about the fields!"

"It can't be raiders," Gytha said. They all glanced towards the horizon, where a pale emptiness told of the sea. "They'd burn the crops and steal the horses. There's a hearthsmoke over there, too . . . it looks like sheer neglect."

"Come on!" said Godwin, and spurred his mount.

When they got to the hall they saw that it was as bad as the fields. The gate was off its hinges and the courtyard was unswept, piled with refuse. The roof thatch looked leaky. Godwin sounded his horn and the doves went up from a cot beside the hall. Voices were uplifted somewhere inside and then Eadgyth came, running down the hall steps to meet them. Her face lit up with joy when she saw who they were.

She too looked neglected. Brand's tenderness rushed up and half closed his throat at the sight of her. She was haggard and thin, and her clothes were the dun-hued coarse woollens women used for dirty work. She had been doing dirty work. She was dusty and her face was smudged. Her feet were in old sandals, one broken thong tied up with cord. Her slender, expressive hands were reddened. Her first words completely belied the gladness in her eyes.

"You mustn't stay! Please, you mustn't stay!" She would not even come near them. "You must go away at once! Don't even dismount!"

"Whyever not?" said Harold, doing it.

"The smallpox! Most of the men have run away and three thralls are dead and so many in the village . . . the thatcher and all his family and the smith, all gone. It hadn't been here for a generation and no one had had it."

"I know trouble when I see it," said Harold firmly, "and for your information, I had it as a small child. We shall help."

"How many are sick now?" Gytha asked.

"Oh, none now. The last was the hayward, and he's better

now. My mother's better, too. She threw it off, though she's weak still and rests a lot. My father had it in the east and I haven't taken it, God be thanked . . ."

"You had cowpox years ago," Gytha said. "Your mother told me. I've had it too. I used to milk the cows at home. People who get that almost never get the smallpox; I don't know why. It sounds as if your epidemic's over, in any case." Everyone began to dismount. "So you've been trying to run the place on a handful of men and nurse the sick as well, have you?"

"We shall invite ourselves to stay," Godwin said. "You need us." He looked towards the hall, where Eadgyth's father had appeared, leaning on his stick. "Stay there, Edric! We're coming in. We've come to relieve the siege!"

Eadgyth was brushing her eyes, wet with thankfulness. Brand led his horse up to her. "Eadgyth!"

"Oh, Brand! Hallo, Brand."

"It feels like a hundred years instead of one. I thought you'd forgotten me."

"I'll never do that, Brand, but this isn't the greeting I'd have liked you to have. But oh, I am glad to see you!"

In the next few hours Brand did a variety of extraordinary, sometimes menial tasks and gloried in them. He swept the yard. He climbed a ladder and plastered sacking and mud as temporary plugs where the roof leaked. He fetched fresh rushes for the hall. He drew water. But he paused in his toil when he saw Eadgyth alone in the herb garden. He went to her. She waited, smiling, and let him kiss her. She had a grimy scarf over her hair and he pulled it off. Her hair looked as tired as the rest of her.

"You haven't had enough to eat." The hand in his was too fragile, too much made of bone.

"We didn't earlier. There was no one to do things—collect eggs or make bread. I had to see to the sick first. But it's better now. We are getting over it. I heard Earl Godwin ordering someone to kill an ox, and his men have bullied ours into going down to the river to fish, so we shall certainly eat well tonight!"

"I want to talk to you," said Brand. "Seriously. At length. And alone. When?"

Eadgyth fiddled with the basil and rosemary in her basket. "I don't know." She seemed to be struggling with some secret, difficult decision. "You came so suddenly, out of nowhere. What shall I do or say? I don't know. Dear Brand. Take these herbs indoors for me, will you? I'll tell you this evening when we can talk. I'll make a plan. I promise."

He took the basket and bore it to the kitchen as if it were a treasure chest, because she had touched it.

In the evening, when a misty dusk was settling on the fenlands and the torches had been kindled in the hall, it was seen that an afternoon of labour had wrought wonders. Deep, fresh rushes swished underfoot instead of trodden, rotten ones. White cloths covered the trestle tables. The air smelt of fresh food instead of sour dirt and disease. And Eadgyth herself, in light green and deep violet, with her thin face washed and amber bracelets on her arms, seemed made new. She smiled a welcome to him as Brand took his place, and he felt more of a king than Edward in his palace, because she had looked at him, at *him*, at him like that, singling him out, and because she had promised to see him alone. He would tell her of Godwin's offer and they would go to her father. He had saved three silver pence and he would buy her an amethyst ring for her left hand. When after the food the lyre went round, he sang a love song. It was for her.

It was a merry evening. Harold, sitting next to Brand, took the lyre after him and sang first a rival love song and then a witty and deadpan tale of a battle hero who feared no man but shook at the knees in the presence of his wife. Everyone roared and stamped, and then Godwin took the instrument and touched the first chords of a well-known lay of the valiant if horizontal deeds of Harald Hardraada and the Empress Zoë of Constantinople.

At the women's table there was a movement of departure; the ladies rose to withdraw. Eadgyth passed close to Brand, and as she did so she paused and put a hand on his shoulder.

"Can you keep a clear brain and when the feast is over come to the wellhead? The moon will be out, I think. The mist is lifting."

He put his hand over hers, rejoicing. Beside him Harold, who was near enough to hear her low-spoken words, looked thunderstruck.

"I will be there," Brand said.

He slipped early out of the hall. He waited, walking about in the courtyard until the sounds of revelry had died down. Then he went softly to the well and sat on the stone parapet, looking at the tranquil reflection of the moon on the water far below. A few people wandered out of the hall and in again, but no one disturbed him. It was peaceful.

As Eadgyth had foretold, the mist was gone. The stars were out and the soft air was full of the scents of early May. He waited in a moonlit stillness so hushed that the blood sang in his ears and he could hear the rhythmic throb of his own pulses. He waited a long time.

How long, he did not know. Serene expectation turned to impatience, to alarm, and at last to despair. She would have come by now had she been able. Her father had found out and stopped her. Or she had changed her mind. His disappointment was so huge that he could scarcely contain it. He wanted to cry. He wanted Eadgyth, with every pore in his skin, with mind and muscle and bone. He walked wretchedly across to the stable where Greedy was stalled and stood for some time with his forehead resting against the pony's rough mane. He had been there for ten minutes when he heard footsteps in the courtyard.

He straightened, wildly hoping, and went to the door. But the girl was a stranger, one of the thrall women. He didn't want her to find him. He thought she might come to the stable and looked about him for a hiding place.

Behind the stable was a lean-to for the corn bins and the hay. A door near Greedy led straight into it. Quietly he lifted the latch.

He held the door open for a few seconds. The two already there did not see him. They were sitting in a patch of moonlight, resting at ease on a pile of hay. They were not making love. Harold sat with his back against the wall and his arms wrapped round Eadgyth, whose head was on his shoulder. Her eyes were closed. The pale moonlight had taken all colour out of their mingled hair, but in his mind Brand saw it—hers red, his golden, fire in the corn.

He shut the door soundlessly. He stumbled into the courtyard. He remembered to shut the stable after him, also soundlessly. They must not hear.

Harold. Looking distastefully back, he recognised the footprints Harold had left over the year gone past. Harold laughing while Eadgyth brandished a bucket at Sweyn. Harold taking her from the mews, claiming her. Eadgyth turning to him when Gytha pressed her to stay. Harold had said to her: no, go home. And she had gone, too proud to stay if he didn't want her. Harold, visiting Norfolk ostensibly only to buy Stormcock. Harold saying: "Half of me wants to marry, the other half wants to be free." Harold standing on and off, maddening her as she had maddened Brand. Harold. For his benefit she had put her hand on Brand's shoulder, made a tryst with him in a voice that the man at his side could hear. He, Brand, was nothing but the hawk to bring down the game. He wanted to vomit.

The girl had not been bound for the stable. She was pulling a pail from the well. She set it down slopping and dipped a drinking beaker in it. He went towards her.

"Give me some water."

She obliged, smiling. She was certainly a thrall, grubby and stringy-haired, but quite young. She was friendly too, and her smile had more than a little come-hither in it.

"What be you at, wandering so late?" she asked, in the thick and almost incomprehensible dialect of the local peasantry. "Looking for some'un? Me?"

"You'd do," said Brand grimly.

The night was not as destructive as it might have been. She was a poor exchange for Eadgyth, but she cooled his enflamed body and gave some balm to his hurt manhood. He was not feeling gentle, but she knew little of gentleness anyway. When he thought himself vengeful, she admired his virility, and because she did not know what had happened to him, her admiration was free of pity. She gave him back strength enough to face the day to come.

When, leaving the byre where they had slept, he saw Harold crossing the dawnlit courtyard, he knew he would need that strength.

He turned away from Harold, but his name was called and perforce he halted. They met and looked at each other.

"I believe I must apologise," Harold said. "I didn't know she had . . . women!" He let the word by itself amount to a condemnation of female deviousness, and a refusal on his own part to be responsible for it.

Brand said stiffly: "There are other women."

This was Harold, Harold Godwinsson, son of his beloved lord, and his own friend beside whom he had fought. This was Harold, who had kept his word and stood between death and Rolf Ericsson, because Brand begged it. Brand stood poised between gratitude and hatred and had no words for either. It was natural, after all, that she should choose Harold. Lovely, flame-haired, swan-necked Eadgyth. She ought to have a man to match her. What could a common housecarle like himself give her, with his dull conversation and his miserable hide or two of land?

"I have just come from my parents," Harold said. "Oh, yes, they're up early! Plenty to do about the hall, they say." He grinned. "My father is furious! I'm surprised you didn't hear him bellowing. But he has consented to the handfasting on the promise that I do not take Eadgyth with me to court."

"Your father objects?" Brand could hardly believe his ears. "But . . . why?"

"Look round you! She may be a thane's daughter, but what sort of a manor is this? And when she marries me she'll be a king's sister-in-law. The king has asked for my sister Edith's hand, did you know? It will be announced when we all go back to Winchester. Eadgyth will be angry at being forbidden the court, but she'll come round. She loves me. Oh, God, I'm a fool. I'm sorry, Brand. I'd better go away before you hit me."

Brand watched him go. He had only spoken the truth. Eadgyth did love him. Brand felt now that he had always known it in waking life, and that his pursuit of her had been only in a dream. He sat through the merrymaking that night, when Godwin put a good face on it and let Eadgyth's father join her hands with Harold's. Like Godwin, and with sympathy towards him, Brand drank a toast that tasted bitter and joined in the cheering. The noise crescendoed in his head and broke in hammer blows of pain.

He wished that he were dead.

8 ❧ Bride of the King

The smallpox came as a relief.

He sickened on shipboard when they were sailing down the coast towards the Sandwich war fleet. Gytha went with him when he was hastily put ashore at Sandwich and rode beside the litter that took him to Godwin's nearby manor. She stayed with him till the climax of the disease was past.

He was aware of her during the dreadful throes when the fever roared through his veins, burning his senses away. He knew he talked to her and told her about Eadgyth and that she seemed to understand. But when he at last emerged from the pit, she had gone. A brother from a local monastery replaced her, bringing food, reading to him to distract his mind from the irritation of the slowly healing rash, tidying his bed. He grew a little stronger and the rash receded. He got out of bed, took his physician's arm into the courtyard. He heard that no one had taken the sickness from him and was glad. He had been housed apart, and Sandwich had in any case had a visitation a few years back. There were few likely victims about.

To his surprise he enjoyed his recovery. The fever had scorched the worst of his grief away. His lax body was too weak to harbour violent passions. He ate and slept and sat in the sun like a lizard, and time rolled over him. But when he was able to ride again and was thinking of trying out his sword-arm, outriders came in at a gallop to say that Godwin and his countess were coming, and that the hall was to be made ready. Brand was at the gate in armour with the other men when they appeared. Gytha waved, pleased, and when he was again sitting in the courtyard awaiting the summons to the late meal, she came out of her bower and sat beside him.

"So you're well again. Good. We almost lost you!"

"You looked after me yourself," he said. "I remember. Thank you."

"I'm a good nurse," said Gytha complacently. "I've had practice enough—measles, coughs, sprains, and fractures. If it isn't my children, it's the men." She studied his face. "You're not much marked. Not that it matters so much with a man. I kept away from Winchester for weeks for fear of infecting Edith. Above all, just now!"

Brand recalled a dim memory from before his illness. "Is she married yet?"

"No, not till next January. The twenty-third. A royal marriage takes time to arrange. And we wouldn't like the groom to change his mind!"

Brand nerved himself. Sooner or later he must face it. "What of Harold?" he said.

Gytha's eyes were kind. "It's done, Brand. Harold has set up his first household in a hall at Saxmundham, and the marriage feast was held there two weeks ago. It was not what his father wished for Harold, but neither of them would be gainsaid. It was by the old rites—her parents like the old ways. King Edward didn't approve at all when he heard it!" He thought she was talking while he recovered himself. "Harold went to her home to fetch her and promised her father to maintain her and their children and guard her from all dangers, and everyone gave gifts to everyone else and got drunk. Then next day we all set off for Saxmundham and had another feast there. Harold hired a bard for the occasion, and he made a wonderful song about her. She's known as Eadgyth of the Swan-Neck, from the Humber down to Andred, now."

Brand was silent.

Gytha said gently: "You will hear all this soon, anyway. It's best to cut off the mortified limb with one axe-blow. I know about it, Brand. You told me in your fever. I am sorry."

"I . . . wish Harold to be happy."

"He is sorry, too. Women will do cruel things in the name of love, Brand. Love itself can be cruel. It will be best, I think, if you do not go to Saxmundham or keep company with Harold for some time. Godwin told me to tell you. My nephew Beorn is soon to take up an earldom in the midland district and will need men. Your friend Peter Longshanks is to go. You are to go with him."

Brand was jolted out of his brooding. "An earldom? Beorn?"

"One for him and one for Harold—Harold's is in East Anglia, Beorn's in Mid-Anglia. Brand . . ."

"Yes?"

"It won't always feel like this. It will pass. There will be other girls."

"What girl would look at me now, me and my pockmarks!" said Brand, suddenly angry.

"Weren't you listening to me? I said, you're hardly marked at all. Didn't that monk give you a mirror? How like a monk! I'll send one to you. You'll see."

He was silent, watching the smoke of the kitchen fire as it rose tranquilly into the windless, subtle blue of the summer evening. "It was like being struck by lightning," he said.

"A bolt of lightning," Gytha said as she stood up, "isn't necessarily the best way of lighting the fire on your hearth. You'll have a hearthfire one day, Brand. And you need not fear meanwhile to meet the men who were in Norfolk with us at that time, either. The news got round that you found other company that night." Brand turned crimson. "Don't look like that! They said it showed the right spirit, that if one torch goes out, the wise man lights another!" It was just like Gytha not only to know what the housecarles were saying over their mead but to quote them. She never, as some of her young women did and as indeed she made Edith do, behaved as if the menfolk were a different species. "The only one to pull a solemn face was my Tostig. He's such a moral youth. How did I ever manage to produce both him and Sweyn? If they sang the deeds of mothers the way they do of warriors, I'd merit a saga for such a feat." She looked down at him with her kind and comprehending smile. "Get your strength soon, Brand, and get back into the busy daily world. That's my advice. Though I'm afraid that you're going to find the subject of marriage somewhat inescapable. Harold's is over, but King Edward's is still to come, and no one even remotely connected with the house of Wessex will have much chance to escape that!"

Gytha was right. If the coronation had inspired excitement, the king's marriage led to something like insanity. The happy madness spread across the land as the autumn drew on, and the word began to go round of what foreign powers would be represented and what gifts they were sending. Young women envied the bride, and middle-aged men, hearing that she was only twenty to the king's forty, said he was a lucky man; how they wished they were kings and could take their pick of the maidens. Prelates who did not think romance worth wasting words on spoke gravely of the benefits a good woman could bring a lonely man, and of the importance of a healthy heir to give the land peace in decades to come. While the merchants, as before, put together the cream of their goods and dreamed of making fortunes.

Even in the nunneries the excitement took hold. In Leominster, Edgiva patiently soaked and scraped calfskins to make vellum for a book to be presented by the abbey to the queen on her wedding day. A queen's task in this world, said the abbess, was to uphold Christian worship and set an example of the devout virtues, to support a husband doubtless beset by many duties and heathen foes. So the book was to be about the conversion of heathen Northumbria, three hundred years before, and was to be copied by the nuns from the writings of a monkish sage called Bede, whom the great King Alfred had translated into English from the Latin. Edgiva had the illustrating to do. She laboured with her most cunning skill, for both king and queen would handle the book, no doubt, and might even keep it in their private chamber. That much share in the life of man and woman she would have.

In Dover, Eric Merchant was flabbergasted to receive a royal order for wine and silks and silver to be sent on approval to Winchester. "The man supplies good merchandise even if he is a fool," Edward had said bluntly. Eric, passing the news to Rolf and to his son-in-law Ragnar, said: "I'll see myself a thane yet. The day is coming. But I'm still sorry you're not one, Ragnar, for Hild's sake."

"Hild doesn't mind," said Ragnar, untroubled. He smiled broadly. Since her marriage, Hild had laughed more than ever before.

"She looks happy," her father agreed. "For which I thank you. Will you come to Winchester with me? Rolf, perhaps . . ."

"Would rather stay here," said Rolf candidly. "Of Winchester I have had enough. And of Gloucester, and of courts altogether. Will Hild go?"

"Hild," said her husband smugly, "won't be travelling far for some time."

Eric blinked, understood, and then shouted. "You sly devil! You never told us! When?"

"March, she says."

"Oh, sweet angels in heaven . . . Rolf, did you hear? Fetch wine, we'll drink to it. My first grandchild. Oh, if only her mother were here. Well, well, my little Hild to have a baby. Well, well, well!"

Brand's hopes of marriage had been wrecked, and he would have gone to his marriage feast so gladly. Edward Cyng's were coming to fruition, borne triumphantly along by a tide of approval and congratulation and universal encouragement, but he did not seem to appreciate his good fortune. For it was perfectly plain that the king, although a willing bridegroom, was entering into marriage for policy more than for love. And far from wishing to deepen his friendship with the vast new family he was acquiring along with his bride, he appeared to be gathering his own friends and such family as he already possessed round him like a protective mantle. Brand wondered at him.

It was still only October. But because of the risk of winter storms, the mainland heads of state had sent their representatives early. They were arriving already from Norway and Denmark, Normandy and Germany, and for each there was a feast of welcome to which the earls and prelates and chief thanes of the realm were bidden.

Beorn, being an earl, was at all the feasts, and his chief followers, Brand among them, were with him. In joining Beorn, Brand found, he had come into new dignities. He was a mere housecarle no longer, but one of his leader's friends, and he had been fitted out accordingly. His old black pony had been retired at last, by Beorn's command, to be replaced by a better mount, and he had been given a set of new armour and a helmet made to measure by Beorn's own blacksmith, who took all his master's men one by one in a hardworking morning and measured their heads with calipers. He had been given new arm-rings of heavy yellow gold, a gold-clasped belt, and a round cloak-brooch of silver and amber to fasten a new tawny cloak. And when he went with his leader to the royal feasts, he found himself seated much higher up the table than ever before, within earshot of much of the high table conversation. Which, when he could keep his mind from nagging painfully at the fact that all this merrymaking was in honour of another man's marriage, was interesting.

The latest arrival was the Norman representative, Edward's old friend Abbot Robert Champart of Jumièges. The feast was taking on a pattern which Brand now recognised, for he had been there when the king's sister, Godgift, with her husband, Eustace, now Count of Boulogne, their two small daughters, and Godgift's two sons, Ralph and Walter, had been feasted ten days earlier. They had been given such marked precedence over the Godwin clan that adverse talk resulted.

It was happening again.

"There is no friend I would rather have at my side," Edward was saying now to Champart, who had the high-backed seat of honour, looking down the hall, which glistened with gems, gold and silver, rich-hued garments, and gleaming silks. "My lords," Edward called to his earls, further along the top table, "this is my best-loved companion of my days in Normandy, Robert Champart! Make him welcome!"

"You must have many friends closer than I, after all these years," said Champart. He was spare of build as he had always been, with his face a fraction more lined. His blue-grey eyes were astute.

"I have a thousand things to talk over with you," Edward insisted. "Old friends are always the best. They're the most thoroughly tested."

The mead was being served and the delicacies were being brought out: roast swan and boars' heads and a huge roasted ox. Heavenly smells floated through the hall.

"Your lands look prosperous enough, and I'm not qualified to advise on matrimony," Champart said, amused.

"Money," said Edward succinctly. "You're qualified to advise on that. I need it. I've earls who can make ships from the air . . . and breathe courage into fleeing men and keep barbarians at bay with a scowl, but none of them can do arithmetic. And I've the saintliest priesthood on earth, but all they say is trust in the lord . . ."

"And in Whom else should we trust?" said Abbot Sparhafoc

gravely. As royal goldsmith he had a place near the top, close enough to join the royal conversation. Kitehawk, a few places above him, nodded. Champart smiled tolerantly.

"The key to prosperity is the treasury," said Edward. "I want it kept full. I need a worthy steward. If I asked you to stay and make your future here as my chief advisor on finance, Robert, would you do it?"

"Are you talking without forethought out of the joy of our re-union?" asked Champart. "Or had you considered it before?" The rest of the top table had become rather quiet, and everyone seemed distracted from the good viands. Godwin and Kitehawk were exchanging looks. This idea was new to them, whether or not it was new to Edward. And it was customary to ask the Witan Council first.

"I have given it much thought," said Edward.

"Then I will consider it. I admire your green kingdom, my lord."

"You'll find our society very unlike that of Normandy," Godwin said, accepting a helping of roast swan. "Few Normans settle happily here. They find us . . . alien. Hard to understand." He fingered his beard and turned to speak down the table to Sparhafoc. "The management of treasure in another sense is your own calling," he remarked. "What are your latest commissions?" Godwin's interest in and furtherance of his kinsman's fortunes was a mild puzzle to most people, who saw little that was compatible between the two of them. Though they could understand just now that Sparhafoc was preferable company to this uppish Norman stranger.

Sparhafoc began to talk with animation of the gold-framed purse and the coronet he was making for the royal bride. As everyone who knew him was aware, Sparhafoc in his workshop was a different man from Sparhafoc the sanctimonious prelate, or Sparhafoc the exceedingly mean manager of his permanently underfed abbey.

"But I am only a craftsman," he said as he finished his description, with a deprecating glance to where the king and Champart were deep in financial mysteries over the swan. "I so often fail to make the profit on my work that I rightly should, my head for figures is so bad. A craftsman and a man of God only. But it would not be fitting for such as I to seek the skills of the treasurer and the power of high office. It would become neither of my professions. A craftsman wastes himself on ambition beyond his workbench, and a man of the Church sins if he indulges in it."

Into the scandalised silence Earl Siward said heartily: "Why is the minstrel silent so long? Has he no songs to sing us of the bridegroom's sinews or the beauty of the bride?"

Beside Brand, his friend Peter Longshanks said comfortably: "Well, it isn't so rare for the bride-ale to start a fight, but usually it doesn't happen till the wedding feast itself, and not between a pair of abbots even then, for the love of heaven! Old Sparhafoc's jealous, by the look of it!"

Brand nodded, unhappily, playing with his meat. He too had found the exchange amusing. It had taken him out of himself. But now the minstrel had begun to sing and was mending the rift at the top table by welding them together in gentle laughter at Godwin's expense, for he was likening the bride Edith to a fair flower in bloom, born of Godwin as the rose is born of the thorn. From the true reason for this splendid gathering, there was no refuge. He thanked heaven Eadgyth was not there. Harold had abided by his promise to his father and left his wife at home. Brand could not be sorry, for to see her as Harold's wife could not give him pleasure.

The January night was cold, biting to the bone, and the dancing, torch-waving throng which escorted Edward to his bridal chamber had made ribald jokes all the way about methods of getting warm. They would have come in with him had he not adroitly elbowed them aside on the threshold and slammed the door in their faces. He paused just inside to brace himself, but it was only a respite. Candlelight shone from the inner room and there, awaiting him, was Edith.

She was in bed, under a rug of glossy wolfskins. In a brazier burned sweet pine cones and applewood above a charcoal foundation, and the hangings round the walls were embroidered with trees in fruit. Champart had brought them, a gift from the Norman duke. Edith's hair had been brushed till it gave back the candlelight, gleaming pale. Edward was suddenly conscious that his own hair was lank and his rib cage too prominent. While his knowledge of women was next to nothing. He stood in mid-floor and his mouth was dry. He hadn't the least idea what to say.

It was absurd. He was the King of England. He was a husband retiring for the night with his wife. The one should be enough to lend him dignity and the other was the most commonplace thing on earth. From end to end of his realm, husbands and wives were retiring peacefully in the selfsame way. Edith was waiting for him to speak first.

He said: "You looked very beautiful today. Very dignified."

"Thank you, my lord."

Dear God. Please help me.

He tried again. "You must not feel shy with me. Were you nervous during the ceremonies?"

"A little. I thought I might make a mistake in the responses, or stammer. There was so much to learn."

Her voice was formal, correct, as if he were a total stranger instead of someone with whom she had talked often and long. It was terrifying. He would sooner face an army of raving Vikings than this. A war cry would sound soothing compared to Edith's cool accents. He shivered. He found that he was genuinely cold. His bare feet in their jewelled sandals were freezing and the gooseflesh was rising on his skin under his blue bedrobe. Without giving himself time to think, he scrambled out of sandals and robe alike and in the manner of one who dives for cover, plunged under the wolfskins.

Edith, becoming human, squeaked that he was like ice and began to chafe his fingers. She essayed a little giggle. He tried, and failed, to giggle back.

He had never been in bed with a woman before. It felt outrageous. He shouldn't have married. He'd had misgivings about it for some time. But with ambassadors landing on every tide and marriage gifts piling up in the royal halls till they looked like warehouses, and bright-haired, self-confident, gold-ornamented, bold-voiced, fully armed Godwins in every corner, he had not thought withdrawal from the contract feasible. Now he knew he had been wrong. He wished he were in his chapel, praying, or reading a book of devotions by candlelight in his old apartment, with his pages in their truckle beds at a respectful distance from him and the guard's boots grating in the courtyard outside. No guard would approach his door so near tonight.

What had he married for? he wondered desperately. He forced himself to admire his bride's hair and stroke it. To get a son. If he could. Yes, if he could. Neither Alfred his brother nor Harthacnut his half brother had ever fathered children, although both had had

mistresses. He had married too to get a circle of kinfolk, to fill the
cold void left by his mother's desertion and Alfred's death. He had
wanted wife and brethren. In Godwin's hall he had seen the close-
ness of blood-kin, the love and trust that could live between them.
He had coveted that.

So he hadn't only married, he'd married Godwin's daughter,
who was here, nestling up to him in this horrifying privacy.

Godwin. The creature of Cnut, the henchman of Emma—whatever Emma might say about it; she had her name to protect—and
the betrayer of Alfred. Godwin's daughter. Who was now looking at
him . . . out of Godwin's hazel eyes. He saw that for the first time.
How could he have missed it before? Dear saints and angels, dear
God in heaven, what had he done?

And what had he still to do? He had a duty now to this Edith
Godwinsdaughter and a duty to his folk, to give them an heir of his
blood. In prayer and fasting, long hours of work and hard days in
the saddle, he was used to making his body obey him. It would have
to obey him now.

He slept presently, in the knowledge of duty carried out and in
the ease of a body which had found its own satisfaction despite the
carping, reluctant mind. But Edith stayed awake.

Edith had needed more than obedience to duty. Edith had
needed courtship and ardour and laughter to bring her into bloom.
She knew that this was not all there was to love; she had heard other
women talking. If this was all that Edward could offer, she ought to
have stayed in her convent. Better nothing at all than this wretched
imitation.

Far away in Leominster, on a hard pallet in a nun's stone cell,
Edgiva too was awake. She was thinking of the queen, that daughter
of an earl, who had been taken from a nunnery in order to marry,
not pushed into one to prevent her. Who was with her husband
now, knowing all that Edgiva would never know, possessed of all
that Edgiva longed for. Such thoughts were forbidden here, but if
you broke rules in your mind, who was to catch you? She let her
imagination wander, changing places with Edith in her dreams.
Quite unaware that Edith, listening to Edward's snores and remembering her quiet convent childhood, would gladly have changed
places with Edgiva.

Part

LEOMINSTER
GUILT
1046–1047

1 ❈ The Enemy Within

It was so hot that before she walked across the open space of grass between the chapel and the dwellinghouse of Leominster Abbey, Abbess Edgiva had to pause and draw breath. The stone-built chapel was so cool, such a refuge. One cursed the stone buildings in winter, but in this scorching July they were a blessing.

Still standing in the chapel porch, Edgiva contemplated her home. The thatcher had come earlier in the year, and above the grey abbey walls the fresh straw shone pale gold in the sunshine. Trim grass, a little browner now than grass should be, but neat, lay below the walls. Grey stone, gold roofs, sky of smooth blue enamel, elms and oaks of deep midsummer green—all were as serene as the windless air and as richly hued as the manuscript of saints' lives which waited her attention in her office. There was no discord except in Edgiva's restless mind, no dull colours save in her black garments. She was weary of both, she thought. And angry.

"You have an unruly mind," the old abbess had once said. That mind was now playing with wild visions of swimming in a cold river, stripped naked, free of hot clinging draperies, and not alone. A most unsuitable thought for an abbess, Edgiva reproved herself. And then thought it all over again.

She was thirty. She had been abbess for a year. The smallpox, sweeping west, had struck her community some time earlier with the destructive force of a tidal wave, brought in by a sick woman who sought shelter there. The convent had a reputation for healing skills and turned no one away.

But the woman died despite their care, and with her died many, too many, of the nuns. The old abbess did not take it, but her life was near its end, she said wryly, without any such violent intervention from heaven. Edgiva, marked by it already, did not take it either, and on her shoulders fell much of the responsibility for nursing the sick and encouraging the well. In the depleted community she found herself a person of importance. On the death of the old abbess she was, to her astonishment, chosen to succeed.

She demurred, and was lectured by the convent's confessor on the need to take up dutifully the burden to which God had called her. He drew a graphic comparison between her situation and that of the young Duke of Normandy, called to his honours at the age of fourteen and mastering his duchy despite his youth and his many foes. How simple a task would hers be beside that! So here she was with her keys of office clanking at her girdle, charged with the care of a dozen souls besides her own—so much had the stricken abbey shrunk—and with the upkeep of their home.

At times she devoted more energy to nagging at the tenants of the abbey farms to render up their dues, and striking canny bargains with sellers of wool and oil and salt, than she did to her manuscripts or her prayers. An abbess needed a head for business more than she needed piety. And an abbess, Edgiva thought resentfully, should also be old. What good were youth and merriment to her? She was expected to set an example of deportment to the giddy young novices. There were only two at present; the sickness had frightened the parents off. No bad thing, perhaps. In this sensuous summer weather, who wanted to set an example of anything to anyone? All she longed to do was bathe and sleep, lie in the sun and dream . . . and dream . . .

She began to walk across the grass, her heavy garments dragging. The ground between the grasses was baked hard and covered with a tracery of tiny cracks. The sun glistened on the wings of swarming ants and the air was full of tiny insects. She was halfway to the nuns' house when the gatehouse bell clanged.

It went on clanging, and she realised that the porteress must have gone off duty. She turned towards the outer gate. The lodge was indeed empty and the door to the roadway shut. An imperious horn had now been added to the bell and indignant rooks were leaving the elms. Edgiva stepped briskly to the entrance and opened it herself.

Outside there appeared to be an army.

A small army. A score or so of men on horseback waited at a polite distance from the convent gate. They were soldiers, faceless behind the nosepieces of their helmets. Even across that careful gap the pungent smell of horseflesh, leather, and sweat came to her. Three or four stood forward of the rest, gathered round a man she thought was a prisoner, as his feet were tied in his stirrups. One man, the one with the horn, was directly in front of her.

She had pushed the two leaves of the door apart but kept the defensive chain in place. Over it, she said: "What is it?"

The man with the horn hung it from his pommel. "Who is in charge here?" he said.

"I am the abbess." Edgiva slid her hands into her sleeves. "What service can this poor house offer?"

"Healing, I hope. Our commander is sick. He has a poisoned sword-cut on his thigh, got fighting the Welsh savages to keep your marches safe. We have heard that there are doctoring skills here."

"There are," said Edgiva. "But this is a house of women. There is a monastery . . ."

"Dame Abbess," said the spokesman earnestly, "he is *ill*. If there is skill to help him in this house, take him in for the love of God. Don't ask him to ride on."

"Three of you may bring him in," said Edgiva, undoing the chain.

They were grateful, inquisitive, rough, courteous, gentle, and clumsy all at once, a bunch of big hirsute housecarles clumping about inside the neat grass courtyard. Edgiva led them to the hospital building, empty at this time, and rang a bell vigorously. It brought three nuns hurrying to her side: the porteress, an elderly nun called Dame Hilda, who had great knowledge of herbs and medicine, and a novice who trotted breathlessly in the rear, carrying an armful of bed linen.

"What's all this about, then?" Dame Hilda took charge at once. The sick man had had his feet tied in order to keep him in the saddle, for he was feeling dizzy. The old nun guided him to a bench, chivvied the novice into making up the bed, and then helped his friends lay him on it. His skin was lead-coloured, with a red surface flush on the cheekbones. He thanked his helpers confusedly, as if not sure where he was. There was a bulge of padding under the tunic that covered his left thigh. Dame Hilda felt his pulse and forehead and sniffed. "How long has he been riding in the sun in this state? Sun's half the mischief, I shouldn't wonder. Did none of you have sense enough to put a scarf over his head? One of you help me get this wound into the light of day."

"We took his helmet off," said one of the men defensively. "He said the weight worried him."

"No doubt. No doubt. And then the heat worried him more." With a small knife Dame Hilda was cutting the man's garments away from his injury. Edgiva came to her aid. The soiled bandage fell away. "We need water," Edgiva said to the novice. "Two big ewers—one hot and one cold—and two basins."

"And herbs," said Dame Hilda without turning round. She recited a list. "And a measure of wine," she added. "And hurry."

The wound was six inches long, deep, swollen, streaked with red, and hot to touch. As they examined it, the man on the bed suddenly opened his eyes, two gleaming hazel slits widening to orbs, and murmured: "Gentle hands. Must be ladies." He managed a grin. His friends crowded round, pleased to hear his voice.

"One of us must stay with him," said the man who had sounded the horn. "He must have a servant."

"As long as it is only one," said the porteress firmly.

"My lad Wulf can stay," said the sufferer weakly. "The rest of you find lodgings . . . Leominster. Axebearer, you come each day to ask after me."

The porteress shooed them out, except for the chosen Wulf, a young housecarle, little more than a boy, who appeared to be a kind of personal servant to the injured leader. Wulf watched anxiously as the novice came back bearing ewers and basins and a bunch of herbs inside one of the basins. Dame Hilda was testing the edge of her knife. The man on the bed also roused himself and regarded these preparations dubiously.

"How did it happen?" asked Dame Hilda. "And how long since?"

"Blasted little Welsh runt had rust on his sword," said the supine commander faintly. "We had a fine victory, but at the end I was running down this scruffy savage and he turns round and sticks his sword in my leg. I saw the rust. They don't even keep their weapons in order. I had his head for it, though. Five days ago. What's that knife for?"

Edgiva said, pouring water: "Come, you weren't afraid of the Welsh."

"I had a sword then," said the patient frankly.

"Wulf," said Dame Hilda, "help us to keep him still."

Cleaning the wound took some time.

"Gentle hands! Did I say *gentle?*" the victim enquired bitterly. Wulf, clutching his master's ankle, whispered miserably to Edgiva: "He won't lose it—lose his leg, I mean—will he?"

"Not if I know my business," said Dame Hilda crisply, over-hearing. "But if you'd left it another day . . ." She shook her head and probed the injury again. The patient muttered an ungrateful prayer that the fiends of hell should snatch him and deliver him from these angels of mercy. "Don't blaspheme," said Dame Hilda. She began to wash the wound out with hot water and wine.

"I beg your pardon, Dame Abbess."

"I'm not the abbess. That's the abbess." Dame Hilda spared a thumb to indicate Edgiva, standing ready with a poultice. At a signal from Dame Hilda, she slapped it into place and the patient yelled. He wiped the sweat off his face. "You can't be an abbess," he said earnestly to Edgiva when he could speak again. "You're too young."

No one answered. Edgiva bound the poultice into place and Dame Hilda stirred herbs in hot water. The novice carefully shredded up more leaves and added them.

"Very well, I'm sorry," he said when Edgiva, still silent, gave him the cup. "I meant no rudeness. I was surprised."

"Drink that," said Edgiva.

"It smells horrible."

"It will ease the fever and help you sleep." She put a hand behind his damp ginger head and raised it. Against her fingers she felt the strong, wiry texture of his hair and the heat of the scalp beneath it. He drank unwillingly, making faces and snorting, while Dame Hilda watched him with the air of a child's nurse seeing that her charge finishes its medicine. Edgiva took back the cup when he had done, wished him good sleep, and withdrew. Dame Hilda and the novice were left to gather up clothes and basins and give Wulf his last instructions before following their abbess.

"How did that one ever turn into a nun?" asked the man on the bed as Edgiva's footsteps faded. "Some man's lost a good wife."

"She has taken the Lord for her husband," said Dame Hilda

crushingly, dropping stray leaves and stalks into the empty ewers. "Sister Elfswith, take the cloths away and boil them."

"That must be a very satisfactory kind of married life," said the patient dryly. "It's a waste."

The ageing Dame Hilda eyed him sternly. "Young man, *I* became a bride of Christ to keep from being the bride of a man. My mother had ten babies in ten years, God rest her soul. She was sick carrying them, screamed bearing them, and cried herself into a frenzy when they died, and most of them did die. On the tenth childbed she died herself. I was the first and I saw it all. My father didn't see it because he amused himself elsewhere while his wife travailed. Do you call that a *satisfactory kind of life?* You men are such fools. Now go to sleep, and while you're waiting for sleep, turn your thoughts to matters more in place under a convent roof than the things you might do with our abbess if she wasn't one. Oh, I can read you! By the way . . ." She gathered up her final oddments and prepared to depart. ". . . Who are you?"

He had shut his eyes obediently when told to sleep. He opened them again. "Sweyn," he said. "Earl Sweyn . . . Godwinsson."

The fever fell on the third day, and the pus by then was coming away properly on the linen pads, drawn out by poultices and herbal packs and copious washings in wine. "Happily for him, he's strong," Dame Hilda remarked, inspecting him on the morning of the fourth day. He was asleep, breathing naturally. He had needed his strength and drawn heavily on it, losing flesh. But the structure of his vigour was there to see—the sturdy bones of the fingers, the wide spring of the ribs, visible because he had pushed off the covers.

"Yes," said Abbess Edgiva, standing at her side and staring down at him. "He is, isn't he?"

Later in the morning the man Axebearer was allowed to bring two other men with him to sit with Sweyn for a while, for he had woken up feeling better and was clearly going to be hard to control during his convalescence. If his friends could talk to him, Edgiva said, they might amuse him and stop him from trying to get up.

So he sat up in the bed while they sat on it, and the hush of the sick chamber was broken by male voices and laughter. They had come straight from a horse fight between two wild little stallions stolen from over the Welsh border. Sweyn had had a proxy bet on the outcome, and although he cursed at missing the contest, he rejoiced noisily to learn that he had won. Axebearer had brought the winnings—a knife with a marten-skull handle and a set of horse-teeth chessmen. Abbess Edgiva, walking back from the lodge where she had spoken with a chapman selling needles and silk thread, heard the noise and went to discover the cause. She found a chess game in progress, Axebearer versus Sweyn, each with an advisor. A warning flush had appeared on Sweyn's forehead, and she shook her head at it. They must go soon and let their leader rest, she said. They could come back tomorrow. She sent for the porteress to see them out and herself went away to prayers and the evening meal.

She was tired. The past four days had been a hard struggle against Sweyn's sickness and against more than sickness. One came to a convent believing that it offered escape from the world of wars and battlefields, but it did not. The battles were different, that was all. Disease was one. Weariness was another. Kneeling in the chapel, praying for the guest's recovery, she remembered a saying of her mother's, that things always came in threes. Behind her closed eyes she thought: It is true. The third enemy is already at my gates and I have no strength left to meet him. Oh God, let Sweyn Godwinsson grow well quickly, quickly, and let him depart from this place.

In the evening, as she left the refectory after the meal, she found Sweyn's servant, Wulf, hovering in the courtyard. "My master wants you. He wants to ask something. Will you come?"

Inside the hospital building the stone walls were tinged with sunset. Sweyn lay on his back, hands behind his head. He did not move as her robes rustled over the threshold. She stopped just inside. "You asked for me. Are you in pain?"

He raised his head. "Good evening, Mother Abbess. No. I have rewarded your skill better than that. But I want some information."

"Information?"

"You had a pedlar here this afternoon, Wulf tells me. Had he come far?"

"East Anglia. Why?"

"Do, please, come right in and sit by me for a while. Wulf, put a stool for the abbess. Pedlars with long journeys behind them are bringers of news. They know what's going on in the world! My men know nothing—they're wrapped up in their horse fights and their dice. I like good sport too, but there are other things. What did your chapman have to tell? Who's at war with whom, out in the world, and who's winning? I want to know."

Edgiva took the stool Wulf offered her. "He had a little gossip but nothing that would interest you greatly, I'm afraid. Very little about your own family, for instance."

"Never mind, just tell me what he did say. It's like being deaf or blind, not to know things. Where is the king now—did he know that?"

"Gloucester, I believe. He came that way." Edgiva smiled. "They always know where the king is. It's magical at times. Your father, Earl Godwin, is in Mid-Anglia. Does he know where you are, by the way?"

"I sent word but there's been no time for a reply. I knew he was with my cousin Beorn, yes. Earl Beorn now! Earl! I can pick him up with one hand."

"Not at the moment," said Edgiva dryly.

"I'd mend faster if you'd let me use my legs."

"Not yet, till we're sure the wound won't open again. The pedlar told me there was a rising in Normandy against the young duke there, but the French king is supporting him. Does that interest you?"

"Very much! So Normandy's trying to buck young William out of the saddle, is she? She'll have a job of it, from all I've heard. He grew up the hard way. Wouldn't know what to do with a mount that behaved. What else?"

Church news came naturally. "Bishop Stigand has been promoted from East Anglia to Winchester." Sweyn looked bored. "There's a rumour that Hardraada is back in Norway."

"True, probably. I heard he was coming. What of the Welsh or the Scots? Any excitement there?"

"No news of the Welsh. Did you kill them all?" Edgiva shifted restlessly on her stool, worried by his bright gaze, too intent for her unremarkable bits of gossip. "The young Scots prince, Malcolm, is at Gloucester, I believe. Earl Siward brought him."

"Oh—yes, he lives with Siward. He's an exile," said Sweyn disparagingly. "You didn't know that?"

"No." She shook her head. "Here, we know so little of the world. Travellers who pass through tell us scraps, that's all. We are supposed to keep our thoughts on heaven, not on the business of the earth."

"But when news is told to you, you listen. What brought you here, Lady Abbess? Do you hate the world and menfolk as that fierce Dame Hilda does?"

"I know little of either," said Edgiva remotely. "My family thought the convent best for me. They thought I would like to learn."

"And did you? Or do you?"

"Yes," said Edgiva. "I could not have studied at home. I have been grateful. And happy."

"What do you study?" asked Sweyn, head on one side.

"Latin, calculation, reading and writing, manuscript making . . ."

"Healing?"

"Yes, that too. And herb growing and embroidery."

"I'm stricken with awe," Sweyn said. His eyes danced. "My feeble brain would never grasp so much. But what do you do with it all? You've shut yourself off from life. No husband. No babies. Not even lovers. What takes their place?"

"The love and praise of God," said Edgiva firmly. "For which we would have no time if we had families. Nor would we have time to learn or heal. If we hadn't given up the world, you might be dead by now."

"Alas," said Sweyn sadly, "very true. But it seems a shame . . . a whole world full of pleasures, out of your reach . . ."

Edgiva rose. "It's plain you're fast recovering, my lord. I'm glad. For it seems to me that unless you can temper your speech to your surroundings, you should find more suitable surroundings soon."

"Oh, you're offended. My deepest apologies, Lady Abbess." He did not sound apologetic. "I talk too much." He moved the bulge of his strapped leg. "I think I'm talking now so as not to think about this. The truth is, there *has* been some pain today. I hoped it would stop, that I had only knocked it, but it hasn't."

Edgiva said: "When was the dressing changed?"

"This morning."

"I can renew it. I'll fetch fresh dressings."

"Wulf can do that. He knows what to get. Wulf, come here!"

Waving away Edgiva's objections, he told Wulf what to fetch and threw off his covers as the boy departed. He started to unfasten the bindings. Clicking her tongue, Edgiva went to him.

She was less gentle than usual and pushed his hand brusquely aside as she took hold of the wrappings. The touch of his skin worried her; she was too much aware of it. She was annoyed that her body should so answer his without the consent of her mind. At close quarters now she was horribly conscious of him—his warmth, the brightness of his eyes, his strong springing hair. Wulf's return was a relief.

She scalded the herbs and brought the basin over. The wound did not look inflamed. Sweyn said: "Am I allowed wine yet? I've had nothing but milk and well water and revolting herb concoctions since I came here."

"Wine's bad for fever."

"I haven't any fever now."

"I suppose you can have a little if you want it. I'll send some later." She applied the cloths with skill. "I can't see much wrong with this."

"I want some wine now. Can't Wulf get it?"

Invalids were often impatient. One tended to humour them. She took her buttery key off its ring. "There's watered wine in the jar nearest the door," she said to Wulf. "And pitchers on the shelf above. You know where the buttery is? Go along, then." Wulf hurried out. Surely, she thought, this taut sense of gathering danger was imaginary, born of her own unschooled longings, her ignorance, her folly. She had known within an hour of Sweyn's arrival that he represented a male world of which she knew nothing, and that this lack of knowledge was perilous. She was like a man going to battle without a shield. But surely the risk she ran was only that of seeming a fool. His talk was only talk; it was part of him and meant nothing unless a woman were both fair and free. She wiped the wound carefully dry, and as she did so Sweyn's fingers closed softly round her wrist.

They were both quite still. Edgiva said warily: "Did I hurt you? I'm sorry."

"It isn't that," said Sweyn. "Give me your hand." He pulled at her wrist, not roughly, but with strength. "Let me guide it." Momentarily she yielded and let him draw her hand upwards. With a shock that stiffened her whole body she found that he was erect. "Take hold of it," he said coaxingly.

The rigid instant passed; she snatched away her hand.

"*This* is a convent. And I am an abbess. And if I were not I would still be a nun. Have you forgotten? How *dare* you?"

"The world gets peopled by that sort of daring. It's quite common." Sweyn shook his head at her. "I hadn't forgotten. But you're a woman as well as an abbess, and I can't forget that either. You've wrapped yourself up in gloomy draperies and said some words about—what is it?—chastity and poverty? What of it? Words don't change anything. You're just what you were before you spoke them. Don't you like me?"

"Like you! I'm ashamed of you, my lord!" The dressing had to be finished. She finished it, her hands shaking.

"Really?" said Sweyn lazily, smiling up at her with eyes so impenitent that she could have slapped him. "Really ashamed of me? Or just ashamed of yourself, of being the way God made you? You nuns! You know so much of so many things and so little about yourselves."

He had been trained in the surprise attack. Before she could move to stop him, or even guess what he intended, he had pulled her down on top of him and stopped her protesting mouth with his.

2 ✠ The Battlefield of Love

The abbess had a room where she could toil in peace at her studies, pray alone, or talk in privacy with nuns and novices. It was square and low-doored with whitewashed walls and stone-flagged floor. In winter it was warmed by an iron brazier. In summer it was a haven of coolness. It held a table and a chair and four wooden stools. A rood hung on the wall and beneath it was a chest containing relics of a saint martyred by the heathen Danes two hundred years before. Shelves held Edgiva's inks and tinctures, quills and brushes, and rolls of prepared vellum. Three tall, narrow windows set close together let in daylight, and with it the scent of the honeysuckle that clung to the wall outside and the hum of a bumblebee among its flowers.

It was Edgiva's own place now, her home, where she could be alone with the manuscripts which were her spirit's outlet. But this evening, as she sat shaking in her chair and told her tale to a sagely nodding Dame Hilda, she felt the air of sanctuary tainted. On the table lay a vellum sheet held down by stones at the corners, its colours drying where the work was finished and faint charcoal outlines inviting her brush to the rest. She had looked forward to completing it. Now it meant nothing.

As she talked she found her eyes going to the iron-hooped chest which held the phial of blood and the lock of hair and the fibula bone of St. Ethelflaed. Ethelflaed must have felt as Edgiva did now, when she took refuge by the altar of her church, and the Danes pursued her there regardless. She had thought that the altar meant safety, but the heathen had not cared. St. Ethelflaed, it was said, had prayed aloud for help and the foremost Dane, grabbing at her, had dropped his dagger. She had snatched it up and plunged it into her own heart. At this point, however, Edgiva's feelings strongly diverged from St. Ethelflaed's, for death, shamefully, was not the desire Sweyn had waked in her. She shut her mind against that shocking truth and tried to listen to Dame Hilda.

"I never had any patience with Ethelflaed," the old nun was remarking incredibly, as if the saint were a particularly silly young novice. "Stupid girl."

Edgiva blinked. "You mean . . . she shouldn't have killed herself?"

"Of course she should. She could hardly have done anything else. But she should have stuck the dagger into the man first. It's always the men who make the trouble—mostly for the women. And when they've got what they want, they aren't grateful. As soon as a girl gets big round the belly, they're off again after another one. If she's a mistress she gets cast off, and if she's a wife he goes and finds a mistress. This one has a bad name with women—you didn't know, perhaps, and I, God forgive me, thought him too sick to be dangerous. And anyway, in a *convent* . . . ! Well, it's natural you're distressed, but there was no harm done, you say? He kissed you? Nothing more?"

"Indeed not! I wrenched myself free and ran. I came straight here and summoned you. No. No harm was done."

It depended what you meant by harm. Two people seemed grappling for possession of Edgiva's one body, an outraged nun and a hungry female animal. "I wasn't careful enough," she said. "That was a fault."

"Perhaps. Tell the confessor. But it's the future that matters. None of us must ever be alone with him again."

"I hope never to see him again!" said Edgiva with passion.

When Dame Hilda had gone, Edgiva knelt down before the rood, elbows on St. Ethelflaed's relic chest. She clasped her hands. But the prayer she wished to make would not be spoken.

She had wanted to say: Forgive me my unseemly lust and help me cast it out. Give me strength to fight.

But the words that sprang into her mouth were of anger and repudiation. "I did not choose to be a nun. I cried out loud: 'I want to marry!' But no one listened. I was forced to take vows with my tongue that I never made in my soul. By what right do You hold me to them? By what right do You condemn me a sinner for being as You made me?"

Sweyn. He was imprinted on her senses, colouring them as her pigments coloured the waiting outlines on her manuscripts. Her skin still felt his warmth, his eyes still looked into hers. She simply wanted him, and it was simple, that was the right word. It was a simple thing . . . to all creation but stupid human folk. It was simple to the roebuck running beside his doe, to the hen bird on her nest. Why did it have to be spoilt for people? Why did God have to interfere? She felt her vows like chains of iron, every word a link.

Sweyn's voice in her mind said: Words don't change anything.

"Oh, God," said Edgiva despairingly. She hammered the top of the relic chest with clenched fists and then, at last, she prayed.

The harbour at Dover lay in blazing sunlight and the glitter of the water hurt the eyes. Air currents there must be, for above the sea the gulls were lazily adrift on them. But no breath stirred the hair of the four men gathered to look at the ship drawn up on the strand. Out in the harbour the bright painted floats of someone's lobster pots, which shouldn't have been there, hardly moved on their lines.

"If you must buy a ship," said Ragnar to his father-in-law "then yes, I grant you, she is a good one. If you *must*."

Eric's announcement that he meant to buy his own vessel had not precisely drawn applause from his family. But he had held to it. He was tired of the cheating captains who stole his goods and told him they'd been washed overboard, tired of leaky tubs that foundered with all hands and his merchandise. He had tried again and again to achieve that third triumphant voyage that would make a thane of him and failed through a series of dishonesties and disasters which ate his hard-garnered capital as well as delaying his promotion. So now, he said, he would have his own ship, sound, manned by men he had chosen. Ragnar and Rolf, now in a comfortable partnership whereby they sent wool to the northlands and brought back ship-masts and weaponry, using hired ships and going themselves only if they felt like it, shrugged. "You'll have the crew eating themselves fat at your expense between trips and laid out drunk when you want them," Ragnar warned.

"You'll have to pay for careening in winter and all the repairs—every single rotten rope," Rolf had added. Eric replied that he had found the ship he wanted and he meant to call her *Hild*.

"A good ship?" *Hild*'s shipwright said now in outraged tones, facing the three of them. "The best I ever build." He was a hulking Flanders-born seaman who looked like a pirate and probably had been. He was the kind of man Eric usually disliked, but the merchant got on with Gudbrand Shipwright because Gudbrand had a true scientific love of the sea and could talk for hours of tides and stars and navigation, where others of his ilk only talked of women, fights, and lawlessness. He had a stock of tall sea tales which the stolid Eric did not believe but nonetheless enjoyed. "She's new," Gudbrand now said. "I build her for an old shipmate of mine and the day he is to take her, what does he do? He goes drinking in her honour and falls out with his mates and there's a fight and a man killed and now he must pay such a weregild he can't pay me. It was a fair fight and it was him or the other man, but still they fine him." He spat into the harbour. "Such silly laws! So here am I with this ship on my hands and no one to buy. So you buy, eh?" He grinned at Eric and tugged at his blond beard. "My beard, it feels dry. We wet it to the bargain, eh?"

"Not so fast," said Eric, his bargaining instincts on top. He looked down at the ship. She was sixty feet long, a broad-beamed trader, but graceful in spite of it, her planking still golden with newness. She had places for twenty pairs of rowers, ornamented oars, and a great proud prow with a dragon's head atop a curving serpentine neck minutely carved with scales.

"That figurehead," said Eric. "Too like a pirate craft."

"All the better. Keep the others off."

"Speed is what keeps off pirates, not dragonheads," said Eric quietly. "There ought to be . . ."

"Speed she has! I build her for speed myself, shape her keel for it! She cut the water like a knife, a shark's fin . . ."

"I want two more pairs of rowers."

Gudbrand made a large gesture with massive shoulders and fleshy hands. "I could, yes. Room there is. It cost you . . . twelve silver pennies more in coin. But I take salt, wine, gemstones, in part payment. There's much work."

"Eight silver pence," said Eric automatically. "There's not that much work. One pair can go *there* . . . there's space. The other . . ."

"For you who are a friend," said Gudbrand, slapping a hand over his heart, "eleven." They had known each other casually for years.

"Nine."

"Agreed. It take a month, maybe two. I have work on hand. New ships for the king. A dozen shipwrights in Dover, but it is me the king's men come to," said Gudbrand immodestly.

"That is all right. I didn't expect much work from her this season. The figurehead can stay."

"By the Skyfather and the Thunder God, I hope so!" Gudbrand was scandalised. "I hire the best craftsman in Kent to make it! He is seaman himself and he make it the very fashion of a sea serpent he see himself one day off Bergen. It was a day of calm and he see this swirling in the water and order his rowers . . ."

"It's time," said Ragnar, amused, "that we all go and wet our beards." They had heard the serpent story before.

"One moment," said Rolf, shading his eyes, "there's some fun going on in the harbour. "Oh, I see. The lobster pots!"

An incoming vessel, one of the coast-hugging traders with half a dozen pairs of rowers which plied round the shores from port to port, had got her oars entangled with the line of one of the illicit pots. A fisherman had appeared on the harbour's wooden jetty, where the deeper-draught ships from the south came in. He was red in the face and bellowing. Answering bellows drifted from the trapped vessel and a crowd of small boys and bystanders had magically appeared at the water's edge, where they stood and made derisive noises.

"Perhaps a fight there will be," said Gudbrand hopefully. "They have cut the lines now."

The oars were plying once again. The craft drew within reach for purposes of lucid verbal exchange, and the two streams of abuse became reciprocal.

"You wantwit rowers couldn't turn an ale barrel round in an ocean and not foul something!"

"If you'd mark your bloody pots or put 'em where they ought to be, out of our way, there'd be nothing to foul!"

"You cut my lines!"

"Did you think we'd hang ourselves in 'em?"

The rowers negotiated another stray line and brought their keel ashore. The fisherman, rushing back along the jetty to get round the beach and meet them, trod on a piece of seaweed, slipped, and went into the sea. Some friends went to rescue him and could be heard, between their whoops of laughter and his curses, dissuading him from a single-handed fight with twelve men.

"There will be no fight," said Gudbrand, disappointed. "But . . ." He brightened. "The ship is landing a passenger, and from that big pack with straps fixed to it, he is a chapman. Come!" He was already striding forward. "Let us get there first and exchange hospitality for news. No doubt your wife would like some farings, eh, Ragnar?"

"Mind you," said the stranger as Gudbrand, beating several other bystanders to it by no more than a nose, began to help him on with his pack, "the fisherman's right. They couldn't turn an ale barrel round in an ocean. I didn't think we'd get here, once or twice. They were drunk all the way."

Eric, coming up, said: "Pedlar, are you?"

"Aye. I took ship to get here for your August fair. I've been over the Welsh March way."

"If you've a mind to make a sale or two," Ragnar said, "you can stay with us tonight. My wife might be a customer and we don't get news from the Marches every day. You'd be welcome."

"I'll be glad of your houseroom." They set off, strolling, away from the waterside. "I carry needles, silks, bead necklaces, belts, combs, gloves. I sell to court ladies and convents—convents like the best, if you can believe it!—and . . ."

"We're all merchants," said Ragnar, amused. "Even Gudbrand here sells ships. We know sales talk when we hear it!"

"Then you know quality too," said the pedlar, undeterred, as they went up the rutted street with the river running beside it. "As for news—Earl Sweyn's taken the edge off the Welsh swords for a bit, which is good hearing. But . . ."—his thin, dark, faintly Phoenician face split into a crescent of a malicious smile—"there's other news of Sweyn. There are odder goings-on in convents than buying first-rate needles, these days."

"Oh, those tales!" Eric was scornful. "Not true, mostly."

"This one is. Oh, this one is. I was at the convent when Earl

Sweyn was sick there, and back again the day after . . . well, it's a
tale best told with a moist throat. The tale of an abbess and an earl."

To their surprise Gudbrand, the hulking, hearty, piratical Gudbrand, stopped short in the dusty road and crossed himself.

"If that *is* true," he said, looking up into the dazzling August
sky, "then there's bad luck coming. God protect us."

By the third hour of Sweyn's feast in celebration of his return to his
hall, the affair was a self-evident success. Egfrith and Olaf, two of
the finest topers in his following, were snoring on the floor. A man
called Helgi Oakenskull had been knocked out in a fuddled argument
with one Thorold, who thenceforth bore the name of Thorold
Cleave-Oak. A Scot called Kenneth and a Kentishman named
Alfmaer were happily drinking a toast to a new-made pact to seduce
or if necessary ravish the daughter of a certain petty Welsh chieftain,
a girl they had never seen but who was reputedly as beautiful as a
black-haired angel. In the morning they would regret their ale-
inspired oaths but, being honest men, would attempt to fulfil them.
They would regret them even more when they learnt that the hidden
daughter was both repulsively ugly and simple-minded to boot.
Sweyn himself, elbows on the scrubbed pine table, was swallowing
drink for drink with his friend Tofig Axebearer. He had already
beaten Axebearer at a trial of strength, elbows supported and right
hands clasped palm to palm.

"You know," Axebearer remarked as the ale beakers were re-
filled, ". . . that was a funny experience, going inside that convent.
Never been in one before."

"They wouldn't have wanted you. Wrong sex." Sweyn chuckled.

"No, no, seriously. *Seriously*. Never knew convents were like
that . . . ladies like that . . . quite happy, doing good, praying,
learning . . . God, *learning*! I heard them pattering away in Latin,
enough to burst your head . . . but nothing else. All given up to
God. One day . . . one day, I'll repent and go on pilgrimage. Die a
good man, if I live long enough . . . ." Axebearer opened his large,
gap-toothed mouth unexpectedly and laughed.

Kenneth and Alfmaer abandoned their own discussion and
asked what they were missing.

"Axebearer's having a fit of virtue," said Sweyn. "Says he'll repent one day and die a good man if he lives long enough."

"What put that in your head, Axebearer?" Kenneth asked when the joke had been duly appreciated.

"Leominster Abbey. All those women who've let go of the world." He shook a thick, solemn finger. "They've found something, must've done. Not a natural way to live. No men, no children . . . women should have children . . ."

"You've always tried to make them happy," said Alfmaer solemnly. Axebearer was not deflected. "Maybe. Maybe. But how do you account for it? Those women . . ."

"Weren't all such ice-maidens," Kenneth said. "Didn't you see the abbess looking at our Lord Godwinsson here when he took leave of her? There's a fine natural lassie wrapped up in those crow's feathers. Hey, Alfmaer, what about that? A quarry for each of us. I for the Welsh girl, you for the abbess."

"I wouldn't go chasing a nun," said Alfmaer, almost shocked into sobriety. "I'd be struck by lightning, like as not. Besides, she wants Godwinsson."

"I tried a bit of wooing while I had the chance," Sweyn admitted. He upended his beaker on the table. A thrall ran up. "Fill it up, boy, we're drinking to a lovely abbess. You drink, too. To Edgiva, learned lady, holy-habited healer, who said no to Sweyn Godwinsson."

"The trouble," said Kenneth earnestly, "was that you were on her ground. Always a drawback, that."

"How d'you mean?" asked Sweyn, interested.

"She was at home. It was her abbey. You were a stranger. You put a horse to graze with another horse, the one that's there already will bully the new one, even if the new one's bigger. Other way round, that's what you need. Now, if you'd brought her here to *your* home . . . Still . . ." Misgiving seized him. "Alfmaer's right. She's a nun."

Sweyn snorted. "You think I'd be struck by lightning? By Odin's Beard and the Mistletoe Spear, I've half a mind to find out!" He sat up straight and hammered the table. "How's that for a wager? That I bring her here and make her love me and the lightning doesn't strike? God's Elbow, Kenneth, you drunken Scots barbarian, if you want to be sick, go outside! He's shocked! He won't take me on. Who will, then? Who will?"

"I will," said Axebearer, watching the Scot unsteadily depart. "My best gold arm-ring to your deerhound?"

"It's done. Agreed."

"You're mad. Both clean crazy," said Alfmaer sadly, shaking his head, and he emptied the remainder of his ale over the recumbent Oakenskull in a spirit of scientific enquiry to see if it would bring him round.

The parting from Sweyn had been worse than anything dreamed by Edgiva in all her life, beyond any grief that hitherto had touched her.

She had sworn not to see him again, but it was more than she could do to let him go without saying farewell to him. Besides, she told herself, he was an earl; he would expect to be sped on his way by the abbess and not by an underling. So she was there at the leave-taking, a ceremonial business with the nuns gathered near the gate, an escort of housecarles in the road outside, and Sweyn presenting gifts to the convent in gratitude for its care of him.

Edgiva went through it with her mind elsewhere, imprisoned in misery. In a moment it would be finished. He would ride away and she would never set eyes on him again. An eternal hell of empty days and dreadful nights stretched before her, in which his voice would speak and his form move in her mind, yet she would be without him, not even daring to speak his name.

She had begun to know that hell already during these days when she, the righteously offended abbess, had kept away from him. But at least he was there; she could feel him through the walls. Once she had heard his voice in the distance. Three times, when the inner gate between the nuns' house and the hospital stood open, she had glimpsed him walking on the grass. After today even those tiny comforts would be lost to her.

The farewells ended at last, as the longest life must end and the hardest death. She returned to her joyless pigments and her account tallies, her cell and her empty prayers. She talked with her nuns, dined, and hoed an onion patch to set an example of humble toil and ease her tumultuous feeling with physical exhaustion. When night came, she slept. But his wraith was at her bedside when the bell called her to devotions before daybreak and went with her to chapel and back again through the dawn. She began the day as one who sets out on a voyage, in a craft with small provision, across an unknown sea.

Afternoon had come again and she was laying down gold leaf on vellum, trying to believe it mattered, when the porteress came unsmilingly to say that a party of Sweyn Godwinsson's men were at the gate demanding audience with her. "Put them in the visitors' room," said Edgiva, rising. "Two of them, that is. The rest must wait outside. No doubt the earl wishes to make some grant to the abbey as a further sign of thanks. I hope he hasn't fallen sick again." Amazing how one's face and voice could so smoothly deny the surging of the blood.

"I hope so, too," said the porteress with meaning. She knew the tale of Sweyn's assault on Edgiva.

But there were twelve men in the audience room when she got there. "They *pushed* their way in!" said the porteress, flushed and indignant. The big burly one called Axebearer, who had been Sweyn's spokesman when they brought him in, stepped forward as Edgiva paused in the doorway. "Abbess Edgiva?" he said in a formal voice.

Something was wrong. His manner was perfectly courteous, but behind the courtesy lay menace, force, something as out of place in this sanctified atmosphere as a wild boar in a cathedral.

"You know me by sight, I think," said Edgiva briskly.

"We are here on the orders of our overlord Sweyn Godwinsson, Earl of the Western March. He desires that you visit him at his Hereford manor. We have come to escort you there."

"*What!*" burst out the porteress.

Axebearer glanced at the two men nearest him. "We don't want the old woman," he said. "Take her out. But keep her with you till we leave."

The porteress was removed, efficiently. Outside, her protests were suddenly cut short, as if someone had put a hand over her mouth. Someone probably had.

"I am to tell you," said Axebearer to Edgiva, "that my lord means you all kindness and hospitality. But you are to come. If not willingly, then by force. We have brought you a pony."

"I can't ride," said Edgiva blankly. They had surrounded her. In her own convent she had become a prisoner.

"You need only sit on the saddle and hold the pommel. We'll lead it."

Edgiva drew herself up. "I want to know what business Lord Sweyn has with me."

Amusement sprang into their faces. Two of them laughed. Axebearer said softly: "Now that is a silly question."

One of the men was opening the door for her. Another gently pushed her. She could walk on her own feet, or be carried. Her heart pounded. She was afraid. She was joyous. She was going to Sweyn. Without having to make the choice herself, without the wilful breaking of vows on her conscience. In their midst, without resistance, she went out of the convent.

Outside in the road waited a group of horses, tails swishing at the flies. Axebearer helped her mount a sturdy bay gelding and put the stirrups right for her. As they began to move off she saw the porteress, freed again, running to the gate with half a dozen flying-robed nuns behind her, their faces aghast. Some of the men blew kisses to them and the gesticulating little group fell back, were shooed back, indeed, by the porteress and Dame Hilda, who was at her side. Dame Hilda was shaking her fist. It struck Edgiva that probably she would never see any of them again. Then they were out of sight.

Afterwards, through all that followed, the best and most beautiful hours and those of the darkest anguish, the ride from Leominster to Hereford stood apart, something to cling to in memory. During that ride, thirteen miles as the crow flew and three dusty hours as a pony jogged, she was out of the ordinary world, between heaven and earth, past and future, Edgiva the abbess and Edgiva Sweyn Godwinsson's woman. If Eve paused between plucking the apple and eating, it was like this. She wanted the ride to last forever, going towards Sweyn but never arriving. For she knew that when she did arrive, the moment she saw the rooftree of Sweyn's hall, the world would crowd back and her longings, becoming fleshly fact, would lose their magic. She would be afraid again and defenceless, and most defenceless of all against herself.

The courtyard of the hall was full of cooking smells, and smoke streamed from the roof vent. The household must be eating. But Axebearer did not take her to the hall. He helped her off the pony and led her instead to one of the lesser buildings, where he beat on the door and called. The door opened and she was pushed in. She heard it shut after her, and she was face to face with Sweyn.

He looked as she had imagined him all through the day and night since they had parted. The sun through a window glittered on his tawny hair. Mischief danced in his eyes, light on a green sea. A table was beside him with wine and food on it, and behind him was a wide padded couch with a glossy rug of deerskins.

He said: "Welcome to your home."

Edgiva said: "I demand to know why I have been brought here in this disgraceful fashion, as if I were under arrest! Do you forget all that I and my convent have done for you?"

Sweyn grinned. Without trying to find words for it, he understood the nature of the barrier between them. Edgiva, bound by vows, by ingrained beliefs and fears of hell, could never of her own will step out of the part of insulted abbess. He must wrench her from it, and to do that he must play the part of a Viking marauder, for most if not all the way. Well, he had Viking marauders among his recent ancestors. He shouldn't find it difficult. It would probably be fun.

In the event, it was a magnificent fight. It was also fairly prolonged, since Sweyn, however strong and determined to have his way, was hampered by trying to disrobe himself as well as Edgiva, and because he did not really want to hurt her. Edgiva, on the other hand, harassed alike by the enemy outside the gates and by treachery within them, could see no way to salvation except by a stalwart attempt to kill Sweyn. She inflicted a good deal of surface damage with a silver candlestick, until Sweyn, tired of being bruised by it, snatched it away and hurled it through the window. Whereupon Edgiva, panting and frantic, her vision blurred by fright, fury, and exhaustion, seized the first portable object within reach, which chanced to be a leg of chicken from the refreshment table, and Sweyn, roaring with laughter, collapsed in a corner in mock alarm.

Edgiva looked down at her assailant, who was peering bright-eyed at her from under his shielding arms, looked at her bizarre and useless weapon and stumbled back. She cursed and threw the stupid chicken leg away. Sweyn instantly uncurled himself and with a smooth enwrapping movement bore her across the room to the bed, on which they landed together with a thud that shook it. With one

arm he held her against him while with the other hand he stripped
off the remainder of their clothing.

"There goes the last of convent; forget it now," he said, as he
threw the fabric on to the floor. "Hush now. Hush, my love."

His warmth lay along her and his strength was round her, and
their bodies were talking to each other, in a language that Dame
Hilda and the old abbess of Leominster had never known. Edgiva's
eyes changed and Sweyn, smiling down into them, watched as her
pupils widened and darkened, filling up with wonder.

"*Now* will you let me in?" he asked her, and he was no longer a
marauder, but spoke as a guest on the threshold, who does not fear
refusal beyond some short-lived jest.

The youth Wulf, shouted for through the window some time
later and ordered to bring more wine and food to Sweyn's apartment, went back to the hall after performing his errand and reported
the scene. "Near carnage it was . . . the table all in splinters and the
wine spilt on the floor, and clothes and robes all torn, all over the
place . . . and I picked up a candlestick *outside*!"

"And them, themselves?" asked Kenneth the Scot with interest.

Wulf said bewilderedly: "They were curled up under the deerskins the way your old Fleetfoot's pups curl up by their dam. After
all that! And laughing fit to burst . . . something to do with her trying to brain him with a leg of chicken! Or that's what I thought they
said." Wulf was young. He added with a snort of incomprehension:
"They looked clean daft to me!"

"Not daft," said Kenneth, amused. "Just in love!"

3 ⚚ "Sweyn Is My Son"

To the great surprise of everyone except the few who knew Edith Godwinsdaughter well, the king's bride was very soon on the friendliest of terms with her mother-in-law.

At the start there were crosscurrents, admittedly. Emma, enthroned on two marriages and five children, sceptred with power, mantled in intrigue, and crowned with more experience of hate, love, triumph, and sorrow than convent-bred Edith knew the world contained, was ready to play the queen to the peasant girl. Her attitude was tempered only by the fact that she was a little sorry for the peasant girl. In Emma's cynical opinion, her royal son Edward was no matrimonial prize.

But convent-bred or not, Edith—as Edward had painfully recognised already—was also Godwin's child. She wore the manners of the convent, the soft voice and restrained movements, as if they were garments. Within them she had other characteristics.

She demonstrated the first within days of her marriage by unexpectedly discovering a talent for dress. Edith from the convent had worn simple clothes with little colour. Edith the queen swished across the hall in trailing skirts of sea-green which picked up the green in her hazel eyes; gleamed at torchlit feasts in silk overtunics of tawny or turquoise which flattered her fine skin and her yellow-golden, burnished ringlets; sparkled in jewellery of amber and garnet and gold. At the same time she revealed a surefooted knowledge of court protocol. Emma, looking for opportunities to patronise, knew in a week that in Edith's clothes or behaviour she wasn't going to find them.

Nor did she find them when it came to discussing the business of the realm. Edith, daughter of the land's foremost earl and a kinswoman of King Cnut, had been very well educated politically. Repeatedly, what Emma began as an instruction session, Queen Maestro to Princess Tyro, ended as an informed dialogue on current affairs between equals, and Emma did not know how it had happened.

Nor was she more successful in her attempts to advise Edith on her conduct as a wife and to probe into her private life with Edward. Edith was unfailingly courteous and unfailingly discreet. Her public manner to Edward was faultless, a mingling of the dignified and the affectionate, and if the marital chamber had not brought her all the joy it should, Edith was not going to talk about it. Not even to Edward's mother.

Well, Emma said cynically to herself, it would be interesting to see how long *that* lasted. If Edward as a husband was turning out adequate by more than a hairsbreadth, then she, Emma, knew nothing of men. But if her guess was right, then Edith was acting gallantly, and Emma liked gallantry.

She could also appreciate cleverness. And there was great cleverness in Edith's gentle but inflexible determination to behave as if her mother-in-law and her husband were an ordinary loving mother and son, like the kind of family she had grown up in. If both were present at any time, she talked cheerfully to either and led them to talk to each other. She proposed joint excursions with such good timing that neither could reasonably refuse. Bemusedly, Edward and Emma found themselves sauntering side by side round abbeys and mints and potteries and weaving sheds, exchanging suitable comments. The court began to say that Edith was a good influence.

As the months lengthened to a year and beyond it, Emma's respect for her daughter-in-law grew. She thought Edward's respect was growing too. Something had been far wrong at the start; the honeymoon air had been quite lacking. Now, she thought, he was warming to his wife. If only . . .

"I have never much enjoyed weaving," said Emma, choosing oatcakes from the tray Rohese held out to her. "Your skills on the loom impress me, Edith. If you ever have to follow your husband into exile as I once went with mine, you'll be able to keep the two of you."

"I expect we'd go to Flanders like everyone else," said Edith, half-serious. She added, wholly serious: "I hope it never happens."

"For your sake, so do I." Emma, seated by a window, glanced through the open shutter and across the courtyard to the hall, where Edward was at that moment in council. The hall shutters too were open and a murmur of voices came through them. "Well, all seems peaceful enough today. Leave that weaving and sit here for a while. You put these idle girls of mine to shame."

"They're not really idle," said Edith mildly, giving her gentle smile to the maligned ones. She sat gracefully on the stool at Emma's feet. "They rise early and attend you faithfully. My own ladies work no harder. As for the weaving I do—it's an excuse to take good care of my hands." She glanced at her smooth-skinned fingers and laughed. "I pretend the rosewater and the unguents are to keep the threads from snagging, not for vanity. But it isn't true!"

"Why should it be? You're not in the convent now. Do you miss the cloister?"

"No. Not now." Edith took a cake and Rohese poured wine. It was the light refreshment they generally had between breakfast and the main meal in late afternoon. "I like visiting religious houses but I wouldn't like to pass a lifetime in one, not now. I enjoyed going to Abingdon last month. All the more because it was only a visit."

"Ah, yes. Abingdon." Emma seemed abstracted. "Where you objected to the food the schoolboys had. Did Edward award them some money for better food? You said you meant to ask him."

"I did. At least, I asked him to award some money of mine. Someone willed me the revenues of a village not long ago. I thought I could spare those easily to feed some children properly." Suddenly Edith's eyes sparkled with anger. "How can they grow up strong on bread and gruel, with meat once a month, if that? I signed the grant two weeks ago and I shall visit Abingdon again, unexpectedly, to see that it has been used well. It was that creature Sparhafoc's fault. There's no real heart in him for all his holy talk."

"You like children," Emma observed. Her tone was quite neutral, but the words hung in the air. She flicked her fingers and the ladies, her own and Edith's, retired with their refreshments to the other end of the chamber. "Have you any signs of pregnancy yet, Edith?" she enquired.

Edith held her wine cup carefully, not clutching it too tightly, not letting her hands shake. "I . . . am afraid not, madam." She put the cup down. "I had hoped . . . this month. But I was late, that was all. I was disappointed."

"So you did have reason," said Emma, breaching the wall she had now besieged for eighteen months, and marching through it into the stronghold, "to think you could be with child? Edward has been carrying out his duties?"

"Yes, madam. Edward is all he should be."

"I'm very glad to hear it. There have been rumours."

"Rumours!"

Edith's voice, startled out of its studied quietness, shot up several notes. Emma permitted a trace of a sour smile to appear.

"Rumours," she repeated. "To the effect that my pious son, in a misplaced zeal for the early Christian virtue of continence, has been pursuing it within his marriage. He has been seen at his devotions in the royal chapel at night long after one might expect him to be at his devotions to his wife. The other theory—there seem to be rival rumours, Edith—is that he isn't able and was praying for virility. And it's no use looking so shocked. Sooner or later you will hear these tales. It may as well be now, from me, in private."

"Edward is regular and careful in his prayers," said Edith indignantly. "And on some saints' anniversaries he keeps all-night vigil. But he does not neglect me. He longs for an heir and does all that is necessary to get one. What tales are these? Who is spreading them?"

"Who? God knows, child. I overhear a little here, people tell me a little there. People do tell me things. I reward them for information and I don't blame the informant if I don't like the news. You relieve my mind. I should like to have grandchildren I can see sometimes, I must say. I must ask Godgift to send her sons on a long visit one day. But returning to you, Edith. I shall not blame you if there is no child. None of my sons have had any. But I shall feel sorry for the lack in your life."

"You are very kind, madam."

"I'm rarely kind. I mean it. Tcha!" Emma made an impatient sound. "If you do have a son, it will be a fine thing for the whole land and for Edward too. He might cling less to his friends. I hear that Robert of Jumièges has agreed to stay here for good, by the way." Emma glanced out of the window again. There was a flurry in the courtyard; a horseman had ridden in in haste and was running, cloak flying, up the steps of the council chamber. Emma smiled. The court, its affairs, its crises, its posthaste messengers and secret manoeuvres, were like food and air to her. This visit to Gloucester with Edith was unusual, a sortie from her Winchester fastness and a stimulating treat. "Someone has arrived with news worth hearing," she remarked in parentheses. "I shall send to find out what it is, presently."

"Jumièges and my husband were friends in Normandy," Edith said. "I think Edward values his advice on financial matters."

"I hope it's worth it. Edward has too many Normans round him. Cnut was clever that way. He used always to give the English preference over the Danes, whatever his private feelings."

"But . . . there are only a handful of Normans."

"In key places, near the throne. And Champart's a climber. Edward thinks he's just a loving friend, but I've met dozens of Champarts in my time. And now I understand he's to be made Bishop of London. Madness! If you get a chance to warn Edward about favouring Normans, do so! Ah!" A fresh set of noises from outside had drawn her attention once more to the courtyard. Edward was striding out of the council chamber and coming towards the bower. "I don't think I shall have to send to hear the news after all," Emma commented. "It's coming of its own accord."

"King Edward!" said a breathless page in the door. He had had to outdistance the king in order to announce him.

Edward, pushing him aside, strode pale-faced into the room. The ladies half rose to greet him and then, as once before, subsided because it seemed unnecessary. He made straight for his wife and stopped in front of her.

"I have some news," he said without preamble. "It ought to interest you, Edith, my dear." He was speaking through his teeth. He paused a moment and then poured it out, beginning in the Norman French he so often used at court and sliding abruptly into the vernacular under the pressure of rage. He often did it when angry, never noticing that it was Emma's trick.

"Your family, my sweet wife Edith, are getting a little above themselves! They think themselves beyond the laws of God and man since they saw you made a queen! The news is about your brother, my dear. Your renowned, handsome, honourable, puissant, *bloody* eldest brother!"

It had been an ecclesiastical council, and the prelates were now crowding into the bower after him. Jumièges was there, his lean face anxious. Alfric Kitehawk of York, Bishop Aldred of Worcester, and Bishop Stigand followed. Abbot Sparhafoc came last, lamenting. ". . . A calamity! So fine a young body! So hopeful a young soul! A terrible, terrible calamity!"

"These things happen." Champart was urbane, trying to nudge Sparhafoc to silence.

"Young men will be young men," Stigand agreed.

"This young man," said the King of England savagely, still glowering at his astonished wife and his tight-mouthed mother, "is unlikely to live to be an old one, unless he mends his manners."

"Come, my lord, it's hardly a killing matter." Stigand's voice was matter-of-fact. It was plain that Edward had erupted out of his council chamber regardless of his friends' attempts to stop him. They were still trying to exercise restraint.

"And if I may say so, my lord," added Champart, taking the liberty of a long-standing friend, "the matter is hardly to be blamed on the queen." Edith shot him a grateful glance. "Your lady is convent-reared. She will share your . . . our . . . horror."

"Will someone please explain," said Emma, her voice scything across the male argument, "what, precisely, has happened? Has the queen's eldest brother done something disgraceful? If so, Edward, you can hardly expect your wife to control her brother's actions when she is weaving cloth for your wardrobe in Gloucester and he is chopping up Welshmen on the marches fifty miles away. What *has* he done, and why do you think it Edith's fault?"

Edward jerked his head at someone hovering in the doorway, and Godwin came slowly into the room. He was alone and bareheaded and his face had the washed-clean look of shock. Sparhafoc started another lament, but a warning hand on his elbow—it was Stigand's hand—silenced him.

"Godwin will tell you," said Edward. "My tongue won't frame the words."

"Father?" said Edith nervously. She had risen as Edward came in; now she remained standing, looking into Godwin's face. "Is Sweyn . . . is he dead?"

"Unfortunately, no," Edward put in.

"Poor boy, far better in his grave than so dishonoured . . ."

"Sparhafoc, be quiet!" Emma snapped. "Godwin?"

Godwin said baldly: "He has abducted an abbess from her nunnery and taken her to his bed."

"An abbess?" Edith spoke in a half whisper, after a pause while the news took hold of her. "Vowed to God? He . . . who was she? Where is she now?"

"Sit down." Her need of his support seemed to steady the earl. He helped Edith into her chair. "She's still with him at his Hereford manor. She was the abbess of Leominster. I have just been to Hereford to see if the tale were true. I got it roundabout . . . from a Bristol merchant who had it from a pedlar. It is true. The place is in an uproar."

"Ha!" Emma suddenly snorted. "I can imagine! Churchmen raising hands to heaven. Beldames prophesying the wrath of God. And much laughter and thigh-slapping in the mead-halls. How did he meet her in the first place?"

"Leominster?" Edith was thinking it out.

Godwin nodded. "You remember Brand Woodcutter? She is his sister."

"Poor Brand."

"The Leominster house is famous for healing," Aldred of Worcester said sombrely to Emma. "Earl Sweyn was cured of a poisoned wound there, after a battle with the Welsh."

"Is he holding her against her will?" Emma asked.

"He must be!" said Edith. "If she is a nun . . ."

"She is staying of her own free will now, whether she went there from choice in the first place or not," said Godwin quietly. "I offered her safe conduct away and she refused." For the life of him he could not quite keep the pride out of his voice, though he saw Edward's face grow colder as he listened. This woman had thrown away all she had—honour and a position and future—for his son's sake. He had made a son as potent as that. "Sweyn talks of marrying her," he said.

"She's married already!" Edward retorted. "To Christ. The laws of King Cnut, who was not even born Christian, forbid that any man should marry a vowed nun. Bring your pup to heel, Godwin. I will not have him fouling altars!" He glared at them all, bracketing Godwin and Edith together with Sweyn as a single undesirable entity.

"It is . . . a terrible thing. I have no words," said Edith.

"My brother-in-law," Edward said bitterly. "One of my own family. My *family!*" Without warning he spun on his heel and marched out. The prelates went slowly after him. Godwin stayed behind, beside his daughter's chair.

"Edward is angry," Emma commented calmly, surveying their stricken faces. "But he'll get over it."

Godwin looked up. "In the name of sheer, simple justice," he said, "he had better!"

And Emma, studying father and daughter, saw that the distress she had attempted to quieten was not what she had thought. They were grieved at Sweyn's perfidy, but Edward's unreasoning anger against themselves had had a different effect. Godwin and Edith, on their own and one another's behalf, were furious.

From the low ridge on which stood Beorn's hall at the place called Bedford, one looked northwards over fields of rye and barley stubble to the dark green oakwood where the pigs rooted in acorn time and beyond that again to the tangled roof of the virgin forest, broken only by patches of bogland, where reflected skies gleamed in the pools. Eastwards there were more pools, and threadlike waterways, and one or two distant wisps of smoke betokening hamlets. Westwards the pools were fewer, and from this vantage point no habitations were visible. The forest rolled on like an ocean till it vanished into haze. Brand looked at this vista and his mind noted these things, as the mind will note irrelevancies when the immediate world is too hard to bear. He was in the company of Godwin and Beorn, and they, with difficulty, were trying to tell him what Sweyn had done to Edgiva.

To tell bad news to anyone it was natural, a kindness, to take him out of the populous hall into the open, where there was some privacy and the wide sky could comfort grief by dwarfing it. They had brought him out to the hillside for this purpose. It felt strange. Godwin was his teacher and nearly his father by now. Beorn was his immediate leader. And they were looking at him with humble hang-dog eyes and asking his forgiveness.

"Sweyn is my son," Godwin was saying, "and Beorn's cousin. We cannot wholly separate ourselves from what he has done. You have the right, if you wish, to leave our service and take what steps

you wish to rescue your sister or take vengeance on Sweyn—or his
kinfolk. We give you that right."

"Only I shan't fight you," said Beorn, trying to lighten the air.
"I shall refuse to fight even if you draw blade on me, Woodcutter. I
won't be yoked in double harness with Sweyn in this, whatever my
uncle here says!"

"Why should I want to fight *you*?" Brand asked. He shook his
head impatiently. "I don't want a feud. What good would it do?"
The idea of feuding with Godwin was in any case unthinkable. One
might as well start a quarrel with the sun in the sky. "Did he take
her by force?" he asked.

"I understand he had her brought to him, but that there had
been something between them before. She admitted that to me. And
now she is staying of her own will. I'm sorry."

"You could challenge Sweyn," Beorn said.

Brand nodded to show understanding. It was not agreement.
To fight Sweyn was nearly as unthinkable as challenging Godwin.
Never before had he seen how this astonishing Godwin power, common to the whole family, of making him feel half his actual height,
could shackle him. He had not even been able to quarrel with
Harold about Eadgyth, and the same pattern was asserting itself
again. Besides . . .

"It wouldn't help Edgiva if I were killed," he said, "and Sweyn
would probably kill me."

Godwin made a despairing gesture, hands to temples, and suddenly laughed. "I know you far too well, Brand, to mistake solid
good sense for timidity. Timid you have never been. But you'll
never make a great warrior, either. Is there no natural boastfulness in
you? Time and again when the lyre's going round, I wonder, when
it gets to you, will we at last hear you make a song of your own doings? But the only time you sang of yourself, it was a tale of how a
mischievous girl made a fool of you!"

Brand looked unhappy. He had done that, it was true, one evening in the mead-hall, after Harold had paid them a visit accompanied by an Eadgyth visibly carrying Harold's child. Brand had ignored her while she was there, but when they had gone a dry, sour
ballad had risen up in him about a girl who led one man on in order
to snare another. It had met with much applause; most of his colleagues knew or guessed its origin. But afterwards he had regretted

it. He found he was not as bitter as he thought. Eadgyth had seemed so unfamiliar, a stranger of no interest to him. His outburst had been the last flicker of feeling, and once it was gone nothing was left but an ashy taste in his mouth.

Godwin said now, reverting to the matter of killing: "One of you would certainly die if you and Sweyn fought over a matter like this." His eyes were grave. "I would not have you killed, Brand. And I would not want you to kill Sweyn, either."

Something of the pain and conflict in Godwin's mind reached Brand. He understood it, for a similar turmoil was troubling his own. He knew what the correct response should be. No vowed nun could be allowed to remain with a lover; it was the duty of both families to drag them apart as soon as possible. Since it was certain that Godwin's interference would be limited to exhortation—for he would never in person take up arms against his son—this duty was now Brand's. He must get together some friends, seize Edgiva, kill Sweyn if possible, and send her back to her convent if they would have her, and, if not, then to her home, her own village, to live out her days as a local wonder, something sneered and pointed at. Edgiva, who hadn't wished to enter the convent, who had cursed him and his silver on the day they took her to Leominster, who had cried out aloud that she wanted marriage.

And Sweyn had a way with him. The chief risk was that he would tire of her and abandon her. In his own heart, which seemed quite unable to produce the officially sanctioned answer, he found only gladness that Edgiva had fled her convent-prison, and fear that one day she might be deserted or thrust back. His decision came out crisply.

"I've had a bad conscience over Edgiva for years. My family used my silver to buy her into that convent, and she didn't want to go. It was the reward King Harefoot paid me for bringing him his father's relics. I am not now going to force her into anything else against her will. She should never have been in Leominster; God never called her. A monk said to me once: 'If God wants you, He'll shout.' He didn't shout for her. What I will demand is an undertaking from your son, Sweyn, that he will treat her well or at least provide for her so that in future she can live in comfort and dignity. I will have his sworn word for that. But if he gives it, she may please herself."

"I don't know," said Godwin, "whether to be stricken with admiration or outrage. Brand, have you no fear of the wrath of God?"

"My sister took her vows under duress. I've heard even a priest say that a promise made by force could lawfully be broken."

Godwin, in whose face relief and something near gratitude could be read, said: "Well, sinners are rarely struck by thunderbolts. Or few of us would stay unblasted. We will get that undertaking, Brand. We'll ride to Hereford together and demand it."

"What about Sandwich?" asked Beorn. "We were to start for the east coast at the end of the week to see the fleet laid up for the winter."

"I hadn't forgotten. We shall make short work of Hereford and come back by way of Bedford to join you. Then we will make straight for Sandwich."

Beorn said: "That's agreeable to me." As they started back to the hall, he added: "Sweyn should marry. He's a nuisance as he is. I'm told that Baldwin of Flanders has some beautiful young daughters."

"From the bottom of my heart," said Sweyn's father, "I hope he doesn't end up in Flanders of necessity. Edward is angrier than I have ever seen him. And not only with Sweyn. He's angry with all Sweyn's house, with me, my little Edith, all Sweyn's brothers, and probably with you as well. I hope the storm blows over. Or Sweyn's crazy navigation may sink him and the rest of us too!"

Edward's anger with Edith had cooled by nightfall. He went to their chamber willing to make friends, only to find that his wife had other opinions. Her silence stretched across the room between them like a pane of invisible, impenetrable, ice-cold glass. Edward tapped on it with a few commonplaces about the warmth of the evening, lost his temper again, and smashed the glass resoundingly with a shout. "What in the name of God is wrong with you?"

"Wrong with *me!*" Edith turned a savage glare on the maid who was brushing out the royal hair, and the girl fled. "Wrong with *you* would be more the way to put it," Edith said, her voice high-pitched. "By what right—or reason—do you hold me accountable for what Sweyn does? And what is this talk of my family getting above themselves? What does *that* mean?"

"What it says! When your brother thinks he can do as he likes, break all the laws of God and man, because his sister is a queen."

"Because I'm a queen?" Edith uttered an astonished sound which resembled laughter, except that there was no mirth in it. "Do you think Sweyn was thinking of me or what I am or am not when he was after this abbess? When Sweyn chases a girl he sees nothing on earth but the girl. If he never stole an abbess before, it was because he never happened to see one he wanted. Most would have sense enough to keep out of his way!"

"Your father was proud of him," said Edward. He sat on the edge of the bed, unlacing his sandals, not looking at her. "I heard it in his voice."

"So now I'm to blame for what my father thinks! Why don't you ask me what I think for once? Am I real to you, Edward? Do you know that there's someone called Edith? Or is all you see a Godwin? Another Godwin?"

"I haven't the least idea what you're talking about. Are you proud of Sweyn?"

"At last! No, I am not. I'm angry and ashamed." Edith began to brush her own hair, which crackled under the violent onslaught, fine strands flying up after the bristles.

"I'm glad to hear it. You bewilder me at times, Edith. I never know what to expect from you. I can never get near enough to you to understand."

"You could try harder." Losing one's temper was like being sick, Edith thought. If you felt sick you could sometimes control it, but once the process had started it went on until everything fermenting in the stomach was emptied out. "And oftener."

"What do you mean by that, may I ask?"

"If you spent less time on your knees of an evening and more time with me, you might come to understand your wife a little. Or at least get an heir, if nothing else!"

"Oh. Yes, I thought this would come in the end. I have never reproached you for that, Edith. I know the failure may be mine. But as for trying, do you suggest I don't?"

"No. You try," said Edith, herself amazed at the wellspring of longing and disappointment within her that was tapped merely by talking of children. She also knew that it was unfair to hold his failure against him. But it was not only barrenness that hurt. "*Oc-*

casionally you try." She had lain waiting for a man who did not come, or fell asleep at once when he did, so often.

"I thought you were a quiet woman, Edith, who would make a gentle, loving wife. Not a screaming virago."

"I . . . am . . . not . . . a . . . virago," said Edith through her teeth. "And I would like to be a loving wife. I would like much more opportunity!"

"You're a Godwin," said Edward with a sigh, and Edith turned her back on him. "You're a great family in some ways," he said to that back. "Gifted, united, beautiful. But demanding. Land, gold, titles, the right to break the law with impunity . . . and now you want my heart and soul. Did they teach you nothing at that convent of yours? Not even that you should not be jealous of your husband's hours of prayer? I never thought that you, of all people, would resent my devotions. Dear God, beloved saints! No, I never thought to hear that."

He threw his discarded footwear across the room and suddenly cast himself back onto the bed, hands to his face. After a while, Edith turned and looked at this attitude of despair. She eyed it with exasperation and then went to him. "I do not reproach you, either, because we have no children," she said quietly. "Edward. Edward? I only ask for your love—and not to be made responsible for the deeds of others, even when they happen to be my kinsfolk. No more than that. How can you say I resent your devotions? I spend hours on my knees myself, and through many of them I pray for you. Edward?" She drew his hands from his face. She thought there were tears in his eyes. She said: "It is sad for us both to be childless. What if you asked your sister Godgift to send one of her sons to us for a long stay? That might comfort us."

It was an olive branch. Edward, after a silence, decided to accept it. He sat up. "She'd send Ralph, I think. He was at our wedding; perhaps you remember. You'd make him welcome?"

"Yes. I liked him."

Edward said: "I do not blame you for what Sweyn did. I was angry and shocked, that's all. I fancy the way the convent is run is much to blame. It should be disbanded and the ladies sent to better houses. The crown can take the lands. Champart will approve! He's always on the watch for ways to swell the treasury."

"Leominster's quite wealthy," said Edith. "More than two hundred plough teams on its lands, I hear, and over twenty sublettings. The revenues should be useful."

"I'll make them over to you," said Edward handsomely.

Edith smiled, thanking him, and waited for a physical gesture of friendship, but none came. They got silently into bed and lay side by side. Edward, tired by the quarrel, fell asleep at once; his breathing deepening into the rhythm of slumber within minutes. Edith gritted her teeth. She was not the maiden wife that rumour alleged, but for all the good Edward's unenthusiastic lovemaking had done her, she might as well be. He had only wakened longings he could not satisfy, and no child had been conceived to compensate her. And the years stretched ahead. Twenty, thirty years they might live together like this. She thought of her own parents, their love and the strength they drew from one another. If ever any bond were forged between her and Edward, it must be made of materials other than desire and offspring, but for a man and a woman what others were there? The desire of heaven and the creation of good works, perhaps?

In every sense of the word it was a barren prospect.

4 ⚜ The Warning of God

They reached Sandwich in late October, glad of the long warm summer which had dried the roads and shrunk the marshes in their path. Brand, with Sweyn's oath safely sworn in the presence of witnesses, was glad to put Hereford behind him and turn instead to the examination of beached ships. It was one of the regular duties for which Beorn was liable, since as well as having his earldom he was now commander of the royal fleet. Godwin had enough to manage with Wessex and the royal housecarles, he said, resigning to make way for his nephew. But he still went to sea at times with Beorn, for the interest of it.

Brand's time with Beorn had been happy. It was exciting. In getting a grip on a new earldom, building a new hall, learning the way about courts and tenancies, dues of service and rents of produce, exploring the paths and waterways, the markets and fairs, and getting to know the local thanes, Beorn had found his life full to brim-over point, and the lives of his followers were likewise. They found their leader trustworthy and generous. He was no sun-god, no lion. He lacked both the inches and the beauty of the Godwinssons; his hair was mouse-blond where theirs was gold or tawny; he was wiry where they were mighty, patient where they were passionate, dogged where they were inspired. He trained youngsters competently without Godwin's occasionally blistering turn of phrase. ("What in God's name are you doing, boy? Fighting an enemy or ploughing a ryefield? Drive it home, boy, drive it home!" Beorn in like case simply twitched the weapon from the inexpert hand and demonstrated.) But this steadiness had its own strength. Sweyn might and did despise it, but Gytha and Godwin both knew its worth and so now did Brand. He had come to consider Beorn as a friend. Although he had fought and ridden at Harold's side, he had never looked on Harold in quite that way. Like all the true Godwins, Harold was too far above him.

With the fleet at rest for the season, they rode on to Dover, where Godwin met Gudbrand Shipwright. Gudbrand had built several of the ships in the fleet. Eric Merchant was visited in order to sample his wine, and he gave them all a kind welcome. Matters were mended now between Brand and Hild's folk, and Eric in any case never held grudges against good customers. Hild and Rolf were safe, and Hild was contented in her marriage. Eric took them to a pony fair in Dover (busily introducing Godwin and Beorn by name to every acquaintance he met) and feasted them afterwards in his hall. By then the weather was breaking.

It had begun to grow dull before they set out to Sandwich. But now the wind veered east and developed an edge that cut through cloaks and gauntlets. Old sailors sniffed it and prophesied a long, bitter winter.

"We'll be brief guests only," Godwin told his host as they prepared for their rest the night after the fair. He and Beorn had twenty or so followers with them, now split up for sleeping purposes between Eric and Ragnar. The two earls themselves were favouring Eric. The town reeve was their usual host, but there was sickness in his hall, a shivering illness with fever and a harsh cough, and it seemed to be contagious. "The roads get waterlogged too fast for delay at this time of year," Godwin explained. "We've already trespassed on you too long."

"You are always welcome," Eric assured him. "It's no trespass. We're always hungry for news, and the tales you bring of doings elsewhere would pay for your lodgings for a twelvemonth."

Wherever one went people were eager for news. Godwin smiled. He had talked at length of the Welsh defeat and given other news of births and deaths and marriages, crops and diseases and miraculous healings—the usual small gossip. But he had not mentioned Sweyn's name; this most interesting topic of all he must withhold. He knew it was being talked about in Dover, but no one would raise it in his hearing.

At the same moment, far away in Hereford, Edgiva, past abbess, present sinner, and future mother, was nerving herself with difficulty to speak not of, but to, Godwin's wayward son.

The large doses of cynical wisdom passed on by that inveterate manhater, Dame Hilda, had had their effect on Edgiva. "If a mistress starts a baby, he'll cast her off, and if a wife starts a baby he'll take a mistress for the same reason. Playthings or breeding stock, that's all we are to them." She had heard Dame Hilda say it not just once but many many times. "I swear that women go straight to heaven when they die," was another of her sayings. "They serve their purgatory here on earth. We should pray in gratitude every day to be safe within convent walls where the men can't get at us!"

Edgiva, even though Sweyn swore he loved her, even though he had said in his own father's presence that he wanted to marry her, recognised her status as that of plaything. She loved Sweyn and, more than that, she needed him. She could not leave him, even under safe-conduct from Godwin, who had offered it to her. She had liked Godwin. People said he was irreligious, but to her that was a blessing. He had treated her courteously, as a woman he thought Sweyn had wronged. That she was also a lapsed nun did not seem to matter to him. But though she was too bonded now to Sweyn to accept his father's help, she did not in her heart trust her lover. The first failure of her monthly course terrified her.

She remembered a neighbour of her mother's at Ashtree. Wulfhild had suffered three terrible births and on finding herself pregnant yet again had grown desperate. Edgiva's mother had made certain recommendations, which worked. Perhaps they would work for Edgiva, too.

But the pennyroyal and the other herbal brews got no results at all, and neither did getting drunk. After that she tried falling off ponies, which was easy enough because Sweyn was teaching her to ride properly so that she could go hawking with him. For the space of a week she suffered a series of mishaps and acquired some fine, plum-coloured bruises. But that was all. She had begun to suspect the truth at the end of September. By the end of October, with two missed courses and several sharp attacks of nausea to her credit, she could hope no more. She must tell Sweyn.

She was afraid. She knew him very well by now. She knew he

must have his way in everything and she knew his power of careless cruelty if denied. She knew he was unfaithful. She could not hold him even now, when she was well and able. She had not enough beauty, she supposed. Her skin was free of spots now and the short convent-cut hair was growing out dark and glossy, but to her life's end she would carry that scattering of pockmarks, and she would have the stocky peasant build and the heavy brows of her family. So how could she hope to keep him when she was past lovemaking? She had learned that in the past others had been brought to this big, comfortable, good-living hall of Sweyn's. He had sent them away when he was tired. Loaded with gold, naturally, and most of them had bought husbands on the strength of it. She could not buy a husband. She was married already, to God. She knew that Brand had made Sweyn promise to provide for her, and that was something, but he could not provide a man for her. That was what she needed most. She admitted it sometimes, to herself, when she was alone. It was Sweyn she loved, but she could do without him at a pinch, if only she had a man of some sort. But without a lover at all, what would her life be? She tried to think what it would be, and was frightened as a child is frightened of the dark.

Sweyn was capable of understanding at times. He did not despise literacy, and when he learned that she had skills in manuscript preparation, he had got her the materials without being asked. He had also got her the materials for gold and silver embroidery, another ability she had learned in Leominster. But none of these had cost him anything that mattered: no sacrifice, no effort. Only an order to his steward.

Sitting in the hall on an October morning, needle in hand, she glanced to where Sweyn with half a dozen men was poring over a rough-drawn map of the Marches, painted on sheepskin and spread over a trestle table. The Axebearer was complaining that the map was inaccurate, and they were arguing good-humouredly. She must, she had decided, tell Sweyn today. She would speak to him when he had finished. She swallowed nervously. At the same moment she heard voices and feet outside, and then an interruption came. A dusty man with a tired, defiant face was being led in. Sweyn left the map and strolled towards him, snapping his fingers at the thralls to bespeak the usual refreshments and seats. The man spoke to Sweyn, softly. She couldn't hear the words, but Sweyn's face stiffened. The man spoke again, at some length. Sweyn turned crimson. He kicked away a bench as the weary stranger was about to sit down on it, and flung away the tray of mead and cold meat that a thrall was offering. The hounds got up from their snoozing and closed eager jaws on the ribs of beef. The dusty man went white.

"By Thunor Boltflinger," said Sweyn, who almost always used pagan oaths, "you dare to come from your oath-breaking master to me with this message and expect me to swallow it? He'll pay his dues, my friend. He'll acknowledge me whether he likes it or not. And he will not tell me how I live my life or who stays in my hall, or who sleeps in my bed. Go back and tell him so, and take a token with you! Kenneth! Axebearer! Here!"

The housecarles closed round. Something hideous was happening, some mushrooming up of savagery in this hall that had been peaceful only moments before. In Edgiva's stomach the thing—she did not think of it as a child—which was growing there seemed enlarging every second, pushing outwards and upwards, forcing her belly into her mouth. She dropped her work, put her hands to her mouth, and ran. Behind her a man screamed and she grabbed the doorpost for support while she vomited. Two thrall women (dirty, draggle-haired, young, and devoted to Sweyn—she hated them) came silently to clear it up. Sweyn was fastidious about such things. During drinking bouts his men were ordered outside if they wanted to be ill. Edgiva went into the open air, shaking. She was still there when the stranger was brought out, half-fainting, and arranged on his mule, where he clung unsteadily to the animal's stiff mane. A cloth, blood-soaked, was tied round his head.

It was very cold. Shivering, whey-faced, Edgiva went back and sat by the fire. She left it before the afternoon meal was served. She could not eat, nor could she now talk to Sweyn. When he came to the sleeping chamber that night she was buried under the rugs, her back towards the door.

"Edgiva," he said as he barred it, "have you anything to tell me?"

He knew, then. She turned over. Impossible in the weak mixture of torchlight and twilight to see his face clearly. He was leisurely taking off his mantle and jewellery, laying his cloak-brooch and arm-rings and finger-ring aside. Edward had made him a gift of jewellery when he became an earl, including a great gold finger-ring with an astonishing green stone in it of fabulous value. An emerald, it was called, and it had been mined in Scotland. Sweyn tossed the flashing heap on top of the chest he had given her for her own, with a lock whose keys she carried at her belt as if she were his wife. She felt sick again.

"It was the end of August, I think, when you last said to me: 'Sweyn, I can't.' And you have this constant sickness. When will it be born? In the summer?"

Edgiva steeled herself. "I think June."

"Why didn't you tell me?"

"I . . . wasn't sure. I know so little about . . ."

"You were bred on a farm, weren't you? Were you afraid to tell me?"

He did not sound angry, only amused. Edgiva sat up straight. Perhaps it wouldn't be so bad. "I was afraid you'd cast me off," she said.

The thrall women had told her about her predecessors. None had lasted beyond a few months. They had enjoyed telling her. Thralls stood in no danger of dismissal; they belonged to Sweyn as his passing loves never could. He always came back to them; they were his daily bread, and if he liked a sweetmeat now and then for a change, let him. They would even make a show of serving Edgiva and her like in order to please him, for it was never for long. Her time would soon be over. Theirs would endure.

"Send you away?" said Sweyn, astounded. "Carrying my child?"

There was an unbelieving moment, as when a painful illness first begins to recede. "You're pleased about the child?" Edgiva asked.

Sweyn suddenly laughed, flinging back his head. "Pleased! I'd begun to think I couldn't, like poor Edward. Listen, Edgiva, my dearest wantwit. I'm the eldest of a large brood. The hall at home was always full of my younger brothers and sisters, tumbling, fighting, wrestling the dogs, grazing their knees, and needing their noses wiped. A hall's only half-alive without brats in it. Oh, why didn't you tell me before? Yes, I'm pleased!"

The wind moaned outside and a freezing draught made him turn to look for the source. "That door's not properly fastened." He went and undid it, the better to slam it again. A few snowflakes whirled in with the wind, to sink and melt on the floor.

"Is it snowing?" asked Edgiva. Her mind was in confusion; relief and thankfulness struggled with an unexpected pain. He was glad of the child. He would not send her away, carrying his child. Would he in time have sent her away had she not conceived? When his father came, he had talked of wanting to marry her, but he had known very well that it was against the law made by King Cnut. Even then she had recognised it for talk pure and simple, pretty words meant to please her, on which he couldn't be forced to act. What did she, Edgiva, really mean to him? A passing pleasure and the vessel to nurture his seed? Was that all?

"It's snowing hard," Sweyn said. He secured the door and came back. "You saw that man in the hall today," he said as he finished undressing. "You knew who he was?"

"No."

"He came from one of my thanes, Alfward—he has a holding about twenty miles from here. He has hives and a weaving shed. He owes me five bolts of cloth every Christmas, four big jars of honey, ten sacks of grain, and a fat sheep. He's sending his dues to my father instead. He won't have me for overlord because, my love, I have defiled a convent of God."

"Because of me!"

"Don't be afraid." He slid in under the rugs. "My thanes don't tell me how I live. But if it snows hard and blocks the roads, I can't send to him to collect my dues. I meant to ride there with my men tomorrow. He'd have come to his senses the day after. But it's nearly a blizzard out there now."

"What did you do to the messenger?" asked Edgiva.

"Amputated his left ear. He can still hear, but he doesn't look as handsome as he did. And it'll be a wasted gesture if this weather lasts."

"It's early in the year for it," said Edgiva. "It probably won't lie."

It was early indeed, but it lay. Lay and deepened as fall succeeded fall. Roads filled up between banks, roads on hillcrests vanished. The frost spread ice in thin brittle sheets over miles of marshland, and silenced streams. Fodder grew scarce. Farmers slaughtered next year's breeding stock as the supplies ran low, used up long before their time. Famished deer walked openly through the habitations of man, willing to trade their wildness for a share of the cattle mangers, and were slaughtered also for their meat. Dead birds, frozen and starved, lay under the trees. The foxes and the stoats alone grew fat, hunting weakened prey. Men trudged the hillsides with spades to dig out their sheep, and sometimes the blizzards came up too quickly and they too died, lost in the whiteness. There had been no winter like it in the memory of living man.

Men and women alike cursed the steel sky and prayed to God and the saints and, when these failed, to older, darker deities, that the frost should break.

But the thaw, when it came, was worse.

On the morning of that day there was no promise of a thaw at first. Hild, struggling with a sick child and ten extra mouths to feed in her husband's modest hall, hardly glanced at the sky when she rose. Her mind was all on the problem of dinner, and what more could be done for small Ragnar, fevered and coughing under his blankets. The epidemic which had started in the town reeve's hall was spreading. Her guests went out to "see what they could find," but it was not with hope that some hours later she heard them come in again and pushed aside the oxhide curtain that divided hall from kitchen, to see what they had brought.

"Venison!" said Brand.

His nose was peeling from the abrasive wind, and he blew on his fingers as he drew off his gauntlets. A pole protruded over his shoulder. Another of Beorn's housecarles had the other end, and between them a fair-sized buck was slung.

"They were looking for scraps near the town," said the housecarle, a fair, stocky, good-natured man with round blue eyes. He was known as Odi Pathfinder, since he had no sense of locality at all and had once got a hunting party lost for forty-eight hours by leading them in all earnestness along the right path in the wrong direction. However, he was a reasonable shot with a bow.

"Bring it through!" Hild held the curtain back.

"How is the child?" Brand asked as they did so.

"Sleeping. One of the women thralls is with him. His breathing was easier this morning, I thought." She looked tired, and her hair escaping from her woollen cap was dull. "What is the weather like?"

"The wind's changing," Pathfinder said. "We met your husband and Gudbrand the shipwright on the way back; they said Alfwold

Reeve was telling owners to bring their ships further up the shore, so someone's foretelling dirty weather. But if it's warmer weather, then it may help your little boy."

It was close to Christmas and they were still in Dover. The snow had come so suddenly that it had blockaded them before they had time to stir. As it was unseasonable at first, they had shrugged their shoulders at it. They would wait till it cleared, Godwin said. But it hadn't cleared, and constant blinding snowstorms with driving winds had made the sea routes as useless for making journeys as the buried roads and frozen rivers. Commerce halted. An itinerant preacher who had also been benighted in Dover was getting large crowds as he went about declaring that the freeze was the wrath of God on the sins of the English folk and would not break until they repented and forswore pagan and sinful ways. He had cited Sweyn Godwinsson several times, to Godwin's fury. Some people were looking sideways at Godwin and his companions now.

The venison was roasting and the smell of it was stealing mouth-wateringly through the tang of woodsmoke from the fire when Godwin himself, with Beorn, Eric, and Ragnar, came in. They were all cloaked, booted, and—as Hild suddenly exclaimed— bespattered with raindrops.

"It is thawing, yes indeed," Godwin said, shaking his cloak out on the threshold. "And the wind is veering west and blowing hard, and the sea's worse than it's been all through the storms so far. The ship's beached as safely as we can manage. We can't do more. What is that wonderful smell?"

Peter Longshanks, with several companions, pushed open the door and came in, letting a howl of wind in at the same time. "You can hear water running in the river!" he cried. "I never heard sweeter music."

"I hope," said Ragnar, "I only hope the sweetness doesn't turn to discord. I've seen sudden thaws before—of much less snow!"

After the food they thought of going out to look at the weather, but one glance through the door discouraged them. Outside was a downpour so heavy that land, sky, and sea were merged in it. Even indoors the fire was fighting for life against water pouring through the smoke vent. Godwin and Eric should have returned to Eric's hall, but Ragnar dissuaded them from leaving the shelter of his. It was possible to keep the fire going by constant stoking with fresh wood, and Ragnar providently had his woodstack in a lean-to adjoining the hall, with a door straight into it. He and Hild themselves were less fortunate and at bedtime had to run for their apartment with rugs thrown over their heads. Those left to sleep in the hall lay down early.

Brand woke in the night and wondered why. He had dropped off to the sound of swishing rain and buffeting wind; now there was quiet. Perhaps the silence itself had roused him. He sat up. The fire was low, glowing deep red; a log reduced to a luminous shell collapsed as he watched. He saw Odi Pathfinder's eyes gleam. Odi was wakeful too on the neighbouring pallet. The stillness felt threatening.

The crash came out of the sky immediately above. It tore and boomed its way down through the clouds, like a boulder hurled through the sky-roof. With it came a blaze of blue light that enwrapped the hall, showed hangings and beams and every straw separate on the floor before it passed. The building shook. A second, lesser crash sounded somewhere. Something had fallen from the roof. A thrall let out a wail of fright. Then the wind came.

It came from a new direction; it had swung northeast, it seemed. It leapt on the hall like a wolf on a doe, shaking it with such fury that the timbers groaned and shutters burst from their catches. Then it passed on, keening, dying away across the town. Another gust followed it, and this one brought the rain in an instant deluge which extinguished the fading fire once and for all. There was a scramble of movement as man after man got up from pallets that no longer promised sleep.

There were no more thunderbolts, but there was enough damage done already to keep sleep away. Someone managed to kindle a torch and someone else tried to restart the fire, not very successfully. The thatched roof had been torn at one end of the hall and rain was coming in; water began to spread over the floor. Odi, who was Norwegian-born, started to tell them a tale of terrible northern winters when folk went to ground in their houses like hibernating badgers, huddled with the dogs and goats and oxen, drinking and singing the dark weeks away while the snow blanketed the halls and kept in the heat. Peter, dashing about with leather buckets to put under the leaks, told him tersely to stop it. "We're in no danger of freezing now! Drowning, yes, possibly!"

At dawn the rain eased to a drizzle but the wind seemed still increasing. The thatch was gone in two more places and they had run out of buckets. Now with the light there was activity outside in the town, and a hammering at the door sent Odi to unbar it. Gudbrand Shipwright and half a dozen men, all hooded and drenched, were outside. Gudbrand's face was urgent.

"Ragnar and Eric, the merchants, where are they?"

"I am here, here, my friend." Eric pushed forward. "And here is Ragnar, come from his sleepinghouse. What is it, Shipwright?"

"The sea never rightly ebbed last night with that wind behind it, that's what it is! And now again the tide is flowing and your fine warehouse by the harbour is in danger, my friends. Empty it before the waters swallow it!"

"The warehouse!" Eric paled. It held not only his own goods but those of fellow merchants who rented space from him. He recognised the faces of some of them among Gudbrand's companions. Then a further thought struck him. "The ship! The *Hild*!"

"Oh, she is safe, we placed her well. But the river is spating and the warehouse will be caught between the tide coming up and the flood coming down. One more hour, or less, and the sea will have it. You come with us to clear it, now, quick!"

Ragnar shouted: "All that can lend a pair of hands, follow us!" and was gone at a run towards the gate, which had stood unfastened all night, since no one felt like crossing the enclosure to shut it or expected robbers in such weather. With the briefest of pauses to seize on mantles and boots, the rest went after him. The run became a thrusting, head-down walk when they were out in the road, for the wind was like a wall. Its voice was deafening, half-human, half-demoniac, and as they neared the harbour they heard the voice of the sea beneath it like the speech of the gods who had carved the earth and conceived the first life and could end them both this morning if they chose.

The sea was in sight before it should have been; huge, grey moors of water moving against the sky, splintering into jagged white crests as they came ashore, and thundering down on whatever lay below. The river, foaming, had overleapt its banks as it surged to meet the sea, and they found themselves wading, forced to turn aside to avoid it, coming to the warehouse by the last tongue of ground that led to its little eminence. From it they could see at least that Gudbrand was right about the ship. The *Hild*, along with several other vessels belonging to provident owners, had been dragged to higher ground to the north and placed with such wisdom that with luck, a very little luck, she would survive.

People were running about in the rain, clutching children, bundles, and baskets; their hair, clothes, and faces streamed with wet. An oxcart was standing near the warehouse. "My thanks, neighbour!" Eric gasped to the fellow merchant who had brought it.

"They're my goods, too," said his neighbour, backing the cart into position.

The warehouse had two doors, on the seaward and the landward sides respectively. They wrenched the landward one open and ran in. Brand, in the forefront, stopped short and looked at the mass of bales and boxes piled on racks and shelves and an upper half floor. He groaned. It would take a week to shift it all and they had, at most, forty-five minutes of grace.

Godwin and Beorn had come with the rest. Godwin took charge. Here within walls at least the gale couldn't slow them down. Under his direction they dragged out casks and sacks and set the ladders which gave access to the upper regions. A human chain was formed to carry goods to the cart; a few folk set off themselves with their property on their backs. A second oxcart arrived as the first one creaked away.

But there was too much. Eric wept aloud with frustration when the river cast the first swirl of water over the floor and purple dyestuff began to run from a sack. Hardly a quarter of the warehouse's contents had been moved.

Ragnar was on a ladder, throwing down fleeces, bales of silk, and bolts of cloth to the waiting hands below. Brand was rolling wine casks towards the human chain, and Godwin and Beorn by the door were stacking spices and dyestuffs on the cart, as much out of the wet as possible. Eric was in a panic, demanding that the most valuable things be loaded first, pulling at the careful stacks in order to check if they were there. Beorn caught Brand's eye over the merchant's burrowing shape and they made faces at each other. Godwin shouted, exhorted, pointed, pushed. The floor was turning to mud as feet under heavy weights slipped and stamped across it.

Something struck the door on the seaward side and water surged under it, green grey and marbled with veins of foam. Godwin thrust the sack he held into Beorn's hands and bellowed: *"Out, everyone! The sea's coming in! Ragnar, get down off there! Outside, all of you!"* The men ran to him with their various burdens and he shooed them out into a world which seemed to be made of water. The oxcart was in retreat, splashing away as fast as it could go towards higher ground. It was raining hard again.

Brand, a wool bale on his back and his arms full of rolled cloth, glanced back as he half ran, half waded, away from the warehouse. He thought something was wrong with his eyes. He was seeing something magnified to ten times its proper size, he thought, or something moving that ought to keep still. Waves were not that big, nor did hillsides travel. He dropped his burdens and fled as the thing showed its white teeth. He heard its roaring descent behind him and fell as something clawed at his knees. There was a tree, well-grown, deep-rooted; by the grace of God there was a tree. He flung his arms round it. Something dragged powerfully at his legs and then let him go. Beorn had fallen too, but he was further ahead and had also found something to clutch. Godwin was with him. He turned round and his face was despairing. Brand slowly did the same. The wave was withdrawing. And as it went, slowly, inexorably, silently, it seemed, for amid the roar of wind and water no other sound could be heard, Eric Merchant's warehouse with three-quarters of the goods—his own and other people's—still within it, dislimned, crumbled, and slid back into the sea. Beams whirled away. Sacks bobbed. Stains of red and yellow and purple dye gleamed briefly and were dispersed.

Ragnar had been inside it.

Hild heard the tale with dignity, her face as still as ice. It had not been only Ragnar. Gudbrand Shipwright was gone too, and three of the housecarles. She grieved for them all, she said, her voice tight.

"How is the child?" Godwin asked her. They were still all soaking wet, but a fire had been lit at last and they stood round it, steaming. The wind, as if satisfied at last with the human sacrifice paid to the elements, was dropping and the tide was losing power. It was turning. The hall was safe. The ship was safe. These at least remained.

"The child . . ." Hild repeated. It was as if she could not quite understand what was said to her. "The priest is with . . . the wandering one who's been preaching in the town. I couldn't find our own priest. He says . . . he says . . ."

"I have children," said Godwin. He seemed surer of what to do than Hild's own father. Eric, stunned by the magnitude of his own loss, could only mumble and pat her shoulder awkwardly. "Take me to see him. Come." He put an arm round Hild and turned her towards the door. "You must try to think of Ragnar as a warrior who died fighting the sea to save his livelihood and yours, as a man might die to protect his lord or his homestead in time of war."

"I need him," said Hild in a whisper as they went towards the chamber where the child lay. "We could spare the goods and the ship, but Ragnar . . . and my child, my little Ragnar . . . the priest says he's dying! How will I live without either of them?"

At the door of the sleepinghouse one of the old female thralls was sitting, and she let them in, but beyond her a tall wild figure rose up and barred their way to the cot where Ragnar Ragnarson lay and from which came the sound of rattling breath. Hild's face grew colder and bleaker even than before. Brand tried to think of words to say to comfort her and could not. The tall figure was that of the itinerant priest. He looked like a scarecrow. He pointed at Godwin with a long, bony forefinger. "Back, you!" he said.

"It's Earl Godwin. Let him see the child," said Hild. She put up a shaking hand to brush hair out of her eyes. Godwin could not cure her child, she knew. He was not a physician. But he could give her his strength, perhaps, in this further anguish.

"I know who he is." The priest had a resonant voice. It almost found an echo in the little cloth-hung room. "And since you also know, why do you bring him here? Why do you have him in your house, knowing what his house has done?"

"I don't understand," said Hild, bewildered.

"He's mad," said Godwin. He moved forward and found the priest's outturned palm against his chest. "I respect madmen," he said. "I pity them. But take away your hand or I knock you down."

"Let him pass!" commanded Hild. "He has a family too and . . ."

"Indeed, he has!" the priest agreed. He raised his voice again to that curious resonance. "And the first-born of that family is his curse and the curse of all this land. Because of what your eldest son has done, my lord Godwin of Wessex, God has sent this curse of snow and storms and death on us. Because your son Sweyn has defiled a bride of God, men's lives have been forfeit this day, by the sea. Others will be forfeit tomorrow, by famine. And this child's will be forfeit before the day is out, by pestilence. Until Sweyn Godwinsson is out of this land, death will be piled on death. Today is the warning of God!" He dropped his hand and laughed. There was true merriment in it, as though the curse were a most amusing joke, and the hair pricked on their scalps. "But come to the cot if you wish," he said, and stood aside. "I have given him the last rites. Even one of the house of Godwin cannot harm him now."

Godwin knocked him down.

5 ✠ The Outcast

The Hundred Court was a formal affair, called every month and ruled by men of rank who stood for the bishops and the earls. Sometimes the bishops and the earls actually attended it. But there was a less formal moot, which summoned itself when needed, an event as natural as the congregation of starlings. And if rank were represented, it was on sufferance, not of right.

It would begin with a murmuring, a small wind through the air of a community, whispering that something must be talked about. It would be said at the market and at mead-time, until someone at last remarked bluntly: "We ought to hold a moot." Then it would become: "We will hold a moot," and finally: "The moot will be at such a time and place." If any who were concerned lived at a distance, word would be got to them by whoever chanced to go that way: pedlar, merchant, priest, or tinker. The moot of Hereford that March was born in such a way.

It was an occasion. A family of charcoal burners whose circuit included Hereford did a special burning for braziers and cooking. Women who still had flour or some honey to spare after the winter's privations baked loaves and honeycakes. The men went to the woods with dogs and bows and brought back hares and venison for the feast. For some of the poorer and less able folk the moot would provide the first square meal in months.

It was a smaller gathering than it should have been. Many faces were missing. Some lay sick, some were dead—the toll of the cold and the hunger which had gripped the land since November. But all came who could, and there were many from beyond Hereford. For this moot concerned all who lay within Sweyn's earldom. Master of ceremonies was a thane called Alfward, and he brought with him as a guest a wild-looking, gaunt-boned wandering priest who had come in from the east during the brief thaw in December.

The day was mild, in the first kindly spell of weather that year, so they gathered in the traditional place, on the common land near the three elms which were a local landmark. The boughs were bare against the dappled sky, but the twig ends were swelling and the rooks were repairing their nests. A fire was made and the meeting sat near it, cloaks spread to protect them from the wet ground. And Thane Alfward stood up to address them.

Alfward was square all over: face, body, fingertips. He had a wind-reddened face and fading flaxen hair. He shoved his thumbs into his belt and stood with feet apart, eyeing the ring of hollowed faces with large, light blue eyes.

"My thanks for letting me speak," he said. "I'll be short. I'm here to say that we should no longer, for our own safety, recognise Sweyn Godwinsson as lord. I myself have not recognised him as such since last October, nor will I, ever. Does anyone here not understand why I will not recognise him? Does anyone not know the reason why we're all here?"

No one seemed in doubt, but he told them all the same. "We who have lived through this foul unnatural winter are only the fortunate few. We've seen our parents, wives, and babies die of chill and plague. We've killed our cattle and next year's calves with them so that we can fill our bellies now. We've eaten corn we should have sown. God alone knows what we'll live on in the year ahead. We've seen earth the likeness of iron. We've seen the land piled with snow and drowned with floodwater and houses swept from riverbanks in the thaw. There's been no winter like it since time began. If God sends the weather, and we know He does, why has He sent this to us? What have we done? Or who are we harbouring?"

They answered him, but not by shouting. It was a muttering, a low hissing. "Sweyn. Sweyn Godwinsson. Godwinsson."

"Sweyn Godwinsson." Alfward's head on its short neck swivelled like an owl's to see all the way round the semicircle of his audience. "He who raped an abbess from the house of God and gave her an unhallowed child. What would make God angrier than that?

For it isn't only here in Sweyn's lands that His wrath has fallen. It's on the whole of the land that holds him. I have a witness to it." He beckoned, and the travelling priest, ragged garments drooping round his lean body, came to his feet. "Ask him," said Alfward, "ask him what happened in the east, among the Kentishmen, the East Saxons, and the Eastern Angles, during this winter past!"

The priest told them. Dover—little though poor Hild Erics-daughter would have believed it—had been a minor sufferer. The slope of the land and the curve of the harbour had kept the seas from damaging more than the immediate shoreline. Further north, where the coasts were flat and the fenlands ran down to the sea, it had been a far worse story. Miles of land had been inundated by that terrible tide, with the wind driving it from behind. People, villages, cattle, and fields had been obliterated. Of those who fled to safety, many had died before they could reach shelter, of exposure in the drenching weather.

The priest was only halfway through his tale when Thane Alfward, watching the moot with round, observant eyes, knew that the motion was carried. There would be no more than token discussion of whether or not they should cast Sweyn out. The real business of the gathering was to settle how.

It was the town reeve of Hereford who remarked, some time later, that Sweyn's father, Earl Godwin, was at Sweyn's hall now and might receive a deputation. "For it's said," he told the assembly, "that the king is in a rage with all the house of Godwin over this thing that Sweyn has done. Godwin of Wessex has the rest of his family to safeguard. Sweyn may be his son—but he has five more. He'll maybe listen to us and persuade Sweyn to go. At least, if we go in orderly fashion, all proper and polite and not threatening anyone with weapons, we'll be heard. I've never heard that Godwin has attacked an honest petitioner. Reckon we can trust him not to harm us, at the least."

They ate before they went, however, and made it a good meal. There was Sweyn to deal with as well as Godwin, and everyone knew that earls and their kind were incalculable. There was always the chance that this meal might be their last.

In Sweyn Godwinsson's hall, usually a place of unashamed revelry, the air was full of unfamiliar embarrassment. Also of curiosity. The thralls and housecarles had one and all found work to do indoors and were doing it earnestly. Never were onions peeled or shields burnished with a closer eye for detail. As Thorold Cleave-Oak said, softly, eyes on his polishing and teeth agleam in pure amusement: "When the family drop their voices, you can hear the ears aflapping."

It was a family conclave. It consisted of Sweyn, his parents, his brothers Harold and Tostig, his cousin Beorn, his mistress Edgiva, and Edgiva's brother Brand, now uncomfortably made a member of this catastrophic inner circle by virtue of his blood-link with her. He felt out of place, unable to grasp that the child she carried was equally Sweyn's baby and his own niece or nephew. Across the space of floor between them where they all sat grouped near the hearthfire, he caught his sister's eye and tried to smile reassurance, but he knew his own uneasiness must show.

Edgiva did not smile in return. The arrival without warning of Sweyn's exalted family had horrified her. She was not frightened of Godwin, whom she remembered as a friend, but she had not known what to say or how to behave with Gytha. True, Gytha had been kind, had said: "Don't be afraid of us—it will be our grandchild, after all," and had asked after Edgiva's health and diet. But now they had embarked on the business for which they had come, and it was becoming plainer and plainer that they were here to separate her from Sweyn. It was also becoming plainer and plainer that any value Edgiva had in their eyes—and, she was quite certain now, in Sweyn's also—was vested in the child she carried. Edgiva sat silent, heavy-browed, and rage and misery seethed within her.

Sweyn was in an impossible mood, full of extravagant oaths, drawling rudenesses skilfully calculated to offend his brothers and lounging in indolent postures with legs outthrust and an arm draped along the back of the settle, of which he was the sole occupant. "So," he was saying now, "my self-confessed well-wishers are here in force to elbow me out of my own home. So now, by the Thunderbolts of Thunor, we know where we stand. I am overcome by all this anxiety for my welfare."

"It's more than you deserve," Tostig growled.

"Some people," said Sweyn, "find your uprightness more annoying than my reclining habits. Have you ever fallen in love, Tostig?"

"No, have you?"

Edgiva bit her lip, hard. So Tostig had seen it too. But he might have spared her that open comment. Godwin's eyes were on her. Of all of them, Sweyn's father seemed to be the only one who did think Edgiva had a status apart from the baby, and feelings that could be hurt. He said now: "You will be quiet, please, Tostig and Sweyn." He did not say it with his accustomed authority, however. It was clear that Godwin was not himself. His powers of command were dimmed. He hated what he was here to do. "Sweyn," he said, "listen. Let me go through it again. And believe me, we are not here to harm you. Before we came, I talked to Bishop Aldred of Worcester and he advises this course. You know he is friendly to you. He says it would be best if you went abroad until the uproar has passed. Feeling in the land is running too high for your safety."

"We will look after Edgiva for you while you are away," Gytha added, "since she clearly can't travel with you. You can leave orders for a proportion of revenues from your estates to be set aside for her maintenance. Brand would accept that as fair provision within the terms of your oath to him, would you not, Brand? We will give Edgiva a roof with us for as long as she needs one." She smiled at Brand and Edgiva. "You can leave Edgiva in my hands," she said to Brand, and he looked at her hands: strong, capable, unadorned, and short-nailed. He need not fear for Edgiva. "It seems very fair. I must thank you," he said correctly.

"So must I," said Sweyn ironically. "It's all thought out to the very last detail, isn't it? A proportion of revenues from *my* estates, eh? And how much mine will they be when I am across the sea? Answer me that!"

"They would be yours as much in your absence as in your presence," said Godwin. "The king has not withdrawn your title. Your sister spoke for you. I should say that he is more likely to withdraw your title if you stay and cause unrest than if you show wisdom and go away for a time."

"It would leave a briefer memory if you went now," Harold said.

"You could go to Normandy to see some action with Duke William," Godwin suggested. "He'll welcome any good sword. A man worth meeting, I fancy." The tale of the fierce, triumphant battle that the young duke had fought at the French king's side at

Val ès Dunes the previous autumn had spread abroad. The Norman duke had never fought on a battlefield before. His name was gathering lustre from that first, lionlike performance.

But not in the eyes of Sweyn Godwinsson. "Don't try to fool me, father!" he said angrily. "Don't dangle William like a bait! Or have my brothers and my dear cousin already fooled *you?*" He scowled at them. "They don't want to help. Do you, Tostig? Do you, Beorn? They want my earldom. Tostig's twenty-three and hasn't an inch of soil to call his own, and no doubt he'll want to marry soon. With his prim ideas, he'll have to. And Beorn's always loathed me. Haven't you, cousin?" He picked a piece of wood from the fuel basket and flung it accurately onto the flames. "Look at the pair of them! Dogs hoping for bones!"

Beorn's hand went to his sword, but he checked himself. "This is a family meeting and the womenfolk are here, or I would answer that with more than words," he said.

There was a pause. Edgiva knotted her fingers and looked down. She dared not meet anyone's eyes for fear of having her mind read. She hated them all, and Sweyn the most. Since the conclave began he had sent her not one single kindly look for herself alone, not uttered one word of concern for her. She needed him. But she detested that need, she would have torn it out of herself and stamped on it if she could. She was not Edgiva to him. She was a vessel, a thing. She wanted to kill him.

"Sweyn," Godwin was saying, "the feeling in the land . . ."

"Because of a bad winter? God's Teeth . . . !"

"It is said," Harold told him, "that God was showing His teeth when he sent us the fanged winds of last winter."

"Has there never been a heavy fall of snow before?"

"Often. But the point isn't whether it was really a divine visitation, but how many believe it was. The answer happens to be about three-fourths of the country."

"You could visit our kinsfolk in Denmark, if Normandy doesn't appeal to you," put in Gytha. "In fact, I wish you would, because it's been too long since . . ."

"Mother," said Sweyn, shaking his head sorrowfully, "mother, dear, you mean well but you must think me a fool if you imagine I am going to go away and leave my dear brothers and my cousin to carve up my lands between them."

"If you ignore Bishop Aldred's advice," said Harold calmly, "then a fool you undoubtedly are."

There was another silence, a taut one. Sweyn was not a man to call a fool in public. Godwin's body tensed, ready to interfere if necessary. They all watched Sweyn's face. In the body of the hall, where the followers of Sweyn and Godwin respectively had been mingled, there was a faint movement. Sweyn's men separated themselves from Godwin's, as curds split off from the whey when thunder turns the milk. Gytha drew breath to speak.

Sweyn, however, spoke first, and what he said was not what anyone expected. It was as if he had not heard Harold, as if his ears had been tuned to some other, farther distant sound. He cocked his head towards the door at a listening angle and said in the tones of the deepest puzzlement, suspicion, and indignation: "What, in the name of the seven stars that guide home sailors and the wolf that waits for mankind, *is that?*"

That was a noise, a rising racket which had been growing for some time, but so gradually that hitherto it had passed unheeded. There were shuffling feet in it, the barking of dogs, raucous protests from someone whose authority was under challenge, and beyond all these, above, below, and all round them, a collective grumbling as from a growing crowd.

The hall door was never barred by day. It opened suddenly and Sweyn's gatekeeper stumbled in, pushed from the rear. He was weaponless and cradling his right elbow. Behind him came a stocky, red-faced man with some signs of rank upon him: an ornate sword-hilt and a gold-clasped belt. After him again pressed a crowd, grimy-faced, with no armour and only staves for weapons. The foremost was brandishing his stave fiercely. It was clear what had happened to the gateward's elbow.

"My lord!" cried the gateward protestingly to Sweyn.

"Alfward!" said Sweyn.

He strode down the hall towards the stocky intruder and stopped in front of him, hands on hips. "Thane Alfward, as I live! You dare to come *here?*"

Alfward bowed, with formality. But when he spoke he did not speak to Sweyn. His eyes slid past the lawful master of the hall and sought and identified Godwin. The Earl of Wessex, responding to it, moved a few paces forward.

"I and my friends," said Alfward, "wish to have audience with you, my lord of Wessex. Immediately. Will you grant it?"

By some unlikely alchemy, achieved by force of will on Godwin's part, mixed with Gytha's appealing eyes on her firstborn, and heated over the smouldering determination of the supplicants, Sweyn's hall became an audience chamber for the Earl of Wessex. He presided from Sweyn's own high-backed chair, and it was seen that his power of command had returned. He was back in his own element.

The others, including Sweyn himself, sat on the benches. The housecarles lined the walls. The petitioners stood in mid-floor with Alfward in front as spokesman and there, standing before Godwin's dais, Alfward made his case.

He got through it unhindered, although Sweyn's fury was palpable, a blast of heat from a rapidly spreading fire. Godwin's face grew troubled again as the thane's voice went on, describing the horrors of the winter, their belief that God had sent it as a curse because of Sweyn's immoral behaviour, their own loathing of that same behaviour, and their refusal to accept him any more as lord.

"So you are asking me," said Godwin at the end, "to dispossess my own son."

"The king is at Gloucester this month," said Alfward. "Within reach. If necessary, we shall go to him."

Godwin passed a hand over his forehead. A moment ago he had been urging flight on Sweyn, but that was out of his care for his son. To urge it now would be to range himself with Sweyn's enemies. Brand found that he could read Godwin with surprising ease, and that he felt sorry for him.

It was Harold who put the matter plainly.

"If these people go to Edward," he said, addressing Sweyn, "it is likely that Edward will listen, with the mood he is in. Then you will lose all title to your lands. But if you leave quietly of your own free will, perhaps you can retain it. Sweyn, you should go."

Beorn and Tostig both nodded, and Tostig spoke quietly to his mother, in a tone of reassurance. Gytha's own eyes were anxiously on Sweyn, and Sweyn's hand was on his sword-hilt. Godwin said:

"You have heard with your own ears now, Sweyn, what you only knew by hearsay before. Do you believe us now?"

Sweyn looked at his housecarles, ranged upon his left. He nodded towards Alfward and his followers. He said in a hoarse voice: "Take them!"

Alfward's rubicund skin turned grey. The housecarles moved smoothly, expertly, between the group of petitioners and the door, with a rattle of drawn weaponry. Godwin stood up quickly. "I am in charge in this hall! Stand still, every one of you!" The housecarles hesitated. They were faced not only with Godwin, whose voice and status had more authority than Sweyn would ever carry, but also with Godwin's own followers, who were watching them, poised, waiting only for their leader's orders to intervene. Brand got Edgiva by the elbow and pulled her back towards the wall and the low door that led to the kitchen quarters. But at the door she would go no further. "I must know what happens," she whispered desperately.

Godwin said grimly: "There will be no killing of unarmed men in my presence."

"Squeamish, father?" said Sweyn pleasantly. "You never used to be. Do you remember Gildenford?"

"Often, in my dreams." Godwin strode forward. Amazingly, his own sword was out. Gytha gritted her teeth but did not speak. He went straight to Sweyn and stood before him. "Thane Alfward," he said without looking round. "Get yourself and your people out of this hall. Your petition is granted. Earl Sweyn will leave Hereford tomorrow. Now go, while you can. Order your men to let them pass, Sweyn, or by God you'll fight your own father over it. And I can still disarm you, my fine bantam cock, at any time I choose!"

"Can you indeed?" said Sweyn.

Brand had heard Gytha say that when Godwin was angry his eyes became greener and the copper lights in his hair grew redder. This phenomenon was happening now. Sweyn's blade was also out. He confronted his father with both hands clasped tightly round the hilt. His knuckles thrusting at the taut skin were bone white. His brothers and Beorn started a wary advance, but Godwin snapped: "Leave him!" The earl walked forward. Sweyn backed. "I don't want to fight you, father," he said warningly.

"No one is forcing you. You have only to do as I bid!" Godwin said savagely. Around them the housecarles, Alfward and his companions, the rest of the family, stood holding their breath. Gytha began to speak, but Godwin briefly caught her eye, sending her, it seemed, some wordless message of reassurance. She was silent.

"I don't want to hurt you, father," said Sweyn coldly.

"Don't you?" said Godwin. He swung up his blade and attacked.

It was a master's onslaught; only a most gifted swordsman could have done it. It was an attack which was neither lethal nor negligible; it was strong enough to force a defence, yet clumsy enough to be withstood with ease. They had no shields; the broad, heavy blades must be sword and shield in one. Godwin led his son's blade in succession high, low, to the left, to the right, up, and up again above one shoulder. Then Godwin had thrown his sword away and dived in under Sweyn's arms, to grip the younger man round the middle. They lurched. Then came the crackling explosion of complete, coordinated movement which Brand remembered so well from his training days with Godwin. Sweyn was in the air. As he hit the floor, Beorn and Harold pounced on him. They dragged him, panting to his feet and held onto him. Godwin surveyed him, hands on hips, exactly as Sweyn had confronted Alfward.

"So I'm still better than you at nearly everything except despoiling maidens, and I give you best there, with the greatest goodwill. Now will you order your men to let these people go, or do I ask Beorn and Harold to go on holding you while I knock some sense into you with my fists? Well?"

Sweyn jerked his head at the men in front of the door. They moved. Alfward and his companions went, at a pace between a walk and run and with an uncertain grip on their dignity. Only Alfward paused at the door to say: "We can trust your word, Earl Godwin? Earl Sweyn will leave Hereford?"

"He'll leave England!" Godwin said. "Yes. You can trust my word."

"It's the most trustworthy word in the land," Sweyn agreed, rigid like an iron post between his brother and his cousin. "As others have discovered. Alfred Atheling for instance."

As the door closed after Alfward, Godwin said: "Let go of him, the two of you."

They did so, warily. Godwin's voice had held a thin, warning note. His eyes were glittering.

"You hardly seem to believe it," he said to Sweyn, "but I only strike helpless men when I must. I have a dislike of it, in fact. So you can save your two-edged comments." And without warning his right hand swept in a savage arc which ended at Sweyn's jaw and lifted him off his feet. He went down on his back with a flat, rafter-shaking thud and lay there winded, mouthing for air. His man Axe-bearer ran to him and knelt beside him.

"Here, sit up." He propped Sweyn up with one arm and drove a heel of the other hand hard into his lord's lower ribs. Sweyn drew a whooping breath and regained the power to speak. He uttered a venom-laden oath.

Godwin said: "The coming of Alfward showed me what I should have known: that there is no choice now for you. If you do not go now, then the king himself will send you. He would have granted that petition, had they made it to him. You will go under guard to Bristol tomorrow. I have a ship there already, waiting for you. I shall send orders to the captain that you are to go to Denmark, to your cousin Sven, Beorn's brother. I hope you agree better with him than you ever have with Beorn. You may travel bound or you may travel free, but travel you will. I do it for your own sake, Sweyn, whether you believe me or not."

Sweyn, fluently, swore at him again.

"I heard you were ill," said Emma, standing over her daughter-in-law's bed. "What is wrong?"

"Nothing of importance," Edith's pale face looked up at her. She lay with her knees drawn to her chest and a rug over her, despite the June warmth. "I shall be better in a little while. It's only stomach cramp."

"Ralph of Mantes is on the road. His foreriders came in half an hour ago. They said he would be here by noon. I shall tell the physician to make you up a draught; you must be up if you can to welcome him. I shall be glad to see my grandson, though I hope Edward has done right. It will be another foreigner, after all."

"I would provide an English grandson for you if I could," said Edith.

"Oh yes, I know. I don't blame you, child. Far from it. I pity you. I think you will have to make up your mind to it, Edith. I doubt if you and Edward will ever give me any grandchildren. Can you face it? I can't believe that any daughter of Gytha and Godwin lacks courage."

"I . . . don't know. I hope . . . every month. But now, again, there's nothing." She had been crying, and if she had told her women that the cramp was the cause, it was a lie.

"Children aren't always a blessing," said the older woman coolly. "They can give you more grief than a foe with a sword in his hand. I know. You can end by hating them as much as any blade-wielding enemy. I may pity you, but don't pity yourself."

"Did you ever hate . . . one of your own children, then?" Edith's eyes were wide.

"Two," said Emma frankly. "Because I loathed their father. The father is the start of it, after all. His daughter I managed to take to but never his sons." She smiled grimly at Edith's appalled expression. It was not the first time that Emma had shocked her daughter-in-law by oblique references to the gossip about herself and Alfred's death. She never spoke Alfred's name. Still less did she, these days, deny the rumours. In some ways, Edith thought, her dragonlike mother-in-law almost enjoyed her stark reputation. Edith herself did not probe. Edward had little enough family as it was; it would do him no service to destroy what shaky links he now had with his alarming mother. The family circle, in Edith's view, was important.

Alone again, she curled up tighter to warm away the pain in her abdomen and tried, as Emma had bidden, not to pity herself or grieve for the children she could not have. But bitterness was hard to avoid. She and Edward had prayed constantly that she might conceive, all to no purpose. Yet somewhere in the land, she knew, Sweyn's woman, the stolen nun, must at this moment be nearing her time. It might have been born already. A child had been granted to them and what had they done to merit such a blessing? She turned over and looked at a patch of sun on the floor. The cramps were easing now, in the sudden way they had. She must call her women soon and get up to welcome Ralph, who would be to Edward the nearest thing he had to a son. She must smile and greet Ralph gladly, show to him the face she must show to all the world: Edith the good queen, devoted to piety and good works, King Edward's helpmeet, comforter, and friend.

But never, she thought, the mother of his children, and only in the simplest physical sense his lover. Their rare and fruitless unions had never had much in them of love. For Edward they were clearly a distasteful duty and for herself they resembled the wakenings of a sick person from slumber into pain. It might be best now if they ceased entirely. She should put away all thoughts of desire, and with them all envy of those who could enjoy it. All thoughts, for instance, of such as Sweyn and Edgiva. Never, she told herself, fighting down a wish to weep again, must she—God forbid!—think of Edgiva and her like with . . . envy.

The idea of envying Edgiva would at that moment have struck those who were caring for her as a harsh, battlefield jest. Only Gytha, perhaps, might have understood and sorrowed for her daughter. While Edith was driving herself to rise and face her full-grown nephew, her newly arriving infant one was still two hours from the light of day, and Edgiva's agony in the guesthouse at Godwin's Winchester hall was so terrible that Gytha had ordered the menfolk to stay out of earshot. Aldith, who had helped to bring most of Godwin's offspring into the world, stood at the bedside murmuring helpful incantations of mingled heathen and Christian origin, and Gytha had no heart to rebuke the heathen element. Let any power be invoked that might come to the aid of this hideous childbed. Edgiva had no strength, it seemed, to expel the child. She even screamed on a note of protest, as though this were something that was being done to her instead of something she should herself be doing.

This was a true assessment, although Edgiva was not in a state to confirm it for them. She had no will either to give life or to hold onto it herself. Her will had lost its power through disuse. She had come passively to Winchester because it was all the shelter that was offered. She had not wished it. She did not wish anything. Sweyn had gone and he had not even said farewell to her. When she woke on the day of his departure, having slept alone in his chamber while Sweyn lay under guard in the hall, she found that he had left already. He had not asked to see her. She guessed, although no one was unkind enough to tell her, that he had been offered a chance to say good-bye and refused it, choosing to make Edgiva the scapegoat for his misfortunes. Nor had any message reached her since. She would have been glad by then to be remembered for the baby's sake alone. It would have been better than nothing. Better than this negation.

The child was born into a hot, airless world. The sun on the thatch above had made the chamber thick with heat. The baby wailed loudly, perhaps in disapproval of these unpleasant conditions, and Aldith said: "Thank God he is strong enough to fight for himself." Then she looked at Edgiva, made a sharp exclamation, and darted forward, grabbing cloths. The smell of blood in the heavy atmosphere became overpowering, a sweet, nauseous stench. Aldith said, working quickly, "I'll do my best, but I've seen this sort of thing too often. Maybe it's as well, seeing who she is and where she ought rightly to be. What'll we call the child?"

"She wanted a Danish name." Gytha was working alongside her. "Sweyn is a Danish name. Godwin suggested Hakon."

The baby was baptised Hakon that same day. The priest went straight from the christening to give Edgiva the last rites, granting them to her at Gytha's prayer, lapsed nun though she might be. Brand sat by her, for she was conscious now and then, and tried to talk life back into her, but she shook her head weakly at him. "I shan't get well and I don't want to. If only Sweyn could come . . . oh, Brand, I want Sweyn so much." Any man would do, she had once thought, but it wasn't true. It was Sweyn alone she longed for, Sweyn alone who could help her now.

Later she said: "He went away without a word to me, did you know that, Brand? Without a single word. I hate him. Hate him. Damn his soul in hell for all eternity."

Part

GOLDEN RING
Summer, 1049

1 ⚹ Supplicant at the Gate

"We have called this council," said Edward, hands clasped before him on the scrubbed plank table, "to consider a request from Henry Emperor of Germany to send him aid in his quarrel with his vassal Baldwin of Flanders. He has a certain right to call on us. He married our half-sister Gunhild, daughter of the Lady Emma and her second husband King Cnut. But there are other sides to the question."

He scanned the table, surveying the Witan Council ranged down its two sides, summoned to London in haste for this meeting. On his immediate left sat Champart, always a valued aide. Champart was cautious and clever, and if he was also ambitious, his ambition was at least limited to himself. He didn't have a growing family of land-hungry sons like Godwin.

Ralph of Mantes, Edward's nephew, was on his right. Edward was pleased with him, a quiet, courteously spoken young man, prettily grateful for his uncle's notice and content with his tiny earldom, carved out of the land that had been abandoned by Sweyn Godwinsson and finally stripped from him when infuriated messages from Sven of Denmark and Baldwin of Flanders made it plain that he was continuing his lawless career abroad. The rest of the land had gone to Harold Godwinsson and Beorn. One must keep the ravenous Godwins quiet somehow. Godwin himself was a few seats down on the right-hand side, with the other earls and facing the Church contingent. The Church was well represented. Aldred of Worcester, Abbot Sparhafoc, Alfric Kitehawk, Eadsige of Canterbury, were all present. Eadsige was back at his duties now after a long illness but still looked a sick man. However, his eyes were sharp enough.

"Since I have summoned you all at short notice," Edward said, "we shall deal with all business in hand that we can, without waiting for the next official meeting. There is the question of designs for the new crown, for instance—Abbot Sparhafoc has them with him—and the grant of a mint to one of our northern towns. But this request from our brother-in-law has first claim on us. What he wishes us to do is to muster our fleet and blockade the Flemish ports. Has anyone any comments?"

At least six people instantly drew breath to speak and Wulf-noth, Godwin's ash-blond youngest son, attending a council for the first time and sharing guard duty with Brand, muttered in Brand's ear: "It's going to be a long, tough session—am I right?"

"I think so," Brand muttered back. He too had recognised the symptoms.

Aldred of Worcester was the first to translate breath into speech, beating Siward and Champart to it by a narrow margin. Aldred considered that his ministry included protecting the bodies of his flock as well as their souls. "A blockade of that size would draw the bulk of all our forces eastwards," he said. "The Welsh are prowling on my borders again, and my agents over the frontier have been bringing in tales of tribesmen slipping southwards through the mountains, and of Viking arms from the Irish settlement being brought in by Gruffyd of South Wales. In other words, I am expecting trouble. My diocese can spare no men and we'd like to think that if we need reinforcements we can get them—that they won't be fighting someone else's wars on the wrong side of England!"

"They'd be handier ready-mustered than if you had to round them up from their homes," Siward of Northumbria broke in. Viking himself to the marrow of his bones, he had never said no to a fight in his life.

"I agree with Siward," said Leofric unexpectedly.

Unexpectedly, because Leofric was notoriously insular and never saw why English armies should fight on anyone's behalf but their own, or in anyone else's territory. But both Ralph of Mantes, whose lands partook of the Welsh borders, and Robert Champart had been nodding their heads while Aldred spoke, and Leofric had been watching them. Siward grinned, reading his fellow earl's mind. Both were foreigners to Leofric, and the alliance of Champart and Mantes was just one more alien backing up another. To support the opposing side was merely instinct as far as Leofric was concerned.

"There are reasons," said Godwin some time later, when the argument had made several useless circles, "to fear that Flanders could be a danger to us in a day to come. A show of power might discourage that."

"Because her ports are open to the ships of Denmark and Norway?" asked Leofric.

"Flemish ports by tradition are open to everyone, my son," said Sparhafoc, as if this were a virtue on the part of the Flemings.

Siward moved restlessly on the bench, which as usual seemed too small for him. "I'm all for getting into a fray rather than staying out," he said. "But why is Godwin, this time? Three years back, Godwin, you wanted to say yes when Danish Sven asked for fifty ships for help against Norway. Well, Sven's your kin by marriage, and that was natural. And last year when Magnus died and Sven saw his chance to grab a bit of Norway instead of having Norway grab at him, you wanted to help him again. Again, natural . . ."

"And I was turned down both times," said Godwin. He looked at Leofric and Champart, who had been the backbone of the opposition. The look at Champart was longer and colder. Leofric's opposition had been impersonal; Champart's had not. Champart's seat beside the king had been Godwin's until that second defeat.

"What I'm getting at is, what's your reason this time, Godwin? Ye've no kin in Germany."

The Witan turned to Godwin. He said: "There was a Viking raid on our shores last year. They were driven off but they took booty, and I hear they sold it in Flanders. Well, they were pirates and of no account in themselves. But they show how the wind lies. Sven had very good reason to fear Norway. We refused him, and because we refused him, all Norway and half Denmark are now in the hands of Magnus's successor, Harald Hardraada. Let me remind you all that Magnus imagined he had a claim to England. King Harald perhaps has inherited Magnus's dreams along with Magnus's kingdom—and when did Hardraada ever have scruples over increasing his possessions at swordpoint? Ask my kinsman Sven! The fewer allies the man Hardraada has, the better. And since Flanders is so well disposed to the Viking folk, let us see that Flanders respects us. Hardraada is such a man . . ."

He left the sentence in the air. He had no need to finish it. Harald of Norway was such a man as might one day attack England purely for the fun of it, with or without an excuse. In the speech of the far north, Hardraada was the word for ruthless, and he had earned that title a dozen times over, in Byzantium and Russia, in war, in gaming, and in his barbarian notions of love.

"All this is supposition," said Champart impatiently. "We talk of what *may* happen. What my lord bishop of Worcester is talking about are things that are happening already, on the Marches . . ."

"Let us remember," said Godwin, pitching his voice accurately just one decibel above that of Champart, "that Hardraada now has all his lands in a state of subjection. He is beginning to have time on his hands."

"And Flanders already bears us some ill will," Harold Godwinsson put in, backing up his father.

Amidst laughter, Champart said: "And whose fault is that?" He gazed round him, urbanely collecting eyes.

Godwin presented a cold profile to him. The very sound of Champart's cultured voice with its clipped Gallic accent, Godwin had been heard to say, put his teeth on edge. The fault he meant was mostly Sweyn Godwinsson's, and Leofric, damn him, was now regaling Bishop Aldred, who hadn't heard them, with the details. Edward's mouth was set in lines of distaste.

"Whose fault it is, is hardly the point," said Godwin sharply. "It is the fact that we must deal with."

". . . Sweyn Godwinsson was blown off course on his way to Denmark and landed up in Flanders. Baldwin took him in—who did he ever not take in?—and he stayed there for some months. *But . . .* Baldwin has daughters. They say William of Normandy's courting Matilda but the other one, Judith, she's not yet betrothed, and it seems Sweyn took a liking to her."

"Dear, dear. Continue." Aldred had an undoubtedly worldly streak in him. He enjoyed a fight and relished a deplorable story. His eyes were sparkling. They were not the only ones, either. To his rage, Godwin saw that even those who had heard the tale before were inclining welcoming ears towards it.

"She's a virtuous maid as well as a lovely one, it seems. When he came on her walking in her father's vineyard and began on his love talk, she led him to look at the fishpond and then, when he tried to embrace her, she pushed him in and ran . . ."

Stifled snorts of merriment, like kettle steam, escaped the audience, now listening without concealment. Godwin's working jaw muscles suggested that he was grinding his teeth.

"She went and told her father," Leofric went on, "and Baldwin ordered Sweyn to get on his way to Denmark. Baldwin hasn't been too sweet on the English altogether, ever since."

"The pure and lovely Judith sounds like a minx to me," whispered Wulfnoth to Brand.

"That's what your mother said," Brand whispered back. "She also said she sounded like an ideal daughter-in-law and she wished Sweyn would marry her!" Once, long ago, Gytha had said the same of Eadgyth. It was a marvel to Brand how that wound had healed. On the rare occasions when he saw Eadgyth now she was only another person, Harold's wife. The enchantress of former days had gone.

Edward was banging on the table. The laughter ceased. He began to review the arguments they had heard. He talked at length while Sparhafoc looked at the cylinder of rolled-up crown designs before him and clearly gave up hope of having them discussed at this session. Edward's voice was dispassionate, what nuances there were suggesting that he thought Godwin's viewpoint good and wished it were Champart's instead. "There is the point," he said at length, "that the matter is military rather than ecclesiastical, and that therefore the view of the earls should have extra weight. The majority of the earls seem in favour of acceptance. However . . ." Edward looked round the table, as if in search of new arguments. His doubt, his reluctance to take Godwin's advice and oppose his most trusted minister, Champart, could be felt by them all. Godwin, back relaxed against the wall behind him and right hand resting on the table, fingers tracing spirals on its surface, was deep in thought. As Edward paused, he said in a colourless voice: "There is clearly a division of opinion. We could adopt an old practice of the Witan and ask our followers to settle the matter at mead-time after the late meal. I believe Earl Siward has already sounded his men, in fact. What is your view, my lord of Northumbria?"

He turned to Siward, handing the suggestion on like a relay runner passing on the token. Siward's fist descended on the table with a crash that shook it. "Aye, I've sounded them. And they're ready. Well fed, in training, longing to get their teeth in something. Don't know how anyone else's men feel. But it's their trade. They ought to talk sense about it."

"I see." Edward nodded. "Very well. The arguments will be put to the men tonight. The meeting will resume tomorrow to deal with unfinished business. Adjourn!"

The vote was taken in the evening, after the meal had been eaten, when the lyre and the mead were going round.

Because, as Siward had said, fighting was their trade and because, like Siward, they had never said no to a challenge in their lives, and because one blockade now was a better prospect for fun than any number of problematical Welshmen in the future, the housecarles of the earls said yes to the emperor, almost to a man. Godwin had known they would.

As a source of entertainment, however, the blockade proved disappointing. Instead of the lively skirmishing with a chance of booty that all the men had hoped for, it was a monumentally dull affair of relays of ships patrolling in the Channel. Baldwin sent a few vessels to harass them and there were some ineffectual exchanges of arrows, rocks, and ruderies. There were no captives, no casualties—except that Harold Godwinsson dislocated a shoulder when he slipped while helping to launch a ship—and no loot.

"And not much competence, either," said Edward coldly. Word had come from the emperor that their mission was over. He thanked them for their help and released them. They were free to go home. But first it was necessary to hold an enquiry into the incident when half a dozen small ships in close formation had slipped through the defences and fled southwards unchallenged. They had come from somewhere north of Flanders, and they had not tried to put in at any Flemish ports. But they had got through without identifying themselves, and that was heinous. At Edward's Sandwich fort, where the fleet was based, Godwin and Beorn, in embarrassing conference with the king, were trying to explain how it had happened.

They held the conference out of doors, the chart unrolled over a small table and weighted down with stones. The sea was in sight, the ships drawn up on the beach. It was a sultry day with a heavy, slopping swell and a steeliness at the edges of the sky. Harold sat on a boulder close by, his left arm bundled in a sling. He had called Brand to him for company and they were talking quietly. Behind them the conference was both tedious and tense.

". . . Mist is an act of God, I am aware." Edward's finger jabbed at the chart. "But if ships had been positioned here and *here* . . ." He took up a lump of charcoal and made marks. ". . . you could have closed in in time. If it gets to Baldwin's ears that six . . . six . . . vessels got through, we shall have done ourselves more harm than good with him. He will think us fools. I should have listened to Champart's advice. We should make more impression on Baldwin by ignoring him."

The back of Godwin's neck was red, not merely from the sun. He said: "I took into account that we must cover all the strait. To concentrate ships there would mean drawing on other squadrons and thinning them out elsewhere."

"No one would question your experience, Godwin," said the king, in a tone which meant that he had every intention of questioning it, "but . . ."

"My lords," came Harold Godwinsson's voice urgently, "I am sorry to interrupt. But a messenger has come in from the west, this page tells me." He pushed the boy forward. "He asks for speech with the king and says he has a pressing reason."

"From the west? The Marches?" Edward looked up. "Bring him here, boy. At once."

But he was almost there already, having got Odi Pathfinder to bring him through the tents that surrounded the fort. He walked behind Odi, leading his pony. He thanked his guide in the broad-vowelled speech of the Welsh March, his voice rough with exhaustion. He was lined and taut with it and a string of clotted blood beads stretched across his forehead. He had had a narrow escape from something or someone lately. He was filthy and—to judge from the involuntary turn of his head as he passed a group of men spitting meat over a brazier—hungry. He pushed his pony's reins into Odi's hands and stumbled forward to kneel before Edward. He said: "*Vikings!*"

Three-quarters of the men in the camp were bred, in part at least, from Danish or Norwegian stock. But the word "Viking" in that context and that tone was a dread-invoker, a spell to conjure hideous images. Whatever their ancestry, almost all had in childhood been told by harassed mothers: "Shut your noise or the Vikings will get you!" In the eye of the mind, all saw the same visions: the bounding berserker shapes with faceless helms and upraised axes, outlined against the glare of burning thatch, and the sprawled bodies mutilated with the sign of the bloody eagle, ribs torn from the spine and wrenched outward in a travesty of wings. They stiffened.

"Up!" Edward gripped the man's shoulder and pulled him to his feet. "No need to kneel. Now tell me. Vikings? Where?"

"Bishop Aldred sent me. Irish Vikings came up Severn River five days ago. Welsh tribesmen joined them, raiding and burning and going towards Gloucester. They put the bishop's men to flight— the ones they couldn't catch and slaughter. I was lucky. I lost my two brothers . . ." His voice faltered. He overcame it and went on, lower, telling of roads crammed with frightened folk driving their beasts before them, looking for safety behind the old patched-up Roman walls at Gloucester. "We need men, quickly. I hardly slept on the way."

"Thank you." Edward beckoned a page. "Take this man and see he has food and drink and a bed. Serve wine from my own supply."

The page led the messenger away and Odi took the pony off to the horse lines. The pony was as foundered as the man, its coat black with sweat and its legs trembling. Edward stood deep in thought, looking at the chart of the Dover strait but not studying it. He said: "By sea or overland? Which? It's a long way." He turned irritably as another page, excited and apprehensive both at once, appeared at his elbow. "Yes?"

"My lord, it's another horseman. The gatewards said I was to tell you that someone is asking to see you, my lord."

"Someone? Who? I don't give audiences to men who won't identify themselves. What's his business? Where's he from? The Marches again?"

The page gulped. He said: "He wouldn't give his name, but I've seen him before. I know him."

"Then who is he?"

"It's Earl Sweyn Godwinsson, my lord."

"Perhaps," suggested Godwin, "I had better find out what he wants."

"You had," Edward agreed. "And you may tell him that if he

sets foot in this camp I'll have him thrown into the sea. Weighted. He was officially outlawed when I heard of his conduct in Flanders and Denmark and he still is!"

"We do not know why he had to leave Denmark!" said Godwin angrily.

"If his activities at Leominster and in Flanders are any guide, we need not waste time wondering. See him. Get rid of him. And get back before the tide turns. I have decided. The Wessex ships are to sail on the tide, go round the coast and up the Bristol Channel. That is, your ships, Earl Beorn's, and Tostig's. Harold's ships had best be put under Tostig's command, since Tostig has the fewest. Harold is unfit for the field. You may catch the raiders coming down the channel if the weather's with you. The wind's lying east now." He glanced up as Harold began a protest. "If it comes to swordplay, Earl Harold, what good will you be? Rest yourself and mend, ready to fight with both hands another time!"

"My lord," said Godwin, "if Sweyn asks . . ."

Edward brought his hand down flat on the chart with a bang. "God's Elbow, Godwin, have I time to trouble with your renegade offspring now? I've invading Vikings on my hands; isn't that enough? Go if you're going but come back on your own! Godwin! *Go!*"

Godwin turned from the king's unyielding profile and walked away. After a pause his nephew and Harold followed him. Brand felt no pity for Sweyn the supplicant at the gate. But for Godwin he was sorry, once again.

He missed their return. As preparations to depart began he was embroiled in a whirl of action and a hubbub of orders which concealed a smooth mobilisation machinery. He was co-opted as Tostig took charge of provisioning and loading all his father's vessels as well as his own, and found himself down on the shore labouring in the afternoon heat. Beorn did not reappear until the work was almost done and the first ships were already being pushed over their rollers into the sea. Not until launching was complete and the three squadrons were well out from the beach, strung in long-drawn-out formations over the water like three flights of geese, did Brand find himself at his leader's side. Beorn had seated himself amidships, a sword upon his knees. He held out a hand for the sand box. "Did you think I'd miss my own ship? It was Sweyn that kept me."

"I know. I was there when the page announced him." Brand

paused, absently continuing to clean his own sword, and then re-membered Hakon. He was entitled to take an interest in Sweyn. "Where is he now?"

"In Sandwich. He leaves the district at dawn. The king has allowed him to rest the night in the town. After that he has four days to get out of the country again. He wanted to be reinstated."

"And King Edward refused?"

"Harold and I refused. Sweyn said if we were willing to hand back the lands we took over from him, perhaps that would persuade the king to forgive him. Which I suppose is possible. My uncle begged us to agree; he thought it might move Edward. I was sorry for my uncle." Beorn sounded unhappy. "He and Aunt Gytha love Sweyn. Well, they would, he's their eldest. I'd do almost anything for them. They trained me, gave me a home as good as my own was, treated me like one of their own sons. But *Sweyn*! It was because of him that my uncle lost his post as commander of the royal guard; did you know?"

Brand shook his head.

"Well, it was. After the king heard Sweyn had been thrown out of Denmark. My uncle was sent for and told that the royal guard would be a separate body henceforth, with every man directly sworn to the king, and Ralph of Mantes as its commander."

"I didn't know. I thought Lord Godwin had just resigned."

"Not quite. He was asked to resign. Ordered to. Ralph of Mantes is just a figurehead, I gather; the men didn't like the change much. Oswald Halfear does most of the work of training and recruit-ment, because they'll follow him. My uncle was very dignified about it. He picked out some of his best men—Halfear was one of them— and commanded them to offer their swords to Edward. The guard's still run in the old way; the same kind of training, and they still have the power to try their own members if one of them is accused of anything. But the men say it isn't the same. It's a shame, for them as well as for my uncle. My uncle," said Beorn, rubbing violently at the blade, "would like to see every Frenchman run out of the country and chased into the Channel, and so would I."

"Every Frenchman?" For a moment Brand did not follow. "You mean . . . Ralph of Mantes? But he seems very harmless."

"He is. Harmless to the point of feebleness. What of it? He's *foreign*. Oh well, all that's beside the point. We were talking of

Sweyn. I'm sorry for my uncle, as I said, but Sweyn's brought him nothing but trouble, if only he'd see it. If he were reinstated, he would just bring more."

"He managed quite well even at a distance, from Flanders and Denmark," Brand said dryly.

"I wish I knew what happened in Denmark," Beorn said thoughtfully. "I wrote to my brother Sven to ask, but Sven wrote back that he did not wish to complain of Sweyn any more to Sweyn's own family and preferred to let the matter drop. Harold agrees with me that we shouldn't have Sweyn home again." Beorn sighed. "And Sweyn's his own brother. Harold kept on saying to Sweyn that he'd done damage enough, and they nearly came to blows. They would have done if Harold hadn't been injured already!"

"Did he have any men with him—Sweyn, I mean?"

Beorn laughed. "No! We all thought he must have them hidden somewhere, but he hadn't. He didn't know for sure where to find his father, whether at Sandwich or Dover or out at sea, or even not with the blockade at all. He knew about the blockade, of course; it's the talk of every port for hundreds of miles. That was Sweyn who slipped past us in the strait. He was proud of that! He sailed on round to Bosham to see if he could get news of us at my uncle's manor there, and when they told him his father was here, he rode off overland on his own. He took a freak into his head to ride by the Pilgrims' Way, clutching a green branch like a palmer, trying to look penitent." Beorn let out another snort of laughter.

"And does he look penitent?"

"No." Seriousness returned. "He doesn't. He looks desperate. It's as well he had no men with him. He's been freebooting in the Channel since he left Denmark, living off merchant ships. I didn't like the look of him, Brand. I tell you, he's more dangerous alone than a whole Viking war-band together. Desperate men often are. Yes. Dangerous. That's the word."

The ship rocked. An uneasy swell rolled against her. Beorn considered the sky. He said in a different but still serious tone of voice: "And I don't much like the look of this weather, either."

2 ✠ "Sweyn Spoke the Truth"

"There in haven stood . . . *pull*!
"The high-prowed vessel . . . *pull*!
"Cold and outward bound . . . *pull*!
"For the Atheling's journey . . . *pull*! . . ."
"We need wind," Beorn muttered, looking aft at the swinging
backs of his rowers as they leant and stretched to the chant of the
steersman. Muscles formed into patterns, melted and re-formed,
called into play and out of it by the oarsmen's reach and pull. Brand,
released from rowing duty for a while, flexed aching, salt-caked
shoulders and agreed. Testing the air with a wetted finger he discovered that what trace of breeze there was had now swung to the west.
They were in haste. The story of *Beowulf* was being chanted abnor-
mally, exhaustingly fast, and still the shores seemed hardly to be
moving. He looked beyond their own ship to where the rest of the
fleet was strung across the sea. Beorn's were leading, augmented by
two ships on loan from the royal fleet; Tostig's and Godwin's squadrons were following. The steersman's voice fell silent as dead King
Scyld on his burning death-ship laden with treasure departed over
the water. Growing hoarse with the shouted rhythm, he took to
beating it out on a drum instead.

"I had meant to put into Dover on the way home," Beorn said.
"I wanted to see Eric Merchant. So much for that! We shall have to
look forward to fighting instead—if we get there before the raiders
leave. I hate this dead weather. They won't plunge too deep inland,
I think. They'll grab what they can carry and go. We'll probably

meet the Viking contingent sailing east to sell their booty in Flanders again. Where does a pirate end and a merchant begin, Brand?"

"Eric isn't a pirate," said Brand. He frowned. As he matured, Brand's face had acquired force. His nose was broad and widesprung at the nostrils and his thick black eyebrows nearly met at the bridge. When he frowned they did meet, darkening his whole face. They had met now. "I saw Eric when I took ship to Dover for provisions, fourteen nights ago," he said.

"How is he?" Since they had been benighted with Eric and fought for his warehouse, Beorn had taken a real if spasmodic interest in the merchant's fortunes. "Has he voyaged into thanehood yet? Or not yet cleared his debts?"

"The debts are paid," said Brand. "But there's other bad news. The *Hild* sailed on that third voyage, this summer, with Eric's son Rolf aboard. And she vanished. She was six weeks overdue when I saw Eric. She was bound for France with a cargo of cloth and skins and leather goods. There was a storm not long after she sailed. There's been no news, no word, nothing. They think she must have foundered. Hild . . ."

He had been more grieved for Hild's sake than he had words for. Her very dignity in the face of this new calamity had made words hard to put together. She had grown very much from the green, dull girl who chattered of thanes and queens on the ride to Edward's coronation. Her life would be a dreary affair now, he thought, with Ragnar and her baby both gone, and nothing to do but care barrenly for her father's hall while Eric muttered over his profit tallies and bartered his soul for a witch's visions. He wondered how much of Eric's total means had been sunk in the *Hild*'s last voyage, a die that had been thrown to win glory, but had turned a useless number up.

"If we catch any Viking ships this voyage," said Beorn, "we'll drown the crew one at a time and take Eric a present of the cargo. Shall we?"

"Yes. *If* we catch them. Most likely they'll be far away before we get there."

They journeyed on, rowing in relays through the night under an ominous, haze-ringed moon, and on through the next day, in thick warm air which lay heavy on the skin but felt scanty in the lungs. The sky slowly dimmed till the part where the sun should be was the colour of breathed-on copper, and elsewhere had dulled to the tone of lead. The sea below it was restive, breaking into tiny stillborn crests. Beorn consulted a chart and exchanged signals with Godwin and Tostig. The leaders' ships drew together and drifted awhile in starfish formation while their captains conferred. The conference over, Beorn said: "We're to run for Pevensey. There's a storm coming up, or none of us has ever seen one."

They were dragging the craft clear of the high-tide mark when the first warning flicker showed on the western horizon, now darkened from lead to black. Godwin led them inland to shelter in his nearby hall. It was not the first time that his string of halls and homesteads along the south coast had provided useful shelter in emergencies. They spent the night under a watertight roof, singing round a fire while the thunder growled outside, and fell asleep to the sound of drenching rain. By morning the worst of the rain was over, but a furious southwest gale was driving jagged seas past the mouth of the bay, sealing the ships in as effectively as though they were landlocked. Some, indeed, had been damaged. Most of the forty-four vessels had been drawn up high enough to be safe, but some half a dozen had been caught by the fierce tide. The sea, having got them, had battered them and then thrown them back as if in disgust, further along the shore. Godwin organised a repair party.

By the second day the rain had stopped entirely and the sky was lifting, but the gale still blew and it was useless to fret about the Vikings, for there was no getting at them through this.

"Or ever at all," Tostig said crossly, regarding the upturned keel of the damaged boat in front of him. Wulfnoth, who had been on Tostig's ship, having insisted on going with his favourite brother, said: "The storm must have driven them back to their own boats by now."

"I know." The wind lifted damp yellow hair from Tostig's scalp. "Hardly a sword unsheathed in the Channel, and now when we have a real foe to fight, we can't get to the battlefield! They must be bound for home by this time."

"And not empty-handed, either," Odi Pathfinder said.

Tostig made an angry noise. "That's true enough!" Then he laughed, struck by another thought. "Unlike my poor brother Sweyn," he said with malice. "He must be furious. I'd be happier if I knew where he was now."

"Behind you, my friend," said Sweyn's voice, softly, amusedly, no more than a few feet off.

They jumped, springing round instinctively to face the voice. Sweyn stepped from behind a sheltering rock. His appearance at the sound of his name, as though Tostig's words had been an incantation, was uncanny. Odi Pathfinder gasped and crossed himself. Sweyn stepped out and laughed.

"No, I'm not the Horned One in person!" He leant against the rock, surveying them. "An army could creep up unheard in this wind!"

Tostig, less impressionable than Odi, stared at his brother with exasperation. "A fine, dramatic appearance! What is it you want?"

"Is my father here?" asked Sweyn.

Odi said: "I'll find him," and hurried off. The rest gathered round in a semicircle, a little wary. Brand thought that now he understood why Beorn had said that Sweyn was dangerous.

For he looked it. Danger breathed out of him. He was as soaked in it as the stained brown mantle he wore had been soaked in sea-water. One wanted to stand out of arm's reach of him and felt it would be unwise to turn one's back.

He had become a sea wolf, a pirate. It needed no explaining. Only an outlaw, one who was hunted as well as hunter, moved like that, prowling rather than walking, checking the space behind him before he relaxed, placing his feet so that he could be balanced and ready to fight or flee at an instant's notice. His face was weathered dark brown with sun and wind, and in his tangled hair the colour had faded. His eyes were bright, predatory, wary, merry, unpitying. He had one gold arm-ring and a belt buckle of gold, and he had kept his emerald finger-ring. His other arm-rings, his mantle-brooch, and his helm ornaments were of copper, and his dagger-hilt was bone. He looked hungry.

"Sweyn!" said Godwin, arriving suddenly at Odi's side. He looked at his son anxiously, unhappily. "So you're here!"

In the hall to which he was taken, Sweyn was taciturn until he had eaten. The look of hunger had told truly. He consumed cold meat and fresh bread and gulped down mead while his kinsmen watched.

They had left the rest of the men on the shore, still repairing

ships. This was again a family conclave. And again, despite his protests, it included Brand. "Where my eldest is concerned, you *are* a
kinsman," Godwin had said, pushing Brand in front of him as they
left the beach. "Don't argue!"

So now he sat with the others, waiting for Sweyn to speak. The
outlaw wiped his mouth and said: "My thanks. I needed that. Father. I couldn't talk to you before as I wanted to, with the king at
your back and the camp buzzing with messengers. I trailed you
along the coast hoping you'd put in somewhere. I could read a storm
coming. Father . . . I need help."

"Tell me," said Godwin. His face had taken on the lines of a
man who has not slept.

"I find," said Sweyn, twisting the ring on his finger so that the
green gem in it winked, "that the life of a sea wolf palls in time. As a
home, the sea lacks charm. The roof leaks and the floor's uneven. Father, I think I have paid God for the treasure I took from His
Leominster storehouse. Whatever the king said when I was at his
gate, surely that wasn't his last word? He had no time to think—not
with news of an attack coming at the same moment. If you were to
plead with him again for me, at a time when he is free to listen . . ."
Suddenly Sweyn's voice had altered. It was now the humble tone of
the prodigal son, incongruously uttered by the sea wolf's harsh
throat. "Father, I beg you to help me. And you, Beorn. Close
friends we have never been. But you were moderately courteous at
Sandwich." He stared at his cousin. "It was Harold . . ."

"Who is not here," observed Tostig. "Did you know he wasn't
here?"

"What if I did?"

"I expect it encouraged you to come and make a nuisance of
yourself, that's all, jumping out from behind rocks and harrying our
father."

"Quiet, Tostig," said Godwin.

"Why?" Tostig demanded. He turned back to his brother. "Sea
roving should suit you to perfection, Sweyn, since you got into it in
the first place through stealing what wasn't yours, as you have just
confessed. What do you think father can do for you with Edward?
He has hardly any power now to do anything for anyone, and whose
fault is that? Yours. You damaged his status and turned the king
away from him, yourself. Why do you ask for his protection now?"

"Can't father speak for himself?" asked Sweyn.

Godwin's voice and face were full of conflict. "I want to help you," he said to Sweyn. "And I will, in any way that is possible. But as I said to you before, at Sandwich, I have your brothers and your sister Edith to consider. It is true that I lack the king's ear now. I do indeed doubt my power to help you back to England and your lands. Other help I can offer you. Gold, enough to start you in a new land, buy you followers and estates. Go and build yourself a new hall, offer your sword to a lord in France or Normandy or the northern lands. Or go to the Holy Land on pilgrimage . . ."

"Perhaps if you did that," said Wulfnoth eagerly, "Edward might feel you had wiped out the past. A pilgrimage is very holy."

"My dear little brother," said Sweyn, vaguely, as one conferring a verbal pat on the head.

"It would do no harm to ask Edward, would it?" said Beorn.

Everyone blinked at him. It was not the sentiment expected from the member of the family who had least cause to love Sweyn, even if he had reportedly been less violent than Harold at the first meeting. "If the king refuses, he refuses," said Beorn, aware of their surprise but paying no heed to it. "But still, would it do any harm to ask?"

"By Ragnorak," said Sweyn, "I hoped I might persuade you, Beorn, at least to agree to such a plea. But I confess I never thought to hear you urge it."

"My lady Gytha is grieving for you," said Beorn simply. "And so is my uncle here, I think. I would lend my voice to your plea for their sakes."

Godwin turned to Brand, who started as his name was spoken. "Brand. Give us your opinion. You have a right to speak. Your sister bore Sweyn's son."

"My son!" Sweyn interrupted. "I heard that the child had been born, no more. It was a son, you say? Did it live? Where is he now? And Edgiva?"

"At last, you think to ask after them!" Tostig said. "Our mother is rearing the boy. We called him Hakon and he is thriving. Edgiva died in childbirth."

"My son!" Sweyn's haggard features had lit up. "Well, Brand? I need to come home doubly now. I must see my boy. You are my . . . not quite my brother-in-law. I loved your sister. Will you speak for me?"

"For you?" said Brand. The memory of Edgiva's last words was still with him. "You can roam the seas all your life or drown in them for all I care. No, I will not!"

They were all staring. Through the sick anger that had welled up in him at those lying words of love, he knew that Godwin's eyes were shocked, full of grief and disappointment. Godwin had looked to Brand for support and not found it. He knew also that Tostig was triumphant and that Beorn, who had expected Brand to follow his lead, could hardly believe his own ears. Sweyn looked stunned.

"Before you left Edgiva," Brand said, "when she was happy with you, I didn't mind. I didn't care. She was forced into that abbey. I was glad to see her out of it. But afterwards, when you went away and never even said farewell to her . . ."—he found that his voice was actually shaking—". . . she cried for you. She told me that in any case it was only the child you cared for, not for her. You say you loved her. I say she died despairing because you didn't. She died cursing you. Her last words were a wish that you should spend eternity in hell." Sweyn's face had blanched. "So, go, Sweyn God-winsson, and be damned, and don't look to me for your salvation. Your son will be cared for, better than you could care for him, never fear."

"Well said!" Tostig applauded. Brand turned away. Godwin put his face in his hands. Sweyn sat quiet, very pale, eyes very bright and fierce. Without speaking he poured himself more mead.

Godwin said at length: "You see the strength of the case against you, Sweyn. Believe me, if I had only you to consider, I would plead for you. But as it is . . . what can you offer to make the plea good? What oaths can you give that would hold you, what sureties that would convince the king of your future good behaviour?"

"*Sureties!*" Sweyn shot to his feet. The violent ambience that went with him everywhere like a portable thunderstorm crackled into life. Something of his desperate hope and his bitter disappointment came to them through it, as if revealed by lightning. He spat on the floor. "*You* talk of sureties, my own father! I wonder you don't talk of my son as a hostage . . . !"

"Well, he is my grandson too," said Godwin reasonably.

Sweyn's hands settled on his hips. He seemed to be taking command of himself. He took up an attitude, feet astride, standing before them. He cocked his head. He allowed an expression of theatrical sorrow to appear on his face. "I had hoped," he said, "that you wouldn't drive me to this."

"Drive you to what?" Tostig asked.

"Suppose," said Sweyn, gently, sweetly, slowly, "that I went to the king myself, father. Suppose I told him what *really* happened at Gildenford?"

"I . . . don't understand you at all," said Godwin in a tight voice when the silence had gone on much too long.

"The king already knows," said Tostig shortly.

"Does he? Not all of it, I think. He doesn't know for sure who sent that letter: his mother in collusion with you, father, his mother in collusion with Harold Harefoot, or all three of you together, or Harefoot and you, or Harefoot on his own. He doesn't *know*."

"He'd hardly take you as an untainted source of information!" said Tostig. "He'd know it was malice talking."

"What if I had proof?"

Godwin said in a hard voice: "Proof?"

"When we were going across the meads at Gildenford to see the ships depart, you asked me a question or two, father. You asked me what happened to the token you sent to the Athelings along with Lady Emma's so-called letter. I said I had taken it from Alfred and cast it into the grave of one of his followers."

"Yes. Well?"

"I was lying. I kept it. It seemed too valuable to throw away, and I thought we might want to repeat the exercise one day with Edward. I have it still. Oh, not here! I've hidden it well. But what if I showed that to the king?"

Tostig and Beorn were on their feet. Wulfnoth looked horrified. Tostig said. "You think we'd let you leave here after such a threat?"

"It would be rather difficult to control me for the rest of my life. Wouldn't it, father? You can overpower me and ship me off again, I suppose, though not to Denmark or Flanders this time . . ."

"Why *were* you thrown out of Denmark?" asked Wulfnoth curiously.

"I had a chess bet with one of Sven's jarls. He lost and delayed payment—he'd wagered an estate. I killed him. Unluckily, he was unarmed at the time."

"Oh, Sweyn!" Wulfnoth was distressed. "You ask us to help

you but you do such terrible things! If only you would go to the Holy Land . . ."

"Keep it up, little brother. You'll make a priest one day. Father, if you did ship me abroad, I might still come back some time unknown to you. If you keep me captive, how long can you hold me? For life? I doubt it. And I don't think you'll kill me. What would mother say? Wouldn't it be easier, much, much easier, just to put my case to the king? That's all I ask. Who would criticise you? I'm your son. It would be natural. Surely you see that?"

"I see you came prepared," said Godwin. "You have thought it all out."

"I'll withdraw," said Sweyn. "You may like time to think about it." As he moved towards the door, his mocking gaze lighted on Brand's face. "You look shocked, Woodcutter," he said lightly. "Have I told you things you didn't know? My staunch, unforgiving Woodcutter. Let me tell you some more. It hardly matters what I tell you now, after all; you know the truth of Gildenford already. But did you also know you were part of the clever plot to catch the Athelings? When my father forged Queen Emma's signature and a token of hers to trap her sons, and got the news that Alfred was coming, he sent a secret messenger north to warn Harefoot, waiting so innocently in Worcester, well out of the way, so that gossip afterwards would say it was Harefoot's spies who told him of the Athelings' coming and not Godwin, who had had no dealings with him. You were that messenger, that so secret courier."

"I carried no message!" Brand snapped defensively.

"Oh yes, you did. The heirlooms you carried were the signal. You were taken on because your home was in the right direction. You had an innocent, open reason to ride that way, and who but you and my father knew of the heirlooms in your saddlebag? You were a nobody. You were the best of all messengers, an unsuspecting dupe . . ."

"It all seems to have been very well planned," said Brand. He had clenched his teeth, as if Sweyn were trying to hurt him physically. He spoke tightly through rigid jaw muscles.

"Oh, it was," said Sweyn, moving gently, closer to the door. "Hardly anyone was in the know but our own kinsfolk and Thane Edwin, who was and is father's man to the death." He shook his head mournfully. "We were all sadly deceived by clerks and messengers who said they came from Emma . . . in the days of her regency she had a habit of giving commands through underlings instead of directly by word of mouth. Perhaps they really came from her; perhaps not. *We* couldn't know. Well, Brand, I wonder if you'll go running to the king with all this tale? There's a pretty problem for you, father. What will you do with Brand?" His hand was on the latch. Godwin put a sudden hand out and gripped Tostig's elbow. He shook his head at Beorn as Beorn stepped sharply forward. "You look upset," said Sweyn kindly to Brand, watching his stricken expression. "When it comes to damning souls to hell, Woodcutter, two can play at it. You owe all that you are to my father. I don't think you'll sell him, myself. But you may suffer. Well, you're his embarrassment, not mine. Father, at daybreak I shall be at the dead tree halfway between here and the shore. Meet me there. Alone. Tell me your decision. Fail or refuse me, and I go to Edward. Bring men with you in the morning, and I shall see them coming and not show myself. Good day to you all."

He was gone. Godwin with a low, decisive "Let him!" held the others at his side. Tostig said as the latch clicked after his elder brother: "*Why* did you let him go? We would have knocked the devil out of him!"

Godwin sighed. "There's a saying about sowing the wind and reaping the storm. And another that barnyard fowls that escape from their pen come home to roost at nightfall. One way or another, it was bound to happen."

"Father," said Tostig, apparently understanding what this meant, "you did what seemed right at the time. Only warlocks can read the future. Why torment yourself?"

Brand tried not to look at Godwin. Something terrible had happened, was still happening, to the earl. Age: five, ten, fifteen years had stamped themselves on him in as many minutes, greying his skin, dulling his eyes, etching lines round his mouth. He put a hand to his eyes and the hand was tremulous.

"Brand," Godwin said presently, "Brand, listen."

"My lord?"

Godwin lowered his hand and looked at Brand directly. "Woodcutter, if what you have heard today is new to you, I will tell you now that Sweyn spoke the truth. And I trust you, I have to trust you, for the sake of the years you have served my house, and the child who is a link of blood between us, not to betray me. Will you swear to keep this knowledge to yourself, for all time?"

There was nothing else to do. "Yes, I swear."

Without speaking, Tostig held out his cross-hilted sword and Brand said it again, his hand upon the hilt. Godwin nodded.

"I have my regrets concerning Gildenford," he said. "But the past can't be undone. God knows, I would have undone it, whatever the cost, before my own son rose up and brandished it in my face."

Brand said nothing. He too was ashamed: for Godwin's guilt, in which, since the speech on coronation eve, he had not believed, and for himself as well, because Godwin was still his lord, and whatever he had done there was in Brand a pity for him that nothing could alter or deny.

3 ✖ "Don't Let It Be True"

"You understand?" Godwin repeated. He, Beorn, Brand, Odi Pathfinder, and Peter Longshanks stood together at the top of the cliff. It was a clear, well-washed morning. An innocent sea sparkled below and a westerly breeze lifted their ponies' thick manes. All Godwin's manors were well stocked with saddle beasts. "You are to ride along the coast, keeping to open ground to make it plain that no one else is with you. Presently Sweyn will join you. He trusts no one now. Not even me." Carefully, Godwin kept expression out of his voice. "I had hard work to convince him that you should have companions, Beorn. I swore on the rood, in the end, that you would go with him in good faith. I would not send you alone. I don't trust Sweyn, either. I never thought it could be so between me and my own son. However. You will ride with him to Bosham, where he says he left his ships and his men. He thinks the men will desert if he leaves them there much longer. You will sail back with him to Sandwich to look for the king. When you find him, Beorn is to put Sweyn's case. Since Edward knows there is no friendship between you, Beorn, and Sweyn, he may be more willing to listen. He'll know it isn't blind love talking, at least." The earl scanned the faces of Beorn's three companions. "Guard your lord well, Woodcutter, Longshanks, Pathfinder. He is in your care. You had better start."

They left Godwin by the dead tree where he had met his son at dawn. Beorn looked back once and waved, but Brand rode on with eyes uncompromisingly fixed between his pony's ears. Later, Beorn rode up beside him and said: "You're silent, Brand."

After a pause nearly long enough to be rude, Brand said: "I didn't know. Till last night I didn't know the truth about Gildenford. That's all."

"I see. I suppose I thought you did. It's common knowledge in the family, except for Edith. We always kept it from Edith. You're part of the family now."

"Lord Godwin always meant that Edith should marry the king, if he could bring it about, I take it." Brand's voice was bitter. "Yes, I see why it was kept from her. The Earl of Wessex is a gifted scheme-maker. Gildenford—and a daughter as a queen."

"You're angry."

"I've looked up to him so long."

"Go on looking up to him. Do you think he did it for fun? He thought, everyone did, that the Athelings were war-bringers. If you think he knew what Harefoot meant to do with Alfred, you're wrong. He offered to arrange ransom terms for the soldiers and he thought Alfred would simply be executed. Harold told me that—he was there. That's part of the truth too. Think about it, Brand."

Brand nodded, silently. He rode more slowly, letting Beorn go ahead. They were all bound together, these Godwins. Even between Sweyn and his father there was a bond still, or Sweyn for all his clever arguments would not have gone free yesterday. They were the insiders, knowing each other's minds, understanding each other's motives. He, the short dark Celt, the country boy, the Woodcutter, might be uncle to a thousand Godwin babies, might look to Godwin of Wessex as a father for a thousand years, and still remain outside.

Ahead, Beorn turned in his saddle and said: "There's a rider coming. It must be Sweyn."

Sweyn descended on them at a gallop, slapped the rump of Pathfinder's pony, which was a slug, and shouted to them to hurry. Talking and thinking alike ended as they spurred their steeds to keep up with him. Later, when he let them slow down to breathe the ponies, Brand found himself a cynical audience at a most impressive Sweyn-style performance, for Sweyn, it seemed, was out to repair his damaged image in their eyes. He was at his most beguiling. He was eager for the latest news and Beorn, politely, also concerned with smooth relations for his uncle's sake, was giving it. It was like a layer of thick, bright paint over rotten planking.

"What is this news from Normandy about William and the girl

he wants to marry? I gather he's got an eye on my pretty Judith's sister Matilda, and he's had a rough rejection. Is it true?"

"Quite true." It was a good story, even better than the one about Sweyn himself and Judith. "Matilda refused him because he's bastard-born, and the next thing was that he arrived at the Flanders court in person, without an escort, burst in, found Matilda and her ladies listening to music, grabbed her by her hair, thrashed her with a stirrup leather, and marched out again. He was on his horse and gone before anyone recovered enough to do anything. Baldwin was away hunting when it happened. When he got back he found the place in an uproar, with Matilda in tears and being given wine possets by her ladies and having to drink them standing up. The tale's gone round every hall from Normandy to Northumbria. We had it from a minstrel who'd been playing to the ladies when William arrived . . . he's been living off it ever since. He hardly has to strum a note for his dinner these days."

Sweyn shouted with laughter. "Serve that haughty little bitch right. Baldwin wanted that marriage, too. Well, he made trouble enough when I made much gentler advances to Judith. Is he going to war with Normandy over it?"

"Oh no, that's the best of the tale. Apparently Matilda was so impressed with William's boldness—if Baldwin had been there he might have been taken and even killed—that she's changed her mind and favours the match! The only hitch now is with the Church. She and William are related, I think."

"Holy angels! Women! I wish him joy of her. She's got cold, cold eyes and a lump of stone where her heart should be, that one. Now, Judith . . ."

He talked on, zestfully. Brand once more let his mount fall back. Earlier in the day he had been told to think. Now he needed to.

He was no rapid thinker. Sweyn's revelations and their full meaning were still only half-seen shapes in the deeps of his mind. He peered at them wretchedly as they jogged on. They made camp for the night in a homesteader's dry, straw-filled barn, and he found himself wakeful long after the others were deep asleep. He was trying to understand his own unhappiness.

He had known for thirteen years that Godwin might have taken a hand, in advance, in the trapping of Alfred Exile. Godwin had sworn otherwise and Brand had believed him, but the rumours had always continued and he had always known that the earl's avowals might, just might, be suspect. He could even understand why. Godwin needed to remove the king's suspicions in order to work with him. It might be sad that he had perjured himself, but it was comprehensible. So was the original offence. Alfred Atheling could have started a war. All right. He knew for certain now that Godwin had laid the snare beforehand, and he knew how and why, and he knew why Godwin had lied about it. Godwin was a man, not a saint. Was he, Brand, a child, that he could not accept these things?

He pulled his cloak more tightly round him. He felt chilled. Pictures swam in his head. The midden of Harefoot's courtyard and the dead Welshman with the flies settling on him. Harefoot's belly laugh and the amazing reward of silver, so huge for the simple service performed. The real nature of that service. The silver which had sold Edgiva into the convent. From which Sweyn had . . .

The memories were like a series of blows. Godwin might talk of reaping the storm but he had not done that bitter scything alone. Edgiva, Sweyn, and Brand himself were also its harvesters. Godwin had used Brand, picked him cold-bloodedly from among Harefoot's men and made of him a tool, and Edgiva's death had come of it.

Damn him for that, for using his follower so. That itself was a betrayal.

He turned over, rustling the straw. Godwin had given, too. He had made Brand into a warrior. And he had lost his own son. One might hate the schemer of Gildenford, but not the Godwin ageing and hurt, at the mercy of the son he had so loved. And had he never plotted against the Athelings, never made use of Brand, Sweyn's downfall at Leominster might not have happened. Dimly it was comforting, a built-in vengeance for Alfred. Perhaps he could let go of it after all. He slept.

He woke at sunrise, feeling lighter. He had made out the haunting shapes last night and found them less evil than he feared. It was all right. He could rest against the weregild that the fates had already demanded of Godwin and need seek no further redress of his own. He could pity Godwin and keep faith with him.

They journeyed on towards Bosham. Sweyn was quieter today, more serious, though still theatrically gracious. Brand watched him sardonically and tried not to think of anything else. They were in sight of Bosham inlet, jogging at ease with helmets off in the warm weather, when a new and this time utterly monstrous implication smote him, turning his bowels into ice water and focussing his eyes into so blind a stare that Longshanks broke off gossiping to Pathfinder to say: "Brand! Are you sick?"

"No." He shook the reins and cantered on, away from them. No. No. Please God, don't let it be true. Godwin can't have done that. How could anyone? Not Godwin, anyway. No. *Please!*

But Godwin had. Must have done. What had Sweyn said? "When my father forged Queen Emma's signature and a token of hers to trap her sons . . ." Godwin had used Emma's name as bait. And for thirteen long years since he had let that charge lie against her name. He had let the rumour spread that she had plotted to murder her own children.

He thought of Gytha and Godwin with their own children. He remembered Gytha, whose love for the erring Sweyn was so great that it moved Beorn to plead for his enemy. How in the name of sweet Mary, mother of Christ, could Godwin be the husband of *Gytha* and use another mother of children in this way?

Well, Emma wasn't Gytha. There had always been ill rumours of her feelings for Ethelred's sons. She had never loved them. She had virtually abandoned them when she married Cnut.

But there was a wide gulf between that and desiring their deaths. That tale sprang from Godwin's trickery. He had made a few small attempts to clear her, Brand recalled. He had implied in that coronation speech that he thought her innocent. He had hinted that she was innocent. When he knew her to be. But he could not say he knew for sure. A man who was innocent himself would not know for sure, would not have been privy to the intimate details of the conspiracy. In the end he had let the wolves have Emma, in order to save himself.

Ahead of them, Sweyn had pulled up. They could see the inlet from here, and the ships drawn up on the mud flats. Sweyn's men seemed to be down there with them; small figures moved about on and among the vessels. "I left them in the homestead," Sweyn said grimly. "I seem to have got back just in time. Wait here. I shall ride ahead and warn them of who you are and why you're here. I wouldn't like you to be attacked." He grinned. "They're a hilt-happy lot and they need some handling."

"And can Sweyn handle them, one wonders?" muttered Long-shanks as Sweyn rode off.

He returned presently and waved them to come on. They trot-ted forward. The men by the ships were awaiting them in a cluster, all faces turned towards them. As the distance narrowed one could see how wild a bunch they were. Little more than Viking raiders themselves.

No wonder Emma had tried to bring over Magnus of Norway to challenge Edward. Brand's mind had slipped away again to his own gnawing problem. Edward had believed that she was his would-be killer, and how she must have hated him for believing it. "She's an Emma," people said all over Christendom of scheming women or unloving mothers, just as they said: "She's a Jezebel," of a wife who was unfaithful. But Emma was not guilty. She had only been branded. By Godwin.

"Down you all get," said Sweyn, swinging a leg over his pony's rump. "And meet my boys."

From his two visits to Sweyn's hall in past years, Brand could identify some of the fierce faces. The man Axebearer was there, in the forefront. His weapons were stuck in his belt and a wolfskin was thrown over his left shoulder. His right side was bare and dirty and bulged with muscles, as though his skin housed a mass of sliding snakes.

Sweyn was presenting his men by name. "Axebearer . . . Ken-neth the Scot . . . Thorold Cleave-Oak . . ." Beorn, when the tale was finished, began to present his. When he got to Brand Woodcut-ter, Axebearer laughed.

"Woodcutter and us have met," he said. He held out his great right hand, palm up, empty, in token of friendship. Brand took it. As he did so, the left hand, gripping a club, swept from under the shrouding wolfskin and struck him over the head.

His first thought on waking was that someone was hammering nails into his skull. Except that at first he could not remember the name of the skull's owner. He tried to get away from the pain, back into the darkness, but the darkness was frightening because that was the place where he had no name. He must struggle into the light and the knowledge of what and who and where he was, however much it hurt.

He fought for it. He was a living thing lost in a void. He was human. He was called . . . called . . . Brand . . . Brand the Woodcutter. He lived in England. He was the sworn man of Godwin and Godwin's kinsman Beorn. He was . . .

Memory poured back into a head that throbbed beyond bearing, as though the bones inside it were being ground together. He was thirsty. He was cramped. No, it wasn't cramp. He was bound. His ankles were fastened together and so were his hands, behind him. He thought someone had just tried to rouse him by throwing cold water over him. He opened his eyes and they were stabbed by starlight. The stars reeled. There came another douche of cold water and some got into his mouth. It was briny. Then he saw that the stars were not moving only in his dazed vision but also because the hard something on which he lay was moving too. They were at sea and the cold douche was shipped water. Against the stars he could see a square sail bellying. Below it, by lantern light, a sailor was checking their course, peering at a lodestone needle afloat on a bowl of water. Sleeping forms lay all about. The lantern light bobbed, wavered, showed him Beorn at his side, bound also and also awake. With the effort of using his eyes, the pain in his head crescendoed to a discord of jangling bells. He rolled over and vomited where he lay.

Some time later he felt impersonal hands on him. They pulled him to a sitting position. Sweyn's voice above him said: "I don't want any of them dead. See to them." A beaker was pushed against his mouth and fresh water ran blessedly down his throat. A covering was put over him. He heard the visitants move away. Beorn's voice said softly: "Brand?"

He made a new effort to use his eyes and found that it was growing light. He could see Peter and Odi lying beyond Beorn. He noted with anger that his arm-rings and weapons were gone and so were theirs. Beorn whispered again: *"Brand!"*

"I'm here," Brand muttered back. "With a filthy headache. I was almost brained. Weren't you?"

"No, just pulled down like a deer and sat on. Sweyn shouted at them not to hit me. He wasn't quite so worried about the rest of you. Though I gather we're all useful and worth preserving up to a point." Beorn's voice was quite expressionless.

The anguish in Brand's head was lessening a little. "It was a trick all along," he said.

"Oh God, yes," said Beorn wearily. "Planned from the day we left Pevensey. He rode ahead to give orders to his men. Hah! They were on the point of deserting. If we'd been a day later, they'd have gone. He's had luck with him. He's been talking to me while you slept . . ."

"Slept! Huh!" said Brand forcefully and at once regretted it.

"I can tell you more. Can you take it in?"

"I can listen."

"It isn't good hearing. Seems we managed between us to convince him all too thoroughly that he stood no chance with the king. We also bred a wish for revenge—on his father, his brothers, and you. We're hostages, Brand. One of you—Odi or Longshanks probably—will be sent to the king and my uncle, saying that if Sweyn isn't pardoned and reinstated the rest of us will be killed. I'll be kept till last."

"But . . . you promised to intercede for him."

"Only for his uncle's sake and Aunt Gytha's, not for his. He's always resented me," said Beorn calmly. "I'm blood-kin to King Cnut, you know. He envies that. Cnut's always been his hero. The hero he can't match. I'm a very good hostage. Highly expendable as far as Sweyn is concerned, loved by my uncle, and fairly in favour with the king since I'm not a real Godwinsson."

"Where are we going?" Brand asked.

"I don't know. Westwards. There's an easterly blowing. I've been watching the stars."

"Then the fleet will be able to sail for the Severn," Brand said, remembering the rightful purpose of the voyage.

"Oh, the raiders! No, that's over. I gather from Sweyn that he didn't tell us all the news at Pevensey . . ."

"*Sweyn*. Damn him!" said Brand, thinking of Sweyn's deliberate charm, all the way to Bosham.

"No doubt damnation will find him one day. But about the raiders. Two hours after we'd gone, four riders came tearing into Sandwich from the west to say that the Vikings had withdrawn. Must have withdrawn before ever we knew they were there. The king's messengers to recall the fleet can't have been far behind Sweyn at Pevensey, I imagine. I suppose Edward would have sent some off. But at least we're not lying here helpless while enemies ravage the west. That's some relief."

"Yes," said Brand mechanically, without having any real feelings in the matter.

Beorn said anxiously: "Brand? They hit you hard, didn't they? You can remember? You know where you are . . . who I am?"

"Yes." Godwin had questioned Harold in the same way, long ago, after another kind of struggle in which Sweyn was involved. "Did Sweyn mean it—about using us as hostages?" he asked. "Or was he throwing dice with words?"

"He meant it," said Beorn quietly.

Brand's head was pulsing again, worsening into a gonging, clanging agony. He couldn't think. He said: "I feel so bloody sick I don't even care." He vomited again.

4 ❦ Glamour Like Armour

They were given attention during the day. One at a time they were unbound for long enough to let them stretch, eat, drink, and relieve themselves. Towards the end of the afternoon the ships lost way in a failing wind. Sweyn let them lie becalmed. He and his men lounged about, drinking. They seemed to be waiting for something.

"If Edward's on the east coast, why are we sailing west?" Brand muttered.

"Sweyn's keeping well away from Edward," Beorn said. "Whoever he puts ashore will have to travel to find the king." He moved, twisting against his bonds. "Oh, if only just one of us could get free! Odi? Peter? Any luck?"

"Been trying for hours. No luck," growled Longshanks.

"Keep trying. I've a plan if we can find a way to use it." Beorn dropped his voice. Sweyn's men were mostly at the other end of the ship, but sound could carry in the quiet. In a half whisper Beorn explained his idea. Pathfinder said he didn't think much of it. It depended first on at least one of them getting free, which seemed impossible, and second on Sweyn's men caring a snap of the fingers what happened to Sweyn. The proper relationship between leader and followers did not seem to be present in this fleet. Desertion had been in the air at Bosham. Sweyn's hold was precarious, to say the least.

A man carrying a water bucket came picking his way along the vessel towards them. There was only one man this time. The rest seemed to be devoting themselves to the ale. He knelt down by

Brand and set his bucket on the boards. Brand looked up at him and stared, amazed.

Well, the world had been nothing but a piling up of surprises, mostly unpleasant, ever since Sweyn popped up at Sandwich. This surprise at least was merely extraordinary, which was an improvement.

"Rolf Ericsson," said Brand to the grimy, seamed, but perfectly familiar face, whose owner was tipping a tin cup into the water for his benefit. "You're supposed to be drowned."

"*Brand!*"

"And Lord Beorn. And Pathfinder and Longshanks, if you look round you. What the devil are you doing among these cutthroats? Your family are frantic."

"I nearly was drowned," Rolf said, speaking low. He loosed Brand's hands and gave him the cup. "We were taken by pirates—this merry crew—off the Brittany coast. They'd chased us miles off course. They were heaving us overboard one by one; great fun they thought that was. They'd do anything for a bit of sport, this bunch—put their own mothers up for auction, I shouldn't wonder. I've seen them play football with a man's head they'd just cut off, and one of them slipped and went overboard and sank and they thought *that* was funny, God help us all. I'd no hope. I was saying my last paternoster. But before they got to me they went aground on a sandbank. It turned out that the only two men in the whole fleet who knew that stretch of coast hadn't been there for years, and the sands had shifted. Well, I'd been there two or three times in the last few years and I knew roughly where the banks were now, and I spoke up. I said if they could refloat her, I could pilot them out. It was a chance to live a bit longer. So when the tide lifted her clear I got them into deep water again and then they decided I was useful enough to keep alive. And here I am, chief advisor on the sandbanks of Brittany, to a pirate fleet. I've been waiting a chance to get away, but it's difficult. On shore we all sleep together and there's always a watch set. I have to fasten your hands again before I loose your feet. They may check on me."

"What's wrong with slipping overside in the night when the coast is handy and swimming for it? You don't spend all your nights ashore, obviously."

"I can't swim." Rolf looked wistful. He added: "They don't

know who I am or that I know you. Sweyn doesn't recognise me. But if I set you free they'd guess who did it. I'm the only one who isn't really one of them. They'd kill me."

Beorn turned his head. "Rolf!"

Rolf looked at him unwillingly. "My lord Beorn?"

"Rolf, listen to me. Sweyn is on this vessel, isn't he?"

"Yes, but . . ."

"Good. Now then, Rolf. While you have the chance, loose us. We will go on looking as if we were tied. Then go to Sweyn and say his cousin and captive Beorn wants to talk to him."

"I can't loose you! I dare not!"

From the other side of Beorn, Odi Pathfinder said: "Gutless nithing!"

Rolf stared at him, like a hunted animal facing the hounds.

"Once Sweyn is within reach you'll have no more to fear," said Beorn, soothingly, his own voice only a little gritty with impatience. "We shall seize him and use him as a hostage for our own safety and yours."

"He may not come alone!"

"Then I trust he won't see we're free."

"I still don't understand," said Peter rather plaintively, "why, if we get loose, we can't just slip overboard."

"They'd pick us out of the water again," said Beorn. "Now, Rolf . . ."

"I can't!"

"Do you want to see your father and Hild again or not?" demanded Brand. His headache had faded during the day, but anger now made it throb again. "They want you, do you forget that? It would be as if you'd returned from the dead. They're mourning you. They've bought Masses for your soul, let me tell you. Stay here and you'll be killed in the end, anyway."

Rolf gulped.

"Remember the warehouse?" said Brand. He snatched hungrily at the food Rolf had brought him. His stomach seemed to be more or less normal once more. "It's your chance to get away, you fool!"

Rolf said wretchedly: "Don't you understand?" and moved closer, to look into Brand's face. Brand dropped the bread he was eating and his grip closed on Rolf's wrist. Rolf jerked back.

"Stand still!" growled Beorn. "If they see you've let yourself be caught, that *will* finish you! Get his knife, Brand."

"I've got it." Brand, with his spare hand, was already slashing through the thongs round his ankles. Rolf, half-paralysed, stood helplessly in his grip. He had made one more attempt to break away but Brand merely twisted a little harder and Rolf's knees gave. "Will you join us, Rolf?" Brand asked. "Or at least swear to keep quiet till we've brought Sweyn here by shouting for him?"

"You'd get them all in a body for sure, doing that," Rolf panted. Brand passed the knife to Beorn, who swiftly set about freeing himself and the others. They were rubbing blood back into constricted muscles and groaning.

"I'll join you," Rolf said sullenly. "What can I lose? You're free and they'll blame me. I'll fetch him."

"What are the chances," Brand muttered as they waited, bonds wound artistically round their wrists and ankles, "for Sweyn to walk into the trap?"

"Poor," said Beorn. "He'll probably get to Sweyn and then stutter and quiver like a jellyfish—he's got as much backbone—and Sweyn will guess something's wrong."

But Sweyn, to their surprise, came without precautions. Rolf was probably always so nervous when addressing his commander that his state of fear now passed unnoticed. Rolf hovered in the rear, standing cautiously back while Sweyn loomed over his cousin, thumbs hooked in his belt. "Well, Beorn? Is your bed on my ship not so cosy as the one you had in my stolen hall?"

"Where are we?" asked Beorn. "And where are we going?" He was sitting up, hands out of sight behind him. Brand grunted and let himself roll closer to Sweyn.

"We're near the mouth of the Dart River. We shall land soon to revictual. We're waiting for the tide. What of it?"

"Sweyn, think again. My words would have weight with the king if anyone's did. I am still willing to forget this—this madness and make that plea on your behalf. What if he did pardon you to save our lives? He could back out of the bargain the minute we were free. And what a list of counts he'd have against you then!"

Sweyn laughed. "I'd see he swore my safety on something that would hold him! Our holy Edward won't forswear an oath taken in a church on a chest of saintly relics, before a horde of witnesses. And that is the only oath that would buy your lives. Don't underestimate me."

He was still laughing when Brand moved, sweeping his feet free

of their pretended bondage. They hooked Sweyn's ankles and top-
pled him. He fell sprawling on top of Beorn and Beorn moved too,
as fast as his long-cramped muscles would allow, to get on top of
Sweyn.

It wasn't fast enough.

Their biggest peril had not been Rolf. It was their own deadly
stiffness. Brand, struggling to his feet, found that he had not got his
sea legs yet and that the ship had more motion than he thought. He
overbalanced against the side. Odi was no better. Peter had been
seized with cramp and was doubled, clutching at a left foot in agonising spasm. Sweyn and Beorn, locked together, rolled away. Sweyn
was shouting and his men were scrambling towards them, leaping
the oars and benches and miscellaneous objects that lay on the deck-
ing, making her rock. Beorn had at least got Sweyn's axe out of his
belt, Brand observed. And now Beorn and Sweyn stood up, face to
face. Sweyn's men halted, surrounding them. There was a pause.

"Grab him!" roared Sweyn, jerking his head at Beorn.

Surprisingly, no one moved. Brand saw that the statement that
this bunch would do anything for a bit of sport was an unholy truth.
Their loyalty to Sweyn was barely skin-deep. They had been ready
to desert him at Bosham and it was plain enough why: there was
hardly a gold arm-ring between them. A leader rewarded his followers with such gifts. They were more than payment, they were a
demonstration that the leader was competent, worth following.
Sweyn had failed that test. They had obeyed him on the shore at
Bosham, seized his prisoners for him, probably because it was a
chance of some rough fun. Now they clearly regarded the sight of
their leader face to face with a furious and axe-brandishing escaped
captive merely as a little more fun. Sweyn swore, colourfully. He
drew his sword.

"You . . . tricky . . . little . . . rat," he said to Beorn.

"Did you think I would wait meekly while you murdered me?"
enquired Beorn. "Even a rat wouldn't be so stupid!"

Before, on this ship, there had been something dispassionate in
the cousins' relationship. They had been trying to make use of each
other, with no pity but not overmuch hatred either. But the short,
violent bodily contact had loosed a deeper, more personal enmity.
The interested throng sensed it and edged back. There was an in-
stinctive grouping to balance the ship. From one of the other ships,

drifting near at hand, came a shout to know what was going on. No one answered.

"You were always second-rate," Beorn said. His knees were flexed. His axe was ready. "You won't follow and you can't lead. You couldn't command your earldom and you can't command these ships. They're dirty and the rigging's unsound and your men are dressed like beggars . . ."

"You lousy interloper!" Sweyn didn't really want to fight; Beorn was too valuable alive. But he was angry and he would break out soon, Brand thought. "Shouldering into our family as if you belonged there!" Sweyn flung his old grudge at his cousin. "You and your boasts about royal relations . . ."

"I wonder what your royal hero Cnut would say of his disciple now?" Beorn said. "A mangy sea wolf whose pack won't obey him, bartering his kin to save his own smelly hide . . ."

Unlike Sweyn, Beorn was longing to fight. But he wanted Sweyn to jump first, to forget himself, to be blinded with rage. Now he had his wish. Sweyn, his skin suffused, sprang. Beorn dodged, swinging the axe. "Nithing!" he taunted.

But after all there were a few pockets of loyalty in Sweyn's band. Axebearer leapt forward, got behind Beorn, and seized his axe arm, wrenching the weapon away. Beorn, weaponless and off-balance, lurched back against the mast. The shouts from the other ships grew louder and now Sweyn's men began flinging back replies. Through it all Beorn's voice went on, in a tirade of provocation. Brand thought he couldn't stop, that the banked up contempt of years couldn't be dammed again once it had started to pour out. "Nithing! Nithing! Nithing! No king would acknowledge you as kinsman, Sweyn, least of all the mighty Cnut! I could lead these ships and make them pay. You can't even keep off a sandbank in calm weather! You can't keep your hands off a woman if your earldom depends on it! You can't . . ."

It was like Sweyn, so very like Sweyn, to throw away his best counter, his most precious hostage, for the sake of a brief satisfaction. Beorn, unarmed, was his to bind and barter with. But Sweyn's bloodshot eyes saw only the face he had hated since they were boys at Winchester, and Beorn had challenged his leadership. Before Beorn could utter the third in his list of things that Sweyn couldn't do, Sweyn had levelled his stout-bladed sword and put his weight behind it, and with a long, steady, killer thrust had driven it through Beorn's body.

Beorn died in less than a minute. Brand saw his mouth open and strength go out of him. He saw his lord's knees buckle and the blood spread over his chest. Sweyn put a foot on the convulsively moving body and pulled out the blade. The blood flooded after it and the outstretched legs shuddered, jerked, and went rigid.

Brand pushed himself from the ship's side where he had been leaning. His balance was steadier now. He began to walk towards Sweyn.

He had no idea what he would do when he got there, but his lord had been slain before his eyes and no man who called himself one would stand by to see that, offering to strike no blow. He had nothing to lose, anyway, any more than Rolf had had a short while since. He would die soon, either on Sweyn's sword or over the side with weights on his feet. He preferred the sword.

Sweyn saw him coming and leant on the blade. "So it's the Woodcutter. Well, well. Come to avenge your master, is that it?" His breath gusted into Brand's face and Brand realised what he had not understood before: that Sweyn was drunk. There were small red veins in the whites of his eyes. At his feet Beorn lay glaring at the sky.

"Yes," said Brand. "That, exactly."

He turned to face the interested half circle of Sweyn's men. He said with dignity, addressing them and not Sweyn, for the power lay with them and not with their so-called leader: "I have a lawful quarrel with Sweyn Godwinsson. Two quarrels. He took my sister from the convent where she was an abbess and gave her a child which killed her. And he has now killed my lord Beorn, who was not armed. I demand the right to challenge him."

They appeared to consider, staring at him. One or two heads nodded. There were affirmative grunts. One of the men turned away to shout to a friend aboard a neighbouring ship, and in answer there came a laugh and then, more distantly, voices calling the news across to yet another vessel. There were seven ships altogether, scattered over a calm sea.

Sweyn said: "You challenge *me*—you, Woodcutter?"

"I do," said Brand with formality.

Axebearer said: "What terms do you propose for the combat, Woodcutter?"

"That the fight be to the death of one of us!" Sweyn declared. Brand glanced at him. He wondered at Sweyn's confidence. He himself might be tired and injured, but he was sober. And he was also coldly, rightfully angry. He had God on his side.

"I agree to that," he said. "Let God decide between us. If I prevail, I demand first that Lord Beorn be given honourable burial. I then demand my life and freedom and the lives and freedom of my companions who were seized with me, and Rolf Ericsson there who is also a prisoner on this ship. And I require the return of the valuables taken from us." He faced the men. "Is that agreeable to you?"

"You kill our leader, you become our leader," one of them offered, grinning. The rest laughed. "A bright idea, Oakenskull!" his neighbour said.

"If I kill your leader I'll leave you to choose another," Brand had a brief, mad vision of himself as a pirate captain, imbuing the name of Woodcutter with a new and terrible significance, and he could not help grinning also. They reciprocated.

Sweyn enquired: "Would you like to be buried at sea or on shore? You may have a last request."

"I've no preference. What's yours?"

The man called Oakenskull interrupted: "We'd best get the ships ashore. Tide's on the turn. They want ground underfoot for a fight."

The shouted news went from ship to ship and the oars came out. They landed on the north side of the estuary and pulled the vessels up. Ashore they found shining stretches of flat, wet sand between the sea and the high-water mark. Smoke from a settlement further inland rose in the evening sky, and some fishing craft which presumably belonged to it lay drawn up not far off. The local inhabitants were not to be seen. If they had watched the landing, the helmets and dragon prows had probably frightened them into hiding. Brand thought about them and felt his will harden still more strongly against Sweyn. How many little hamlets had Godwin's savage firstborn raided since he was outlawed? And how many of his victims had had faces, voices, daily lives like those of Brand's own family far away in Worcestershire?

Beorn's body was brought ashore, respectfully enough, and laid on the ground. Brand straightened it. The others had been bound again, Rolf with them. The crew had grasped that it was he who had freed the prisoners. If Woodcutter lost the contest, they said, they were promising themselves some fun with him.

Axebearer brought Brand's helm and weapons. He weighed his axe in his hand; the feel of it was as welcome on his palm as water on a drought-stricken tongue. But Sweyn liked swordplay better and was already testing his blade-edge. It was going to be sword against axe. Brand pushed his arm through his shield-straps, bent his knees, twisted his shoulders, gingerly shook his head. It stood the treatment tolerably well. He checked a start as Sweyn suddenly let out a yell and leapt in the air, landing with a thud on the firm sand, feet apart, and glittered his eyes at Brand over the curve of his shield.

Axebearer had somehow put himself in charge. He placed them, facing each other, as Godwin had placed the contestants at the coronation feast. The other men formed a wide ring. They were ready to start.

Brand, studying his foe, noting the ale-tremble in his hands and wondering how much this would or would not offset his own stiffness, did not notice that Sweyn's old advantage, that of being a sacrosanct member of the house of Godwin, untouchable as if garbed in magic armour, was gone. Sweyn now was no more than an opponent, with a certain measure of skill, with a certain weight and a certain reach encompassed by a body this much tall, that much broad, and smelling of poor-quality drink.

But if Brand did not notice this loss of his enemy's finest weapon, the enemy did. Without knowing the cause, Brand read a sudden doubt in his foe's face as they looked at each other and rejoiced at it.

From a safe distance, Axebearer said: *"Begin!"*

It was difficult—fortunately—to keep in mind the real nature of the fight once it had started. It was so familiar. The grinding ring of metal and the sparks. The feints, dodges, attacks, and parries— shield up, down, over the head, left side, right. The adversary's eyes with their unintended warnings. The scrape-scuff of feet, the deepening breath. He had done it all a hundred thousand times, in practice and in earnest. He had done it with Godwin on the training ground—no, he must not think of Godwin now—and he had done it at Harold's side, against the Welsh. It was real then, as now. Except that then he had others alongside, a friendly sword to swing in on his behalf if he slipped. Here there were no helpers. Only eyes that watched.

As they moved, sidestepping, revolving, he caught glimpses of the audience. He saw Axebearer, his eyes intent, nonpartisan, an expert watching experts. He saw the others, the ones unknown to him, avid, encouraging, hostile, appreciative, absorbed. Once he was near to Peter and Odi. Peter's face was hopeful and Odi's, alarmingly, was trusting. A moment later he saw Rolf, whose face was a mask of fear and despair. Rolf was a pessimist.

Not without reason. Sweyn had got past his guard already and blood was coursing down his thigh. It couldn't be much; he felt little pain and no weakness. But his guard hadn't been good enough. Forget the wound. But keep your mind, your eyes, on Sweyn. Keep the shield up and the axe swinging.

There had never been anything in the world but this. The past was gone and the future would never come. Sweyn's shape was burnt into his sight: long shield, battered helm, gleaming eyes, and sandy, matted beard; the sinewy hands, their backs coated with ginger fuzz, wielding the sword on which Beorn's blood had dried; the cross-gartered legs, muscle-knotted, always planted apart, never off-balance, leaping or landing both together. Sweyn was drunk, but not too drunk for that.

He felt his own breath begin to rasp. But a glimpse of Beorn's body, as the audience moved to keep out of their way, stiffened him again. Sweyn read the flare in his eyes and responded. He bounded and yelled, feinted low, struck high, quickening the pace. Brand's left foot landed in something that slithered. Seaweed. He lost and regained his footing in a space of half a second but as he did so, Sweyn's sweeping blade clanged against his helmet.

He sprang back. Sweyn's face was a wavering oval beyond a spray of white, glittering specks. Pain flooded into his skull and swelled it. He parried a blow automatically and feebly. Sweyn's eyes widened in joy and he whooped, closing in. Brand stumbled backwards again and Sweyn's face, with death in it, smiled beyond the sparkling specks.

In the eye of the mind, small, distant, but clear-cut, he saw a picture. Green grass, blue sky, himself with a clumsy, unfamiliar

weapon, struggling up with ringing ears from the restful turf,
dragged up by Godwin's relentless eyes and Godwin's commanding
voice, to face once more the menace of Godwin's flashing sword.
"To hell with your head," said that faraway Godwin. "Forget it.
You'll have to forget worse than that one day if you want to live.
Throw the pain aside. Attend to me! I'm going to kill you!" And the
blade caught the sun as it fell, calculatedly, to stop within inches of
his wincing scalp.

What Godwin had demanded of him then, what he had learned
with so much struggle to give, now came instinctively. His eyes
cleared because he ordered them to clear. He drove forward. The
pain was still there, like a voice shouting at him, but he would not
listen. In turn he feinted, drew the guardian shield upwards in front
of Sweyn's face and then struck beneath it. Sweyn gave ground, got
his shield there in time, but now was defending. They were shield to
shield. Brand's left foot groped forward inside his enemy's stance,
found an ankle, hooked, and dragged. Sweyn momentarily wavered
and Brand used his shield to thrust. Sweyn went over backwards
and fell spreadeagled on the sand. Brand pulled out his own sword
and stood over his adversary, and the end of the sword rested lightly
on Sweyn's jugular. The axe he had dropped, and Sweyn's sword
lay on the sand beside him. Sweyn could not reach either. He was in
Brand's hands.

And Brand hesitated.

He did not know why. He looked down. Sweyn, but for the
rapid rise and fall of his rasping chest, was relaxed, lying as if in a
most comfortable bed. Very slowly, so as not to alarm the man
standing over him, he drew up his right arm and made a pillow of it.
He smiled. He said: "I congratulate you, Woodcutter. You have
chopped Sweyn Godwinsson down. Why are you waiting?"

Brand wanted to curse. Had he had the power, he would have
wished them both back to the practice field, where after defeating
your man you let him up and you went off with arms round each
other's shoulders to hold an inquest on the fight across friendly
beakers of mead. He wanted to let Sweyn go, to walk off basking in
having bested his mighty lord's magnificent son. He saw now that
Sweyn had lost his glamour and so had given away the victory. And
he also saw that the glamour was kindled anew. Sweyn, smiling,
self-possessed, almost inviting the sword-thrust, had rekindled it.

He had done it on purpose. He was gambling for his life. And for all his mild, amused eyes, he was wary and dangerous. One moment off guard . . .

"Strike, Brand, *strike!*" whispered Odi's voice from close at hand.

"You may have your life on terms," he said to Sweyn. "The terms must be fulfilled before you rise from the sand."

The hazel eyes widened. "Indeed? How magnanimous of you!"

"Your credit's gone," said Brand coldly. "You'll be a leader without followers, a captain with no ship. I wish you joy of my big-heartedness." Without taking his eyes from Sweyn's, he called: "Axebearer!"

"Here." Axebearer stepped forward.

"You and the rest agreed to my terms. Do you now agree that the combat is mine?"

A chorus assured him that they did.

"Good. First, release the three prisoners. Second, commandeer one of those small fishing boats and put it in the water for them. Third, collect all the goods, the weapons, the belts, and rings you took from us, and put them in the boat. Fourth, give me an undertaking that my lord Beorn will be buried with honour, in hallowed ground, with his sword at his side. Well?"

They gave him their promise and obeyed his first three orders at once, while he still stood holding the sword at Sweyn's throat. The strain told. It seemed long until his friends and their goods were in the boat. A tremor began in the back of Brand's legs and the sweat rolled down his spine. The sword seemed to grow heavy. "One more thing," he said, directly to Sweyn this time, "that gold arm-ring of yours. And your emerald finger-ring. I'll have those, as souvenirs. And you've a gold chain round your neck, I see. What's on it?"

"Only a spare ring," said Sweyn sullenly.

"I'll have them all."

Getting Sweyn's valuables away from him was a fraught business, but it kept Sweyn's mind occupied while the others were boarding their craft. Ring and arm-ring were passed up slowly into Brand's hand. Also slowly, Sweyn drew the chain over his head and the ring that hung on it came into view, a fine piece of craftsmanship in thick yellow gold, set with a red stone, deep as blood. Sweyn withheld it a moment from Brand's waiting fingers, looked at him consideringly, and with a flick of his wrist sent ring and chain flying through the air towards the water, which was nearer now.

"You can go and dive for it!" he said venomously.

"I see," said Brand. He in turn considered Sweyn, and for the first and last time in his life allowed himself the doubtful pleasure of tormenting a captive, recompensing himself because he could not kill. He changed his grip on the sword and let his face take on the look of one who doubts his chosen course, is on the point of changing his mind. He saw the fear begin at last in Sweyn's eyes, now that the battle heat had died. He let it grow while Sweyn's heart shook his thorax, once, twice, three times, four. Then he laughed, threw the sword into the air so that descending it would scatter the audience and give them something to think about besides his movements, and he ran for the water. He was in it, and swimming hard in pursuit of his friends' departing boat, before they knew what he meant to do.

But no missiles followed him and no one else made for the boats. His friends saw him coming and rested on their oars to wait for him. They backwatered as he neared them and Pathfinder, leaning out, hauled him aboard. He lay in the bottom of the boat choking, his thigh wound burning in the brine. They pulled across the estuary to where a stretch of sand and shingle promised a safe landing and another distant drift of woodsmoke suggested habitations. He sat up presently, retching a little from the seawater he had swallowed while swimming when too exhausted, rightly, to keep afloat. He wondered if his head were going to split. It felt as though it might. They all gazed at him. Rolf's expression was almost doglike. Odi, that simple fellow, said: "We never doubted you'd lay the drunken fool on his back but why didn't you kill him?"

Longshanks said, fumbling inside his shirt: "This fell into the boat as we were pushing off. It looks valuable. You'd best have it." He extended a grimy palm. In it lay a clasped gold chain, and threaded on the chain was a ring of thick yellow gold with a stone of blood-red garnet.

5 ❧ *As the Falcon Returns*

"They've cheated us, the bastards! So! What do we do now?"
With great disdain, Odi Pathfinder twirled a dented, discoloured
copper arm-ring on his hand and tossed it away.

Peter shot out a retrieving hand and grabbed it back from the
air. "Even copper's still worth something." He looked at Brand. "But
not much. Well, what do we do? Odi's right. We must decide."

They sat, Brand, Odi, Peter, and Rolf, leaning their backs
against the hermit's hut which had sheltered them for the night.
They could look out from here across the estuary to the strand
where Sweyn's ships had been. The ships had gone now. At the feet
of the quartet lay the leather bag in which had been the valuables
whose return Brand had demanded. Only the items on top, two gold
arm-rings and an amethyst and silver brooch, were their own goods.
The rest of the weight had been made up with cheap jewellery of
copper and polished bone.

Brand said wearily and truthfully: "I have not thought." He had
slept away the worst of his headache, and Rolf had cleaned and
dressed his thigh wound, which was not now troubling him much.
But his spirit was ailing and he wished they would not all look to
him as a leader. He did not feel like one.

He felt only desolate.

During the uncomfortable night they had spent in the wattle
and daub dwelling of a misanthropic and lice-ridden hermit who had
only let them in under menaces, knowledge had flowered in Brand.
Beorn was gone and with him had gone Brand's last bond to the

house of Godwin. For he could not return to Godwin now. Whether his greatest grief was for Beorn's death or Godwin's guilt, Brand himself did not know. But what he did know was that even Edgiva's death had not mattered as this loss did. His daily life had not been shaped round Edgiva as it had been shaped round Beorn and Godwin. Without them his life had fallen apart like a set of clothes with nobody inside. He said fumblingly: "We must get the news to Godwin. We might find him at Sandwich, if the king's messengers did recall him. We need a ship."

"We must return the boat we used last night," Rolf said. "There's a village over there. And fishing boats. We might find a coastal trader there, going round the coast towards the east. We might get passages . . ."

"What do we pay for them with?" asked Peter sourly. He kicked the dully gleaming pile of copper. "Pretty seashells?"

"I have the things I took from Sweyn . . ." Brand began.

"I've got some silver," said Rolf.

They looked at him in astonishment. He took a small pouch from his belt and slid a handful of silver pence onto his palm.

"Did the pirates pay you for your pilot services?" Peter asked disbelievingly.

"No. But there was a fight once over some valuables on a ship we seized and this was dropped. I picked it up." They eyed him with a mixture of the contempt a warrior feels for a tradesman and the respect a human being feels for anyone who not only survives against odds but also makes a profit out of it. "There's enough here for our passages," he said. "And Brand has earned his winnings."

Brand nodded. His mind was beginning to work again. "I shall go ashore at Dover and be there at Rolf's homecoming. Odi and Peter, I want you to take the news to the earl. I . . . have too many quarrels now with that house. I shall leave its service. You two must go on to Sandwich. You will pick up the trail there. You can get horses there. I suppose the horses we rode to Bosham were left at the manor."

He could not and would not meet Godwin again. He would send word, as the proprieties required, that he was seeking a new lord, and if he could find a literate priest with writing materials in the township over the estuary, he would send that word in a letter.

But more than that he would not do. "I expect Rolf's silver will run to a couple of nags," he said.

He put his head in his hands and his temples throbbed again. There were causes for which you might, even should, leave your lord, acts which placed him beyond the reach of any man's loyalty. Brand knew that. But what the laws did not tell him, what no one had told him, was what to do when your lord had placed himself outside the love of God and man, when to serve him any longer would be to outrage your own spirit, and when in spite of all that you still loved him.

Gytha had never liked her husband's London hall. It lay on the south bank of the river, with a view of the water, and it was spacious and stoutly built; but it was made of stone, which she considered a chilly, unnatural material for a home. They went there every Lent for the king's Lenten Council, but otherwise she avoided it. Except at times such as this, when she was awaiting Godwin's return from Sandwich.

London itself she liked. Here were excellent churches in which to worship and first-class merchandise to inspect. It was an opportunity to take her current batch of young ladies to the finest markets and warehouses and thus further their education. By the time Gytha had finished with a girl, she would know to the last fraction of a penny what she should pay for any cloth or bowl or spoon in her own hall when she had one, and how to make sure that she got what she was paying for.

Today's lesson had already embraced a potter's shop and a silversmith and had now moved out into the market and the ancient art of haggling. The stalls were crowded, noisy, and cheerful, providing a kaleidoscope of smells, as spices yielded to the pungency of pigs, and pigs in turn to the tang of leather. She was expounding to her four companions on the quality of some calfskins which were hanging up complete, while her bored escort hovered at a distance, when the trumpet sounded.

It was strident, ear-splitting, instantly silencing the vendors and chattering customers for a hundred yards all round. Turning, Gytha saw a rostrum being set up in a clear space in the middle of the market and a man in the dress of a royal messenger mounting it. The trumpet rang out again and the man shouted to the crowd to draw near, there was news of great importance to them.

At a signal from Gytha, her escort of housecarles made a path for her and her ladies through the throng. They came to rest not far from the rostrum. The crowd closed in behind them.

They were trapped, therefore, unable to miss a word of the message and equally unable to turn away in horror when the messenger unrolled a great scroll bearing the king's seal and proclaimed in a powerful voice that for reason of his having foully and unlawfully murdered his cousin Earl Beorn of Mid-Anglia, the former Earl Sweyn of the Marches was declared nithing, outlaw, and wolfshead, and by order of the king, his Witan, and the unanimous vote of all the housecarles of the royal bodyguard was banished from the shores of England for the rest of his life. No one might succour him if they wished to keep their life and limb secure, but any who encountered him within the boundaries of England might kill him with impunity, on sight.

When he had finished, and the crowd began to break up, Gytha's men needed no signal to tell them that they should escort their mistress home.

She went home like a sleepwalker, not answering her ladies when they spoke to her. The courtyard there was full of men and horses and Tostig was at the gate, looking out for her.

"Father is home," he said. "Mother . . . we have . . . some sad news for you. You'll find him in your bower chamber."

Gytha spoke for the first time. "Sad news? Yes, I know. I've already heard it."

In the privacy of her bower, alone with Godwin, she gave way at last and cried as he had rarely known her do, while he told her the story as Odi Pathfinder and Peter Longshanks had told it to him.

"Brand Woodcutter has left my service through it," he said. "He sent me a letter saying it was because he had quarrelled with my son and tried to kill him, but I think it was because of what Sweyn told him of Gildenford. That hurt him too much. I saw his face when Sweyn was talking. He took an oath of secrecy and I trust him with it, but . . . Gytha, it may be best now that Sweyn makes a new beginning in some other land. He is alive at least and he has a few men with him."

Gytha said: "I know he is alive. But Beorn . . . isn't."

Godwin nodded. She had seen, then, the real victim in this hateful tale. Gytha's sight was at times clear to the point of cruelty. It could be a doubtful blessing, he thought. Her mind and her natural heart could be set at odds by it.

Gytha drew away from him and went to where a pitcher of cold water stood. She began to bathe her face.

"I've wondered, at times, when the first would go," she said. "Most parents lose more than one as children, but all that were born to us living, we've reared. And Beorn as well. I thought of him as a son, you know."

"Yes. So did I."

"Where is he buried?"

"At Bosham. But Harold and Gyrth have gone to fetch his body home. Odi and Longshanks went with them."

"Was Sweyn condemned by a sitting of the royal bodyguard?" Gytha asked. "The proclamation sounded like that."

"Yes. He used to be one of them and Edward decided to act as if he still were and let them judge him. That was fair of Edward. He was furious and wouldn't trust his own judgment. There was nothing I could do, Gytha. The men's vote was unanimous. And if I had been one of them, I would have voted the same way, I admit it."

"Yes, I know."

"I didn't protest," said Godwin, making a further admission. "I had Edith to think of, remember. Is Edith in London, by the way?"

"Yes. I saw her a few days ago. No, there's no sign of any child." Godwin never mentioned his daughter without asking that at least by implication. "They don't even live as man and wife now," Gytha said sadly. "They seem to be friends—close friends, even. But it's a strange kind of wifehood for her."

Their eyes met, momentarily bright as they recalled their own warm marriage from the first joyful night after Cnut himself had lit them to their chamber and informed them with a completely straight face that no one would mind if they were late to breakfast next day. They had gone into each other's arms so naturally, so gladly, it was as though they had known each other in some past life. They were sorry for Edith.

Godwin said: "I used to think that if Edith had no sons, then Edward might nominate one of our boys to succeed him. They're known to the folk, they understand the administration of the land,

and it's according to custom that a king without sons or brothers can choose a brother-in-law. But now . . ."

"No, I think not now," Gytha agreed. "Sweyn has wrecked that hope for himself and all of them."

"I wonder what the king will do?" Godwin was instinctively trying to change the subject from Sweyn. "Ralph is no use. He's too gentle-spoken and eager to please to make a king. My old hound-bitch would make a better one. What's more, he knows it himself. He's said repeatedly that he doesn't wish to be the heir."

Gytha said shakily: "I love Sweyn, and I wish so much he could come home, but if he walked through that door now I should probably kill him! When I think how we reared him, and what he's done to Beorn now and all of us—I feel torn in two!"

"Don't, love," said Godwin as she buried her face in his shoulder. "Oh, Gytha, dear heart. Don't."

"And where the hell are *you* going?" Godwin demanded.

In the late evening sunshine, Tostig was in the courtyard tightening the girths of a grey pony. He stroked the sturdy neck affectionately. "I bought him this afternoon. I call him Prince. A good-looking animal don't you think?"

"Answer me, damn you!"

Godwin was drunk. His movements were heavy and he put a hand on the stable wall to keep himself upright. Tostig looked at him thoughtfully and said: "Flanders."

"*Flanders?* Now? Alone? It's nearly dusk."

"I feel like it. I'm off adventuring and I want an adventurous start. There'll be a moon." His foot was in the stirrup.

"What in Woden's name are you going to Flanders *for?*"

"To put right the harm Sweyn's done to our credit. Maybe Baldwin will be willing to make peace now, since we showed our teeth blockading him. I'm going to marry Judith."

"You're . . . *what?*" Godwin let out a yelp of laughter. "Without an escort? Where's your mule-train of expensive presents?"

"It's a very good idea, a marriage with Judith," Tostig said reasonably. "All the more if William of Normandy marries her sister. Baldwin and William is a hefty little alliance if you like. The Normans," said Tostig judicially, "have a tradition of friendly welcomes to passing Vikings, just as the Flemings have. Nice for the Vikings to have so many friendly ports just on the other side of the channel from us. It might give Hardraada ideas. In self-defence we should join the partnership. And if half the tales Sweyn told about Judith are true, it'll be a good marriage for me as well. She's lovely, chaste, and she pushed Sweyn into a pond. What more could I want in a wife?"

"But you won't get a wife if you go like a vagabond! You . . . !"

"I'll get to know her first before I talk of marriage. My name isn't Tostig if in the end she doesn't urge the marriage herself and plead my cause with Baldwin. She'll be in love with me."

Godwin barked with laughter. "You'll come back with a flea in your ear. And it's a pity. You're right. It would have been a good idea."

"You think," said Tostig, now mounted and looking down at his father, "that I'm such a poor figure of a man that I can't make Judith look at me?"

Godwin gazed back at him blearily. "How can I tell? I'm not a maiden. Well, I can't stop you. Tell Baldwin, if it ever gets so far, that we'll make his daughter welcome. I'll tell your mother where you've gone. Might make her smile."

"Breaking her heart for Sweyn, is she? I'm sorry. I would have said good-bye, but she's in her chamber and won't see anyone."

"I know. We had been talking . . ."—Godwin belched—". . . of Sweyn and Beorn earlier. I wish you success, Tostig. Wish . . . wish you weren't going off alone. Ought to have company. Wish Woodcutter were here. I'd send him with you. Reliable fellow."

Tostig adjusted his stirrups and prepared to move off. "That's a strange thing about Brand," he said. "No one knows where he is now. Odi said he insisted on landing at Dover, and that's the last anyone heard. Pathfinder was puzzled, did he tell you?"

Godwin shook his head.

"He said he could understand Brand wanting to be there for such a homecoming, with Rolf Ericsson returning from the dead, but Brand was so insistent, so urgent, so set on it that Odi thought there was more to it than that, only he didn't know what it could be. Brand didn't tell them any more."

Brand had not told them because he himself did not know. His own urgency had at times bewildered even him. When he disembarked at Dover he was still quite unaware that as the falcon returns to the falconer's wrist, he was going to Hild.

WEREGILD
1049–1052

1 ⚔ Another Man's Debt

He did not know that it was Hild he wanted. Her image had grown in his mind without his noticing it, grown with every visit he had made to Dover since the day of the flooding. To himself he thought only that he was bringing Rolf home and that Rolf's family might shelter him until he had decided what to do next. But when she had finished hugging her brother and turned to Brand, he found to his amazement that to a man weary and soul-sick as he now was, Hild was rest and healing. And that in his heart he had known it and come to her for help.

She had and always would have the candour and practicality of the girl he had ridden with on the road to Winchester. But to it now had been added knowledge of laughter and deep affection, and the immense dignity of sorrow. She thanked him for Rolf's safe return, gracefully, warmly. Then she looked hard into his face, took his fingers between her thin, firm ones, and said concernedly: "Brand, are you ill? You look so pale and your hands feel hot. What is it?"

"I don't know," he said, and gave way to the thing he had been fighting off for days, letting her push him onto a stool. His legs shook and his stomach was uneasy. His head ached. His injuries were better; this did not seem to be part of them. It came from some deeper place within him. "I'm tired and thirsty," he said. "Can I have something to drink?"

Hild made up a bed for him in the main guesthouse. It hadn't had much use lately, he thought vaguely through the mists of sickness, watching her go round with a long-handled broom, knocking cobwebs down from the corners. Rolf helped him undress and Hild brought him a herbal posset to drink. His throat had apparently been scrubbed raw and he was cold. He asked for rugs. When he at last began to doze under the pile of furs they heaped over him it was not comfortable sleep but was shot through with violent dreams. He fought an insubstantial opponent who was now Sweyn, now Godwin, now small and distant, now swollen to the size of a giant. Sweyn held out a handful of jewellery: gold, garnet, emerald. The jewels flashed and glowed and came nearer and nearer, shining straight into his eyes until his sight went out. He woke with a cry to find himself sweat-drenched and trembling. He heard footsteps and the creak of a door, and Hild was there, taper in hand, a background of stars behind her. "Brand? Did you call?"

"I was dreaming." He was husky. It was hard to speak. "I am sorry. Did I wake you?"

"I wasn't sleeping." She came nearer and he saw that she was indeed fully dressed. "I was praying before I lay down; I always do, for the souls of Ragnar and our son. But not for Rolf any more, thanks to you." She felt his forehead. "Good, you're sweating. I'll get you another warm drink."

He drank the mulled wine gratefully when she brought it and curled down under the rugs again. He hoped he wouldn't be ill for long; he had too much to decide. Where to sell his sword. And what to do with the hideous knowledge he now carried locked within him. Should he be silent and leave Emma under an unjust suspicion till she died? Or speak, forswear his oath, and betray Godwin and all his house? But he couldn't decide now, and the very effort of thinking had made his head hammer again. He turned his face into the pillow and fell back once more into the haunted world of fever-dreams. The next time Hild came to him, he did not know her.

The fever persisted for more than a week. Hild tended him with ceaseless patience, bringing him drinks, aromatic vapours to inhale to ease his throat and the grating chest he now developed, fresh bedding, and food when at last the heat in his body subsided and he could take nourishment again. By then he had no more strength in his limbs than an infant and had to be helped to a chair while Rolf and Hild changed his pallet and sheets for him. As soon as he was capable of worrying about anything, he was distressed.

"You shouldn't do such jobs for me, they're thralls' work."

"We haven't any thralls," said Hild, punching pillows.

"But you used to have. Why not now?"

"According to my father," said Rolf, tugging at the pallet, "we can't afford them."

Brand thought about it. "Because you lost the ship? I'm a burden on you. I must get well quickly."

"Fool," said Rolf amiably, lending a shoulder to steer him back to bed.

Hild said: "We're glad of you or any guest. We eat better then. Get well quickly by all means! But then stay on with us and join us at table. Don't leave till you have to."

"My father doesn't like to seem mean," explained Rolf. "Guests force him to provide square meals."

He had two things to worry about now: his own future and Hild's. But despite his anxiety he did slowly mend, and as soon as he could sit in the hall he did so and questioned Hild as she went about her work. "Why is there no help for you? Do you have to market and cook and spread straw and spin on your own?"

"Almost. The neighbours help sometimes or lend us a thrall for a day. But I'm strong, you know."

"Look here," said Brand as belligerently as his weakened state allowed, "are you as poor as you appear? Your father does nothing but count tallies and frown, and I overheard you yesterday saying that the kitchen roof leaks but that you can't get it repaired. Tell me!"

Hild sighed. "When we lost the ship, when Rolf was taken, we lost nearly all we had, just as we did when the warehouse went. But we did have just a little left. We had some stuff stored apart from what was on the ship, and just before Rolf sailed he bought some land and leased it out. There are produce rents from that. And we had friends who were very kind. We could have started again, paid off our debts, and still had enough to eat and wear and keep a thrall or two. Things need not have been so bad; even the people we owed to understood. But my father wants to back one more voyage, to make himself a thane. You remember his old ambition! So now he grudges every penny that doesn't go into his coffers. He works all day and half the night. It's better since Rolf came home. Rolf says he had enough of bad biscuits and high meat on the pirate ships and wants some good victuals now. But . . ." She saw Brand's brows draw together. ". . . oh, Brand, don't blame my father. He's had so many sorrows, and becoming a thane is the dream of his life. He's not willing to give in now when there's only one more voyage to make. He's not willing to be cheated by . . . pirates!"

"What about plans for you?" Brand demanded. "It's over two years since you were widowed. Isn't it time your father found you someone else?"

"Who else is there, Brand? I've no portion. All that Ragnar left was in the business he had with my father. And who would marry me for nothing?"

"Or look after your father's hall if you left it?" Brand asked coldly.

"Brand, don't. Will you be all right if I leave you now? The cow wants milking."

"Quite all right. Go and milk her." He watched her walk away. She was far too thin and far too tired. His old, dead love for Eadgyth had never been more real than on the day he found her overworked and hungry and struggling with a smallpox epidemic. Now it was Hild who was in trouble and Hild who was fighting back with the same courage and toil, and once again love was springing up in him.

He waited till he could once more walk through the town and bear his armour's weight. Then on a morning which was cool—for it was now October—but also bright and calm, he took Hild out onto the cliffs.

She protested that the hall must be swept and the butter churned, but Brand simply removed the broom from her grasp and said: "To blazes with the butter," and towed her out of the hall. They halted high above the sparkling, crinkled sea. "Why did you bring me up here?" Hild asked doubtfully.

With the formality that always seized on him at important moments, Brand said: "I must make it plain; I am a landless soldier who has not even a lord of his own now. Earl Beorn is dead and I cannot return to Earl Godwin. Never mind why not. I mean to go to the king's court and offer my sword there, and if it is refused, to any leader I find who may have a use for me. Whomever I join, I shall be only one of the ordinary housecarles, sleeping in the hall with the rest and eating low down at the table. I may get a grant of land one day, but it will take time. But will you marry me and share what little I can offer? You will have a roof and enough to eat. A good leader doesn't starve his men or their kinfolk. And if God wills it I will give you new children. I know what little Ragnar's death meant for you. Hild, will you come?"

"Why can't you go back to Godwin?" enquired Hild, striking home at once to the one unexplained mystery in Brand's whole speech.

"Oh, *God!*" Brand said, and sat down among the tussocks of grass and the sea pinks and glowered out at the sea.

Hild waited. Presently he said: "Answer my question first. Will you be my wife?"

"Yes," said Hild serenely, as if surprised that he should doubt it. "Of course. But if you have a feud now with Earl Godwin, I must know about it. Your counsel is safe with me." She sat down beside him. "Safer than Queen Emma's was. But those days are far behind me; I am not so foolish now. Brand, since you have been here, something has been worrying you halfway to madness. What is it?"

He told her. She listened, watching the seagulls that rode the winds around the tall cliffs. "And the king?" she said when he had finished. "When you take your sword to Edward, will you take this news to him with it? Why King Edward?"

"It seemed—fitting," Brand said. His brown eyes were unhappy. "Godwin has injured Edward and Queen Emma, hatefully. If I were to serve them . . ."

"Paying someone else's debt? Yes, I see. But will you tell what you know?"

Brand put his head in his hands. She had pointed, unerringly, to the question that was still unresolved. "I don't know. I don't *know*. What's right? The Lady Emma is innocent. Surely they both have a right to my knowledge. But I . . . owe Godwin something." He told her of the moment in his fight with Sweyn, when his memories of Godwin's training had kept him fighting in the moment of defeat. "And above that," he said at length, "I promised him my silence. I gave him my oath, and he trusted me with it, out of his hands."

"Then there's no more to be said." Hild stood up with an air of finality. "Well, is there? An oath is an oath. No one would ever have credited those tales about Emma if she had been any sort of mother to her sons. I knew her! I never found it at all hard to believe she'd plotted to kill them. I'm quite sure she was capable of it even if she didn't do it. You needn't break your word and your heart for *her* sake. She can take care of herself, that one."

Brand suddenly laughed, feeling his heart expand and lighten, as if a brisk wind had dispersed a heavy fog. "Do you hate her still?" he asked.

"No. But I can't pity her, either. Anyway, it would only be your word against Godwin's—his sons would all say what he wanted them to say—and he's outwitted cleverer foes than you. Keep your secret, my dear. You won't forgive yourself, ever, if you don't. Anyway, it was all so long ago it might have happened to different people."

She wasn't beautiful. There was nothing flamelike in Hild, nothing to set a man's soul ablaze. She was the bread of life and not the wine.

But one could live without wine more easily than without bread. Above all, Brand could, for he was much the same kind of person as Hild. It was the Godwins and their ilk who represented the wine in the male world. Hild was Brand's sort. She understood his trouble and had shown him where his peace must lie.

She said thoughtfully, as he stood up, "People used to say you would never marry and neither would your lord Beorn, because you filled that place for one another."

Brand's mouth dropped open.

"You hadn't heard that? Some of the men you had with you the winter of the floods used to say it."

He had actually felt for his sword-hilt. "I had *not* heard it. And if I had, I would have killed the man who said it."

"I didn't believe it," said Hild. "But I'm glad you didn't marry before. I hope my father permits it! I want to leave Dover. There's nothing here but memories."

"Your father?" snorted Brand. He took her hand and they began to walk, in step, into the cool, steady wind. "You're a widow, not a young girl. You can choose for yourself. We shall tell him we intend to marry, not ask him if we can. Listen—let me get to the bottom of this. Why didn't you believe the tales about me and Lord Beorn?"

"I knew you well—fairly well. I know you had courted a young woman at one time and been unhappy at losing her. And I'd seen you with Beorn. I couldn't imagine you loving him as if he were a woman. If you ever loved any man that way, it wouldn't have been Beorn."

Brand stopped dead. "What does that mean?"

Hild's voice was placid and matter-of-fact, but she took his breath away. "It would have been Godwin," she explained.

He opened his mouth in outrage but her gently amused expression stopped him. "I only meant," she said gravely, "that although it has nothing to do with your body, you love Godwin. Don't you?"

In early spring they set out for London, knowing that King Edward would be there for the 1050 Lenten Council. There were four of them.

The arrival just before Christmas of Peter Longshanks and Odi Pathfinder, armed with several precious keepsakes from Beorn's treasure (sent by Gytha), had done much to reconcile Eric to his daughter's loss. They, with Brand and Rolf, had planned a new ship, the *Bridegift*, to replace the lost *Hild*, and the gold helped hire the labour. Eric passed from grumbling acquiescence to near-enthusiasm very swiftly.

The pair said they had come because Brand had fought to save their lives and henceforth they wished to be his followers. Waving aside his protests, they said that if he wished to seek a new lord they would help. Three swords were better than one and they would enhance his value.

So in the end he allowed them to put their hands between his and promise to follow him, and he used some more of the gold in making gifts to them, as a leader should: new swords with Rhineland blades and gemmed hilts from a Dover workshop. With the very last of the gold he bought ponies for himself and Hild. He was anxious at first in case Hild did not want to go again to the court, but she smiled and said that this time she would not have to serve Emma, and besides, she was a grown woman now, and wiser, as she had already told him.

They rode through bright blustery weather over roads hard to travel at times because of flooding. It would have been a slow ride in any case, for Hild thought she was pregnant. Nor did Brand wish to hurry, now that the time had come. He was not sure how easy it would be to find employment when he got there. Nor was Long-

shanks. Only Odi Pathfinder, whose happy-go-lucky nature sometimes bordered on the chuckleheaded, who had once lost his
comrades in a forest for two days and a night, out of sheer over-
optimism, said it was sure to be simple.

For once Odi was right.

They crossed the Thames by ferry, passing into the town of
London, where houses, halls, and churches gathered in the shelter of
the ancient walls. They made for the king's great hall. They found it
in a state of confusion, crowded with the earls and prelates who had
come for the Witan Council, which was already several days under
way and still seething daily as various thanes and smaller fry, concerned only with the less important business at the council's tail end,
continued to arrive. A thane's party had ridden in just ahead of
Brand's, filling up the compound with men, horses, and strident
dispute over lodgings and stabling. The gatehouse guard halted
Brand's quartet with lowered pikes; they waited, listening to the din
beyond the gate and wondering if there could possibly be room in all
that chaos for four more.

"Whose folk are you?"

"No one's yet," said Brand. He took off his helmet. "Alfhelm,
don't you know me? I trained with you under Earl Godwin, years
since. We want to offer our swords if there's a use for them. I fought
Sweyn Godwinsson in a quarrel and I've parted with his father accordingly. These two are my followers and this is my wife."

"Brand Woodcutter! Aye, I mind you well enough." His years
in the south had mended Brand's accent, but Alfhelm was a younger
son of an exceedingly parochial northern thane, and nothing on earth
would ever mend his. "So will Oswald Halfear—and he's the man
you want. He's over at the horse lines. The stables have overflowed.
Try him. And—glad to see you again, Woodcutter." The pikes were
raised.

They found Halfear issuing orders on the vexed question of
where the newly arrived thane's horses were to be put, when he had
come with twenty more than anyone expected. He greeted Brand
with surprise and pleasure and seemed to welcome the interruption.
Skinny, knotted, and apparently unchanged since Brand first saw
him at Winchester, he took them to a small building which seemed
to be his headquarters and there consulted a clerk who sat at a desk
studying notched tally sticks and rolls of parchment. There were

many companies of men in the royal household, apart from the exalted royal bodyguard.

"You will unquestionably be welcome, if there's room," Oswald said. "That tale about Sweyn Godwinsson's got round! And we don't take every stray soldier without a lord who passes by, believe me! But I don't think we need test your handiness with a sword. And your own men go where you go. I know them as well as I know you, anyway." He exchanged gossip with Longshanks and Pathfinder, while the clerk consulted his records.

The clerk said at last, in a precise, legal voice: "We have had two older men retire to their holdings in this year past. They have not yet been replaced. Nor have two others who died of the shivering fever last winter. There are four vacancies."

"That's settled, then," said Halfear. "There'll be an oath-taking ceremony later, after the evening meal. You'll be under Sergeant Arnulf and I shall have to present you to him before the oath-taking, of course, but I don't expect him to object to you. For the moment I'll show you where you'll live. This is your wife, you say, Brand?" He scanned Hild from head to foot but appeared pleased with what he saw. "Can you weave and embroider?" he asked her. "The soldiers' womenfolk mostly help with the business of keeping the court clad. She'll have to share your pallet in the hall, you realise that?"

"I can weave and do anything in that way that's needed," Hild said. "And live in the hall with Brand as well as anywhere."

"Very well." Oswald nodded. "In that case, we'll get your names entered and then I'll find someone to show you round."

Presently they were crossing the courtyard at the heels of the serving man Halfear had found to guide them, going to the hall to see their quarters, astonished at the ease of their enterprise. The hall door opened as they approached, and they paused to let those who were coming out have right of way down the steps. There were five men together, laughing over some private joke as they descended.

Chief among them, topping the others by half a head, laughing the loudest, blue-cloaked, gold-laden, and jewel-bright, his ginger hair and beard combed sleek and his hazel green eyes dancing, in person, was Sweyn Godwinsson.

2 ✹ A Man in Need of an Heir

"I wonder, often, if I did right to bring him back," said Edward in French, wiping a spatter of mud out of his eyes and reining back his excited pony.

He was only half-serious. The fact that Sweyn Godwinsson, mounted on a flamboyant half-Barb, had just overtaken the king and Champart in the hunting field and splashed them both extensively with mire in the process, could hardly be classed as treason.

"Oh, I think so," said Champart gently, guiding his own mount skilfully round the edge of another patch of mud. "He's no great man and he knows it. And that has certain advantages, *n'est-ce pas?*"

They smiled at each other like boys in conspiracy, like the boys they had once been, when Robert was a young clerk and Edward a youth with high birth and no prospects. Robert had not then thought the lonely, studious prince would one day hold a realm; still less that he would summon his friend to his side to help him and raise that friend to an archbishopric as a reward. For Eadsige, tired and ailing, had gone to his God at last and left Canterbury untenanted. Indeed, Robert had had a choice of archbishoprics. Alfric Kitehawk had been stricken with sickness out of nowhere and had died in the same year. "But I prefer Canterbury to York," Robert had said. "Canterbury is nearer to the court."

There were mutterings about preference for Normans, but Robert pretended not to hear them. People would adapt in time.

"It is a safeguard against Godwin, as you say," Edward agreed, referring now to Sweyn Godwinsson.

The return of Sweyn, to the amazement not only of Brand but of the public at large when the criers went out to spread the news, had been largely at Champart's instigation, though Godwin had begun it.

The first step had been made two Christmases ago, towards the end of the Yuletide feast, when Godwin sought private audience of Edward and found himself instead face to face with a politely smiling Robert who said in French that the king's duties were daily growing more onerous and that he had been compelled to delegate some of them. So that in future he, Robert Champart, would interview applicants for audience before it was granted and was empowered to save the king trouble by dealing with a number of matters himself.

Godwin said in English: "I am not going to pass messages to my son-in-law through any middleman! Where is the king?"

"In council at the moment. Plans for a new abbey near London. To be called the West Minster, I believe." Robert had a gracious air, of one who favours a subordinate with a harmless glimpse into great men's affairs. After a pause long enough for the full enjoyment of Godwin's bunching jaw and right-hand muscles, he added: "But please do rest assured, Lord Godwin, that I will faithfully report all you have to say and that the king will see you if he feels it appropriate . . ."

"If the king has time to listen to you while you report to him faithfully, he has the time to listen to me while I say exactly the same things! And I prefer to talk in English. It is my mother tongue and this is my native land. I repeat: where is the king?"

"I repeat: in council," said Robert, smiling.

In the end, seething, Godwin had made his plea through Robert. It was an appeal for Sweyn's forgiveness and reinstatement. Godwin would pay Beorn's weregild gladly, he said. Sweyn was living abroad, lonely and penitent, according to Aldred of Worcester, who had met him while travelling in Germany and learned that nearly all his followers had left him, so that he was now little more than a penniless vagabond. Aldred managed to be present when Robert presented the plea and lent his support. Sweyn had had so bitter a lesson, he said, that his future might well be an utter contrast to his past, if only the king of his Christian mercy would be pleased to let him prove it.

"Well?" Edward had demanded of Champart. "Give me your opinion."

And Robert, consideringly, replied: "I would have Sweyn Godwinsson back here for no cause except one. But that one carries weight. You have neither son nor brethren, my lord. By the custom of this land . . ." His voice was carefully neutral, concealing his views on barbarous traditions. ". . . any suitable successor may be nominated, and a brother-in-law might be thought a proper choice, often preferable to a descendant of some remoter branch of the royal house. But you will hardly want a Godwinsson as your heir . . ."

"By the Rood, no!" said Edward feelingly.

". . . With Sweyn here in England, the eldest available Godwinsson, you cannot be pressed to have one. His history debars him from it and his presence debars his younger brothers. To select one of them might cause trouble, even fighting. So you would have every excuse to dismiss the Godwin family from the running altogether and I would be no honest advisor or friend, my lord, if I did not tell you plainly that you are beginning to need that excuse. Few now hope to see an heir born of your loins and many look to the house of Godwin to supply one instead." He added after a pause: "If Godwin pays a sufficient weregild, I would suggest that you consider it. The treasury can always do with a little extra."

And after a little thought Edward had nodded. "It shall be done," he said. "At the next Lenten Council. Get the clerks to draw the documents up."

They smiled at each other now, remembering how Harold's face had darkened at that council table when he heard the news and how his father had looked at him and looked quickly away.

"Harold had hopes," Edward had commented afterwards, joining Champart in the whitewashed cell of a room that was Robert's office at the London court, "which his father no doubt put into his head. Now he is angry with his father for despoiling them."

"What a sad thing, my friend," said Champart in Sparhafoc's accents, "that brother should leap at brother's throat and seek to profit by his downfall. Alas!"

"They're fortunate to have brothers," Edward snapped. "I miss Alfred still." He added, faintly reproving, "Sparhafoc is no favourite of yours, I know. But I have found him worthy enough. I try to be fair, Champart. And not to waste ability because its owner is backed by or related to someone I dislike, such as Godwin. Where is the list of items for tomorrow? Have you a copy here?"

Robert rooted in his document chest and found a scroll. "The first item is the pruning of our mercenary fleet. You may want to study that." He watched as Edward unrolled the parchment and frowned at it.

"You feel the pruning is justified, Robert?"

"I can't feel that our present permanent sea force is justified. I'm putting this forward as an economy measure. Godwin will make a to-do about Hardraada, but I can see no real menace from Norway. She has internal troubles of her own. And Godwin has a private axe to sharpen. Since he took back Earl Beorn's empty post as fleet commander, the fleet has been his chief claim to status—and a great enhancement of his power. But can we really afford to keep on an expensive force that we never use, simply to protect Earl Godwin's status—and his power?"

And their eyes had met, in perfect understanding, just as they were doing now, as stirrup to stirrup they loped along the muddy track between the oak boles.

Ahead the trees thinned, oak yielding to ash and sycamore and a grove of silver birch. Hounds gave tongue in the distance.

They spurred forward. The trees to the right ended and from them, suddenly, burst a foam-flecked buck. They swerved to avoid crossing its line, and as they did so an arrow singing from behind a bush passed within six inches of Edward's head and buried itself vibrating in a tussock of grass by the track.

They stopped. Horsemen appearing apparently from nowhere converged on the arrow's source. Two flung themselves out of their saddles and darted into the thicket. They emerged hauling a terrified assistant huntsman. The sweat of his fear plastered his flaxen hair to his forehead.

"I didn't mean it! I didn't know you'd come out of the trees like that! I was aiming at the deer!" He was on the verge of vomiting.

"Let him go!" Edward ordered. The captors obeyed unwillingly, glaring at their prey. Leofric, who had been among the riders who galloped to the king's aid, glowered red-faced at the culprit. Harold rode up beside the king as if to safeguard him from any further attack.

"Stand up, fellow! Stop gibbering!" Edward commanded. "I know you aimed at the buck. If you wanted to kill me you'd have picked a time and place when I was first alone and second standing still and third in full view. I know quite well that you couldn't see me coming or even hear me above the hound noise. Next time you go out with a bow make sure you loose your arrows where they can't be run into by a careless king. You can go."

There was a pause.

"I said," said Edward pleasantly, "that he could go. Will you all be good enough to stand back and let him. What is it, Leofric?"

The Earl of Mercia was simmering. "I beg your pardon, my lord, but what sort of example is this? It's yourself he's almost killed!"

"It's an example of mercy and justice, I hope," Edward said.

After another pause, Harold said: "My lord king is right. Stand back, all of you."

They stood back. Edward waved away the huntsman's gabbling thanks and watched him scuttle away. "Leofric," said the king, "innocent men will not walk in fear in my realm, not even stupid ones. And it was, as you yourself reminded me, my person that the arrow nearly struck, not yours. Mind your own business. Shall we get after the hounds? They may have brought that deer to bay by now and I have a fancy for venison tonight."

"I trust you realise," said Champart as he and Edward later rode homewards, jogging at ease behind the crowd of houndsmen and falconers, "that in telling that fool how he would have gone about it had he really meant to kill you, you have offered anyone who's interested a set of instructions for compassing your death?"

"Have I? I only said what any intelligent man would know. A hunting accident would be an ideal way to get rid of me. Real accidents are so common. Does anyone want to murder me, do you know?"

"No. Though there is always the chance that it might occur to—perhaps—one of the house of Wessex. If anything happened to you while the heirship was in doubt, one of them might rally support and seize power. They have not been overscrupulous in the past, have they? What you need," said Champart calmly, "is an official heir. Elsewhere."

A man in need of an heir customarily turns to his wife for assistance. Edward, doeskin hunting boots removed and face laved in warm water, duly made his way towards his queen's apartments. He had humour enough in him to see the comedy. Edith would help if she could; he always took his problems to her. But she could only help with words. Together they might choose an heir but they would not try to make one.

In the last three years they had reshaped their marriage. It had been by tacit consent, for they never discussed it. On the night of their quarrel over Sweyn, Edith had begun to see her road. On the day when Ralph of Mantes came, she had resolved to follow it.

It took courage. It had given pain, like the straining of hitherto unused muscles. It still did at times. Now as she sat drying her long hair, quiet under the hands of her ladies as they towelled and combed, absently reminding the most junior of them to remove the messy bowl of wood-ash and water in which the washing had been done, she was going through one of her times of distress. Had Edward, she wondered, any idea of the struggle through which she was passing? Probably not, and it was beyond her to explain to him.

The decision had been only the first step. Next came the quiet, imperceptible, inch-by-inch withdrawal of herself from him. Lying apart from him in the bed, offering no caresses of welcome or parting, darting no glances of invitation. Union grew infrequent—or more infrequent, for it had never been regular. At the end of a year or so, Edward caught a cold and coughed in the night. He apologised for disturbing her and moved into the adjoining anteroom to sleep. It involved the to-do which attended even the most temporary arrangements of royalty; hangings were fetched, woodwork newpainted, so that the chamber should be fit for him. It was made very fit. When he was better, he stayed there. With that, the first half of her task was done.

Thereafter, gradually, stone on stone, they began to build a new edifice of marriage founded not on the shared bed but on the sharing of duties, Royal visits, appearances, audiences, charities, and the founding of churches became their cement. Edward, to whom sex had never been much more than a nuisance, was grateful for what seemed his wife's good understanding. Edith redoubled her efforts to be the royal helpmeet: to see that her modest husband appeared in audience dressed like a king instead of being outdone by his ushers, unobtrusively to manage his household, to see the women petitioners, to be his companion, his memory, and at times his deputy. It began to be said that the royal pair were an example to all in their piety and devotion and chastity. Once the news of the separate bedchambers became widely known, the prelates gave great admiration to the chastity.

Edward was pleased with their new reputation. Edith also expressed satisfaction. Alone in her bed at night, after her ladies were asleep, she would cry her pain away if she liked. To live month by month and be always disappointed had been bad enough. But to have no hope at all, she learnt, was worse. The sight of a woman expecting a child was like a stab in the vitals. For a long time she shamelessly avoided it.

But one could not avoid it for life and none of Edith's kinsfolk lacked valour. Nor did Edward himself; it was a virtue she valued in him. She could not, either practically or for the sake of her own self-respect, remain besieged for ever. She must face the enemy. When a young man called Brand Woodcutter, whom she remembered as one of her father's men and recognised as a connection through Sweyn's son, came to the court accompanied by his pregnant wife, Hild, Edith learned that Hild had been to court before and asked her to be one of her ladies.

Hild's own calm, uncomplicated nature was pleasing to her mistress, which helped. Edith managed to ask kindly after her health as the months went on and to make the right noises over the girl-child which Hild bore in October. But when she heard that Hild was pregnant again, it was all she could do for a time to speak to her civilly, and today for the first time she had faced the necessity of uttering congratulations and, once more, enquiring after Hild's well-being. The effort had been agonising. The foe was untrustworthy, it seemed, liable to draw a knife at any time, even in mid-truce. On the plea that Hild looked tired and ought to rest more, Edith would not let her comb the royal hair today.

Edward arrived unheralded, as he often did. Pages, ushers, and similar servants spent much time running about in the vain attempt to get to the king's destination before the king did, in order to announce him. They were constantly foiled, as he frequently did not say where he was going. He waved dismissal at the ladies, who withdrew to the far end of the bower, and took the comb in his own hands, sitting down on a stool beside Edith.

"My dear, I need your advice."

Edith smiled. She lifted a half-finished glove and a threaded needle from the wicker workbox beside her. "Yes? The new abbey? Or is it the crown? I saw Abbot Sparhafoc earlier. He told me you had given him a definite commission at last, and he showed me the jewels you had chosen. It will be a beautiful thing."

"It's neither the abbey nor the crown." Edward smiled too. "What a long face Robert pulled over that crown. Too expensive, he said. But I think he objects to Sparhafoc having the honour. He didn't want Sparhafoc succeeding him as Bishop of London, either. Said he wasn't sincere enough. Well, Robert isn't always right. But I think he was talking wisely on another subject, today. He . . . reminded me that men are mortal."

Edith's needle hesitated. "Men are mortal? But we all know that, surely? What did he mean?"

Edward said slowly, choosing his words: "He meant that it would . . . cause confusion if I were to die and leave the succession in doubt."

Edith sat quite still, looking down at the tiny, perfect stitches of the thin gold thread. Her hair, light as down and flaxen gold in shade, drifted round her. It was nearly dry. Edward was still gently combing it. But its beauty could not touch him. "The Witan would choose a successor," she said.

"I think that if I left no instructions, there might be factions among them. Fighting, even. There should be one man who stands out clearly as my preferred choice. Now, what should I do?"

Without a single trumpet note of warning, the enemy leapt from ambush.

"We could try again," said Edith.

She felt his mind recoil, felt his hands drop away from her hair. "I didn't mean that," he said. He got up.

It was so easy, with Edward, to make mistakes. Like missing one's footing on steep stairs in the dark. He was so unlike any member of her own family. Where she looked for kindness in him, she found resentment, and where she expected a hand outstretched, she encountered a withdrawal.

"I am sorry, Edward. I misunderstood you."

He took the stool again. "It would not be wise," he said, "there might be no child. There never was before. And that would make you unhappy again." His nostrils curled fastidiously. "The carnal side of marriage surely doesn't please you for its own sake?"

Edith put her work on her lap and took hold of the sides of her chair, as though a gale were trying to blow her off it. They were going to quarrel. She could not stop it. She was tired of agreeing with Edward for the sake of appearances. "Why should it not? It's hallowed by the Church. My own parents weren't ashamed of it!"

"They had children from it. It had purpose."

"They didn't think of it in that way. They loved each other. I once heard my father complain that children came too easily. He said he had too many."

"There, madam, many people would wholeheartedly agree with him!"

"I have often wondered," said Edith, beginning roughly to braid her own hair, "whether you forswore my bed purely to seek spiritual growth or as some kind of revenge on my father."

"This is not like you, Edith. You pain me very much. My mother used to fling insults at my father in just the same way. Why should you think I want revenge on your father or suppose I wish to achieve it through you?"

Edith refused to quail. "You hate my father," she said. "Why did you marry me in the first place?"

"Because you were—I thought—sweet and gentle and would be the kind of wife I needed. And because I desired to bury my past differences with your father. But at that time I didn't know half the ambition and arrogance of your family, or the termagant you can be." He was silent a moment, fighting his anger down. He said: "One successor I will *not* consider is one of your brothers, my dear. I have heard it suggested, but I will not have it."

"Just as well we have no child, then!" Edith said. She started on the other plait. "Since it would have been my father's grandson as well as your son."

"It would have been my mother's grandson too," Edward said

acidly. "I would have forgiven it its grandparents. But it does not exist and now isn't likely to."

"If it was a son in the first place," Edith added caustically.

She braided more carefully, thinking. During the hard, nerve-stretching year while she was dividing herself from him, there had been many short-lived storms such as this, born mainly of the conflict between her chosen course and her desired one. She had learned to finish such quarrels quickly, before too much harm was done. She said in a different, lighter tone: "Your sister Godgift left sons. Ralph is already here and he has a brother in France. What about them?"

"Ralph has already said no and I believe he knows his own faults and is showing wisdom." Edward had also learned the technique of the cut-off quarrel. "Walter, I hear, has a similar temperament. Certainly, I doubt if he would have the personality to overcome the drawback of being foreign-bred. No. They look good candidates on the face of it, but they don't stand close scrutiny."

Edith was in command of herself again, her anguish battened down and her mind engaged in the problem. She said: "Do you think the matter as urgent as Champart apparently does? Or could it wait on the nurturing of a child? Not ours, don't misunderstand me."

"Healthy men have been struck down between sunrise and sunset before now," said Edward. "But one must have some faith in God. I can afford a little time for solving the problem aright, yes." He had the good taste not to mention certain personal precautions he had already devised against the chance of murder. They included a carefully leaked rumour that should he die questionably, all the Godwin family but Edith would be instantly banished from the land.

"Because your sister Godgift left two daughters as well," Edith was saying. "Eustace's children. One is married to a Norman, I believe . . ."

"This year. But he's quite obscure and without ambition, I believe, and will probably want his children reared in Normandy."

"I know. But the other one . . . she must be almost marriageable by now. Now if she came to England and were suitably married here and had a son . . . he could be brought up here as your heir. A well-chosen husband—say Siward's son—would be a shield against . . . any other ambitious men."

Edward looked at her, the coldness of annoyance fading and a smile of approval replacing it. His trust in her was justified after all.

"You ought to be on my Witan Council," he said. "You have more good sense than all of them put together at times. I shall consult them about this. Edith—it may well be the answer."

His exit from the bower coincided with Queen Emma's entry into it. Although most of her life these days was a retired one in her Winchester home, Emma still joined the court now and then, at Christmas and sometimes during Lent, so that she could stay over Easter. She came in attended by her own train of ladies and exchanged short greetings with her son as he passed through the doorway. Emma, striking in green and violet shades of a brightness which belied her lined face and shadowed eyes, thoughtfully considered Edith and took the stool that Edward had vacated. Her ladies went to join Edith's, in response to a tapped signal from the stick on which Emma leant.

"Edward seems animated," she said.

"Yes." Edith was often glad of her astringent mother-in-law's viewpoints. She told her of the conversation she and Edward had just finished. "So I pleased him in the end," she said, "though it's a poor scheme. It offers no protection for the peace of the realm if . . . anything happened to Edward soon, and that is what Champart fears, I think. But it pleased Edward. I try so hard, madam. But . . . he still believes my father was party to his brother's death, I think. He never says so aloud, but it's always there. We can't really draw near each other."

"And was your father guilty?" Emma asked. "Do you know?"

"I was told no. I was told that he was indeed taken by surprise, that he was not expecting Harefoot's men. But . . ." She fell silent.

"But you have wondered? So have I. I don't mean to hurt you, Edith. We will not discuss this unless you wish. We have managed very well without discussing it so far."

"Whatever my father did, I know he had reasons for," said Edith. "I could bear the truth, if only I knew for sure what it was. But I don't."

"Edward still thinks I was a party as well," Emma said ruminatively. "I've got used to it over the years, although at times I wish very much to make my peace with him before I die. My mirror tells me things that make me wonder how much older I shall grow."

"Madam . . . surely. The Atheling was your own son. Edward *can't* truly believe . . ."

"So you do me the honour of believing me innocent?"

Edith said truthfully: "You have never tried hard to convince me and I have few facts on which to judge for myself. But I do believe you innocent. I know you quite well now. And that is why I can't understand that Edward . . ."

"Listen, my child. You say you can bear the truth if you know what it is. Well, I don't know it either, but I can say this. If I did not send that letter, who did? It was either Harefoot on his own or Harefoot in concert with your father. And the latter is likelier, because it was a cleverer plan than Harefoot, who was a perfect fool, was capable of conceiving—although his mother might have done, I would admit that—and because the captives were so neatly parcelled, ready for seizure at Gildenford. Which *was* Godwin's doing; Elfgift couldn't have organised that. Edith, I only speak of these things because I want you to understand what it is that gnaws so at Edward. I have a poor opinion of him in some ways, but here I pity him. If I know little of the truth of Gildenford, he knows still less. If you are sure that someone has sinned against you, in time you may forgive them. But when you only *think* they have, there is no escape. It will haunt you forever. He does not *know* what my part was: he does not *know* what your father's was. Now do you see?"

"I . . . there's a saying, madam, that if you know the truth, it will make you free."

"Yes. It will. And I," said Emma with real bitterness, "may never have that freedom. Nor will Edward."

She turned away from Edith, in time to observe a small disturbance among the ladies at the other end of the room. Nominally they were out of earshot, but one never knew for sure. However, if they had been eavesdropping, they had a distraction now.

"Edith," said Emma, "Edith, I have never really approved of Dame Hild as a choice for one of your women. I knew her as a girl, and a sillier one I never met. But as one woman to another I feel that someone should take her to her quarters. She is obviously unwell."

In his whitewashed office, Robert Champart walked back and forth, dictating slowly to his clerk, who sat with rapidly scratching quill,

setting in black, elegant script the official invitation for Eustace of
Boulogne to visit the king his brother-in-law and bring his daughter
the Lady Alys, with a view to arranging her marriage in England. It
was a difficult letter to frame, for there must be hints of the high sta-
tion perhaps awaiting a son born of the marriage, without any too
definite promise. That would be premature. They must look at Alys
first. Champart mulled over alternative phrases and wished the heirship could be settled on someone already in existence. One of the
king's nephews, for instance, or his cousin, William of Normandy.
Champart personally liked the idea of William, a proved and able
ruler as well as a member of the royal family. However . . .

He said: "No, delete that sentence. You will have to make a fair
copy of this, so don't be too particular about your lettering. Is it
crossed out? Very well, put this instead . . ."

In the long run, it proved not only a difficult letter but also a
momentous one. Although in the short run no one would have
thought so, for Eustace's daughter proved unmarriageable, and the
only immediate effect of her visit was that Eric of Dover very nearly
had his hall burnt down.

3 ✖ "Your Daughter Is Dying"

Eric Merchant of Dover was tired.

With a couple of wooden screens he had made a tiny office in a corner of his rebuilt warehouse and here he sat at a pinewood table, his coffer open beside him and tally sticks trewn about the table. When raising a business from ruin one must watch over every last drop of wine and thread of silk, that not one farthing of profit be lost. It was a task he insisted on doing himself, for Rolf in his opinion was too careless, to apt to think approximate quantities would do. He let Rolf have his way in many things these days. He was too weary to argue over Rolf's insistence that the market for silk and perfume was growing, while the market for ship-masts and sword-blades was less, since times were peaceful and much of the royal fleet disbanded. He was even willing to admit that Rolf might be right. But for his own self-respect he must keep a grip on some part of the business, and the keeping of the accounts was that part. Rolf, he told himself, would very soon be in trouble if he did not.

But today his head ached and a most unwonted rebellion was growing in him against this endless toil, this pursuit of a goal which lately had grown more and more unreal. Without noticing it, he had ceased to work and was sitting at his table, looking at the notched tally sticks blankly and thinking.

His thoughts were so alien to him that they frightened him. He wondered if he were ill. He was forty-five now, an age that many never reached. He had been twenty-eight when that gipsy woman told his fortune and thus sold him into thralldom to a merciless ambition. He could still hear her whispering through her gap-teeth that his destiny would be powerful, *"something that you do will change the course of the world."* She had not actually said: "You will be a thane," but fortune-tellers always talked in riddles. He'd done wrong to listen, perhaps. Witchcraft, the priests called it.

But she must have meant he would gain rank, or how else could he exercise the power she promised him? Small merchants could change the course of the world about as easily as they could alter the direction of the winds on which their ships depended.

The sun, which had been shining onto his table through an unshuttered window, had moved away. The draught from the window was cold. He must rouse himself, go back to his hall, and eat the food cooked by the thralls Rolf had insisted on buying after Hild's departure, deaf to his father's protests about expense, ruthlessly rifling the coffer which held Eric's tomorrow. "And when guests break their journey at the sight of your fine rooftree, which you built to show your rank and encourage grand wayfarers, let me remind you, do you think I am going to cook their dinners for them?" Rolf had demanded and Eric, lacking the energy to argue about that either, had given in. The thralls would be at the kitchen fires now.

And he did not want to be bothered, either to put away the tallies or to rise from his stool or to walk up the hill to his home. Any more than he wanted to be bothered with counting quantities or making more profit or turning himself into a thane. Bewildered by his own dullness, he felt his forehead and pulse. His skin was cool and his blood-beat steady. He was not, apparently, feverish. But something must be wrong with him, he thought in perplexity.

It wasn't the first attack. That had struck weeks ago when he was walking by the harbour, looking for the *Bridegift*'s return from a trip to Marseilles. On that warm May evening, the harbour was wide awake at dusk. Lanterns were lit in the alehouses and hung about their doors, and from several taverns came singing. As he walked on the shore he passed near a stall still selling whelks and mussels, and the vendor's voice at close quarters startled him with a raucous invitation to buy. The lanterns and the singing, the stall-holder's shouts and the footsteps of the many strollers mingled together in an affirmation of the vigour of human life. On his right hand, that was. But on the other side, on his left, set against them like the dark night behind the twinkling stars, was the sea.

He had turned to gaze at that sea. Huge, restless, darkening with the sky, alien to the life of the shore, indifferent to it and twenty thousand times more powerful: it had been there before the first man was made from dust and it would be there still when the last man had returned to it. It endured the land but was not bound by it. He had with his own eyes seen the sea repossess itself of the land, once. It was to the busy ephemeral alehouses and whelk stalls what death was to life: the antithesis and the end.

It was also infinitely attractive.

It was this that shocked and terrified him. He felt in himself a turning away from the cheerful human harbour life towards that dark engulfing sea, as though towards coolness and rest. No more tallies, it murmured. No more dreary hoarding of silver, no more haggling. Rest. Sleep in the spacious sonorous deeps. He could have cast himself down on the beach and slept until the tide washed over him. He wanted to.

Instead he fled, leaving the shore at a pace one dignified hairsbreadth slower than a run, his heart jolting with fright.

And now the enemy had found him out in his fastness, at his desk in his warehouse in the midst of all his goods. He ought to consult a physician. And that, he thought, as he began at last to stow away the tallies, would cost more silver.

The walk home, embarked on at last, led uphill past small unfenced dwellings, each with its patch of land for corn or herbs and an animal or two. The tall gable end of his hall beckoned him on. He had built it thus with the witch's prophecy in mind, as Rolf had said. Had he, he suddenly asked himself, all these years been goblin-led?

Perhaps he ought to retire. He worried at the problem as he went, at war within himself. It would mean surrendering his dreams forever and for that he was not yet ready. He would think about it later, after a meal and a beaker of cold ale in the quiet of his big, underoccupied home. He quickened pace, rounding the last corner.

He came in sight of the gate. It stood wide, which was as it should be. But the courtyard beyond it was busy, which was not. Eric, stopping short, counted two, three, four, five horses' rumps with swishing tails; then, as he hurried on again in breathless indignation, an unmistakeably French soldier, in chain mail and a shiny conical helmet, passed across the entrance. Raised voices could be heard within; an impassioned disagreement was in progress somewhere. He thrust his way between two large horses which were blocking both his path and his view, and came upon the trouble source. Rolf was already there. With him, their expressions anxious, were Harold Godwinsson and Brand.

Brand was at that moment suffering from a weariness of heart at least the equal of Eric's. One thing that he had hoped to find as a lowly housecarle in Edward's service was the peace of obscurity. He had had enough of being an unwilling member of Godwin's exalted, perilous family circle. But the honour of defeating Sweyn had picked him out as if he stood in a shaft of sunlight. And now here he was again, with responsibility heavy upon him, trying to avert a riot with half the great names of the land involved. It wasn't, he considered crossly, fair.

He had been pleased enough at first to find himself promoted and placed in charge of those of the court housecarles who went with Siward of Northumbria, Siward's son Osbern, and the Northumbrian followers to meet Eustace of Boulogne and Alys his daughter at Dover. It was action, something to take his mind from Hild's present ill health and his own sense of guilt concerning it. She had been taken sick one day in the queen's apartments, and when Brand came to her in the communal sleepinghouse where they, along with other families, had been given quarters since Hild's new pregnancy began, she said: "It was the Lady Emma. Brand, are we right to hide what we know, after all? The king still thinks she led Atheling Alfred to his death and he will neither forgive nor forget . . ."

"Emma?" he said angrily, caught by surprise at this sudden reversal of Hild's opinions. "What is Emma to you? She bullied and insulted you when you served her, didn't she?"

"Yes. But this was . . . pitiful."

"Pitiful! So should I be with a broken oath, betraying the man I owe my very life to! You yourself said I must keep my word, have you forgotten?"

He spoke with a violence he knew Hild's mild words did not

merit. It came from his own deep-buried doubts, which he would not admit now, even to himself. Afterwards, because she was crying and would not let him comfort her, he put on his finest clothes and went to the evening feast with Sweyn's emerald on one hand and Sweyn's garnet on the other to show that he was a notable warrior and no weakling to be swayed by female vapours. In the morning Hild seemed better and did not mention the dispute. Yet it still lay between them, and in succeeding weeks she was prone to bouts of sickness, which she had not undergone when she was carrying little Elfhild.

This journey, he thought, might do them both good. When he returned, they might have had time to forget everything except that they missed each other. Then they would be happy again.

So he had set out willingly, proud of the honour of leadership. On learning that they and Count Eustace had arrived in Dover on the same day and that the resultant mass of men was too much for Alfwold Reeve's hall, Brand, still proudly, said: "My father-in-law owns the next biggest hall in Dover," and forthwith started out for Eric's house with the overflow, thirty-two in all, at his heels—royal housecarles, Northumbrians, and Frenchmen.

To encounter, literally in the gateway of Eric's house, Harold and Gyrth Godwinsson, bent on the same errand of seeking lodgings. They were discussing the matter with Rolf Ericsson, who appeared to be acting host, while a good forty Wessex housecarles were unsaddling in the courtyard.

Brand had seen the Godwins often at court and even spoken to them sometimes, but on the whole he avoided them. He reined in, embarrassed. Harold turned to him, smiling. "Brand! What brings you here?" His eyes travelled to Brand's companions. "Not a desire for a roof, I hope!"

"I am in charge of these men from Count Eustace of Boulogne's and Earl Siward's retinues, and we are indeed in need of a roof," Brand said. "We may be in Dover for some days—the count's daughter was ill on the voyage. The count is the king's kinsman and it is hoped . . ."

His voice faded a little, for the purpose of Eustace's visit was known to be a slight to the Godwins. Harold took him smoothly up. ". . . hoped to marry the Lady Alys to Osbern Siwardsson. We know that." His eyes twinkled. He and Brand liked each other and if the Godwin family secretly resented the honour done to Siward, it was hardly Brand's fault.

"But Brand," Harold went on, "Gyrth and I are here to escort the Lady Judith of Flanders, who is to marry Tostig my brother. On arrival we heard that the reeve's house was full. The Flemings will expect proper treatment. The alliance is valuable. We may be here for some days too. The Flemish ships are not yet in." He added, with gentle amusement, "And you must admit we were here first."

"Eric's hall can't hold both parties," Brand agreed unhappily. "Where is Eric?"

He and Harold both gazed at the hall, as if hoping it would prove to be made of cats' sinews and would stretch. It remained obstinately wooden: large, but not large enough. Rolf also looked at it. "My father is at his warehouse, and in his absence I am host," he said. "It is true that we cannot accommodate a second influx. We lack service, for one thing. Brand, I am extremely sorry to seem churlish. Could I suggest that there are thanes' houses and the homes of respectable townsmen, all of good standing, where your companions could lodge, very comfortably?"

One of Eustace's contingent, a young, English-speaking knight, interposed. "As guests of the king, on an official visit, we *naturellement* take precedence over those of an earl." He was a thin-nostrilled, supercilious young man who had already been offended because Brand had been detailed to guide them, while Earl Siward took his boots off in the reeve's hall. "It is unfitting for us to be lodged in lesser houses," he said.

"Eric Merchant is not a nobleman," said Brand, seizing thankfully on what looked like a way out. "But thanes are men of rank, of course. We will make enquiries among them. If you will follow me . . ."

The supercilious young knight had been running an eye over the lofty roof of Eric's hall. He now slid his feet out of his stirrups and rested a gloved hand on his pommel, preparatory to dismounting. "Not at all," he said, his inflexion discouragingly soft. "I think this hall will suit us very well. It is these others who must leave."

Brand, twisting quickly in his saddle, barked: "Stay where you are!" to the housecarles in his group. They obeyed him, some of them grinning. They had apparently not taken to the Frenchmen and did not wish to support them. But he had no power to command Eustace's men, and they were throwing their mounts' reins to the English riders and springing to the ground. The Wessex men, already in possession of courtyard and hall, took in the situation and coalesced. Gyrth, looking grave, hurried over to them; he could be heard attempting, unsuccessfully, to preach forbearance. Harold leant peacefully against his horse's shoulder and did nothing. There was a brief scrimmage at the hall doorway; then, the attacking Frenchmen were through it and in, and the rest of the Wessex men rushed in after them, carrying Gyrth along.

"Dear, dear," said Harold. "I am extremely sorry, Brand. And Rolf. But you can hardly blame my followers, can you?"

Rolf opened his mouth to speak, but his words were drowned as two things happened simultaneously. One was the arrival of Eric, puffing, crimson, annoyed, and loudly demanding an explanation. The other, to judge from the quality of the noise within the hall, was the outbreak of a full-scale war.

It had the true ring of battle about it: cries and screams, the clash of blades and the whoops of encouragement, and a crashing of objects thrown or overturned. The hall door burst open and two men hurtled out of it backwards. They picked themselves up and rushed inside again, yelling. Both had their swords out. Eric stood still, glaring and gasping. He stared from Brand to Harold to the swinging door of the hall. The building seemed on the verge of eruption, like a grumbling volcano.

"What *is* it? What is going on? Who are all these people? Why do you stand there and do nothing?" The last sentence was directed at Rolf.

"What can I do?" Rolf asked reasonably. He flinched as the uproar reached a new crescendo.

"Fool of a boy!" screamed Eric, and made for the hall. Perforce, the others went with him. As they set foot on the lowest step to the open door, a drift of smoke came out to meet them.

The nature of the din changed at the same moment. As they pushed their way in, they were in time to see the violent quarrel which had been in progress inside dissolve and realign itself against the common foe of fire. Someone in the melee had kicked a log out of the fireplace and it had kindled the rushes and some of the hangings.

Gyrth had shouted the alarm and set the example by stamping on
the smouldering reeds, and now the others were following his lead.
Eric, his hands to his mouth, watched the interior of his home con-
verted in the space of moments to a state of charred confusion. A
ruined tapestry, blackened and sparkling along one edge, fell at his
feet. He trod on the embers, almost crying. "They're the only tapestries I have! Rolf, are you mad? Can you not be trusted to keep my
gates for half a day?" He waved distracted arms and banged ineffec-
tually on the gatepost. "I am at my wits' end! Oh, I shall retire! At
the end of the season, I shall retire! You shall do as you please! You
shall burn down the hall and present my goods to the first pirate
you meet and I shall say nothing! I wash my hands of you!"

Rolf, unmoved by this outrageous implication, brushed soot off
his tunic and considered the scene. Harold, Gyrth, and Brand had
plunged into the midst of it and begun to sort out their respective
bands of men. Tempers seemed to have cooled. Miraculously, since
almost every man in the hall had his blade out, few seemed to be
much hurt. One housecarle clutched an arm which ran blood, and a
friend was helping him staunch it. A young knight with a forefinger
half off was looking green and had sat down. All other damage
seemed superficial. Quiet had fallen. Even the supercilious knight,
still warily stirring a smoking heap of fabric with the toe of his boot,
was subdued.

Brand, addressing the Frenchmen, said: "I very much regret
that I brought you here, but I did not know that the hall was taken.
I have no doubt that room can be found for you all with thanes of
good standing, and the burgesses of this town. This hall in its
present state can hardly accommodate you suitably now! I hope that
Eric Merchant, who owns it, will be properly recompensed for the
damage. Now please be good enough to follow me." He paused and
then repeated it all in his halting French. Mercifully, no one objected, and the knights moved to join him without further demur.
One of them said, in his own tongue: "We are sorry." He looked rue-
fully round him. "We did not quite understand. We are strangers
here."

One of the Wessex men muttered: "Foreigners!"

"I would be glad," said Brand hastily, before anything else
could go wrong, "If you would remount your horses and come with
me."

Rolf came with him to the gate. Brand tried to apologise, but

Eric's remarkably unruffled son cut the apologies short. "Oh, it isn't as bad as it looks! A few reeds and worn-out tapestries; what's so terrible? And at the end of it all, my father says he will retire. I have been trying to get him to do that for months. This has tilted the balance, perhaps. I think he meant it. This outsize hall is all part of his ambition. He has talked once or twice of going to live in Ragnar's old hall—it's let but that can soon be changed—and now maybe he'll really go! And if he gives up this house, he will surrender the business with it. And I want the business. I can run it better without him." He grinned and Brand noticed for the first time that Rolf, since his sojourn with the pirates, had changed. His expression was sharper, shrewder, than before, and his eyes were more calculating. "I'm not so very sorry this has happened," Rolf remarked.

"I see," said Brand, mounting. "Well, I wish you good day."

Thank the saints, he thought as he rode away, that he had got Hild out of this house of warring generations, and commerce that left no room for anything else. Dear Hild. If she were too kind to hate Emma for old injuries, was that not fitting in a woman? He honoured her for her goodness. And when he went home he would make it up to her.

"I feel much better now, madam. It was kind of you to enquire. I am sorry to be such a nuisance."

"Nuisance, child? Where's the nuisance? This court is overrun with servants and thralls who haven't enough to do. Rest as long as you like. Have you all you need?" Emma, leaning on her stick, looked keenly round the apartment. It was August, so no brazier was lit, but one stood fuelled, ready in case of an unseasonable chill. The rushes were sweet with rosemary. Furs lay piled at the end of the bed in case the sufferer wanted them, and the two French ladies who attended her were seated close by. One had a book to read to the invalid and the other a jug of wine in case she felt thirsty. The king's physician had been to see her and gone away to make up a mixture which he said would relieve the cough. In the midst of it all Emma's granddaughter Alys sat, bright-eyed, with red-stained cheekbones, trying to strangle her bouts of coughing, surrounded by every comfort the court of England could offer, possessed of everything but hope, the saddest object in Edward's Gloucester residence, and the most bitter disappointment.

Emma, assured that nothing was lacking that human aid could

give, pronounced a blessing and left. Queen Edith joined her outside, and with their ladies following a few tactful paces behind them,
they moved away from the buildings towards the fishpool, a favourite place for walking now that flowers had been planted near it
and a narrow path paved. It had been Edith's doing. After the
sickroom, the west-country air was as sweet as new milk and as clean
as spring water.

"Poor child," said Emma. "Poor, poor child. Her father must be
out of his mind and Edward little better. To drag her all this way,
talking about marriage! Marriage! Well, you said yourself it was a
poor scheme, founding a succession on a boy not yet conceived! But
at least you didn't know how sickly Alys was! Eustace did!"

On a bench by the pool she seated herself. Edith sat by her.
Their ladies strolled round the verge, looking at the trout. The two
queens were private together.

"If only Edward had consulted me!" Emma tapped an angry
stick. "But he wouldn't, of course!" She had invited herself to Gloucester on hearing of Alys's expected arrival, and the whole court
knew it. Edward was not pleased.

"Alys may recover," suggested Edith.

Emma shook her head. "I've seen a lot of death. I can read it
when it's written on a face, and it's written on hers. I give her till
Christmas at the most. She's already spitting blood. Well, at least
she can die in peace here. Maybe those stupid men have done that
much between them. From what her women say, her stepmother ig-
nores her; she only cares for her own baby. And as for her father
. . . ! All she ever gets from him is: 'Try harder, you won't get well if
you don't get up; stop that coughing because it annoys me; don't
spend all day in bed, I won't tolerate laziness!' " Emma's voice produced a startling mockery of Eustace's loud, bluff tones. "Ordering
her up out of her coffin, he'll be! I've wondered, ever since he came,
what kind of life my daughter had with him." Her mouth twisted a
little. "Though Godgift was always strong, mind and body. She
could manage him, perhaps. All the same, she wouldn't be the first
woman to die in childbirth because she was tired of being alive. A
shame her boy didn't live, he might have saved Alys this journey.
Well, I'll protect the poor child if I can. They say," Emma added
thoughtfully, "that he's not such a hero on the battlefield, either, for
all his big muscles and his loud voice."

"Even if she were well," said Edith, "one couldn't be sure . . ."

Emma's stick jabbed the water and a trout fled. "How true! No, one can't be sure. Children may not come, or they're girls instead of boys, or they're boys and they die young. Boys often do die young," said Emma with contempt. "Weaklings. I heard that Edward has set Godgift's sons by her first husband aside as possibilities, by the way. Showing sense for once. *They're* weaklings . . . not physically, but that isn't all there is to a man. If he asks your advice again, Edith, and he may do when he sees how ill Alys is, you had best suggest my great-nephew William. He may be Norman and foreign-bred, but at least he's capable!"

"There is a branch in Hungary, is there not?" asked Edith. "I had forgotten them when Edward talked to me . . . descendants of King Ethelred's first marriage before he married you, I believe. If a foreign-bred heir would be acceptable at all, what about them?" She stared at the trout pool. "No one here wants a foreigner," she said. "We hoped to marry Alys to Siward's son. Their children would have been . . . nearly home produce!"

"The other branch is at the Magyar court, you are correct," Emma said. "There's a grandson of Ethelred's, and his family. But they may well be too foreign by now. You are correct there too. And we know nothing about them. At least William we know something about, and one of the things we know is that he's a strong ruler. There is nothing against him but his Norman upbringing. But what are the alternatives? One of your own brothers could provide an English succession, but Edward will never consent to that."

"No," agreed Edith, and with the candour she felt free to use only in Emma's company, added in a tone of frank regret: "Sweyn put an end to that."

Emma smiled grimly, but their talk was at an end, for the sound of feet and male voices was approaching. Ralph of Mantes and Count Eustace were sauntering towards them, fresh from hawking, a falcon still on Eustace's arm.

"How is my sister, grandmamma?" Ralph asked, his round, pleasant features serious. He had been distressed by Alys's malady.

Eustace of Boulogne laughed. He was black-haired and florid and growing massive in his thirties. But he kept limber with hunting and his gold-ringed arms were filled out with muscle. His health was aggressive. It was five years since Eustace of Boulogne had last had a cold. "Alys is well enough, boy. She makes too much of little ailments, but a husband will take her mind off them. We'd best be talking of marriage dates soon, what do you say, Lady Emma? I've come a long way to see my daughter married."

Emma glared at her son-in-law. "Your daughter isn't going to be married."

"Eh? What do you mean?"

"I mean, your daughter isn't going to be married!" said Emma wrathfully. "You've come a long way, Eustace, for nothing, and you may as well go home. Why did you ever start out, with that poor child? Your daughter, Eustace, is *dying*!"

4 ✠ *The Day of Destiny*

Eric the Merchant's day of destiny was a fair day in August—tranquil, warm and blue, with a trace of mist in the early hours. The sea at dawn was coloured turquoise tipped with silver, and across it the path of the rising sun lay flashing gold. But if its beauty seemed to Eric charged with the unearthly, and significant of mighty changes, he did not pay the idea much attention. It was of a kind alien to him, and besides, he had work to do.

Not that he felt very much like doing it. A consignment of silks and gemstones had come, to be taken to London by ship for Rolf to sell there. It must be sorted, valued, and put aboard. Eric slid from his pallet, fussing. He hoped the hired oarsmen were all honest. He hoped that the rest of the cargo, which was largely wine, would travel well. He heard that these heavy red wines—it was another of Rolf's new ventures—sometimes didn't. He dressed and broke his fast quickly, looking with distaste at the blackened fire-marks on the walls of his hall, and the bare places where the ruined tapestries had been. Nothing had been done about them yet. He could not summon the energy, for all Rolf's urging. He would move to the other hall soon, as he had said on the day of the disaster. He would give up merchanting.

He was still in the grip of the inertia which had come on him that day in his warehouse. He was even late in rising. Rolf had gone out some time ago. With reluctance and weariness in his step, Eric at last went after him.

Even the exceptional quality of the new consignment could not rouse him. His mind refused to make its accustomed leap from merchandise in the present to profit in the future, but instead lingered foolishly on the beauty of garnet and amethyst, and on the texture and charm of the little crystal bottles and the carved ivory ornaments which formed a makeweight part of the package. He was like a traveller who had passed irrevocably from one kind of country— a forest like Andred, perhaps—to some other, quite different, kind, like a seashore or a plain. He was distrait, and when Rolf suggested asking prices, his father did not question them.

Loading went ahead. Rolf would sleep on board tonight, ready for a dawn departure. A number of other merchants who had stakes in the mixed cargo would go with him. The harbour was busy, Eric noted. Count Eustace's ships, which had lain there since the count's memorable arrival, were presumably being made ready for the homeward journey. The men were scrubbing planks and checking ropes. Dover was obviously in for another visitation. Mercifully, the Flemings had come and gone without incident. They had arrived late, tired and seasick after a bad crossing, stayed in the town only briefly, and paid their bills honestly. Eric had had to house six. As guests they had been quiet enough. But these days even such visitors as the Flemings were not welcome to him. He hoped devoutly that Eustace's returning retinue would keep away from him. He had not even troubled to seek a glimpse of Tostig Godwinsson's Flemish bride as she rode out of Dover, though Rolf said she was beautiful.

"Have to find you a wife some time, Rolf," he had said shortly, "if female charms are impressing you so much."

"Some other time," said Rolf. He had a standing arrangement with a girl in a harbour tavern and was perfectly content with it.

The work finished at last, Rolf said: "Father, go home. It's midafternoon and you've toiled since daybreak. Make the thralls serve you a good, hot meal and get some rest."

"You are sure there's no more to do? You have the tallies safe?"

"Three times checked," said Rolf firmly. "And the cargo is well stowed. I suppose we *might* meet a tempest sailing up the Thames!"

"Then godspeed and a safe, profitable journey," Eric said, and parted from him with a brief embrace. The hall, when he got back to it, was quiet and empty, as he had wished it to be on the day when it was so stormily invaded. He sat down to a meal of roast goose wing and cabbage cooked in meat juice, with strong, sweet mead to wash it down.

He was still at his platter of goose and cabbage when the hammering at the outer gate began.

He laid down the trencher of bread on which his next mouthful was poised. Steaming and inviting though it was, he set it back on the board. The noise grew louder and he heard the elderly thrall, Wyn, grumbling as she passed the hall door on her way to answer it. "All right, all right!" Her voice was raised as she crossed the courtyard. "Can't hobble no faster! Who's there, then? Who's there?"

The answer, Eric realised with a sinking of the heart and a surge of anger in the veins, was in French. He went to the door to hear better. The demands were now being couched in ill-pronounced English; evidently Wyn had failed to understand the first ones. She had also failed to open the gate. She was looking round at Eric for his guidance.

"We are the men of Count Eustace of Boulogne! We need lodgings for the night! We catch the tide tomorrow! Open up!"

Eric wiped his mouth and walked scowling across to join Wyn. The sight of his gate, firmly barred as it was now kept most of the time, cheered him. It gave him a sense of protection.

"There are other halls in this town!" He shouted back at the importunate ones.

The hammering began again. Something heavy and metallic was being used, by the sound of it. "We want to stay *here*!" That was in a voice that struck him as familiar. He associated it with a cold and arrogant face, belonging to a young Norman knight, the ringleader of the uproar last time. "We were turned out of here for lesser men once!" the voice reminded him. "This time we want our rights!"

The blood pounded in Eric's ears. "What rights? This is my house!" he retorted.

"And there's naught for them to eat, neither," muttered Wyn.

"No stranger has any rights in my hall!" Eric growled in reply.

"Open up!" It was the young knight's voice again. "Are the count's men, the king's guests, to be kept waiting in the road until dark?"

"If you want to wait, that's your affair!" shouted Eric. The stout oaken bars on the gate gave him courage. "There's room with the thanes where you stayed last time. But you don't come in here! You did damage enough to take months to put right!"

The pounding resumed again and now there was no doubt of

the instrument, for several curved axe-blades this time penetrated the wood. The gate had not really been built with assault in mind, and it consisted of only one stout layer of wood. Two, with the grain running opposite ways, would have been needed to defy an axe. Before Eric's horrifed eyes, the timber began to split. Behind him, Wyn whimpered.

Eric himself began to shake. But help was being roused. The two male thralls, Wyn's elderly husband and her simple-minded but harmless and hulking son, had come to his side clutching staves, and the old man had also brought Eric's sword. It spent most of its time hanging unused on the wall, and Eric was anything but practised with it; but still it was there, reassuring to feel in his hand, and thank the saints he had always kept it in good order. He took it gratefully. The old man was now climbing on a pile of empty barrels and shouting to someone over the palisade on the far side. Answering shouts announced that the neighbours were taking a hand. Sounds of altercation, local voices mingling with the French ones, rose on the other side of the gate. There was a pause.

The young knight spoke again, more or less pacifically this time. "We are of course sorry for the damage done last time. There will be no repetition. But we insist that you lodge us this time. Be so good as to open this gate and admit us."

Eric hesitated, looking doubtfully at his sword.

The knight, as a manipulator of men, had no great future before him. He now added a rider. "Refuse and we break in! Take your choice!"

That settled it.

"My choice is to sleep in my own house without guests to-night!" Eric retorted. The idea of allowing the Frenchmen to enter was now infuriating and terrifying in equal degrees. "This is my hall and none has any rights here but me!" he bellowed.

"Go to it, Eric!" cried a friendly voice outside. It was that of a local thane. "They're not lodging with us, either! We had our fill of them last time, like you!"

A consensus of agreement rose into the air following this announcement. It explained why the Frenchmen were so determined to lodge with Eric. They had evidently outworn their welcome too thoroughly the first time and were now desperate for a roof. It hardened his resolve that the roof should not be his, and the knowledge that he was not defending his house unaided steadied his nerve.

"I'm taking no guests in tonight!" he reiterated.

There was a scuffle outside, some French oaths, some running feet, and some laughter from farther away. But the attack on the gate redoubled, and Eric quaked afresh as axe-heads broke through in a dozen places with ominous splits below them.

"Best let them in," quavered Wyn. "They'll maybe quieten if we do."

"No!" Eric gripped his sword with both hands. The hulking young thrall came to stand beside him. "They won't quieten," Eric said. "They'll more likely kill us."

The gateposts swayed again and the earth at the base of the left-hand one moved. It gave suddenly and the gate fell in, dragging the other post with it. It revealed the street outside, with a crowd of helmeted soldiers and another crowd of glowering townsfolk beyond them. Half a dozen knights leapt over the debris and faced him. He stood his ground, frightened but obstinate.

"Leave my courtyard at once!"

"Where we come from, peasant," said the young knight with contempt, "no man holds property except by leave of his lord and no serf calls any courtyard his. The lord and any guests of his have rights there whenever they choose. The king is your lord and we are his guests. Now stand out of our way. You lodge us well, we'll pay fairly. Obstruct us further and you'll learn your place. What's for dinner here tonight?"

"Blood pudding and bone meal!" said Eric. He was on the edge of death but he could not turn away from it. The undertow of some monstrous tide had hold of him. His inertia had turned morbid, put it beyond his power to change his chosen course. Blindly he confronted the cold-eyed knights with the faces of metal, nosepieces and cheekflaps, because he could not think of anything else to do. It actually cost less effort of will to go on being furious than to stop. "And it'll be your blood and your bones," he said. "Peasant, am I?" The word the young knight had used was the French term for a thrall.

The knight stepped forward and Eric struck him with the flat of his sword. It clanged on the Frenchman's chain mail. In the mixed crowd beyond the gate he saw staves and swords lifted in a clattering thicket, and somewhere there was the snort and tramp of horses;

more French soldiers were arriving to uphold their friends, no doubt. Someone gave an old Dover war cry and it was answered. The young thrall struck out with the stave and two French knights felled him. The thrall screamed and blood spattered over Eric's feet. In an instant the courtyard became full of fighting, struggling, bawling men. He found that he was holding his sword correctly, was using it, and had found a mark with it somewhere in the offensive young knight's body. A good blade in a strong hand could pierce chain mail. He was stronger than he thought, he told himself. He had long despised the men of the sword and put his faith in the abacus instead, but his ancestors had been bladesmen and it seemed that they were with him now, telling him what to do. He smelt blood. It was that of the young knight, who had fallen on top of him, knocking him to his knees. As he pushed the body aside and struggled up, someone above him cried: *"Roger! Roger est mort!"* and he was ringed by hard, iron-helmed, iron-faced soldiers. He heard Dover voices behind them, but help could not reach him now. Wyn was somewhere among them, crying her fallen son's name.

A mailed hand shot out and wrenched away his sword. He tried to get out his belt-knife, but it was too late. Still, he swore in the metal faces. His ancestral voices were not silenced. They sang in his blood and in his ears, deep and compulsive as the deep rhythms of the sea.

"So they give churls weapons here, do they?" one of the soldiers said coolly, raising his own weapon.

Eric, sinking to the earth of the courtyard with his body wavering to water and the bright sky dimming above him and a pain beyond belief thrusting, thrusting into his side, was aware that he was dying after all with his fortune unfulfilled, that the witch had lied indeed, and that all the years of his life had been thrown away. But it was only a momentary despair. As his world went out, it ceased to matter, for the sea he had yearned for had him at last —huge, powerful, shadowy, and eternal—and its song was of slumber and its tides were rocking him into peace.

His short despair was in any case misplaced. As the course of a river may be turned by a boulder rolled into its path, so the course of history, in a torrent of old hatreds and new ambitions, now poured down against Eric Merchant's defence of his gates, and the channel that the stream would run in was forever changed.

Tostig's wedding feast, after being delayed first by two guests who could not come at the time first mooted, and then by Judith succumbing to a feverish chill, was now safely under way and turning out a zestfully overcrowded success. Gytha of Wessex sat where she could keep an eye on the servers and hoped that the supplies of ale would last. They should: such a brewing had rarely been seen even on Edward's coronation eve. But the consumption was heavy. Siward of Northumbria, for one thing, was drinking enough for a dozen.

Siward, his tongue well loosened by the bride-ale, was dominating the company at this moment, stating—rather to Gytha's indignation—that they used to have merrier times at these affairs when he was young.

"No wedding . . . if you believe me . . . no wedding was reckoned lawful till one fight had broken out, one mad oath had been sworn, and one guest had dropped dead of apoplexy, as young Harthacnut did!" He regarded with disapproval the bright garments and curled hair of the younger generation of males. "Young men aren't what they were in my day!"

"Hmm," said a woman near Gytha. "Some of the womenfolk don't regret the change. We'll keep our men longer this way."

"Yes," said Gytha, and sent up a silent prayer of thanks for the thirty happy years she had had with Godwin and could not now be robbed of, whatever lay ahead. She did not herself know why those words "whatever lay ahead" had drifted into her mind. She would have liked to think about it and find out, but her youngest daughter, Elfgiva, sitting beside her, was speaking. "I wish Edith were here, mother. It's a shame we're not all present."

"To be the wife of the king means that one must always put the king's business first," said Gytha quickly. She knew it was not quite that; Edward would have sent Edith or come with her, had this been a wedding in a household he thought friendly. But the gulf between him and his wife's kin was widening, year by year, and not all Edith's efforts or Godwin's patient service could prevent it. *Whatever lay ahead.* It was from Edith's absence, and the cause of it, that that thought had come.

Elfgiva said suddenly: "Mother, are you well?" and Gytha hurriedly collected herself. She smiled at her daughter. It was usually she who asked Elfgiva that question, for alone of all the family, Elfgiva was not strong. "I was . . . looking back and remembering my own marriage feast, my dear."

At least all the others were here. At the chief table sat Tostig, sturdy and yellow-curled, with Judith beside him in white and blue; her amber-toned hair was veiled, to be admired by Tostig only from now on. She was a lively girl, laughing with her groom. Gytha was pleased with Judith.

The match was politically valuable; also, the two were in love. Baldwin, learning that the penniless young stranger to whom he had given casual shelter as to so many others was in fact a son of Godwin's and moreover that he had been covertly courting Judith, had sat down heavily on the nearest bench, gasping with astonishment. Then, suddenly appreciative, he had roared with laughter and consented. He had sent Judith off royally arrayed, doing honour to her new family. She was chuckling now at Tostig's realistic mimicry of the Abbot Sparhafoc's reaction when Champart, returning from Rome whence he had travelled to get papal confirmation of his own appointment to Canterbury and Sparhafoc's to London, had announced that the pope had refused to ratify the abbot's.

"Oh, my brother in Christ," Sparhafoc had said, "that you should commit such injustice towards me that never harmed you!"

"It's the pope's blessing that is withheld, not mine," Champart had pointed out.

"But since he has never met me, to whom did he look for a reference?" Sparhafoc had said sorrowfully.

Edward had upheld Sparhafoc, who still held the London bishopric, pope or no pope. People still, however, tended to call him "abbot." It annoyed him.

Tostig's keening rendition rose above the general talk, and Judith's eyes were on him in such frank appreciation that Sweyn shouted down the table: "Tostig, you'd better take her to your chamber! See how she looks at you! You shouldn't let dinner stand when it's ready to eat. But mind she doesn't take you near a fishpond on the way!"

"She wouldn't trip *me* into a pond, would you, darling?" said Tostig smugly. "But . . ."—he cocked his head at the sound of a horn outside—". . . we can't leave the feast while the guests are still arriving. Who will this be, I wonder?"

But the door was already being thrust open and the new arrivals were entering unheralded. Elfgiva caught her breath and said: "But mother, they're not . . ."

"Not guests," said Gytha. *Whatever lay ahead.* Foreboding rose up in her. Six housecarles were escorting a thane, and she knew the thane. Thored of Alford, he was called, and he had once organised the slaughter of six hundred men on a hillside at Gildenford. And although he had once done Godwin a service of a sort, he was not Godwin's friend.

Thored was handing a scroll to the earl, speaking as he did so in a rumbling undertone. The hall had become quiet, sensing something wrong. Gytha caught the words "King Edward."

Godwin read the scroll. His face hardened, lost colour. He spoke, and his voice rang through the hall although he did not shout. "This is my son's marriage feast. Does the king know that?"

"Yes, my lord," said Thored, and shrugged, take it or leave it, as once at Gildenford he had shrugged before he said: "I can use force."

"And I am expected to abandon my guests? Like that? *Now?*"

"Yes, my lord."

"What is this affray the letter mentions, between the count's men and the Dover folk? Why is it so urgent?"

"I am only the king's messenger," said Thored. "He said your presence was required at once. I know no more than that."

Gytha had sat still throughout this exchange. This, for sure, was the start of the unknown thing she had feared. From this moment on her husband, her sons, were setting course for sorrow. The hall in its bridal garlands became full of evil images—of flowers that wilted and shadows that made young faces old. As Godwin came to her she knew that her eyes were frightened, and it did not help that when he saw it he showed no surprise and uttered no reassurance.

"Gytha, I am summoned to the king at Gloucester. Harold will ride with me and wait for me outside the town. My town of Dover has been up in arms against a royal visitor, I hear, and I am to answer for it. It must be serious or I wouldn't be called from a wedding feast."

Gytha said: "Take enough men."

5 ✖ Unlawful Command

Edward was in one of his cold rages: white face, mouth in a thin straight line, eyes stone-pale. He sat motionless, awaiting Godwin. Among the silent housecarles Brand felt that an unwary movement, a scraped boot or a cough, could call upon the culprit's head a royal anathema like a bolt of lightning. By contrast, Eustace of Boulogne would not sit down but was stamping about the hall in a bull-fury, his thick neck suffused. The wounded Frenchmen, however, arranged on benches along one wall as a display of human evidence, seemed pleased with him. He was showing concern for them, they considered. They all sported gruesome bandages, three had arms in slings, and four were on pallet stretchers. They were not, moreover, the only casualties.

"The coffins," said Edward to his father-in-law without preamble as Godwin strode up the hall to within speaking distance, "are in the chapel."

"You may see them if you wish," said Robert Champart, seated near the king's chair. Bishop Stigand and Sparhafoc were also present, seated apart, grave-faced. Brand saw Stigand shoot a glance of warning at Godwin. Stigand was always the peacemaker. But peace would take a deal of making this time. Edward's face was proof of that.

And Godwin too was angry. He had taken off his helmet, but he gripped it under his right arm as though ready to don it at an instant's notice. His mouth tightened when Edward spoke. He was about to reply when Eustace marched up to him and got in first.

"What have you to say for the behaviour of your township, Godwin, earl and upholder of the king's peace?" He thrust his head forward. "Eh? Well? Look at my men here! What have you to say?"

"That the men of Dover seem to have given a good account of themselves," said Godwin bluntly. "Why did they find it necessary?"

The replies were noisy and confused. Eustace and his men all shouted at once. "Lawful request . . . unprovoked attack . . . ought to be wearing woad . . . low-born upstarts . . ." were among the more lucid phrases. Godwin waited until the uproar had faded and then said to Edward: "I would like to hear the tale from the beginning."

Edward said shortly: "My lord Eustace's men needed lodgings in Dover before they sailed for home. The Dover citizens first refused them and then set upon them. As hospitality to the traveller is a first law in a civilised land, and hospitality to the king's own kinsmen doubly so, their actions cannot be defended. The men of Dover are out of hand, it seems."

Stigand, who had been fidgeting his feet, said: "My lord, I think there may be another side to it."

Eustace glared. Edward said: "Well? Speak your mind, bishop."

"I believe that when my lord Eustace passed through Dover with his men on their way here, there was some kind of accident. A fire was started in one of their hosts' halls. The one where the trouble began this time, as far as I can make out. The townsfolk may have been nervous . . . armed men can be alarming to them, you know. And fear can make men violent."

Eustace had been slowly swelling up during this gentle exposition. He now burst out. "I know about the accident! A little fire, quickly put out. The hall was scarcely damaged, no one hurt beyond a scratch or a blister or two! A common domestic incident! And God's Teeth, we were ready to compensate! Is that an excuse for *this*?" He pointed a thick forefinger at his damaged knights. "For this, *I* want compensation!"

Godwin said: "What compensation are you asking, my lord Eustace?"

Edward stood up.

"The razing of the town of Dover to the ground, my lord," he said.

Godwin stared at him. He said: "I did not hear you correctly, my lord. Please repeat that."

Edward did so.

"That is absurd," said Godwin evenly.

"Is it?" The king's anger seemed tinged now with triumph. "I have watched you, Godwin, through many years. I have seen how your ambition led you. First you dreamed of your grandchild as my heir. Then of the succession for a son of your own. You have fed your sons on such imaginings! And I have watched your jealousy grow, jealousy of anyone else I dare to make my friend, of those who were my friends when I was an exile, when if I had set foot within reach of you, you would have sold me to death or torment! I know what happened at Dover and so do you! You gave orders, did you not? That the followers of Count Eustace, whom you hate because I saw in his family a chance to find an heir of my own blood, should not be made welcome. A petty, spiteful act. You wanted my lord of Boulogne's men insulted and treated as nithings and left to camp by the roadside, to gratify your hatred, your ambition, and your resentment, the puny rages of your greedy, grasping, mean little soul!"

"Nonsense," said Godwin, still calm. He had spent the time of Edward's enormous outburst in thoughtfully scanning faces for the origin of the king's remarkable theory, and in a secret—but not secret enough—flash of joy in someone's eyes, he had found it. "More of your poison?" he asked Champart. "I heard the other tale you put about, that I was plotting against the king's life, and I found its source. I take it that this is another lie in the same series."

Champart looked taken aback. Sparhafoc, predictably, looked shocked. Stigand momentarily smiled.

"I see," said Godwin, "that it is. Or you would deny it. So you're still churchman enough to recognise the sin of lying on a few occasions!"

Edward spun round, swished his long mantle out of the way of his heels, and resumed his seat. He raised a hand, palm out, and commanded: "Quiet!" Silence fell.

"We have heard enough squabbling. There is no doubt of the truth. Godwin, you are here to learn what reparation is demanded, not to argue a case for your barbarians, or to make counteraccusations. You yourself shall be my instrument to exact retribution for the crime you yourself ordered. You will take a force of men—the royal household shall lend you some if necessary!—and you will sack Dover. Burn every house and every blade of corn. Slaughter every cow and hen and pig and burn the carcasses. Kill those who resist you. Drive the rest forth to find shelter where they may, or sell themselves to get it. I will myself set a new fort there and begin the town anew with trustier inhabitants. You have leave to go now. You may return when the work is done, and report upon it."

"My lord," said Stigand desperately, "as a Christian king . . ."

"You have leave to go, Godwin," said the king once again. He ignored Stigand.

"I will *not* go," said Godwin coldly.

The hall held its breath. Even Eustace was silent. Brand found his limbs suddenly ashake with longing to leave the ranks of the royal housecarles and once again stand beside Godwin. So heartily did he uphold Godwin now. Thank God he had not yielded to Hild's urging and betrayed his erstwhile lord. For now he could only honour him. Godwin was speaking again.

"My lord, this is a judgment given in anger, and it is not just. It is not just that a whole town should suffer for the deeds of the few, that children and maidens and wives and old men and babies should be cast into the wilderness. I pray you to take further thought. Let us let the matter rest until tomorrow."

"We have taken enough thought." Edward's voice was remote. "The judgment is final. Will you, or will you not, obey?"

"Sweet saints!" Brand whispered, imploringly, within himself. "Don't let him yield! Hild's brother lives there. And Dover's people are Godwin's own folk!"

"I am your sworn man, my lord Edward," said Godwin's steady voice. "Your right hand in any lawful command you give me. But this is not a lawful command. It runs contrary to the laws of God, made for Christian men. I cannot obey it. I am responsible for the safety of the folk of Dover. They pay their dues to me, they answer my calls to arms, and they look to me for safeguarding. I would be a forsworn nithing if I abandoned them."

Edward stared at him, frozenly. Godwin's head went back. He returned to the king a look as cold and hard as Edward's own, swung round, and strode out of the hall. He was gone before anyone moved or spoke. Edward gave no order to prevent him. Godwin's men were outside, with his horse. From within the hall, the departing hoof-beats could be heard. Sparhafoc was the first to break the silence.

"Oh, it grieves me to speak so to those who are greater than I. But it is true that he has Dover in his keeping as a shepherd has his sheep. How can he play the wolf to them?"

"I had a tame raven once," said Champart, "that croaked words the way you do, without understanding. Look into your own heart and see if you uphold him out of virtue or the lesser motive of fearing your noble kinsman may lose his power. Remember you are the king's man first and Godwin's cousin second, Sparhafoc. Get back to London, my friend, and make the crown which is your business. You're a good enough goldsmith, at least. Keep to that."

The tight-strung atmosphere in the hall eased. Exchanges between Champart and Sparhafoc, and the sound of Sparhafoc in sanctimonious harangue, were part of the normal world, were something to smile at. The anger seemed to have gone out of Edward. He said: "Yes, return to London, Sparhafoc. You have spoken your mind. You can go with your conscience clear." The king sounded abstracted. He was not, it seemed, really interested in Sparhafoc. He was thinking. But he roused suddenly as Stigand rose, and followed the Bishop of London towards the door. "Stigand!"

Stigand turned. "I too wish to leave, my lord," he said quietly. "On this matter I sympathise with Bishop Sparhafoc. And with Godwin. I too say that this judgment was ill-done."

"You will remain, Stigand! We may need you!" Edward snapped. "As for your opinions on our judgment, when did we request them?" He tapped the arms of his chair meditatively. "Word must be sent to Leofric and Siward to muster their men and come to us. The more men there are here, the fewer Godwin can get his hands on."

"You think he'll call his army out?" Eustace demanded, brows beetling. He looked bewildered. The wrongs of his men had been somehow edged aside and he did not understand how.

"Of course," said Edward, looking pleased about it. "In his place, wouldn't you?"

As Edith had long known, and Alys in her sick chamber was now discovering, the tough and astringent mother of the king could be tender towards woes if she thought them big enough to warrant it. Her presence now was comfort and support to Edith, down whose face tears of helpless fury streamed as she sat storming on the settle in Emma's apartment.

"If he were ten thousand times my husband, how can I be with him in this?" she demanded. "He has summoned my father like a thrall and accused him of things he has not done, and given him orders that would shame a Viking berserker on a raid! There's no love or duty in the world would make me support him now! I know he still grieves for Alfred! Well, I have brothers, too. I understand. But to order the sacking of a town full of innocent people is just as wicked as what was done to Alfred! What's the difference? He calls himself a Christian king. All piety and good works and hours spent before the altar at nights, even when we were first married! And now this! *Christian*! *Pious*! He's cruel and vicious and *weak*!" Sobbing frantically, Edith hammered her fists on the settle. "*Weak*!" she wailed again.

"I know," said Emma grimly. "So was Ethelred."

Edith gulped, wiping her face.

"But he's cleverer than his father was," Emma added thoughtfully. "One must admit that."

"Cleverer? To think my father would obey that vile command? What was clever in that?"

"But, my dear daughter," said Emma with twisted amusement in her voice, "he didn't think it. That was the cleverness. He knew your father would defy him. That was what the order intended to provoke. If Godwin had gone off and sacked Dover, believe me, my dear, my son would have had a seizure out of shock!"

Edith was open-mouthed. "But . . . why . . . what?"

"He may be all the terrible things you have just said, but this particular affair isn't proof of them. It was merely a ruse to make your father take a stand against him. I am sorry, my dear. If it's any comfort to you, Dover was never in much danger. It's your father who is in danger. And maybe . . . you."

They sat with the letter between them, which Hild had just read aloud. The merchant who had brought it from Dover had gone. "My father . . ." Hild said.

"But Rolf is safe, since he sent the letter," Brand said. "And he says your father died quickly, with a fine, gallant finish that you can be proud of."

"Godwin wouldn't sack Dover," said Hild, eyes brimming. "I'm grateful for that. You were right to keep your oath, after all. But . . . will the king do it instead?"

"I think not. He has his hands full with Godwin now. Hild, he was magnificent. Godwin, I mean. I never loved him as I did today! You should have seen him, standing up to the king for the sake of the Dover folk!"

"I know. And Rolf in Dover is safe because of it." She let Brand put his arms round her. Resting her head against him, she said: "It's queer that my father . . . almost started the fighting, from what the letter says. He was a very peaceable man, you know. He only wanted to be a merchant thane and now he's dead, disappointed. The prophecy won't come true after all. You knew about that? That a gipsy once told him he would change the course of history?"

"Yes, Rolf told me. But . . ." Brand was thoughtful. "That fight he started . . . it does sound as though he began it . . . ! Because of that, the Earl of Wessex and the King of England are calling their men to arms. God knows what the outcome will be. But it's just possible, Hild, my love, that change the course of history is exactly what your father has done, after all!"

6 ✕ "My Lord...
There Is Something More"

The royal hall by the silver-flowing Thames was unlike any other hall in England. The palisade that guarded it was ordinary enough—stout stakes close-pressed together and pointed on top, with a ditch on either side of the bank that carried them. But the hall itself was stone-built, plastered white within and elegantly decorated with religious murals. The guest and sleeping quarters adjoined it. The lamp and torch brackets were many of them gilded, and the place was full of finely carved settles, the most costly embroidered hangings, and the sleekest furs. It was a rather unlikely place to choose for making a stand against a foe. "Too ladylike and much too pious-looking," said Siward of Northumbria frankly, arriving last, since he had to journey from the north to answer the royal summons.

The bustle of his coming had barely subsided. Brand, who had been renewing his acquaintance with friends among Siward's men over ale and chicken legs, had laughed at the old earl's disparagements. It was the first time he had felt like laughing for what seemed a century, he confided to Longshanks and Pathfinder, and another century would probably pass before he laughed again.

Edward was pacing the floor of the hall, pausing now and then to look out at the shining river. On the far bank, to the east, hung a smoky fume from the forges and cooking fires of the encampment

round Godwin's Southwark hall. The sides had polarised. Stigand of
Winchester, whose arrival had coincided with Siward's, and who
had not changed out of his travel-stained clothes yet, was trying de-
terminedly to talk to the back of Edward's head.

"Your lady mother has been installed in the main guest chamber, my lord, on Queen Edith's orders. She stood up well to the
journey by litter. She is tired, but no worse, the physician says."

"I am grateful, of course, for the care you take of my family,
Stigand," said Edward, still contemplating the river. "But she was
safer in Winchester."

"I doubt it, my lord. We could spare only a handful of men to
guard her, and Godwin might have thought her a worthwhile . . . er
. . . pawn."

"She'd be quite at home with the Earl of Wessex. They're old
comrades in conspiracy."

"My son!" said Aldred of Worcester with gentle protest from
the window where he too watched the smoke of Godwin's muster.
Edward snorted.

They were not alone in the hall. At its inmost end, with a chess
game between them to which they were not attending properly, sat
an elderly housecarle in the character of a guard, and Wulfnoth
Godwinsson. Wulfnoth, his nineteen-year-old face sullen, would not
respond to the other man's attempts to be friendly. Nearby sat a
young nursemaid with three-year-old Hakon Sweynsson on her
knee, trying to amuse him with a toy horse. And because of Hakon,
Brand had come back to the hall, leaving his friends, although he
was not on duty. Since Hakon's arrival two days ago, his anxious
uncle had dogged the nursemaid's steps. Brand did not really fear
that Edward would harm so young a child, even though Hakon was
nominally a hostage. But he had to know, by the day, by the hour,
that Hakon was still safe.

"In fact," Stigand was saying, "it would be proper to send hostages to Godwin, though I would not recommend that the Lady
Emma be one of them! He will not come to his trial unless we send
sureties and an oath of safe-conduct. He says he wishes to clear himself of the charge of treachery and to make his peace with you, but
he dare not come with only the twelve men you permit him and no
other safeguard. So he said this morning when I broke my journey
to speak with him."

"I'm not in the habit of treachery," said Edward. He turned his

back to the window, a winter man: grey cloak, silvered hair, pale
face, pale eyes, voice of ice. "But if he refuses to stand his trial,
I shall be pleased enough. What is this news that Sweyn is still
with him? I outlawed Sweyn outright. He should be at sea by
now."

"He won't leave his father," said Stigand firmly. "Which I can
admire."

"Godwin has dazzled you, I'm afraid, as he has dazzled so
many," said Robert Champart, seated behind a table strewn with
maps and tallies. "No doubt his real reason for refusing to face trial
is that he fears the verdict. He dare not swear his innocence before
God, or put it to the ordeal."

"He gave hostages to prove his good faith," said Aldred.

"Knowing that the king, more honour to him for it, would be
unwilling to injure such young folk." Champart dipped his quill and
resumed the figurework on which he was engaged. "He's a fox, our
Godwin. Don't let him fool you. You can trust no one of that house.
Our lord Edward made Godwin's cousin Sparhafoc the royal goldsmith, a high honour! But Sparhafoc has gone to Godwin's camp.
He is supposed to be starting work on the king's new crown. One
wonders if he means to make it in Godwin's workshop! I can only
hope it isn't poisoned!"

A door crashing back and heavy footsteps heralded the appearance of Siward, fresh from a bath and a change of garments. His
tread shook the floor as he strode in. His fur mantle was thrown
back from one shoulder to show his armour under it; his wiry grey
hair and beard were combed tidily. He was in good order from head
to heels, except for his temper.

"So!" He stopped short to survey the tense prelates and the
pale, distant king. "We're all here! Eustace is down in the courtyard
trying to turn squads of raw peasant fyrdmen into warriors and beat
their ploughshares into swords for them! Leofric's got his men at axe-
play so hard there won't be a sharp edge among them if it gets to
real fighting! And when the wind's in the right quarter there's
enough clanging and shouting from Godwin's direction to make it
plain he's doing the same thing. I'm a warrior and I don't turn down
a good fight in a hurry, but I never saw a madder mustering than
this. Two sides are sitting opposite each other making faces, and it's
plain neither wants to fight. So shouldn't we all stop and think what
we're doing?"

"Waiting for Godwin to lay down his arms and come to trial," said Stigand. "As for not wanting to fight, we've half the men in England camped round these two halls. If it comes to war, we'd lose most of them."

"Aye, I know. And then the land lies open to any interested marauder—like that Hardraada, for instance—like a naked man asleep." Siward threw himself into a seat. "I'm just an ignorant berserker. What I can't make out is what Godwin's *done*!"

Champart tried to enlighten him, but he cut the prelate short. "No, you've said your bit before. Now I'll say mine. I know about the Dover affair. Well, maybe they gave offence and maybe not, but Godwin'd not sack his own town. He couldn't obey that and stay honest, so he disobeyed and called his men up in self-defence. In the same circumstances I'd have done the selfsame thing and so would you all. Would you sack Worcester on anyone's orders, Bishop Aldred?"

"No," said Aldred.

"You forget," said Champart. "Godwin ordered the Dover folk to shut their doors to Eustace's men in the first place."

"He did not. That's a lie," said Siward.

Aldred said: "Do you know that or only guess it?"

"I know it, damn ye!" The Earl of Northumbria jerked a thumb unexpectedly towards Brand, who caught the gesture with the tail of his eye and stood up uneasily. "My men were talking to *him* a while ago and now they've talked to me. He's got a wife from Dover and she's had news from a brother there. Here, you!" barked Siward. "Come here!"

Brand came slowly forward. "Tell us," said Edward quietly, "what you know of Dover and how you know it."

"My wife's father was killed in the trouble and her brother sent word to tell her. He said that their father died quickly and that . . ."

"Not that!" said Siward testily. "We can guess all that. How did the message say the fighting started? Did it tell you that?"

"Yes. Rolf said his father was frightened by some of Count Eustace's men when they demanded lodgings." He shot a quick look at the king but Edward's face was blank. He was clearly listening, however. Embarrassingly, they all were. "It is true that they stayed at his father's hall on the journey in and caused a fire there. I was present when it happened. Rolf says his father was afraid to let them in again. That's how it began."

"There was no word of orders from Earl Godwin?"

Brand shook his head.

"Well," said Siward, "it makes sense to me. It makes a lot more sense than Godwin giving the townsfolk daft orders. If our count's men went throwing their weight about in Dover, shouting and giving offence to freemen who weren't their chattels, and got a bellyful of pikeheads for it, that's no fault of Godwin's. Most men say please when they ask for a bed." He grinned. "I've a nice polished skull on my doorpost at home, let me tell ye. Its owner tried asking for a lodging in a way I reckoned a mite rude. He got a bed all right! Six feet long, six feet deep, and a trifle damp, in a handy bit of ground." He looked straight at Edward, bluff, hulking, genial, completely honest and quite unimpressed by Edward's royal estate. "If you want my advice, my lord," he said, "we'll all pack up and go home."

Champart said: "We had information that the resistance was made on Godwin's orders, from what we thought a reliable source."

"Ah. Nameless, no doubt. Never trust a man who won't give his name. It's hard, later on, to find him again if ye need to make him repeat himself," said Siward. "Or," he added deliberately, "to prove that he exists."

Edward said, cutting in: "This man here is related to the boy Hakon Sweynsson, is he not? Brand Woodcutter? Brand, attend me to my chamber. I have questions for you."

The king's apartment smelt of new tapestry and glowed with its unfaded silks. The rushes were deep and a small brazier with a fir-cone blaze in it dispersed the faint September chill. On one wall there were no hangings; a rood hung there above a little altar. Edward knelt briefly before it while Brand stood stiffly near the door. He had never been alone with Edward before, or even been addressed directly by him.

Never until now, either, had he looked closely at the king, this man to whom he had sworn himself. Edward hitherto had been a remote figure, a proper person to serve, but an office rather than a man of flesh with griefs and sorrows and doubts. Lately indeed, menacing the people of Dover, he had acquired a stark air. Now, seeing Edward as a man for the first time, Brand read weariness and conflict in his king's face. For the first time he felt a movement in him of unforced loyalty, of kindness for his royal lord. In spite of Godwin. In spite of Dover. It was difficult to serve two lords, he thought.

Rising from his prayer, Edward said: "The message your wife had from Dover. Did it speak the truth?"

"I should think so, sir."

Edward went to the brazier and stood holding a hand above it, palm down. "You used to serve Earl Godwin, I believe."

"Yes, my lord."

"Give me your opinion of him."

"He taught me all I know of warfare. He is a good teacher. He . . ." Brand was bad at this and knew it. He turned to stock phrases, the common words of praise that every bard put into his songs. "He's open-handed . . . brave. Men follow him willingly." Edward said nothing and he tried again. And this time, unexpectedly, words rose up from his heart. "He seems so alive. As much more alive than an ordinary man, as an ordinary man is more alive than a corpse."

"He has much that I lack," said Edward surprisingly. He moved his hand to and fro. "I try to be a good man. I pray and fast. I give alms to the poor and live cleanly and praise God. When I raise my new West Minster it will be a house of prayer and praise forever. But I have no power to spellbind men. They obey the kingship, not Edward Ethelredson. Few love me. Godwin hardly believes in God at all, and men fling their love before his feet." He spoke wonderingly. Then he smiled. "Perhaps one can have the love of God or man, but not both. Would that be it?"

"My lord of Wessex has little of either now, I think," said Brand with honesty. "Many of his followers have come over to you, have they not?"

"Yes, that's true. I could take him by force if I chose. He has only a few in his camp compared to the numbers in mine. But it could do great harm to the manpower of my realm, and I hesitate. And this information which Earl Siward has just wrung out of you—or rather, the lack of it, for it's what the message does not say that matters—makes me hesitate afresh. Our information was incorrect, perhaps."

He would not discuss the source of it with this mere housecarle.

The question of whether Champart had been misinformed or had lied must wait. He added: "It is possible that Godwin has been unjustly accused. Others have said so."

Brand was silent. The king and his wife Edith were not on speaking terms over this very question, and the whole court knew it. Edith was here in London for her own safety, but she kept to her apartments and never entered the main hall. Her anger was having an effect, perhaps. Edward seemed almost looking for a way to yield with grace.

"Why did you leave Godwin?" the king asked suddenly.

Brand's mouth felt dry. Edward's voice was casual but his light eyes were probing. As if he sensed the presence of secret knowledge in Brand's mind.

"I had a quarrel with Sweyn Godwinsson. I fought him. After that I thought it more fitting to find a new lord. I had been with Earl Beorn, not Godwin himself, for a long time, anyway, and Earl Beorn was killed by Sweyn."

"Ah, yes." Edward looked at him curiously. "Yes, I know who you are. It was your sister that Sweyn took from her abbey. Hakon is your nephew. You had much against Sweyn and you defeated him. Yet you let him live. Why?"

"I bargained his life for the lives of some prisoners of his, who were my friends." Brand had no words for the Godwin glamour, for saying that to put out the life of a Godwin was like putting out the sun. "I knew him as a boy," he said. He added: "I did take his gold off him, what there was of it." He held out his hands on which the emerald and the garnet both shone. "There was an arm-ring and these two finger-rings." Edward moved courteously from the brazier to look. He said: "I gave him that emerald in the first place. So it ended up with you! Well, you won it fairly, all honour to you. The other's a remarkable piece of craftsmanship. It reminds me . . ."

He had leant closer as he spoke. Now he ceased speaking and raised his eyes very slowly to Brand's face. Brand stood rigid. They had been, for just a few easy moments, two men together. Now once again it was king and housecarle, and he did not know why. He felt the distance between them widen, sensed some gathering force of anger in the man before him. He looked down at the garnet ring. The stone was set to form the eye of a serpent, a scaly golden serpent which was swallowing its own tail. Edward said in a voice as bleak as his wintry eyes: "Where in the name of God did you get that ring?"

Since Brand had just told him, it was a hard question to answer respectfully. Woodenly he replied: "From Sweyn Godwinsson, my lord. He had it on a chain round his neck."

"Give it me."

Obediently, Brand drew it off and put it in the outstretched palm. Edward turned it over. He walked away and paced the chamber for a while, as if he were alone. Then he knelt by the rood again and to Brand's astonishment began once more to pray. He remained kneeling for a long time, head buried in his arms. Then he rose, grim-faced, picked up a hand bell, and rang it. A page came, running.

"Fetch me the Lady Emma," said King Edward. "Quickly." As the page hastened away he said: "I was displeased with Bishop Stigand for bringing her here. But now I see the hand of God was guiding him."

They waited. The fir cones crackled and Edward's feet whispered in the rushes as he continued uneasily with his pacing. Presently they heard the slow tapping of Emma's stick and a murmur of female voices. The queen mother entered, attended by three women. Edward said: "Be seated, mother. And tell your ladies to wait outside. You will ring when you want them."

"Edward, what is all this about?" Emma sat with her back very straight and her black eyes regarding him sharply. The ladies withdrew, clicking the door latch softly behind them. Emma added less sharply: "Are you sick, Edward? You look strange."

Edward stood in front of her and did not seem to know what to say. The bones of his lean face seemed to be pushing their way through his colourless skin. "I feel strange," he said. "Unreal, as if all this were a dream. Mother . . ."

"Yes, Edward?"

He still did not speak, and Emma remarked: "It is a long time since you said mother to me in that way, Edward. The last time was when you were about five. After that it was always 'father.' Something has happened. What?"

He looked as if he were afraid of her. He said: "You always swore that the ring you brought from Normandy, a marriage gift from your brother, never left your finger. Although I saw it with my own eyes, when your messenger came to Rouen. When Alfred and I were invited to join you in Winchester. You sent it as your token."

"I did not send it and it never did leave my finger," said Emma firmly. She held out her left hand. The garnet shone on her middle finger. "There it is still. What of it?"

Edward licked his lips. "I think perhaps . . . you . . . told the truth."

Emma's eyes narrowed. She leant forward, one hand on top of the other on the knob of her stick. They were like a witch's hands, wrinkled and bony. *She's old,* Brand thought. *Old and ill. What is Edward about?*

"So you think I was telling the truth, do you, eh? After all this time? All these years you've sworn that Harefoot sent the ring back to me after Alfred was dead. Bah! You thought I conspired with Elfgift's by-blow! That you—or anyone—could believe that has been a wonder and an amazement to me! But since you have believed it without difficulty for fifteen years, why alter your mind now?"

Edward gestured towards Brand. "This man, Brand Woodcutter, took this from Sweyn Godwinsson after a fight with him." He held out the garnet ring. His hand was trembling. Brand glanced at him for permission and moved to see better. Emma drew her own ring off and compared them. Her breath was sharply indrawn.

"They're not identical," she said. "But good enough. Someone who hadn't seen the ring for years could be deceived. Humph!" She replaced her own jewel and stared unamiably at her son. Edward waited. "So. Fifteen years ago I asserted the truth but only now are you convinced! It isn't me you believe. It's this evidence from outside me. My oath was not good enough."

"I saw what appeared to be your ring in Rouen. Mother, you always loved Harthacnut best. It wasn't so hard to believe you would sacrifice us for him. That was what I thought. That you wished his rivals removed. You hadn't seen us or tried to see us since we were children. You were never very kind. You loathed the man who fathered us." His voice cracked. "I loved him and you hated me the more for that. Why should I not believe this thing of you? But I know now that I wronged you in doing so. I am not so dishonest. I owe you . . ." It was hard for him to say it; his Adam's apple jolted in his throat as he swallowed between phrases. ". . . I owe you an apology."

There was a pause. Then: "Fifteen years of torment," said Emma slowly. "Fif . . . teen . . . years." She tapped her stick with each syllable to emphasise it. "All wiped out in a milk-and-water little phrase, eh? 'I owe you an apology!' " She mimicked him ruthlessly. Brand, hideously embarrassed, began a retreat towards the door, but a javelin glance from Emma halted him. "I want to ask you some questions!" she barked. She turned back to Edward, pointing her stick at him as if to transfix him with it. "Years of torment, I said. To be accused of selling my own son's life. What do you know of having children, Edward? You can't even get them. A woman with a child may love it or hate it. Mothers have drowned screaming brats or beaten out the brains of sons who looked like obnoxious fathers. But that's in passion. Women don't scheme in cold blood to have their children murdered by someone else when they've grown up! That's a monster's act. Worse. Even the monster Grendel loved her son. And that is the accusation you have held over my head, Edward, my dear little boy. Bah! And now you gracefully change your mind and decide I am innocent after all . . ."

Edward said: "Can't we . . .?"

"*You're* the innocent," said Emma with malice. "You're easy to convince! I wish I'd known before how easy! I suppose I should tell myself that you're glad to be convinced because you hated thinking ill of me. But you haven't hated it—you've enjoyed it. You're not easy to convince because you want to be convinced, but because you're a simpleton! I always said so. So there's another ring in this world like the one my brother gave me, with a serpent swallowing its tail and a red stone for an eye! What of it? There are probably twenty. I never hid the ring. I showed it to all who wished to see it. Many have held it and even tried it on. Some maybe remembered it well enough to have it copied more or less. In fact, I know they did. So what have you proved? Nothing. Gytha of Wessex saw it often. Perhaps she had one made like it and gave it to her son."

"Gytha of Wessex?" said Edward slowly. "That . . . fits. The workmanship too . . ." His face grew sombre. He said: "It's like the work of Godwin's cousin Sparhafoc. Whom I have promoted and entrusted with my crown! Dear God!"

A memory swam into Brand's mind, of a monk thrown from his pony on the road near Godwin's hall. A monk he had never forgotten, who had foretold the grief Eadgyth would bring him and spoken the wisest words he had ever heard concerning the life of religion. Whose saddlebag had burst open, revealing astonishing treasures, among them a set of gold and garnet jewellery, including a marvellous ring. For Gytha, the monk had said.

He had never seen Gytha wear it, or any other ring. Her hands were always free of ornament or encumbrance. He had been new to Godwin's household when he saw that ring. It must have been before the Atheling died.

Before Godwin went away to Gildenford. Yes. It fitted.

"I see," said Emma, nodding. "A plot between Godwin and Harefoot, and then the ring passed somehow into Sweyn's hands. Hmm." The blaze of anger had faded, to be replaced by what looked like dispassionate intellectual seeking. A clawlike forefinger beckoned to the unhappy Brand. His stomach had gone tight. "You! You say you took it from Godwinsson. Tell me about it."

Brand began the story of the quarrel once more. "And you didn't kill him?" said Emma inevitably. She registered surprise in exactly the same way as Edward, with raised brows forming exactly the same lines in her forehead.

Brand explained all over again. "I traded his life for the other lives in the power of his men and I took his valuables," he recited. "This was among the things I took."

"Did he never try to get it back? You have both been at court at the same time. He must have had opportunity. When did all this happen? If it had a guilty meaning for him, he must have tried to regain the ring."

"He tried to keep it from me in the first place," Brand said slowly. "He threw it away as I reached my hand for it. My friends were in the boat then, pushing off. It fell into the boat and my friends gave it back to me later."

"I must hear about this fight in fuller detail one day," said Emma. "It sounds material for a saga. Hmm. The ring was important to Sweyn, undoubtedly. Did he ever realise you had got it back?"

"I think . . . not," said Brand slowly. "I wear it only now and then and I have had little to do with Sweyn Godwinsson since his return. We would hardly be on friendly terms. No. I think he still thinks it is lying in the sea."

Edward, who had been standing between Brand and the rood,

now moved. Brand's eyes rested on the crucified figure. Wordlessly he pleaded with it: Even in answering these questions, I have come near to betraying my oath. I do not grudge this wronged woman her acquittal but . . . no more. God have mercy on me, no more. Let her ask me no more questions.

But Edward's face still wore a questing look. He did not sense the unspoken petition. He said: "I thought the ring was the only one. I never thought there might be others. If Sweyn's mother gave it him, that would be reason enough for him to value it, to wish to keep it out of unfriendly hands. Gytha of Wessex is loved by all her children." Emma's lips tightened. "No, it proves nothing."

"And final, unquestionable proof you must have, mustn't you? said Emma murderously. "Never, never, not even now will you take *my* word for it! And if I produced a thousand honest men to swear to my innocence, I don't believe for one moment you'd take their oaths either! If I swore to you on my relics, of half the saints in Christendom, would that make you believe me? Well, Edward? Would it?"

"Oh, you'd swear your innocence," said Edward disgustedly. He turned away. "On such a charge—who would not?"

"And who would make such a charge to begin with? Only you. You look like your father. You behave like your father. Just as foolish and just as cold. Now do you see why I hated him?"

The last words came out between her teeth. Edward said: "Calm yourself, mother. You will become ill."

"You may as well not trouble to call me mother. And how much would you care if I did become ill? You'd rejoice!"

On the last word her voice cracked, a transition from strength to weakness as shocking as if one of the Standing Stones on Salisbury Plain had suddenly splintered into pebbles. The parchment skin over the strong bone structure crumpled and folded. The hard mouth shook. Tears ran from Emma of Normandy's black falcon's eyes. The stick in her hand began to tremble and clattered on the floor. "You are the last of all my children!" she burst out. "The rest are dead. All gone, sons and daughters alike! I had hoped to make . . . make my peace with you before I joined them. I had hoped, Edward. And today I thought the time had come." She put a hand to her chest as if her heartbeat were too violent and she wished to steady it. A bluish tinge came to her lips.

Brand started forward. "Madam, may I call your women?"

She shook her head. And then she turned and laid her forehead against the chairback in an attitude of abandoned grief at once so desperate and so unlike the Emma of Normandy the world was used to that it was intolerable to watch. She wept, aloud, like a bereaved and helpless child, and in Brand dread became a certainty.

"Should you tell what you know to your new lord if it would help him?" Beorn had asked of Godwin once, speaking of secret knowledge a man might have of a previous leader. "Only if it was knowledge of some deed so abominable that no oath could stand in respect of it," Godwin had said. "And what sort of thing would that be?" Harold had asked. And Godwin had said: "You will know an abomination if ever you meet one."

He would not define it. He had no need to. For it was true: when you saw an abomination you recognised it and Brand had recognised it now. It was this: this tired, sick old woman protesting her innocence of a monstrous crime and weeping out her heart because her last living son would not believe her. Whatever Emma had done, or failed to do, in the past, it did not merit this, this cruelty to her in the weakness of old age, as fragile and as pitiful as the weakness of infancy. Her next words made it worse.

She said, through her sobbing: "You will not believe this either, but after Cnut was gone I thought of sending for you, you and Alfred. But I never did because I feared the outcome. I feared Harefoot and what he might do, and you were not able to raise a proper army. I didn't then fear Godwin; I didn't know he would join with Elfgift's son. He gave her up a few weeks after we were married . . ." Her hearers suddenly realised that "he" now was Cnut. ". . . He loved me by then. But in those first weeks I bit my bed linen, many nights, that the women shouldn't hear me crying, because he was with her and not with me. I didn't think Godwin would turn to her son. But I knew Harefoot was dangerous and I did not call you, although I was lonely, because I was *afraid for you!*" The frantic weeping overmastered her again.

Brand's own heart was hammering and his eyes were hot. He had no real choices before him now. He could not choose whether to be a betrayer or not. He could only choose whom to betray: Godwin who was guilty, or this aged, grief-racked woman who was not. He heard his own voice, hoarsely, saying: "My lord . . . there is something more . . ."

Emma, still weeping exhaustedly, had been taken away by her women. She and Edward had embraced, awkwardly, and Edward had kissed his mother with formality on her damp brow. Brand stood in the middle of the room, silently awaiting his doom. Edward faced him. "You have known then, for two years past, and said nothing?"

"I did not know I had proof, sir. I didn't know what the ring was. I had no proof beyond my word, and my oath is nothing against that of Earl Godwin. Also, I swore to him that I would keep his counsel. I have broken that vow now." He had reported, as nearly word for word as he could manage, that scene at Pevensey when Sweyn threatened his father with disclosure. He felt unclean.

"I respect that you had an oath and tried to keep it. You may leave now. Go back to your place among the men and keep your face out of my sight until I begin to forget your features. One day I may learn to be grateful to you. On your way out, find my page and tell him I want Bishop Stigand and Bishop Champart here, quickly." He laughed, not very merrily, and Brand went to the door. "I was on the verge of pardoning Godwin," Edward said. "But I have changed my mind."

Champart did not need a page's services to find him, for Brand met him in the passage outside and gave him the king's summons. He went to Edward's chamber instantly.

"Ah, Robert." Edward greeted him with his head on one side and with a grim look on his face that made a wary one appear on Champart's. "I don't know," said Edward, "whether you were misled when you repeated that tale that Godwin gave orders for Dover to insult my guests, or whether you invented it out of hatred for Godwin. And I am not asking." Champart was silent, waiting tautly. "But," said Edward genially, "it hardly matters. Your instinct is sound as always, my friend. You knew that Godwin had to be removed by one means or another and wisely saw to it." Champart's rigid muscles relaxed. "You were right about Sparhafoc too. He and Godwin alike were in the plot against me and my brother. You're a good friend, Robert," said the king, placing an arm about his old comrade's shoulders.

The anger and the fear in Godwin's hall at Southwark were like a fog in the air. Gytha was mainly responsible for this. She knelt amidst chaotic confusion: bundles of tied-together tapestries, half-filled chests, piles of clothing, and baskets of oddments. She was trying to direct the thralls to pack them properly. Her ladies had long since been sent to their homes and even her daughters had been hurriedly despatched back to the nuns who had educated them. Godwin sat at a table with lists of names on a parchment in front of him. His eyes were red-rimmed, as if he had not slept. He said, patiently, not raising his head: "Do you blame me that I defied the king, then? Would you have had me turn my men on Dover?" He stared at the parchment. "Because personally I prefer them to desert me for Edward, than that. And most of them have. Not one in twenty of these names is still in my camp."

"I would not have had them turn on Dover, no, of course not." Gytha's plaits, which she had not troubled to bind round her head today, swung to and fro as she struggled to strap up a chest herself. "But I blame you that you let your son and grandson go to him! They were my son and grandson too. You should have consulted me. And I would have said *no!*" The strap broke. Harold, who was sharpening blades on a whetstone, dropped the dagger he was working on and went to her, brushing aside the dithering thralls. They were too upset and frightened to be useful. "You agreed to send them with Stigand and the king's men while I was in my bower!" Gytha flung at her husband. She sat back on her heels. "I was not even called to say farewell till they were mounted and it was too late!"

"It was easier for you if we did it that way. And Wulfnoth went of his own choice. I wanted to make peace, to show my goodwill. Wulfnoth said he would go as my surety. And I sent Hakon with him because I do not think Edward will harm any child so young. Sweyn is Hakon's father and he agreed."

From where he stood by a window, Sweyn nodded. "Edward won't hurt either of them," he said.

"Wulfnoth was not afraid," Godwin said. "He rode off in the midst of the royal housecarles as if it were beneath him to speak to them."

"Wulfnoth isn't a young child! Wulfnoth's nineteen!" said Gytha. "And even with Hakon . . . what makes you so sure you can trust Edward? Edward's father killed a woman hostage once. King Forkbeard's sister. Edward is like his father."

Godwin sighed. "Gytha . . . Gytha, my love, I was trying to

build a hope of peace between me and the king. To assure him of my good faith, to save the futures of us all. Edward's no savage. I hoped, if I made a gesture . . . Wulfnoth offered, and Hakon's infancy is his protection . . ." His voice trailed away. He looked at Gytha, but she would not look at him.

"There's still hope," said Gyrth, who was by the door, surveying the surrounding camp. Only the family and a few thralls were in the hall. The rest of the muster was camped outside it, with tents and cooking fires. "If Bishop Stigand persuades him to let you go to the palace with a proper escort, and if you swear enough solemn oaths that Dover was not a planned insult . . ."

Leofwin strolled down the hall to look over his brother's shoulder. "Stigand's here now!" he exclaimed. "That is Stigand, surely? He's riding in . . . Sparhafoc's met him at the gate! They'll be here in a moment. Then we'll know!"

They knew, indeed, as soon as Stigand was inside and they saw his face. Godwin did not stir from where he sat, but waited for the bishop to approach him. Gytha left her packing and went, at last, to stand beside her husband. Sparhafoc, who had already heard the news, whatever it was, hovered nearby, twisting his hands. Tostig and Judith, who had been wandering in the camp, came in quietly after Stigand and stood waiting, close together. The bishop had left his escort outside. He stood isolated, before their watching eyes. He said: "My lord . . ." and stopped.

"Yes?" Godwin laid down his goosefeather pen and placed his hands flat on the table before him. "You have seen the king on my behalf as I asked? You told him I desired peace and would meet him and make my case under fair and safe conditions? What does he answer?"

"That you can have peace, my lord . . ." The Godwins gasped and looked at each other, hope leaping in their eyes, smiles on the verge of breaking forth. Then they saw Stigand's face again and checked. ". . . That you can have peace," said the bishop dully, "and pardon, if . . . if . . ."

"Get on with it!" shouted Sweyn.

"If you will first restore Atheling Alfred and all his followers, safe and unharmed," said Stigand all in a rush, and a tear rolled down his nose. "I tried," he said wretchedly. "I did indeed try. This is madness, senseless, foolish. Edward needs his earls. He needs you. Your loyalty is unquestioned, I know. I thought he knew too, in his heart. I thought he would make peace with you."

There was a still and deadly quietness in the hall. Gytha looked thoughtfully at her husband. Godwin's face was frozen. His eyes glittered. His frustration, his anger at the ruin of his last hopes and the resurrection of this ancient grievance, sparkled in them. Then fury swept up in him like a storm and springing to his feet he hurled the table over. Ink, quill, sand, and parchment cascaded to the floor. He kicked the fallen table out of the way and strode across the hall. He whirled round again and strode back. He struck his fist on the wall and the blood smeared his hand where it had hit the stone.

"Why?" he bellowed at Stigand. "Why in God's name does he bring that up—now?"

Stigand said: "He has learned, my lord . . . he has learned . . . he knows now for sure what happened at Gildenford. He knows of the trap you and King Harold Harefoot set." He glanced towards Sparhafoc. "I think he knows of your part too, my lord bishop." There was no accusation in Stigand's voice, only unhappiness and a bald air of statement. "You lent your skill, did you not, to create a garnet ring with a serpent hoop, to resemble Lady Emma's? Edward will never forgive either of you now."

Gytha put a hand on Godwin's shoulder, drawing near to him. Her anger was forgotten. Though not its cause. "And Wulfnoth?" she said. "And Hakon?"

The bishop said with compassion: "He still holds them. But he will not harm them. I promise you."

"How did he learn it?" Godwin demanded. *"How?"*

"There's a man in his service who was once in yours. He knew. He told the king. Brand Woodcutter, his name is."

"Brand!" cried Sweyn and Harold simultaneously, though in differing tones of voice. Sweyn's said: We might have known. Harold's said: It can't be.

Godwin said: "I trusted him."

"There is more," Stigand informed him. "My message has another clause." Another tear appeared at the corner of his eye. He had striven hard with Edward against this judgment, for whatever Godwin had done fifteen years ago, it was not in Stigand's view in the interests either of Edward or of England that he should be cast out now. His sense of failure burdened him.

"Another clause?" said Harold sharply.

"Banishment," said Stigand. "A royal courier is on my heels with it in official form. They were drawing it up when I left. Unless you come to trial with twelve men only, unless you will accept that, then you must leave the country. You have five days to present yourself for trial or to depart. Or else he will have your head."

Gytha the practical dropped her hand from Godwin's back and walked once more to her chests and coffers. "Fill them!" she snapped at the thralls. "Hurry! Pull yourselves together! No one wants *your* heads!" Over her shoulder she said dryly: "It seems that like others before us we are bound for the most hospitable court in Christendom and the sooner the better. Will your father receive us, Judith?"

"Flight," said Godwin, as if the word tasted unpleasant. "Like a panic-stricken peasant bolting from a battle!" He looked at the still-open door through which the smokes of Edward's camp could be seen blurring the sky, dark grey on light.

"If you stay, what can you do?" asked Gytha. "He outnumbers us now and he will not negotiate. Shall we form a shield-ring and die gallantly, or go to Flanders and live to come home again perhaps? I see no other alternatives. Not now. Now that he knows."

As if she had accused him, Godwin said: "At the time the safety of the kingdom seemed to hang on it."

"I know." Gytha nodded. "But it doesn't matter now. What we have to deal with now is *this*. We *must* go. It could mean your life . . . any of our lives! *Godwin!*"

It was both a clarion call and an appeal. Leofwin said: "We ought to start at once. And we should disband the men. What we still have left of them!"

Godwin's face looked as Brand had once seen it, aged suddenly, as if twenty years had passed in the space of a minute. He looked desperately tired. He said: "Then do it."

"So he's gone. Well, well." Edward surveyed his hall. "My world looks bigger already, without that devil and his greedy demon family sucking my life away. I have sent his daughter back to the convent where she was reared. I'll have no more Godwins near me."

"No, my lord," agreed Bishop Stigand, controlling a smile. He had been regaled already with the tale of Edith's departure, having met Siward on the way in. It hadn't taken place quite as Edward described it.

"My lord," Edith had said, arriving unannounced in the royal presence with her travelling mantle already round her shoulders and two ladies at her heels clutching bundles. "My lord, I desire to return to my convent to ensure my safety while these troubled times last. Also, since my husband is at war with my father and I owe love and duty to both, I cannot choose the company of either. Have I your permission to withdraw?"

"Madam, you have," said Edward, perforce. Horses and escort were prepared and at the door. "I wish you godspeed."

"I thank you, my lord," said Edith, frigidly courteous, and swept out carrying the honours of the engagement with her.

Robert Champart, not interested in Edith, had another matter on his mind. "Where is Abbot . . . no, *Bishop*—Sparhafoc, Stigand? He was with Godwin. And he had the gold and gems for the new crown in his possession. I sent yesterday to his London palace and found out."

Stigand considered him coldly. In his opinion, Champart was a climbing Norman weed in the tidy English garden and a very questionable influence on the king. It did not seem to Stigand that either Edward or Champart were blameless in this sorry affair, and for the chief victim, Emma, he felt great pity. She lay sick now and perhaps dying, through the shock of a reconciliation which had proved more deeply wounding even than her long estrangement from her son, when at least the vicious charges were rarely voiced. His opinion of Sparhafoc was not high either, but he was going to enjoy this.

"I regret to say," he replied, "that King Edward must use his old crown for some time to come. I too have been to the palace of the See of London. Some of the thralls Godwin left behind were tattling and I was intrigued by what I heard. Bishop Sparhafoc went away with Godwin. And I understand that he has taken all the small movable treasures of the See, and the gold and the jewels for the crown, with him!"

7 ✖ The Most Hospitable Court in Christendom

"Certain preparations I advise in advance," said the harsh-featured young man with the thick, close-cropped black hair. His face bore a strong resemblance to Emma's. He had the same strong mouth—he was clean-shaven—and the same dark hawk eyes. Just now they were swooping from one valuable object to another in Edward's Winchester hall, as if estimating the worth of the tapestries, the Byzantine silver plate, and the drinking goblets. "There is no hurry, of course. We may hope that many years of vigour lie before you yet, Cousin Edward."

"What preparations had you in mind?" Edward enquired graciously. He signalled a page for more wine.

"If one day I am to come to England as its king, then I shall one day come with a Norman following. I shall—we all shall—appear very strange beings with our French speech and manners and buildings. Your court hears our tongue and sees our clothes, but not your people, the people I shall rule. I wish to come as a friend, a lawful leader, not an enemy. It will be wise to accustom them beforehand. And it may also be as well," said William of Normandy, closing in for the kill, "to be ready for the faction who will resist the strangers, whatever preparations we make." He smiled, teeth glinting. "I know men. There will be trouble. I suggest that a few castles with Norman castellans be placed at strategic points during the next few years. Thus people will grow used to us and I shall establish bases here against my coming. Dover is an obvious place, being a main port. Where else do you recommend?"

"The Welsh Marches?" said Edward. "I have a nephew there already—Ralph of Mantes. You can trust him. He could be the first of the castellans. A chain of strongholds would be useful there against the Welsh in any case . . ."

William smiled, apparently at the prospect of subduing the Welsh, and refused the wine a page was now proffering. "No—thank you—a single cup after dinner is enough for me. There is one more thing . . ."

"Yes?" said Edward. This cousin of his, he thought, his mother's great-nephew, would make a kingly king one day, for all the base blood on his distaff side. He had a keen mind and a valiant spirit, and they were lodged in a powerful body. And his wife would never have to cajole him into dressing royally; he was sombrely magnificent by preference in his crimson tunic and purple mantle. For once Edward felt conscious of his own plain dress. Had Edith been there she would have urged him to wear more impressive garments. At times, he missed Edith.

"Hostages," said the Duke of Normandy, leaning back and putting his square, strong fingertips together. "Not that I doubt your good faith, but Earl Godwin has a following here still. Hostages of some value to the earl would act as a check on his supporters and on him. Are any such still in England? I heard something about a grandson—Sweyn's child, I believe—and perhaps a son?" He looked enquiringly at his host.

Edward wondered how he did it. Wulfnoth and Hakon had been kept out of William's way. William had a ruthless reputation, and on the eve of his landing Edward had belatedly realised that this was all he knew of the Norman kinsman to whom he had so blithely willed his crown, since Alys of Boulogne was dead and Godgift's sons had not a spark of ambition between them. He had picked William for his record of strength and, a little, because it would please his mother Emma and he owed her some reparation. But would this unknown ruthless William regard the two remaining members of the Godwin clan as dangerous and demand their summary removal? Or even arrange for it? Better if he knew nothing of their presence in England. But he had found out after all.

"They're my surety for Godwin's good behaviour," Edward said cautiously. "They are, as you say, Sweyn's son Hakon and Godwin's youngest son, Wulfnoth. Hakon is a child still. I have them living quietly under guard."

"I suggest you hand them to me." William saw his cousin's alarm and added swiftly: "They will be perfectly safe, I assure you. I have better uses for them than stretching their necks. I will introduce them to Norman ways and bring them with me when I come. To have friends of Godwin's blood will help me build a bridge between myself and my opponents."

Edward said reluctantly: "You wish to see them?"

"If they are here."

Edward signed to the page again. "I will send for them."

"Where, by the way, is Godwin now?" William asked as the page trotted away on his errand. "I had heard that he went to Flanders."

"He is still there, I understand. But two of his sons—Harold and Leofwin—went the opposite way and are reported to be in Ireland, touting for support among the Irish Vikings. Who will fight anyone for the amusement of it," said the king with disapproval.

"I hope to have links of my own soon with Flanders," said William. "Though not with Ireland. But Baldwin at least may be careful how much help he gives to Godwin."

A small guesthouse had been set apart for the two young hostages and in it with them lived Brand Woodcutter and his wife. Since Brand was Hakon's uncle, it was natural for Hakon to be in his care, and since Brand was also a questionable character now, it kept all the doubtfuls together. He was allowed to take Wulfnoth hawking sometimes but an escort went with them, and although his own comings and goings were not questioned, he had been withdrawn from normal duties. Hild did not seem anxious, but she rarely worried long about anything and to her the care of Hakon and Elfhild and the new baby girl Edgiva were all-absorbing. Brand was glad of her calm, for it steadied him. She had not lost it even on the day when he came to her from the king's presence and put his face in her lap and told her he had betrayed his one-time lord.

"God will pardon you," she said gently. "I know why you did it and so does He. I urged it once for the very same reason; do you remember? But it was not so necessary then. This time it was. You mustn't grieve."

But the summons to the royal apartment startled them both and even Hild's eyes widened. Wulfnoth was the one who said calmly: "We had best not keep my lord waiting," and comforted Hakon, who howled at being interrupted in mid-meal, by promising him a piggy-back ride. Wulfnoth had matured during his months of captivity. He had started out sullen, proud, and bitterly resentful of Brand, but since then he had apparently reached some understanding of Brand's actions. Brand thought Hild had had a hand in that. He was grateful to her, for it had turned Wulfnoth from an enemy into a genuine member of their curious household. He was excellent with the children, fond of Hild, and at least able to endure life under one roof with Hild's husband.

They threaded their way among the scattered buildings of the royal complex, an oddly assorted quartet led by a page in red and white silk. Wulfnoth followed with Hakon on his shoulders and Brand, in armour, brought up the rear. In Edward's chamber they found the king seated beside his ducal guest. They had withdrawn from the hall in order to interview the hostages in more privacy.

Brand regarded William with interest. He had seen the duke only at a distance so far, but the whole world knew his fame. Brand knew, like everyone else, of William's lawgiving and the mastery he had won over his barons, which had brought peace and safety to Norman peasants who had never known it before. He knew of the young duke's magnanimity to foes who had yielded to him. And he knew of the men in the town of Alençon who lived their days out crippled, seated in chairs and fed like babies by their kin because they had no feet or hands. They had rebelled and from the walls of their besieged town had sneered at William's mother because she was a tanner's daughter and not a noblewoman, and because she was not married to his father, and thus he had avenged her.

William considered them with equal interest, sitting on an oak settle, with one ankle across the other knee and an arm stretched along the settle back.

"This is Brand Woodcutter, of whom I have been telling you," Edward said in French. "The child is Hakon and the fair young man is Wulfnoth Godwinsson."

"*Bien*." William's eyes shifted first to Wulfnoth's ash-fair head and then to Hakon's ginger one. "Hakon. Come here."

Hakon understood the beckoning finger, if not the French words. Wulfnoth with some misgiving set him down and the small boy toddled forward. He seemed favourably impressed by William, who placed him on his knee and let him examine a jewelled cloak-clasp. Over the sandy head William said: "I repeat, cousin, you need not fear for them."

Edward addressed Wulfnoth. "It is my decision," he said, "that you, Wulfnoth, and your nephew Hakon should return to Rouen with Duke William." Wulfnoth's neck muscles visibly stiffened. "The duke has been declared my lawful heir," the king said steadily. "It will be put formally to the Witan tomorrow, but they will accept it."

He had mooted it already, before inviting William. "We need an heir," Leofric had said moodily. "I am no lover of foreigners but he is of the king's blood and competent. Frankly, I'd vote for anyone short of the devil, just to get it settled!"

"It is the custom," Edward went on, with an impersonal pitch to his voice, as though he were addressing a public meeting, "when a named successor is not of the direct line, to send some of those who will be his future ministers to him to be trained."

"And to be sureties against a change of heart," said Wulfnoth grimly, also in French. His youthful arrogance had returned. He held himself stiffly. His blue eyes met William's black ones with an unfriendly, direct stare. "I understand."

"Do you?" William said. "Your king's way of putting it is nearer the truth. You are a fighting man's son, are you not? We will teach you to be at home in some fine new ways of war. You will like Normandy. Do you want to kick your heels here as a courtier for ever? You are a surety only in the sense that you are my cousin's public declaration that he has made a certain promise to me. Should he ever rescind it, I have proof that it was made. I can summon support. I do not have to kill you to make you valuable to me in that event."

"I will go to Normandy if the king commands it," said Wulfnoth. "My family is loyal to King Edward." Edward's face remainded closed. "But Hakon is too young. He has been snatched from one home already. He is only four."

"As to that," said Edward, "I can reassure you. Brand Wood-cutter!"

Brand started. He felt ill at ease. Since he had entered, William had glanced at him repeatedly, piercingly, as if making some silent evaluation of him—as if, Brand thought resentfully, the duke were a slavemaster like a merchant he had once seen at Bristol, weighing up the points of a consignment for export.

Edward continued: "Duke William knows who you are, Brand. I have told him your history. He knows you are Hakon's kinsman and he also knows that, worthy as your service to me has been, your blood-link with Godwin and your former service to him make you something of an embarrassment to me now. And he is aware that you and your wife, Hild, have the care of Hakon Sweynsson. He wishes to offer you a new service now, with him."

It was still a formal delivery, as if the king were reciting something learned by rote. Translated, it meant: I no longer want you here. I don't want to be revenged on you either. Duke William is prepared to take you off my hands. I have given you to him.

As Harefoot had given him to Godwin, long ago.

William said: "Woodcutter, tell me your tale yourself. Beginning with how you got your name."

Brand did as he was bidden. The story came easily now; he could even manage it in his hesitant French. Edward helped with translation where it was needed. He had had to tell it so many times, Brand thought. To Hild, to Edward, to Emma. At the end William, who had listened expressionlessly, handed Hakon back to Wulfnoth and said: "Brand, come here to me. Now, will you place your hands between mine and be my man till death or I release you? You are a loyal follower, it seems to me, despite your broken oath. You will find me a loyal lord also, and generous when well served."

Brand hesitated. He thought of his mother and brother whom he might not see again if he went so far away, and of Hild who must be dragged with him to a strange country. He thought of the strangeness of Normandy from all he heard, its cold stone buildings, its stark unlettered men, its monkish haircuts and garlic-flavoured food. He thought of Edward's bitterness against him and of Hakon, all that remained of Edgiva, lonely and afraid in the hands of strangers in an unfamiliar place, unless Brand travelled with him.

It was for Hakon's sake mainly that he knelt at length and gave his fealty to William, and on the backs of his hands the Norman's palms were warm and steady and hilt-hardened.

"Your complaints," said Godwin to his kinsman Sparhafoc, for whom he no longer had to pretend any liking, "are becoming tedious. Change your tone or shut your mouth." For years it had nagged at him, the small uneasy thought that one day, perhaps, Sparhafoc might conveniently discover to the king that a garnet ring he had once made for Godwin had a special meaning. Now it did not matter and he could detest his unlovable cousin to his heart's content. It was hardly a consolation in the circumstances, but any tiny pleasures at the moment were better than none. "I did my best for you in the good days," Godwin said. "You shared my good fortune, so why repine so much over sharing the bad? You were handsomely paid for one garnet ring!"

Gytha said wearily: "We must be nearly there. Look, I can see the towers! That's the most hospitable court in Christendom, just ahead!"

The party riding slowly into Bruges consisted of the aged chaplain Ethelnoth, Godwin and Gytha, Gyrth, Tostig and Judith, Sweyn, one female thrall, half a dozen faithful housecarles, and the ex-Bishop of London. They were all tired, dishevelled, and saddlesore. Ethelnoth was miserable because Sparhafoc had usurped his business of shriving the Godwins. The housecarles were irritable because the baggage mules hired to carry Godwin's and Sparhafoc's treasures were balky under the weight. Sweyn was in a condition of melodramatic grief, talking of going to the Holy Land as a pilgrim seeking to wipe out his sins. "So much of our trouble stems from me," he said.

"Getting religious in your old age?" Tostig mocked the first time Sweyn broke out in this vein, but Godwin snapped: "Will you boys do nothing, ever, but bicker?" and Tostig was quiet.

Harold and Leofwin were not here. In a final, hurried conclave it had been settled that they should make for Ireland to split any pursuit and double the family's chance of finding future allies. Thinking of the future, planning for the future, was their support now, all that any of them had left to hold them steady.

For the most part they had travelled with little grumbling, except from Sparhafoc. Godwin's sharp speech silenced him now for about half a mile—to everyone's relief, for his constant complaints about their bad luck, the bad roads, the straight-shouldered horse, and the wet weather had got on all their nerves. But as they neared

Baldwin's gate the laments broke out again, and it was Sparha-foc's voice which first drew Count Baldwin out to the steps of his hall.

He stood there astonished while his eyes took in the travel-stained figures and the sweaty animals and the grim look on God-win's face in a single comprehensive glance. His brows rose. He advanced down the steps, tall, well dressed, and courtly, a considerable contrast to his visitors, just as Tostig swung out of his saddle, the first to do so, and turned to help down Judith.

"My dear daughter," said Baldwin with urbane tactfulness, "I never thought to see you again so soon. And Tostig, my upstanding son-in-law! Delightful!"

"Oh, father, can't you *see* we're fugitives!" wailed Judith. She was dirty and exhausted and her head had ached grindingly ever since the stormy Channel voyage. She was also wet and cold. "This isn't just a friendly visit! We're homeless! We've been thrown out of England!" She buried her face in Tostig's chest and sobbed.

"Dear saints defend us," said Baldwin calmly. "Well, as long as you are getting comfort in your husband's arms rather than mine, we can assume that one thing at least is as it should be. Take her inside, Tostig. She must rest. And now, my lord Godwin . . . Lady Gytha . . . down you come." He snapped his fingers at hovering grooms and servants. "Take these horses, unload the mules, and bring the goods into the hall. Get bedchambers prepared and bring hot water, hot towels, wine, and food to the hall. Quickly!" He turned back to his quests. "You are all extremely welcome, my friends, whatever the circumstances. Come inside now, out of this vile weather."

"And now," said Godwin to Gytha as they walked on the frosty grass of late winter with nearly six months of Baldwin's hospitality behind them, "William is on his way here."

He stared at the trampled tiltyard where, in the Norman fashion, Baldwin trained his men in the art of mounted warfare, throwing javelins at targets and riding at a mark with spears. He was not seeing it. "His messenger came in this morning. His messengers, I should say. It was a fine array of men and horses, as befits William's new honours. Edward has made him his heir." He paused to let Gytha grasp it before adding the second, grimmer piece of news. "As for sureties, he has sent our son and our grandson to Rouen.

They are out of Edward's hands, for which I'm grateful, but they are sureties now for our support of William's claim. And if we ever return to England, they will not be there to meet us."

Gytha did not speak, but took his arm and held it tightly.

"He will be another guest of Count Baldwin and we owe Baldwin much. And the boys are in his hands. We shall have to be polite to him, my Gytha. Very, very polite."

The seer in Gytha was crying out warnings of disaster, but she said flatly: "Perhaps it's as well that Sweyn has gone. He never found his passions easy to rule. I wonder what sort of a companion Sparhafoc is making?"

"As a barefoot pilgrim walking to Jerusalem, Sweyn ought to learn a certain amount of patience!" Godwin said, not without humour. "And Sparhafoc will have something to complain about at last!"

"He went as much for our sake as his own," Gytha said. "He holds himself to blame that we are here. Sweyn, I mean. Because of Edgiva and because of Beorn. He thought we should have more chance of reinstatement if he were far away. He said that to me."

"I could certainly imagine him saying something offensive to William, were he here," Godwin agreed. "But . . . what do you think, my pious Gytha? Will Sweyn's expiation of blistered feet and hunger and weariness alter heaven's—or Edward's—frowns back into smiles for us?"

"No," said Gytha. "Not now. Not now that he has smiled at William."

But if Godwin's arrival had caused one furor, William's caused twenty. Since he was betrothed to Baldwin's other daughter, Matilda, he had every right and reason to visit Bruges, but what set the court whispering was that he was the newly pronounced heir of English Edward, and therefore a natural rival to the whole house of Godwin, and that his most probable reason for descending on Flanders at this precise moment was in all likelihood a wish to inspect his opposition. Matilda, as it were, was a bonus.

He came resplendent in red and gold, riding a sorrel Barbary stallion and followed by twenty mailed knights and soldiers. Among them, anonymous in helm and nosepiece and not quite certain yet of his seat on the destrier he had been given, isolated in the midst of all the colloquial Norman voices, was Brand Woodcutter. Odi Pathfinder was with him. Longshanks had gone with Hild and the boys direct to Rouen.

Brand was unhappy. He had not been parted from Hild for any long periods since their marriage, and he was lonely. He hoped that with the children and Wulfnoth, and Longshanks to guard them all, Hild was not suffering too much in the same way; but remembering her sorrow at their parting, he doubted it.

It was astounding, he thought, how solitary one could feel in the midst of people. For the courtyard at Bruges when they rode in was seething. Grooms, porters, maids, pages, were lined up in readiness. Those with no claim to a part in the welcoming ceremonies were peering out of windows and round corners. It was Lady Matilda this time who descended the steps to greet the august guest. She did so with dignity (Judith greeting Tostig in like circumstances would have run), stepping gravely across the flagstones to meet her betrothed, and resting her hands on William's forearms to exchange a formal kiss. But he turned it into a fierce embrace. They were well matched, sharing the same vein of violence under a schooled and splendid surface. She was small in stature but straight as an ash spear, and proud. She said to him, standing back at last with her headdress just a little askew: "I hear great news of you."

"England on a golden platter," he said. "Regard it as a marriage gift, Mald, my sweeting. The pope will not oppose us much longer now, with his nonsense of remote relationship. I am not a man to offend these days."

"Ah," said Baldwin, emerging in his daughter's wake. "Duke William. We have looked for you all day. We have a feast set up for tonight, my lord. I have arranged lodgings for your men. You'll be glad of some refreshment."

Brand, left behind with the others, went first to the stable to see his horse bestowed and then to the well to wash off the grime of the road. They piled their belongings in the guardhouse. They would sleep in the hall tonight after the feast had been cleared away, he gathered from the talk around him. And tomorrow the duke had ordered a practice in Baldwin's tiltyard. This was an ordeal in prospect, a return to the days of his raw recruithood. He had had a few attempts at managing a spear from the back of his destrier and the others had said that he would soon manage it as well as they did, but it seemed to him an unnatural manner of fighting. And the tiltyard, by all accounts, had special horrors. There was a device there, he understood, a crude painted man-at-arms which fell over if you speared it squarely through the heart, but swung round on a pivot if you were off-centre and hit you with the flat of a massive wooden sword. But perhaps he had misunderstood his colleagues' French or they were misleading him for fun. He wished his French were better. Living in the midst of it, with no other means of communication, had shown him how limited it really was. Only Odi, who hardly had a word of it, was worse off.

He made an excuse that he wished to return to the stables, and wandered away from the others, glad to be free of the nasal voices for a while. Hild would not have this problem, at least. Bred in a crossroads port like Dover, she spoke French fluently. He wondered how soon they would go to Rouen. William might stay here a long time, he supposed. After all, he was betrothed to Matilda and it was spring now. He would want to hunt and hawk with her, perhaps. He had no clear idea of why William wished to visit Flanders, apart from Matilda. His fellows did not talk much to him of their duke's affairs, because these might need lengthy explanations to this Englishman without a grounding in matters Norman, and with his limited vocabulary he might not understand. Most conversations concerned horses or fighting or women, in which discussions Brand could hold his own, more or less. Later it might be different. They liked him well enough and his handling of a sword had won their respect at the first practice.

He found the deserted tiltyard and leant on the fence. The wooden enemy was depressingly all that he had been told. He was not looking forward to tomorrow. Turning at last, he walked away and as he rounded the corner of an outlying stable block he came face to face with Godwin.

It was a blow to the belly, huge, numbing, delivered without warning by a cosmic fist. Because of the language barrier, Brand had remained ignorant of Godwin's whereabouts. Even before he joined William at Winchester, he had been isolated from his fellows and out of touch with the grapevine. He had heard only that his former lord had left the country, and Ireland had been mentioned, which made him think that Godwin had fled there. This was like encountering the ghost of a man he had murdered.

He stopped, looking at the man in front of him, wondering if Godwin knew the part he had played in the earl's exile. Godwin looked back him, at first without recognition. To Odi's disgust, Brand had shaved his face. He said it made him feel more at home among the shaven Normans and more comfortable when wearing their style of helmet. But recognition did come presently. And with it came a flickering in Godwin's eyes of menace and anger from which it was difficult not to make a physical retreat. Godwin's right hand, which had been swinging at his side, moved up and rested on his sword-hilt. Brand wanted to speak but could not think of anything to say. He knew very well that for all his guilt and all his sorrow, if the same circumstances arose again tomorrow, he would do the same thing again. He would reveal the truth to Edward all over again. He waited, silent and rigid, for Godwin to speak or act. He did not touch his own sword-hilt. If Godwin chose to lift a blade against him, he was lost in any case. On the edge of an abyss, he waited.

The anger died in Godwin's eyes, or was masked out. The earl's hand fell back from the hilt. He moved his gaze to the path that lay ahead of him, and as if Brand were not there, he walked past and on his way.

Turning his head, Brand watched his retreat. At the end of the stable block Godwin turned not towards the courtyard but to a gate, beyond which could be glimpsed a garden and the gleam of a pool. Deserted, it seemed. Godwin, his figure growing smaller as the distance lengthened, walked to the edge of the pool, the same one perhaps which had witnessed Judith's famous rejection of Sweyn, long ago, when Godwin was still Wessex. He stopped there and stood motionless, looking down into the water.

Had he turned that way because he sought solitude? Gone there to stand upon the grass, alone, and remember all that he had lost, all that Brand had done to him?

Motionless himself, on the path where Godwin had left him, Brand discovered that though he no longer saw Godwin as greater than himself, he still had not lost one iota of his love for him. It was a love that now contained pity, that was all. And it was a love that could still be hurt when Godwin walked by him as though he did not exist.

Godwin had not asked for an explanation. What explanation

could heal such injuries as Brand had given his lord? Yet he was entitled to one.

Brand thought: there is nothing I could say to him that would
not also be an accusation. Nothing I can say that would stitch the
wound and not inflame it. But even as he thought, his feet, as if possessed of a contrary opinion of their own, had begun with purpose to
carry him back along the path.

Not to Godwin. The stony figure by the pool was unap-
proachable. But in the courtyard he found a page hurrying towards
the guest chambers with an armful of fresh linen, and stopped him.

"Tell me, do you know if Lord Harold, son of Earl Godwin, is
here with his father?"

"They say Earl Harold is in Ireland," said the page. "Earl Godwin has two sons here with him, and his countess." He added, being
young enough to like showing off his knowledge: "The eldest son,
Earl Sweyn, has gone on pilgrimage."

Brand thought quickly. With the younger Godwins he had
never had the quality of friendship he had known with Harold. He
said: "The Lady Gytha is here, you say?"

"*Oui*, she is in her chamber with the ladies Judith and Mathilde.
I took mulled wine there not half an hour ago."

"Could you take a message to her?"

The page's knowledgeable eyes travelled up and down Brand's
homespun figure and seemed to ask what business he could have
even with an ex-Countess of Wessex. Brand felt his skin grow warm,
but he would not be deflected.

"Well, could you?"

"I might."

"The message is simply this. A man called Brand Woodcutter
begs permission to speak to her. I will wait here for her reply."

The page considered him doubtfully for another moment, then
nodded and went. Brand withdrew to the side of the courtyard and
waited, watching the archway through which the page had vanished.
He watched it so intently that he did not see Gytha herself emerge
from a different doorway and did not know she was there until she
she spoke to him.

"Brand? The page said you were asking for me. You look different without your beard."

"My lady!" Brand spun round.

"Come with me," said Gytha.

She led him to a small private chapel that Baldwin had attached to the rear of his main hall. It was not empty. Two or three others were there in silent prayer. But its acoustics swallowed sound and it was remote from the constant traffic of hall and courtyard. A little way inside, close to a mural of saints bound for Paradise, Gytha paused and turned to him.

"Well, Brand Woodcutter?" she said.

She looker older. There was little lustre now in her hair and many lines upon her face. They grey wool mantle she wore gave her no colour. But the bones of her face were still lovely and her eyes with their elusive colour between grey and blue were still clear under their slanting brows. They regarded him with cool enquiry.

Brand said: "I would have come to Earl Harold, but he is in Ireland, I believe. When I learned that Earl Godwin was here, I knew I must speak to one of you."

"Have you seen my husband?"

"Yes. He did not speak to me. I would not expect him to. But . . ."

"Yes, Brand? Go on."

She had answered his appeal for speech with her. But she would give him no more help. She waited for him to continue.

"My lady," said Brand rapidly, "I know well what has happened to you, and that I had a part in it. I saw in my lord Godwin's face that the story was known to him . . ."

"Yes. We know. You swore an oath to keep my husband's counsel in the matter of Gildenford. You did not keep it."

Brand gathered his dignity, to set it against hers. "I could not keep it. And it seems to me that my lord Godwin—and his house —are entitled to ask why. And to be told."

"So you would excuse yourself to us?"

"No. Not excuse." He heard a trace of anger in his own voice. These Godwins condemned him, did they? Well, since he had caused them to be thrown out of their home and their country, stripped of all their honours, that was understandable. But had they no awareness of their own part in their downfall? Were they utterly blind to what they had done? Who were they to cry nithing and oath-breaker? Alfred Atheling had trusted Godwin by all accounts, and Emma, heartbroken, falsely accused Emma, had thought Godwin was her sworn man. "I do not need to excuse myself," he said, staring straight into those cool, sea-colour eyes. "I am sorry that what I did led to this but I am not ashamed that I did it. And you have the right to know *why* I did it, and by God, I have the right to tell you! It was this."

Shortly, almost brusquely, he spoke of the ring, of Edward's recognition of it, of Emma's grief. "I owed her nothing," he said at the end, "and I know how much I owe to you and Lord Godwin. I shall never forget it. But she was innocent. Could I betray that, either?" He remembered as he spoke that Gytha had sat beside him when he tossed in fever with the smallpox, and that she had heard his lament for Eadgyth and tried to give him hope of a new life. It was difficult to speak as he was speaking to her, and his own voice sounded harsher because of it.

Gytha turned away and looked through a narrow window. "And we are not innocent? You have not said it, but you mean it."

Brand could not reply.

Weariness crossed Gytha's face as she turned back to him again, the shadow of old age cast ahead of its coming. "No, you wouldn't say it. But there is truth in it. Or I would not have come out in person to you when your message reached me. Indeed, I would not have talked with you at all. But as it was, I wanted to hear what you would say, Brand. And I preferred that others should not listen. I make no excuses, either, Brand. At the time we thought we had done right. It was I who borrowed the Lady Emma's ring and told the pattern to Sparhafoc the goldsmith, that he might make the false token. You met his messengers, the day Gunhild was born." She paused. "Even now," she said slowly, "who is to say what would have happened if the Atheling had come to Winchester? But Emma . . . no, we did not foresee how it would be for her. In your place . . . God knows what I would have done. Perhaps what you did. Perhaps. At least, you need not think I hate you. I will tell Godwin what you have said. Tell me something else, Brand. Tell me why you're here, clean-shaven and wearing Norman armour. Have you become Duke William's man?"

Brand nodded. "Hild and I had care of little Hakon. Hakon and Wulfnoth have gone to Rouen to live in Duke William's castle . . ."

He hesitated, questioningly. Gytha said: "I know."

"King Edward sent us with them. It meant I had to become

Duke William's follower. I shall rejoin them when he goes back to Rouen."

Gytha remarked: "Our forefathers believed, you know, that there were three strange sisters who spent their days in weaving the fates of men. Sometimes I believe it too! And I think they are weaving a powerful fate for that Norman duke and that his will be the design that rules the future. It comforts me a little that my son and my grandson will have friends near them while they are in the hands of Normandy."

Glad to be able to say something reassuring, Brand said: "I don't think he'll harm them. He said he would not . . . I heard him say it. He said . . ."—his brow furrowed with the effort of verbatim recollection—". . . that . . . that they were a public declaration that a promise had been made to him. If ever it is withdrawn, then he has evidence that it was made, and so he could win support. He would not need to kill them. He promised them a good future in Normandy."

Gytha's eyes widened. "You relieve me, Brand." She seemed to be thinking. Then, for the first time, a faint smile appeared on her face. She contemplated the mural at her side. "Brand . . . what of those two followers of yours, Longshanks and Pathfinder? The two who left our household and turned up alongside you when you came to King Edward's court. Are they with you?"

"Odi Pathfinder is."

"Would you still be willing to do us some service, Brand? A little compensation, shall we say?"

"I . . . don't quite understand, my lady."

"Would you leave Pathfinder with us? We may have need of him. If he agrees, of course."

"So you're not coming on to Normandy with me, Odi?" Brand, his saddle over his arm, on his way to prepare for the ordeal of the tilt-yard, found Odi walking in the same direction and fell in beside him. "I am sorry. I shall miss you and so will Hild and Peter when I arrive without you."

"I am also sorry," said Odi. "But these Normans with their queer tongue and queerer food are more than I can stomach. And . . ."—his voice dropped—". . . I can't like that Norman duke either, no matter how highly men speak of him. I was glad of this chance. And I don't hold with fighting on horseback. You're done for if you fall off in the middle of a herd of plunging stallions."

"There, I would agree with you," said Brand gloomily. He added: "I noticed that so far you'd dodged out of any suggestion that you might learn mounted warfare too! But I hope to live long enough for us to meet again one day."

"I, too," said Odi.

Brand was a little late at the tiltyard, having been delayed by Pathfinder. When he reached it, the others were already cantering round and round the trampled ring, weighing javelins and warming up their mounts. The sergeant in charge was examining the wooden figure and positioning it carefully and William himself was sitting on his horse near the gateway, watching his men prepare. As Brand apologetically sidled his horse past the duke, a gloved hand rose from William's knee and caught Brand's bridle.

"I hear you have had speech with Lady Gytha, then, Woodcutter? And that when you left her, you were smiling. And I saw with my own eyes, last night in the hall, that you watched her constantly with the expression of a son looking at a greatly honoured mother. Have you made your peace with the house of Godwin then? Do you still wish to come to Normandy?"

It was as hard to speak boldly to William as it had ever been to speak so to one of the Godwins. Though not for quite the same reason. Duke William did not dazzle. He simply overpowered. It was clear that he wished for boldness now, but Brand hesitated. William saw it.

"I don't always maim men for speaking the truth. Did the Lady Gytha by any chance ask you to safeguard her boy and her grandchild from me?"

One learned, under Godwin, that a first law of warfare and strategy was to keep one step ahead of the enemy. William apparently preferred to be a dozen steps ahead. Brand felt his mouth opening and then pulled himself quickly together. He said: "The little boy Hakon is my own nephew in any case. I would naturally feel protective towards him. But yes, she did say . . . that she was glad I was with them." He gathered his courage. "On the day I was first brought to you, my lord, you declared that they would be safe. It is true that if they were in danger . . . my oath of fealty to you would be in danger too. And I do not want to break my oath again. So . . . are they indeed safe?"

He hoped William had understood. He knew his accent was bad and he had groped for several words. But the duke was listening closely and had followed most of it, it seemed.

He said: "I spoke the truth, Woodcutter. If any man attempts to usurp my rightful honours, it is on that man I shall visit my anger. England belongs to me now and in due time I shall claim it, but I trust without shedding Wulfnoth's blood, or that of your beloved Hakon." His lupine smile showed, briefly. "I am capable of defending my rights without them, I assure you. So you will remain with me?"

"I will remain," said Brand.

"And keep your oath of fealty?"

"I betray no oath from choice," said Brand.

That much at least was true, even if he was betraying William again by accident at this very moment. His farewell to Odi Pathfinder in the stableyard had not been necessary because Brand was leaving, for William expected to stay a fortnight in Flanders yet. It was Odi who was going, on an errand for Godwin. Godwin needed a man who was English in speech and loyalty, yet was not known to be a follower of his, and few such were to be found in Flanders. But Odi matched the requirements, and being known only as Brand's companion, he might depart without arousing the interest of William's ubiquitous intelligence service. And Odi, simple fellow that he was, had seen no need to keep secret from Brand, his friend and leader, the service that Godwin wanted of him. He had turned to Brand, less than half an hour ago, to ask advice on the best way to undertake a journey to Ireland. He was anxious not to fail or lose his way, for the message he bore was important.

It had simply not occurred to the Pathfinder that a message from Godwin to Harold, arranging a rendezvous at sea, must be, could only be, the first step of a campaign to regain Godwin's power at home. Nor had the uncomplicated Odi grasped either that since William was now the heir to England, and since Brand was now William's man, Brand was hardly the right repository for such a secret.

Brand only hoped his friend would get to Ireland safely and that no one would ever know they had talked of it together. William's fresh assurances of the hostages' safety was a greater relief than William could possibly guess. If Godwin were seeking reinstatement, it wasn't in order to uphold any claims from Normandy.

"I shall serve you as well as I am able, my lord," he said now to William, and he hoped that God, if no one else, would recognise that for truth.

He could not tell William what he knew. He could not betray Godwin a second time. It seemed that for all his striving after honesty and his wish to serve his leader with a whole heart, as Godwin and before that his father had taught him, he was irredeemably committed to a career of deception.